VOLUME 4

FUJINO OMORI

ILLUSTRATION BY
KIYOTAKA HAIMURA

CHARACTER DESIGN BY
SUZUHITO YASUDA

NEW YORK

IS IT WRONG TO TRY TO PICK UP GIRLS IN A DUNGEON?
ON THE SIDE: SWORD ORATORIA, Volume 4
FUJINO OMORI

Translation by Liv Sommerlot
Cover art by Kiyotaka Haimura

This book is a work of fiction. Names, characters, places, and incidents are the product of the author's imagination or are used fictitiously. Any resemblance to actual events, locales, or persons, living or dead, is coincidental.

DUNGEON NI DEAI WO MOTOMERU NO WA MACHIGATTEIRUDAROUKA GAIDEN SWORD ORATORIA vol. 4
Copyright © 2015 Fujino Omori
Illustration copyright © Kiyotaka Haimura
Original Character Design © Suzuhito Yasuda
All rights reserved.
Original Japanese edition published in 2015 by SB Creative Corp.
This English edition is published by arrangement with SB Creative Corp., Tokyo, in care of Tuttle-Mori Agency, Inc., Tokyo.

Yen On
1290 Avenue of the Americas
New York, NY 10104

Visit us at yenpress.com
facebook.com/yenpress
twitter.com/yenpress
yenpress.tumblr.com
instagram.com/yenpress

First Yen On Edition: October 2017

Yen On is an imprint of Yen Press, LLC.
The Yen On name and logo are trademarks of Yen Press, LLC.

The publisher is not responsible for websites (or their content) that are not owned by the publisher.

Library of Congress Cataloging-in-Publication Data
Names: Ōmori, Fujino, author. | Haimura, Kiyotaka, 1973– illustrator. | Yasuda, Suzuhito, designer.
Title: Is it wrong to try to pick up girls in a dungeon? on the side: sword oratoria / story by Fujino Omori ; illustration by Kiyotaka Haimura ; orginal design by Suzuhito Yasuda.
Other titles: Danjon ni deai o motomeru no wa machigatteirudarouka gaiden sword oratoria. English.
Description: New York, NY : Yen On, 2016– | Series: Is it wrong to try to pick up girls in a dungeon? on the side: sword oratoria
Identifiers: LCCN 2016023729 | ISBN 9780316315333 (v. 1 : pbk.) | ISBN 9780316318167 (v. 2 : pbk.) | ISBN 9780316318181 (v. 3 : pbk.) | ISBN 9780316318228 (v. 4 : pbk.)
Subjects: CYAC: Fantasy.
Classification: LCC PZ7.1.O54 Isg 2016 | DDC [Fic]—dc23
LC record available at https://lccn.loc.gov/2016023729

ISBNs: 978-0-316-31822-8 (paperback)
978-0-316-31823-5 (ebook)

1 3 5 7 9 10 8 6 4 2

LSC-C

Printed in the United States of America

VOLUME 4

FUJINO OMORI

ILLUSTRATION BY **KIYOTAKA HAIMURA**
CHARACTER DESIGN BY **SUZUHITO YASUDA**

THE MORNING OF THE DECISION...?

Гэта казка іншага сям'і.

І ...... раніцай рашэннем?

Darkness blanketed the night sky.

Everything was painted black to the north, south, and west, including directly overhead. Not even the eastern horizon showed traces of the sun's first light.

It was during the ephemeral time between midnight and dawn—no longer the same day but not yet late enough to be called morning.

Aiz had woken early, even compared to her normal routine. At the moment, she stood atop the great walls of the Labyrinth City Orario.

"...Maybe I'm a little...tired," she mumbled, already clad in her lightweight set of armor and toting her trusted sword, Desperate. Indeed, the golden eyes framed by golden locks appeared decidedly heavy on the girl covered in silver.

Stretched out below her was the vast metropolis of Orario, the sight carrying a sense of tranquility. Magic-stone lamps were scattered about like a sea of stars, their glow all but faded. The only remaining light came from South Main Street—home to the Shopping District with its theaters and casinos, the Pleasure Quarter—sometimes better known as the Night District—running along the boulevard's eastern border, and the Industrial District to the northeast—host to the tireless production of magic-stone goods day in and day out.

Aiz gazed blankly once more across the great city and its extinguished lights.

"..."

Closing her eyes as though surrendering herself to the chill of the night breeze, she attempted to shake off her residual fatigue. At the same time, she recalled how exactly she had arrived at this spot on the city walls, the particulars playing out behind her eyelids.

Earlier that day—yesterday, by this point—after what seemed like an eternity, Aiz had finally been able to apologize to that boy with the white hair, Bell Cranell. At last she'd expressed to him the feelings that had been building up since that fight with the minotaur. The grand game of cat and mouse—or cat and rabbit, as it were—had come to a close, and the two of them had reconciled, though perhaps that was too strong a word. Still, the misunderstanding between them had been cleared up.

And yet, the connection between the two of them had yet to dissolve.

It would seem that Bell, in his quest to become stronger, had come to look up to Aiz as a sort of mentor.

It was true that the boy didn't have anyone else. As the sole member of an insignificant familia, there were no other adventurers to teach him about fighting. He had mentioned yesterday, while completely red-faced and sputtering in front of her, that he'd been diving into the Dungeon time and again with nothing but his self-taught skills. Put less charitably, he was still a complete amateur.

Unwilling to let that continue, Aiz had voluntarily offered to instruct him on combat techniques.

I empathize with your dedication. It moved me.

This was her explanation to the boy for why it seemed as though she were lending a hand to another familia.

While her words weren't entirely false, they weren't the truth, either.

The real reason Aiz had offered to help the boy was to learn his secret—to discover what was behind his extraordinary, remarkable growth.

Despite having been an adventurer for little more than a month, Bell's growth was unprecedented. His achievements and combat results were enough to earn a second glance from Aiz, and her interest had yet to wane. She needed to know how he did it—how he'd managed to progress so quickly that he could already venture into the upper levels.

Because she would be taking on the fifty-ninth floor in only a week's time.

She wasn't about to give in to the hybrid Levis's threat.

And because…it was what she craved.

More than anything, Aiz sought power, and for that she needed to know everything about Bell Cranell's growth…and she needed to surpass it.

And yet…

It was self-serving. A selfishness that was both stubborn and ugly.

The boy would suspect nothing, believing Aiz was teaching him out of the goodness of her heart, while in actuality she'd be lying through her teeth.

The guilt gnawed at her.

Pushing aside those thoughts, Aiz opened her golden eyes and directed her gaze toward the ground.

Her heart twisted in her chest, aching beneath the silver gleam of her armor—*I need to at least reciprocate*, she told herself, as though trying to excuse her behavior.

She knew there was no stopping herself. Not when this secret could grant her every wish.

Thus, she'd simply have to help the boy achieve his goal, as well.

Whether this was truly for his sake or just a way to ensure she could live with herself, she didn't know.

But maybe, maybe if I repay him in every way I can…

—And so she made that her oath to herself. An oath carved into her very heart.

Running a hand along the hilt of her sword, she thought of those eyes, those rubellite eyes, like a rabbit's. She let her gaze rise, her expression stern.

Indeed, there was no reason to prolong this guilt any further. Starting today, she'd need to wake up early to train Bell in the ways of combat—she couldn't let anyone see where she was going, after all.

"I just need to give it everything I've got…"

Little Aiz cheering her on from within, she silently hardened her resolve again.

The location Aiz had chosen for Bell's training—the spot on the northwestern wall she was currently occupying—was a sort of secret hideaway she'd discovered some time ago. She'd happened upon this breach in the city's fortifications around the time she'd first joined *Loki Familia*. The sophomoric Aiz had fled here often after quarrels with the other members—mostly in the form of one-sided spats with Riveria.

There were traces of someone having lived here: a room of rocks, like a living space of sorts, complete with a shower and the like. Aiz had heard that there was even a goddess in Orario forced to live in an abandoned church, though it was nothing but a rumor. Perhaps this shelter in the city walls belonged to a god unknown even in Orario or a vagrant of sorts.

There was no way Aiz could let the upper echelons of *Loki Familia* know about what she was doing or that she had any connection to someone of another familia. No, this needed to be kept secret even from Tiona and the others.

If she was found out, there was no doubt Aiz's little training sessions would be brought to an immediate halt. She'd be scolded, lectured, and the whole thing would spiral into a much bigger incident than just helping a young boy.

But this place would be fine. Atop these walls outmatched in height by naught but Babel Tower itself, she wasn't likely to be seen.

"…Still…"

Aiz was brimming with drive to teach Bell, and she'd clearly arrived at the wall too early.

She'd been too nervous, or something resembling that, to sleep. All wrapped in her covers, she felt her eyes had simply refused to close.

Even now, her heart continued to beat erratically in her chest. Excitement? Unease? She wasn't quite sure, but either way, her meeting time with Bell couldn't come soon enough.

And yet.

Aiz let her gaze drop to the stone pavement below, a mutter escaping her lips.

"What exactly…am I supposed to teach him…?"

While she had plenty of enthusiasm, there was a concerning lack of content.

She'd never trained anyone before. In the past, she had always been too focused on improving herself. Indeed, only a scant few years ago, her seniors in *Loki Familia* had still been training her—Finn, Gareth, Riveria, and everyone else.

And now someone like her was going to be a teacher.

While she was the one who originally suggested it, that didn't make the incredible discomfort she felt any less real.

What exactly should she teach him?

Aiz found herself at a complete loss, her eyes shifting back and forth fruitlessly. There was no one she could ask about it, either. Not even Little Aiz inside her knew the answer, already fast asleep and curled up in her bed.

Wandering aimlessly through the labyrinth her heart had become since yesterday, she had yet to discover a way out.

As she stood there, the perplexities of her situation confounding her still, the appointed time of her training session drew nearer, bringing with it the biting chill of predawn wind, which passed by her with a wispy giggle.

After a moment, there came a soft *achoo*.

Aiz had mumbled something affirmative beneath her breath, then let out a tiny sneeze.

FIRST
CHAPTER

AND

THE BOY ...

Гэта казка іншага сям'і.

Хлопчык

The city was asleep.

Not a single light flickered within the whole of Twilight Manor, home of *Loki Familia*.

The residential building and its surroundings ran thick with shadow. Members of the familia stood watch at the main gate in sets of two despite assurances from their patron deity that "'S all good, don't worry 'bout it." Even now, guards were changing shifts—from a mixed set of humans to a female elf and animal-person pair. Within the manor itself, magic-stone lamps flickered unsteadily throughout the hallways like candlesticks.

Accompanying the main building were many towers, thrust upward like spears at the ready. One such tower was the maiden tower, where only the most beautiful of women, scouted by Loki herself, resided.

It was from within that gloom that a silhouette emerged.

Out slipped a leg in frilly pajamas, descending to the floor below. There was a rustle of cloth, hidden in a darkness as black as the world beyond the window's pulled-back curtains.

The shadowy figure changed clothes, careful to be silent lest it awaken its roommates, still fast asleep in their beds. Then it slipped out the door and into the night.

"I can't believe I've woken this early..." Lefiya mumbled to herself upon exiting the room, her long golden ponytail swishing behind her.

It had already been four days since their confrontation with Levis and her creatures down on the twenty-fourth floor.

After succumbing to Mind Down and resting for nearly three days straight, Lefiya had never been more awake. Feeling refreshed and rejuvenated, unable to sleep even a moment longer, she felt her elven ears twitch back and forth as she tiptoed down the narrow hallway.

Might as well take this opportunity to train, right?

She curled her hands into two tight fists, brimming with determination.

The incident on the twenty-fourth floor had reminded her of how powerless she really was. It reaffirmed her resolve to become stronger, not only to ensure she'd never drag down her seniors in *Loki Familia* but for her own sake, as well.

A flame sparked in her azure eyes.

This early, I might even get the chance to train with Miss Aiz!

Her usual dignified, composed elven countenance dissipated in an instant.

There was no one Lefiya looked up to more than the golden-haired, golden-eyed swordswoman. She never missed a training session, waking up in the wee hours morning after morning to hone her blade work. If Lefiya left now, there was a chance she could spend time with her dazzling goddess. Feeling just a tad bit sneaky, or maybe more than a little, her feet seemed to be practically skipping as she hurried along.

Training so early, Lefiya? I'm impressed. Oh, Miss Aiz! This is nothing! I still have so much to learn, so at least this much is expected. Eh-heh-heh, but I do enjoy praise…

Lefiya wore a little grin as the "Eh-heh-heh" slipped from her lips in reality, as well.

In a delightful mood, she steered herself toward Aiz's usual training spot in the courtyard.

"Hmm…This is strange. Perhaps I am too early, after all?"

Lefiya peered down from the bridge connecting the tower, searching for her golden-haired, golden-eyed warrior in the courtyard below. Strangely, she was nowhere to be found. The magic-stone pole lamps hadn't even been lit yet, leaving the grass of the courtyard still bathed in darkness. Lefiya cocked her head in curiosity. True, the short hand on the timepiece had yet to reach three. Perhaps even Aiz had her limits.

Lefiya drooped in the middle of the bridge, gloom weighing heavily on her shoulders. Finally, she renewed her resolve, intent on starting her training alone all the same.

"Huh? Miss Aiz?"

At that exact moment, Lefiya caught a glimpse of the very person she was looking for.

Not in the courtyard but in a space behind the manor, situated neatly between its towers. Already clad in her lightweight armor and sword hanging from her side, she was acting shifty—checking first left, right, then back again before leaping noiselessly atop the wall surrounding the manor.

"?!"

The sight of Aiz sneaking out without going through the gate caused Lefiya's big blue eyes to grow as wide as saucers.

The sole witness to this suspicious behavior, Lefiya couldn't help but worry that Aiz might be headed to the Dungeon all by herself, and she took off after her idol in a fit of worry.

Leaping nimbly from the bridge, she headed for the garden. There would be no time for fetching her staff as she took off at a gallop and quickly cleared the wall.

It was dark and cold as she ran through the city streets.

Before long, Lefiya realized that Aiz's destination was not, in fact, the center of the city where Babel Tower sealed the massive hole leading into the Dungeon.

Instead, the elusive figure trailing golden locks seemed to be headed toward a district in the northwest.

Where on earth could she be off to this early in the morning...?

Tiny puffs of white air rose from her lips before melting into the shadows as she pushed her legs as fast as they could go.

Stopping for just a moment to ask for directions from a demi-human and a group of drunken, stumbling adventurers, she followed in Aiz's wake. Try as she might, however, she couldn't keep up, and eventually she lost sight of her mark altogether.

Lefiya came to a stop near the northwestern wall, struggling to catch her breath.

"I was so sure she came this way..."

The stone path she'd reached was enclosed on all sides by houses. She paused to examine her surroundings and the ornate magic-stone lamp poles all neatly aligned before taking off at a run once more.

She left the main street behind, dashing first onto a rather wide but tidy backstreet before disappearing down a complex web of small alleyways.

Lefiya blindly chased that shadow for twenty or thirty minutes, wrestling with the ever-branching roads. She didn't even know what she was doing anymore, yet she couldn't seem to stop herself. She had to find Aiz.

Before she knew it, a considerable amount of time had passed.

Head on a swivel and mind consumed by the frantic search, Lefiya sailed around the nearest corner and found herself face-to-face with an oncoming body.

"Eeek!"

"Whoa!"

There was a sharp *crack* as their heads collided. Both parties landed hard on their rumps.

They were motionless for a few moments, teary-eyed and groaning as they held their heads in pain.

Of all the—!

As a Level 3 adventurer, she couldn't believe that she had ended up splayed out on the ground like an utter klutz. It was her own fault, really. She'd gotten too caught up in her chase, unable to think of anything except Aiz.

"I'm very sor—"

"P-pardon me, ma'am!"

Her apology was cut short by an even louder one, and the speaker got to his feet in a hurry.

Upon peering upward, her eyes met those of a boy.

A rubellite-eyed, white-haired human boy.

He had the most cherubic of features, his hair reminiscent of the pure-white snow that often painted the landscape of elven villages in the woods Lefiya had once called home. He was young—there

weren't any men in her familia who were younger—and slim, his features lean and slender.

Lefiya couldn't help but wonder if their ages weren't so different. The boy, on the other hand, simply reached his hand toward her.

"Are you all right…? Ah—"

But then his outstretched hand suddenly stopped short.

Reflected in those ruby eyes of his were the decidedly pointy, decidedly twitchy ears of an elf. Like Filvis from *Dionysus Familia*, prideful elves loathed skin-to-skin contact with anyone they didn't approve of. While this didn't hold true for their entire race, the number of elves who couldn't get over their discomfort was considerable.

As though familiar with it himself, the boy hesitated, unsure whether or not he should retract his hand.

All Lefiya could do was sigh. She could see in his face how distraught he was. Not wanting to be misunderstood due to the habits of other elves, she took the boy's hand herself.

He was surprised, for sure, but not to the point that she couldn't use his hand to pull herself to her feet.

She took a moment to dust herself off before meeting those rubellite eyes again.

"Thank you very much! And I do apologize. I wasn't watching where I was going."

"N-no, I—! I was the one who should have been more careful…"

Lefiya delivered her apology with a smile while the boy could only stumble over his words in response.

One might actually think the boy had never even spoken to a girl before from the way his face heated up, especially contrasted with Lefiya's calm, very elven demeanor. His discomfort was palpable.

There was something authentic about him. A simple sort of humbleness. From the look of his lightweight armor, he must be an adventurer.

As all these thoughts ran through her mind, however, another joined them.

Oh, right—Aiz!

Practically bent forward in her urgency, she quickly asked whether or not he'd noticed someone matching Aiz's description nearby.

"Golden hair and golden eyes…?"

"Exactly! The Sword Princess! Aiz Wallenstein! You're an adventurer, no? Surely you know her! Have you seen her?"

She could feel the desperation building in her voice.

The boy, however, was silent, and Lefiya could have sworn she saw the beginnings of sweat forming on his temple.

"You're, uh…not from *Loki Familia*, are you?"

Lefiya's brow creased. *Where'd that come from?* "…? I am, yes. Why?"

The corners of the boy's mouth twitched. It was almost as if he was hiding something. The hints of perspiration on his face quickly became full-fledged beads.

*Wait a minute…*Lefiya's eyes narrowed, her demeanor shifting. *There's something quite suspicious about this…*

Now she was certain he was covering something up.

"You know something, yes? Tell me what you know about Miss Aiz!" She was practically shouting at this point.

The boy didn't waste a second—he turned tail and bolted.

"You—!"

The way his white hair fluttered in his escape reminded Lefiya of a bounding rabbit.

Not about to be outdone by a human, no matter how fast his legs could apparently go, Lefiya shot off after him like an arrow.

"You come back heeeeeeeeeere!!"

"Eeeeeeeeeeeeeeeeeeeeeeep!"

Amid the silent streets, its residents still fast asleep, the chase had begun.

His head start vanished in an instant. After throwing a glance over his shoulder only to see Lefiya gaining on him, the boy gave another startled *eep*.

He couldn't have been higher than Level 1, that much was certain, which meant he was no match for the speed of a Level 3 like Lefiya, even if she was a magic user. The distance between them grew shorter, shorter, and shorter.

He definitely knew something about Aiz and what she was doing all the way out here in the wee hours of the morning—it was written all over his face.

Lefiya could feel it in her gut. The polite and sincere nice-guy bit had been nothing but an act. She revised her evaluation, seeing him now as nothing but a rude, insolent boy concealing information about her precious Aiz.

Her eyes narrowed like brilliant deep-blue razors, the rabbit in her sights.

"Eeeeeeeeeeep!"

"You little—!!"

Around and around and around they went through that chaotic disarray of back alleys. Why hadn't she caught up with him yet?

She willed her legs to move faster, her eyes glued to the boy's back and her mind screaming.

—*He's used to this!*

The way he used the complicated back roads to his advantage, almost as though he'd been trained by Daedalus himself, and that explosive dash of his—

Lefiya found herself at a loss. What kind of monsters had hounded him at Level 1 that he needed to be this good at running away?

Still, she was close. She had only about five meders left.

No matter what he did, at this point, there was no way he could shake her.

Gotcha! No sooner had the thought entered her head, however, than the boy leaped down a new street.

"Wh-where'd he go?!"

In the instant it took Lefiya's field of vision to shift to this new alleyway, the boy had simply vanished.

Where is he?! She was in a panic now. Head whipping from side to side, she discovered the entrance to another side corridor and tore down it in a flash, arms swinging wildly.

Caught up in her search for Aiz, she neglected to fully take in her surroundings. Failed to closely examine the small enclosure, hidden in the shadows of the nearby buildings like a blind spot.

And she never noticed the old stone well, its bucket rattling from its pulley…but no one in sight touching it.

"Good…morning?"

"Haah, haah, haah…! G-good morning!!"

"…Is everything all right?"

"Oh, sure…I'm fine! Just had a…a bit of a run-in…with a forest fairy…"

"A forest…fairy?"

"So beautiful but so terrifying…!"

"Are you…sure you're all right?"

"If I could…sit down for a little bit…"

"Right, of course…"

And thus the first act atop the city walls came to a close.

The real training, however, had yet to begin.

"Haah, haah, haah…!"

Three hours must have passed since she started chasing after that boy, the sun now peeking out from below the horizon and the sky a gentle pink. Lefiya's shoulders heaved with every breath.

It would seem so much time spent running was too much even for a Level 3. Her stamina was depleted, her skin soaked with sweat, and her body teetered in exhaustion.

"Where in the world is he…?!"

The lovely elf girl had nearly worn herself out.

As fruitless as her persistent efforts to find Aiz and the boy had become, she couldn't give up.

It was at that moment, however, that she felt someone's presence behind her.

Two someones, actually.

With a little gasp—and a sudden feeling of foreboding—she quickly dove behind the nearest cover she could find.

Peeping her head out just enough to have a look, she felt her heart stop.

It was her target. The boy with the white hair. And practically hanging off his shoulder was none other than Aiz.

Whaaaaaaaaaaaaaaaaaaaaaaaaaaat—?!

With a mighty *ZAP*, a colossal lightning bolt seemed to strike the top of her head.

Her every muscle frozen in shock, Lefiya found herself rooted to the spot, skin cold and clammy.

Had she looked closely, she would have noticed Aiz was simply lending the boy an arm—he was quite bedraggled and altogether spent by this point, after all. But Lefiya was not examining closely. No, those blue eyes of hers saw nothing but a passionate, intimate embrace.

Someone somewhere was laughing at her, their mocking voice, real or not, ringing in her ears. She was nothing more than a living statue in the shadows.

Aiz, on the other hand, completely oblivious to her junior's turmoil, walked right past Lefiya in her despondent heartache, consoling the boy all the while.

That night, as the members of *Loki Familia* were helping themselves to supper in a corner of their large mess hall, a certain elven maiden was wallowing in a cloud of misery, avoiding all eye contact with her peers.

"…What happened to her?"

"No idea…"

Tione and Tiona could be heard whispering back and forth, the two of them huddled together in front of Lefiya as though conducting some sort of secret meeting. And, indeed, Lefiya's head was curved at an unnatural angle that was almost gruesome. Even Aiz, sitting next to the two Amazonian sisters, had finally noticed Lefiya's distressed aura. It puzzled her.

Every girl in the hall and even the guys currently congregating around Bete and Raul were visibly whispering, elbowing one another, and generally keeping their distance from the dejected elf.

"...Lefi...ya? Is everything all right?"

Girding herself against the oppressive miasma enveloping the girl, Aiz took a step toward Lefiya—an act that garnered the admiring gazes of her peers. The trembling hesitation in her voice was audible.

Lefiya didn't respond, not even lifting her head.

Just as Aiz was getting truly worried about the girl's state of mind, Lefiya posed a question calmly, gently, in a husky timbre practically squeezed from her throat.

"What were you doing with that human this morning, Miss Aiz?"

"?!"

Aiz was overwhelmed by an incredible sense of enmity and menace...*How does she know?!*

Lefiya just sat there, waiting for Aiz's response, with her head bowed, her eyes hidden beneath her bangs, and extraordinary gloom emanating from her every pore.

The incriminating silence only heightened Aiz's turmoil. She could feel everyone's eyes and attention on her back. She needed to do something. Grabbing Lefiya's hand, she quickly pulled her out of the mess hall.

"L-Lefiya...how did you know...?"

She took Lefiya to an empty room, still very much on edge.

It was rare to see Aiz so visibly shaken. Lefiya, on the other hand, had yet to lift her head.

As the pressure continued to throw Aiz's consciousness into disarray, Lefiya finally parted her lips in response.

"This morning, I chased you to the northwestern part of town... It was there that I witnessed a goddess of the sword with beautiful golden hair and eyes in the arms of an unknown human boy."

"?!"

"Miss Aiz, you wouldn't...happen to have some sort of long-lost sister, would you? Or perhaps I was hallucinating...? I...I have been thinking about it all day, Miss Aiz, and I still have yet to come up with an explanation that makes sense..."

"L-Lefiya, try and...calm down for a moment, would you?"

"If that really was you, Miss Aiz...I...I—!!"

The pressure in the room multiplied exponentially.

Lefiya drew closer. The veteran top-class adventurer was sweating. She could feel the elf's shadow consuming her.

When she slowly raised her head, there were tears in those brilliant azure eyes.

At any moment, it seemed she would fling herself upon Aiz in a sobbing fit like a child who'd lost her most precious, admired, beloved sister for some reason, and Aiz was terrified.

There was no longer any way for her to hide what she'd done. It was that frightening thought that prompted her to spill everything.

"......You were training on top of the wall?"

"Y-yes."

"...Then who was that boy holding you?"

"Um...But he was having trouble walking, so I simply lent him my shoulder..."

It didn't take long before the interrogation made the situation crystal clear.

The black cloud of miasmatic anguish exuding from Lefiya steadily dissipated, and light returned to her vacant eyes.

"So...what you are saying is that...you are going to be training this human before the expedition begins?"

Aiz nodded. Now that Lefiya had returned to her normal, calm self, she let out a sigh of relief as she smoothed down the front of her clothes.

T-to think that boy would ask someone from another familia to train him. For free, even! Does he have no sense?!

Of course, that didn't prevent a different concern from forming in the back of Lefiya's mind.

Camaraderie between gods and their familias' members was understandable, but this? This went far beyond the scope of simple kindness. And of all the possibilities, *Hestia Familia*? *Just who are they?!*

And even then there was the issue of their differing social statuses.

On the one hand, there was this lower-class adventurer from an insignificant familia, and on the other was not only a top-class adventurer but one of the leaders of the strongest factions in the entire city to boot.

Anyone else listening to this would surely tell him to "learn his place."

This is insane! Unbelievable! Outrageous!!

All manner of curses rang through her head, the face of that white-haired boy rising in her mind.

The impudence of that boy! All alone with Miss Aiz like that! I am so…so…JEALOUS!!

That was the reason, ultimately.

That boy was monopolizing her Aiz for personal early morning training.

Lefiya's entire being curdled with envy at the mere thought of that nameless white-haired boy.

"Um…I think you may have gotten the wrong impression. I was the one who offered to train him…It's not his fault. He wouldn't be involved if not for me." Seeing the resentment and jealousy playing out like a wordless soliloquy on Lefiya's face, Aiz quickly tried to intervene.

The desperate way Aiz tried to cover for the boy, however, only worsened Lefiya's mood, expressed as a guttural "Gnkk…"

Look at her, so concerned for him. Does that boy know how lucky he is? Does he?!

"Please, Lefiya. Don't tell Loki, Finn…anyone about this, okay?"

That beautiful curve of her brows. That golden tremble of her eyes.

Do you really want to train him that much, Miss Aiz? the voice in her head implored weakly, frailly, as she trembled in silence.

She tried to keep her emotions from rushing out, but she couldn't bear it any longer.

The jealousy welling up inside finally exploded, her voice rising as she hardened her resolve.

"If…if you want me to keep this secret, you will have to do something for me!"

No one would have believed that Lefiya, now completely red in the face, had demanded something from the person she admired more than anyone in the world.

It completely blindsided Aiz. A mutiny like this, or resistance rather, was the last thing she'd expected, and it shocked her.

Seeing the look on Aiz's face made Lefiya's heart ache, but there was no turning back now.

"Y-you must train me, as well! Just like that human! Only you and me! Alone!!"

The words crackled on her tongue, her face a brilliant shade of red.

All Aiz could do for a moment was blink in silence.

Then, finally, she nodded ever so slightly.

"If that's what you want…"

"R-really?!"

Aiz nodded again. "Yes…It's all right."

"Y-yes!"

Lefiya gave a little leap right there on the floor, her hands clasped tightly in front of her. Her long bright sunny locks swirled around from her prancing, revealing the light-pink flush of her soft cheeks.

She was positively beaming. Her earlier jealousy, the boy—everything else was forgotten.

And all her beloved Aiz could do was stare in confusion as the elf girl twirled around and around and around.

Thus, in return for keeping the practice atop the city walls a secret, Aiz came to train not one but two.

Only six days remained until the day of the expedition.

This marked the second day of their training.

Same as the day before, Aiz had been conducting the breeze with her scabbard atop the city walls since the early hours of the morning.

The wind shrieked, and in every fading flash of her vigorous slashing was the white-haired Bell.

"Make every move count. Think before you move. Use the space to your advantage."

"R-right!"

Aiz emphasized each word with a jab of her scabbard as Bell moved to block each attack with his dagger. It was an intense back-and-forth, or perhaps it would be more accurately described as fending off a one-sided assault. Their feet moved like lightning as the scrimmage continued.

After worrying all day yesterday, she'd finally decided on what to teach.

They'd practice dueling.

There was no way someone with her limited conversational skills would be able to instruct anyone using her words. It wasn't possible to convey everything she knew about combat. After countless failures on the first day, she offered him a new proposal and said only one thing:

"Let's fight."

Their weapons clashed, the two of them reading each other's movements, looking for anything they could use to their advantage.

She told Bell to get a feel for everything she did during their practice battle, and then to steal everything he could.

Aiz might have been using only her scabbard, but Bell wielded a real dagger fit for use in the Dungeon, so it was about as close to a real battle as they could get. She tried just hard enough to distill any unfounded fears the boy might have, not even allowing him to fight back as she peppered him with blows from her relatively harmless scabbard.

"Flailing wildly in an attempt to block…won't help."

"Ngh?!"

"Connect each block with your next move, whether attacking or changing position."

Of course, Aiz wasn't going to leave everything up to Bell to learn himself.

She made sure to point out anything she noticed as the two of them fought, interjecting words of advice between jabs. Even though she rarely spoke, Aiz still managed to provide him the minimum degree of instruction.

Whenever he exposed an opening or made a poorly conceived move, Aiz imbued her scabbard with her thoughts and struck his body as though warning him.

How strange…

In the dim light of the still-distant sunrise, Aiz took the opportunity to examine Bell, who was frantically attempting to block her every attack.

Finn, Gareth, and Riveria had drilled the same basics of combat into her some nine years before, when she was learning the ways of adventurers as well as absorbing their wisdom. Now she was the mentor.

As Aiz recalled all these somewhat poignant memories, she saw her young self reflected in the boy in front of her. Determined to stand and face her despite his ragged breathing, he seemed to transform into an inflexible golden-haired, golden-eyed girl who hated to lose. Meanwhile, she'd become Finn, with his carrot-and-stick approach, as well as Gareth, hearty in every word and action. Most of all, she was Riveria, the severe disciplinarian.

Her hands didn't stop. Everything those mentors had taught her was coming back to her. She could see the mock battles especially clearly.

But only doing this together wasn't enough.

Guiding his movements, she made sure he was following her every step as she attacked.

Finn and the others had done this much, at least, to instruct the young girl she'd once been.

But I can't yet match something like that...

She couldn't mimic them. It was absolutely impossible for her to stand in the same league.

And as Bell's breathing grew more and more ragged, even more so than yesterday, all Aiz could do was utter a silent apology.

There was a reason Finn, Gareth, and Riveria were the leaders of *Loki Familia.*

They'd shown her patience through the many arguments shared together and given all their guidance freely despite her childish resistance. The more she came to understand their degree of accomplishment, the more she felt the full weight of her own immaturity press down on her.

So she assigned herself a new mission. She would, of course, help Bell hone his skills through this training, but she would also be polishing her own at the same time.

Her scabbard collided with Bell's dagger, causing a dull *thud*.

"Mm…Well done."

"Y-you mean it?!"

He'd blocked it quite well, actually. Referencing the way Finn had spurred her on with both praise and criticism, Aiz made sure to do the same.

The words made him so happy, Bell all but forgot the pain and exhaustion, his face brightening with an almost visible shine.

All Aiz could see was a rabbit perking up at a carrot dangled in front of its face, and the thought brought a tiny smile to her lips.

Bell blushed instantly. Aiz cocked her head just slightly in confusion.

"Shall we rest for a bit?"

"Oh, uh…sure." He wheezed in response, shoulders heaving with his every breath.

Aiz lowered her scabbard as Bell did the same with his dagger.

The two of them stood facing each other, five steps apart atop the wide city wall, as the breeze cooled their hot skin.

He's improved since yesterday…

Aiz watched as Bell wiped the sweat from his face.

Compared to the first day, there was a dramatic difference in his movements—well, perhaps that was a bit of an overstatement, but the change was certainly visible. Whether or not this was due to his uncanny growth, however, Aiz couldn't be certain.

There was a kind of simpleminded intensity radiating from him. As though he clung to her every word, taking everything she'd told him and reexamining it endlessly.

That being said, there was no way he could go beyond her instructions or surpass her expectations. Still, he was doing well.

He needs to focus on defense…After that, technique and strategy.

She'd evaluated him yesterday—the first day of their training— identifying and pointing out his current level and weaknesses.

The problem was that Bell Cranell was a coward.

It wasn't necessarily a bad thing. In fact, it actually had some advantages when it came to solo trips into the Dungeon. When it came to combat, however, that cowardice led to one major problem: Bell was more apt to flee than fight. Fearing enemy attacks and the pain they might bring, he often took off like a frightened rabbit. This explained why his evasion skills were more developed than his defensive skills.

Aiz made it her top priority to teach him how to properly defend.

Actually, what she really wanted to do was pass on her technique of deflecting and eluding incoming attacks.

When they started, there had remained a mere seven days to train him before *Loki Familia*'s expedition. If she could impress upon him even a fraction of all the defensive skills, methods, and strategies she hoped to teach, then one way or another, she could make it work.

His shortcomings. Areas of improvement. Strengths.

She carefully considered each of them in turn, going over everything she already knew about the boy.

He does have…one thing going for him…

His ability to flee from danger—practically a specialty at this point—was impressive even by Aiz's standards.

While this was likely due to his craven nature, it was still a splendid weapon of his.

Bell's strategy in fights fundamentally boiled down to a hit-and-run approach.

After taking into account his disposition, constitution, familia, and aptitude with his weapon, that wasn't necessarily a poor decision.

But if he could only harness the courage he'd shown earlier…

After peeling off that shell of his…things could get interesting, Aiz's intuition was telling her.

The first topics that rose to Aiz's mind were speed and quantity of attacks. Making full use of both would give him a fierce attack—a rush.

If he could learn to use two weapons at once, a dagger in each hand, that would be perfect.

Striking from the front with great agility. Truly, this was Aiz's preferred style.

—She had thought that far before gasping involuntarily.

Was that all right? Molding the boy in her own image? *No, no! I can't, I can't!* Her head throbbed from the inner turmoil.

What discipline to follow was Bell's decision.

Forcing her ideals onto someone else was simply unacceptable. Even more so when it came to combat.

Her only job was to teach him the basics, not lead him, and she needed to remember that.

"Still...he could be interested," she muttered beneath her breath.

Once Bell's breathing had finally settled back into a steady pace, Aiz explained what she'd observed from their duel.

"I'm a...coward..."

Bell's shoulders gave the slightest of shudders.

That reaction was enough for Aiz to realize she'd hit the nail on the head.

"You're still...worried about that? What I said yesterday...?"

"No, I mean, it's...well......yeah." Bell's gaze went first left, then right, before finally dropping to the ground. His voice seemed liable to disappear back down his throat.

The pathetic sight brought with it the sting of her own failure, and Aiz furrowed her brows.

You're...a coward.

There's something that you're afraid of.

I don't know what it is that frightens you but...when the time comes, you'll only be able to run away.

That's what she'd told him yesterday before plunging head-on into their duel.

What she'd unearthed and revealed to him.

No doubt, her words had hit quite close to home.

Which would explain his newfound refusal to retreat—to the point of reckless abandon—meeting every one of Aiz's blows as though shying away would spell disgrace.

Aiz's tactless commentary had burrowed its way deep inside him, where the resentment and shame continued to weigh heavily on his shoulders even now.

I hurt him again...

Aiz was beginning to get an idea of just what it was Bell feared so much.

Though there wasn't much she could do until she knew for sure, it was clear that the scar was deep—some sort of trauma, almost—and it wasn't something he would easily overcome.

And here Aiz was brazenly provoking him despite how much he was subconsciously suffering. Was she really so incompetent?

Or was it just that Bell didn't want to hear that from her?

That he was a coward.

Perhaps he wanted to scream at her how he was no coward.

All Aiz saw standing in front of her was a young boy giving his all to be strong...even as his torment and shame trampled him.

"...Mhn, uh...What I said earlier? About you being a coward? That...was wrong."

She couldn't take it any longer. It was unbearable seeing him like that.

To unravel his misunderstanding, as though caressing those pitiable cheeks, she tried to speak her mind.

"I don't think...you're pitiful, useless, or anything like that. I know yesterday...I called you a coward, but it's important that..."

Her words were broken, faltering, and her voice grew softer and softer, heavy with emotion. Bell's distraught face rose to meet hers.

As those entreating rubellite eyes trembled with feeling, the words became harder and harder for Aiz to find.

Frustrated at her inability to express herself, she closed her eyes, taking a deep breath.

"...While cowardice should not be confused with caution..."

She prefaced her thoughts with the words she remembered Finn, Gareth, and Riveria told her once.

"Sometimes...being afraid of something can save your party in the Dungeon."

"..."

"Really, people who feel no fear at all are more dangerous."

—Someone like me, said the voice from deep inside her, but she continued, Bell hanging on her every word.

"Which is why it's important...that you're not ashamed to be afraid. Okay?"

"Miss Aiz..."

"I don't want you to ever forget that."

Now that she'd gotten the words out there, she couldn't stop them, and Bell continued to gaze up at her, wide-eyed, opposite her, as she shifted the focus back to her with just four words:

"The way I did."

"Huh?!"

"I did nothing but worry Riveria and the others. I got my friends involved yet felt nothing. That doesn't make me an adventurer...that makes me nothing but a monster."

Aiz lowered her head. She had long since become numb to fear or terror in her quest for power.

Letting the thoughts of her past drift through her mind, well aware that she could never change from the foolish girl she'd become, she gave Bell her advice.

"Don't become like me."

The self-deprecating girl could see nothing but her feet now.

The voice spilling from her throat seemed so distant, a dim shadow settling on her slim shoulders.

She no longer noticed Bell in front of her, her vision now completely occupied by the rocks of the wall beneath her.

"...Th-that's not true!!"

The loud voice shook her from her reverie.

"A monster wouldn't have been able to save me!"

Aiz's head snapped up to find Bell leaning forcefully in her direction. The words continued to shoot from his mouth with uncanny boldness.

"The way you rescued me was amazing! Like a hero out of those stories I heard as a kid! And so beautiful, too! You...You're the one who gave me my dream of becoming an adventurer! So when you say things like that, I-I mean, it's like...well...you know...?"

As if taken aback by his own ramblings, Bell's words grew increasingly incoherent, and his face turned a brilliant pink.

Aiz felt her own face heating from the unadulterated praise and adoration.

Such candor and sincerity. As Aiz stood there in amazement, her cheeks growing warmer, she couldn't help but reaffirm her belief that this boy was exactly the same as she had been once upon a time.

Her lips curved up in a tiny arc.

She saw herself, eyes shining as her mother told a story.

She remembered her dreams, full of heroes and adventure.

Wonderful, sweet memories of her childhood, called forth by the boy standing before her.

From deep within the frozen recesses of her heart, a tiny flame flickered.

"Thank you…"

The slight curve of her lips erupted into a full, wide smile. The white rabbit had soothed her heart.

For just a moment, Bell was stunned. Then the embarrassment welled up inside him ridiculously quickly, and he could not bring himself to look at Aiz's face. His eyes wandered this way and that, focusing on everything but her.

Finally, he responded with a shy laugh of his own, happy that he'd been able to bring a smile to Aiz's face.

"…Shall we continue with our training, then?"

"S-sure!"

Aiz felt a small tingle deep inside as the faintest traces of light appeared along the eastern horizon.

Pale-pink light dyed the tips of the distant mountains as dawn's glow slowly overtook the dark cerulean sky. As Aiz gazed out across that magnificent scenery, she brought her scabbard to the ready.

Bell followed up with another energetic reply, and their training began anew.

…He's gotten better.

Aiz's eyes narrowed, following Bell's movements, as she became the Sword Princess once again.

While he still wasn't able to block every one of hers attacks, he wasn't just flailing wildly anymore. Face hardened like he was possessed, Bell chased every one of Aiz's slashes, carefully reading her timing and slipping his dagger into any openings.

Her words must have hit home, since Bell's tendency to leap forward recklessly had all but vanished.

Seeing the difference her words had made gave Aiz a wonderful feeling of accomplishment as his teacher.

—*I-I did it.*

Being someone normally so bad with words only reinforced her satisfaction; Little Aiz inside her raised both hands in triumph.

Her joy was so great, in fact, that quite suddenly, without warning, she gave it everything she had.

Her scabbard became a blur, each slash faster than the next.

"Nngh!!"

"Ah."

Her scabbard collided with the side of Bell's head, and with a strangled cry he tumbled to the hard stone. There was a loud *thud*.

And now the boy was splayed out on the ground, his body slack.

She'd knocked him out cold.

"N-not again…" Aiz muttered before dashing to his side.

This was what happened as soon as she got careless. It would seem that as someone with zero teaching experience, she couldn't properly adjust the strength of her attacks, after all.

Calming herself, she took a knee beside Bell, still sprawled faceup on his back. She reached out, fully prepared to take him in her arms in an act of gallant bravado.

Until—

She realized with a start…

"This feels…"

Passed out in her lap. Eyes closed as though sleeping.

Aiz suddenly had the very strong feeling that this had happened before.

Not more than a week prior, down on the fifth floor of the Dungeon, after succumbing to a bout of Mind Down, he'd been passed out just like this.

That's right—the situation was almost exactly the same as when she had done as Riveria said and laid his head in her lap, only to have him dash off at top speed!

*   *   *

Whereupon she'd turned bright red and been heavily criticized by Riveria.

What was it that elegant high elf had told her? "Men usually adore this kind of thing! You're probably just doing it wrong!" It might as well have happened yesterday, the way that memory was burned into the back of her mind.

Of course, Riveria had only been giving her a hard time, struggling to hold back a grin all the while. Aiz, on the other hand, had taken her words as gospel.

Gulp.

Body trembling slightly, she shifted toward Bell.

She couldn't just end things here. *Watch out, Riveria! Watch out, white rabbit!* It was time for her unyielding, indomitable spirit to shine. Her revenge was nigh.

Failure was not an option. Not this time.

Ever so slowly, Aiz took a hold of Bell's head and positioned it atop her thighs.

"Mmhn…" Bell murmured.

That same weight and pressure.

As she knelt with Bell's head in her lap, embarrassment she was entirely unaccustomed to washed over her, and a touch of pink brightened her cheeks.

All the while, the eastern sky silently grew brighter and brighter.

Night turned to morning, and the horizon displayed the most beautiful fairy-tale-like colors, the light wrapping itself around Aiz's shoulders as she gently stroked Bell's forehead and cheeks.

There was something so innocent about that sleeping face, and it brought a small smile to her lips. It really did feel as though her heart had been given a good cleansing.

Was this the way her parents had felt when they'd put her to bed so many years ago?

She ran her fingers through his soft white hair, letting his heartbeat guide her into a relaxing sense of calm.

Forgetting why the two of them were up on the city walls in the first place, with Bell's head on her lap, she let herself enjoy the moment to her heart's content.

"Mmn…" Bell murmured again, right before his eyelids fluttered.

Aiz drew in a gasp, freezing momentarily before flinging her hands behind her back.

And then she waited, face revealing none of her inner turmoil.

She held her breath as Bell's eyes slid open ever so slowly—

"W-waaaah!"

As soon as he realized the situation, Bell sprang from her lap with a scream.

Aiz's shoulders drooped as she watched him scuttle away.

Am I really as bad at this as Riveria said…?

On the other hand, Bell paid Aiz no attention and didn't stop running until he'd made it to a distant corner, face flushed with his back pressed up against a parapet.

"Wh-why a lap pillow?!"

But all Aiz could think about in response to Bell's vigorously sputtered question was how awful she must have been.

She couldn't tell him that she was bitter about losing to Riveria and had wanted to even the score.

Something deep inside her chest reverberated with a weak groan.

"I thought maybe…it would help you recover…more quickly…"

Unable to even glance in his general direction, she struggled to throw together an excuse.

Her response was met with a suitably suspicious look from Bell.

"…Sorry." She uttered a meek apology, head drooping.

Aiz confessed the lie she'd just told him, still kneeling upon the stone.

"Actually…I just wanted to do it to you…"

After hearing her true intentions, Bell turned a brilliant shade of red.

"She doesn't know what she's saying…she doesn't know what she's saying…she doesn't know what she's saying…!"

Aiz was the kind of person who couldn't help but misinterpret things, but what she said had completely shaken Bell and broken him. Again and again he repeated something to himself, both hands cradling his head.

Aiz cocked her head to the side as she watched Bell struggle with waves of emotional turmoil, warning himself to not misunderstand.

Seeing his strange behavior, Aiz asked tentatively, "You didn't like it...after all, then?"

"Ehhhh?!"

Bell's head shot up.

Next thing she knew, his already flushed face grew even darker as his hands leaped up in frantic denial.

"I don't hate it at all! In fact, it's more like a-a side benefit? I-I mean, no! No, that's not what I meant! Forget that! I mean, I did enjoy it, but—Wait, I didn't mean that in a weird way...!"

He rattled off one thing after another, unable to communicate his thoughts while his face became redder than an apple.

"Then...will you let me try it on you again?"

"More than let you, I want you to do it, but...it's just that, you know, it'd be embarrassing and pathetic...I mean, it's really only something you do when someone's passed out and there's no other option, right—?!"

"So...as long as I only do it when you're unconscious, it's fine, right?"

"Huh?"

Aiz rose to her feet in one swift motion, readying her scabbard.

Her golden eyes bored into Bell with intense desire.

Aiz's spirit was unwilling to yield to Riveria's evaluation, but more important, a wish to hold the white rabbit in her lap once more bloomed inside. Her heart would be soothed and she would ruffle his soft white fur.

Bit by bit.

She steadily whittled down the distance between them.

The strange atmosphere she'd created was too much for Bell to stay silent. "M-Miss Aiz? Miss Aiz?! Why are you looking at me like that?!"

"You're imagining things."

Bell fearfully readied his dagger and prepared to back up, only to realize he was already against the wall. There was nowhere to run.

Eyes glimmering with an all-consuming longing, Aiz eliminated any doubts the boy had as she practically flew toward him.

Not even two seconds went by before Bell's shrieking "Gaaahhh!!" rose into the sky.

Several minutes later...

Bell was, once again, passed out cold with his head neatly positioned in Aiz's lap. She ran her fingers through his bangs over and over, a blissfully satisfied look on her face.

A few more minutes later...

Aiz started with a gasp—she'd completely forgotten the original purpose of their training.

When at last the boy's eyes reopened, she peppered him with apologies.

Traditionally, magic tests—often referred to as a magic user's combat training—were held within the Dungeon.

It went without saying that tossing spells around in the middle of the city would pose a threat to civilians and city property alike, which in turn would invite Guild involvement.

Hosting it in the Dungeon, however, with its rampant monster spawning, guaranteed that at worst, only other adventurers would get involved. Magic users who wanted to practice avoided the established routes, venturing deep into the Dungeon to ensure members of other familias wouldn't get caught in their spell effects (or overhear their magical chants).

"I'll be in your care, Miss Aiz!"

Ever her usual self, Lefiya stood ready to go into one of the western chambers on the Dungeon's fifth floor.

Six days remained until the expedition.

As adventurers began venturing into the Dungeon in droves, the elven magic user hurried to the innermost room of the floor. In front of her stood Aiz, fresh from her second day of training with Bell.

The large squared space they currently occupied had only one exit. There wasn't a single soul in sight, making it the perfect place to try a few spells in complete secrecy. It was first-come, first-served when it came to spots as ideal as this for spell training. Speed was key.

While altercations between magic users looking for training spots were rare—they tended to be intellectuals, after all—the same couldn't be said when it came to the throng of low-level adventurers trying to nab the prime locations for grinding.

"But I really am sorry for making you join me. You're training even me..." Lefiya gripped her staff.

"Don't worry about it." Aiz shook her head, still clad in her light-weight armor and sword at her side. She would be training both Bell and Lefiya until the day of the expedition, the young boy in the early morning and her elven admirer from day till dusk.

Despite feeling apologetic at dragging her straight to the Dungeon after their breakfast together, Lefiya couldn't fight back the sheer excitement at being there with Aiz.

Sure, she felt a little put out at getting Aiz after that boy, but the fact that she'd have the Sword Princess all to herself for the whole day more than made up for it.

How about that? Do you see now? Are you jealous?!

She didn't even need to know a name to egg him on in her mind.

The pointless inner conflict had her feeling not only motivated but triumphant as well. She was with her glorious idol, after all.

Lefiya waited impatiently for her training to begin, gladder than ever that she'd requested Aiz.

"Let's start, then..."

"Yes, ma'am!"

"...So...what should we do?"

"..."

Lefiya almost fell to her knees. She had already failed before she could even begin.

"Is there anything I can teach you? I'm a sword fighter, after all..."

The two reached the same fundamental issue, though it was too late to worry about it.

Beyond the how-tos of adventuring, there really wasn't much a swordswoman could teach a magic user. The practical skills and combat methods of a caster like Lefiya, focused on chanting techniques and ranged attacks from the rear guard, did not have a great deal of overlap with a swordswoman like Aiz, who focused on hand-to-hand combat on the front line.

"I've been thinking about what I could do with you since yesterday... but I couldn't come up with anything," Aiz confessed weakly, her head hung in apology. Her brain was already pushed to its limits coming up with a training regimen for Bell.

Indeed, if Lefiya truly wanted to polish her skills as a magic user, she'd have better luck continuing under Riveria's tutelage. That would have been much more helpful.

Lefiya could feel the inklings of shame building like sweat beneath her collar. She'd been focused solely on being with Aiz and hadn't considered much else.

A heavy quiet settled over the two of them as their gazes drifted toward the ground.

Not even the far-off cry of a monster could break the silence.

Finally, Lefiya couldn't bear it any longer. "What, uh...what kinds of things are you doing with that human?"

"Mostly we've just been having practice duels..." Aiz began.

But before she'd finished her thought, she suddenly understood, and she took on a considering expression.

"...Has Riveria covered Concurrent Casting with you yet, Lefiya?"

A look of surprise crossed Lefiya's face, and then she nodded stiffly.

"Th-the basics of it, yes. Though I am...not very good..." she confessed, cheeks tinted pink with shame.

She'd been given the general knowledge but had yet to really put it into practice. As it stood now, she couldn't handle much more than a brisk walk or light run while chanting.

According to Riveria, her "mind and spirit weren't ready," which was why the high elf had been having her meditate to train her inner self.

In reality, Concurrent Casting was more of a pipe dream for Lefiya, with training to hasten her chanting time requiring most of her efforts. Shaving off even a single second meant that much less of a burden for her party members. After all, one second in the Dungeon could mean the difference between victory and defeat. Chanting skills weren't just important for a magic user, they were their everything.

"It's 'cause yer head's as soft as tofu, Lefiya!" Loki had once told her, whatever that meant.

Hence why she was studying the way of the "unshakable tree," as Riveria called it. So she could keep her cool no matter the situation and prevent an Ignis Fatuus from occurring when she used magic.

While Lefiya shamefully explained all her faults and shortcomings and everything she'd been taught, Aiz merely nodded, deep in thought.

Aiz pondered scrupulously, her eyes never leaving Lefiya's. "…I'm not sure if mixing in my teachings with Riveria's will be a good thing or not, but why don't we try practicing some Concurrent Casting? In an actual battle," she added, making Lefiya stop short.

"If you can manage that, you should even be able to fight on your own…I think."

Lefiya gulped audibly.

Being able to use Concurrent Casting would practically make her a mobile artillery battery. It was what every rearguard magic user dreamed of.

And Aiz had a chance to capitalize on Lefiya's solid foundation to get a bit of sword practice while providing instruction—an arrangement that would mutually benefit both sides.

At the very least, something would change, Lefiya thought almost hopefully.

"Of course, it could be that Riveria only decided to teach you Concurrent Casting to instill a bit of confidence in you…"

"…"

"Which isn't necessarily the wrong idea…I'm just worried about doing something unnecessary. What do you think?" Aiz pondered, leaving the final decision to Lefiya.

As those golden eyes peered into her own, Lefiya's gaze fell, and she gripped her staff tightly in both hands.

Aiz was right. There was no doubt Riveria had made the correct decision in disciplining Lefiya's immature spirit, instilling some self-confidence, and helping her grow as a magic user.

But when? When would that confidence finally come?

At what point could she say with absolute faith that she was no longer a burden to Aiz, Riveria, Tiona and Tione, and all the others—a feat that seemed no less difficult than scaling the world's tallest mountain?

In a year?

Five years?

Ten? Twenty?

She couldn't wait—that would be too long.

No matter how tall that mountain, if she didn't aim for the top regardless of how she appeared to others, she'd never be able to stand among those women.

The disappointment she'd been down on the twenty-fourth floor, the cowardice she'd shown during the Monsterphilia...If only she had mastered Concurrent Casting at the time. Lefiya pondered what might have been.

Then she wouldn't have held the others back. At the very least, she could have been a greater asset to them.

Even if there was risk, Lefiya wanted to give everything she had—not for the future but for *now*.

Raising her head, she looked Aiz straight in the eye.

"Please give me training in Concurrent Casting! Please help me practice!" Lefiya's voice rang out, filled with determination.

She would master Concurrent Casting.

Her goal was to become a moving fortress.

And as Lefiya stood there, eyes brimming with courage, Aiz nodded.

"Understood."

The two women faced each other, weapons at the ready and their expressions the embodiment of solemnity.

"See if you can chant and dodge my strikes at the same time."

"Yes, ma'am!"

Thrusting Desperate into the ground next to her, Aiz readied her scabbard.

Following Aiz's lead, Lefiya, too, readied her staff. Thinking back on everything Riveria had taught her about the basics of Concurrent Casting, she prepared her mind for both chanting and moving.

Knowing she'd have her Magic to fall back on, she focused first on the physical act of moving—lips included. It would be very remiss of her to forget that.

Nerves of steel. An unshakable tree.

Levying her nervousness, she took off with a start, first chant already on her lips.

"*Unlea—*"

Lefiya barely had time to begin her backward leap when an attack came from the front at an almost superhuman speed.

"Huh?"

The scabbard hit her square in the side before the air could even finish passing her lips.

She let out an unnatural groan.

"Oh."

With a single explosive blow from the Sword Princess, Lefiya went flying through the air, and her staff sailed skyward.

Aiz, on the other hand, stood frozen in the middle of her attack, scabbard still in its final position.

Lefiya tumbled across the floor of the Dungeon before coming to a stop. She moaned despondently with her arms clutching her abdomen.

"L-Lefiya!"

Aiz rushed to the girl's side, an apology already on her lips.

Lefiya had managed only two syllables of her chant. Aiz broke into a sweat, fearing she might have caused an Ignis Fatuus.

The young elf continued groaning in agony from the floor, her body trembling.

"I'm really sorry, Lefiya...I went at you like I was still training that boy."

But as soon as she heard Aiz's words, Lefiya's eyebrows twitched upward in anger.

That boy could refer to none other than the white-haired brat who'd stolen her Aiz away from her…

Lefiya's face was heating up. Doing her best to shake off the bitter resentment building inside her, she pushed herself to her feet with an energetic pop.

"I am…completely fine! So…keep coming like that!"

"A-all right," Aiz managed, stunned.

Lefiya's face was all (forced) smiles even as she cradled her side with one hand. Her drive to succeed had only intensified, reinforced by the burning enmity she felt for Bell.

Fetching her staff from the ground, she did her best to compose herself.

Then readied herself for her next bout of Concurrent Casting.

"Huh?!"

But.

"Ack!"

Unfortunately.

"Eeeeeeek!!"

She couldn't make even a little progress.

"U-unleashed pillar of—nngah!"

Lefiya's body finally crumpled after her chant was painfully interrupted by Aiz's scabbard.

Her legs simply gave out, and she dropped on her rump to the floor with a tiny *thud*. She let her staff slip from her hands as her chest heaved in and out.

She couldn't complete a single spell.

Even with Aiz going easy on her, she was spending so much effort watching out for incoming attacks that she couldn't complete even the most basic spell. It felt as though all she was accomplishing was practice for preventing an Ignis Fatuus backfire.

While she certainly wasn't about to pass out as easily as a lower-class adventurer like Bell, she was clearly running on fumes by this point.

"I'm sorry, Lefiya…" Aiz's gaze was fixed to the floor in front of the downed elf. "I overestimated myself…I shouldn't have meddled with things I know nothing about…It's just like Riveria said…" Aiz's voice dripped with remorse. She didn't know anything about magic users or the ideal way to give instruction on Concurrent Casting. She was nothing but an amateur.

Upon hearing Aiz's apology and sigh directed at her unsightly, even disheveled self, Lefiya's lips slowly parted.

"Miss Aiz...can I just ask...how that human is faring?" she asked, eyes boring holes through the floor.

Aiz cocked her head to the side. It took her a moment to respond.

Finally: "He's very earnest. He tries so hard. And he's incredibly honest..." As she relayed everything she'd seen, heard, and felt during the boy's training, she couldn't help the small smile that formed on her lips. "His growth is unprecedented...and I believe he has considerable room to grow even further," she concluded, wonder tangible in her voice. In her mind, she thought back to the boy's training session and the glimpse she had caught of his astonishing growth on only their second day. He had hung so fiercely on her every word, sunk his teeth into her every instruction.

Hearing this, Lefiya's hands hit the floor with a mighty slap.

"?!"

The impact and power of a Level 3 left a crack in the Dungeon floor and rising wisps of smoke.

Lefiya's body began to shake.

Her despair had reached its peak.

I couldn't do...a single thing...

While I've been doing nothing but making a disgrace of myself, that boy has only improved?!

Fiery heat engulfed her body. The relentless waves of boiling-hot rage only further fostered the uncontrollable trembling of her every muscle.

In her mind, she could see him. He dashed ahead of her, wearing a disgustingly refreshing smile as he said, *Giving up already? Well then, I'll be going on ahead!*

Grrrrr......!! Her mind sputtered in barely repressed, incomprehensible fury.

Her pathetic state was unforgivable.

She wouldn't tolerate it anymore.

Not when that boy was working hard enough to earn recognition from Aiz already!

—*I won't lose! I won't!*

This was the moment that human boy became Lefiya's rival.

Roaring from the depths of her lungs, she flung herself to her feet.

Her eyes narrowed, displaying a mettle not present during her training with Riveria, shining with an overpowering determination that seemed enough to pierce through the Dungeon's walls.

"I can still go on. Please continue!"

Aiz stared at the girl for a moment in wide-eyed amazement before finally smiling.

With a nod, she readied her scabbard, and Lefiya's Concurrent Casting practice began anew.

Refusing to shrink back from attack after attack, Lefiya continued her song and chants, blue eyes blazing all the while.

"Hey, Riveria. What's Lefiya been up to lately?"

Tiona was covered from head to toe in blood and wounds.

"Shouldn't I be asking you that question…?" Riveria sighed from her position on the couch. One hand held a cup of tea while the other pressed lightly at the spot between her closed eyes.

Five days remained until the expedition.

They were in the parlor room of Twilight Manor, home of *Loki Familia*, just a bit before noon. The majority of members had already left for the day, leaving Riveria alone to rest in the lounge overlooking the street. Until two twin Amazonian sisters had appeared, their matching pareu-style skirts looking decidedly worse for wear.

A lingering heat wafted up from their exposed dark skin as Tiona's semi-short mop and Tione's long silken tresses both swayed softly.

"Tione and I were sparring! Sparring!"

"We were both feeling a little discouraged after Aiz's last level-up. Couldn't just leave it at that, now, could we?"

Tione's slumped shoulders looked mildly out of place juxtaposed

with Tiona's overly cheerful exaltation. Of course, they were referring to Aiz's recent progress to Level 6.

"Indeed, but we all have our limits..." Riveria sighed again, her
eyes taking in the mangled state of both their bodies.

This wasn't unusual for the twins. Inseparable as they'd been since
birth, they were always attempting to help bolster each other's skills,
from sparring matches like this to sisterly catfights, and even included
worryingly almost-literal fights to the death. Riveria knew this.

While she had no problem with the two of them duking it out,
there was a point where the risk of danger became too high.

"You aren't the only ones. It seems the entire familia has gotten
itself into a training craze. Honestly, and right before the expedition, too..."

Indeed, the entire faction was feeling the effects of Aiz's recent
growth, ushering in a slew of intensive practice regimens. From the
lower-class members to the upper echelons, it was like they were all
ablaze, everyone inspired to achieve the same greatness as the beautifully powerful face of the familia—the Sword Princess.

This was why the manor was so empty at the moment. Everyone
was off in the Dungeon or undergoing harsh training trying to follow in her footsteps.

The second-in-command of *Loki Familia* sighed in an attempt to
flush out her worries.

"I bet Lefiya's probably training, too." Tiona thought back first to
the deadly aura Lefiya had exuded that one night at dinner and then
to the extraordinary new burst of enthusiasm she had been displaying recently. Could Aiz have something to do with that?

"Come to think of it, Aiz has seemed a little off lately, too, hasn't
she?" Tione mused beside her sister.

"You know anything, Riveria?"

"I am just as in the dark as you two..."

Though even as she said it, Riveria's mind drifted back to her
memories of the day prior.

Lefiya had approached her in need of learning materials. This by
itself wasn't at all unusual, but there'd been something about her,

like she was possessed by some horrifying demon. The change had been enough to make even Riveria hesitate.

Lefiya had spent the entire night rooted to her desk, paging through book after book. She'd always been a little zealous, but her desperately repeating sessions of trial and error went beyond her normal efforts.

Perhaps she has found a good rival to spar with.

Riveria might not have lived as long as a god, but she was a high elf and had lived her fair share of years—she recognized this kind of change when she saw it.

"More important…Do something about your appearance, you two." Riveria unsubtly brought up the twins' disheveled condition.

It wouldn't have surprised her if the "sparring" the two had done wasn't closer to that of an actual battle, considering their blood-stained skin and messy clothes, hair, and faces.

Elves were naturally fastidious, and for Riveria, looking at the two of them right now was positively agonizing.

"Meh. We're just resting a bit before we have another go. Why bother?"

"Yeah, it'd be a pain anyway."

All Riveria could do was let out another sigh at the blithe and optimistic Amazonian sisters.

Standing up from the sofa, she took Tione's hand and forced her onto a nearby chair.

"What are you doing?"

"You want to look like a lady for Finn, yes? Then you should at least do something about your hair."

Riveria circled around behind the girl and started combing her long, dark hair. Using one of the combs in the parlor room, she tamed Tione's unkempt hair bit by bit.

"You're actually quite…good at this, Riveria. I'd always thought that, as a high elf, you'd have servants to do these kinds of things for you."

"It was when I was looking after Aiz. That girl…She didn't give a single thought to her hair. Things got to the point where I couldn't take it any longer. I ended up learning," Riveria explained with a wry smile. Her eyes narrowed as her thoughts drifted back to memories from many years ago.

Tione's own eyes slowly closed. The feeling of Riveria's hands softly threading through her hair was a bit ticklish, but it was so wonderful at the same time.

"No fair! Do me next, Riveria!"

"All right, all right, just give me a moment." Riveria's eyes softened with a smile as she shook her head, clucking her tongue. *These girls.*

Helpless between the almost catlike Amazonian sisters in their capriciousness, Riveria wove the tines through Tiona's long hair with gentle *swish-swish*es that seemed to fill the room.

"Hey, Riveria?"

"What is it?"

"You knew Aiz since she was little, right? Like…around the time she entered the familia?" Tiona asked slowly, watching over her sister from the nearby chair.

"I did," Riveria replied, not even turning her head.

It had been almost nine years since that day. Aiz had been only seven.

"Did you know Aria?"

Riveria's hand came to an abrupt stop.

"Riveria…?" Tione turned around in her seat, eyeing the elf suspiciously.

Riveria, on the other hand, turned her jade-colored eyes toward Tiona.

"Where did you hear that name?"

"Lefiya…She said Aiz was called that during that time down on the eighteenth and twenty-fourth floors," Tiona explained sincerely, her eyes now fixed on Riveria. The two sisters intently watched the high elf, her beauty surpassing even that of goddesses.

"Seems like a lot of weird stuff has been happening lately. New species of monsters, whatever it was that happened to Bete and the others on the twenty-fourth floor…I can't be sure, but it seems like something serious is going on."

The viola attacks that'd plagued them since the Monsterphilia.

The battle that had broken out surrounding Hashana's control of the crystal-orb fetus down in Rivira on the eighteenth floor and the chance encounter with that monster-manipulating tamer woman, the creature Levis.

Then on the twenty-fourth floor, as if that wasn't already enough, the remnants of the shadowy Evils faction had decided to make an appearance, along with their schemes to destroy Orario.

Tiona crossed her legs atop the sofa, trembling slightly as she relayed each event in turn.

"It almost makes me wonder whether Aiz being called 'Aria' by those thugs has something to do with, you know, everything that's been going on lately."

"..."

"I mean, Aria's the name of the main character in that legend, right? But that couldn't possibly have anything to do with Aiz..."

As Tiona trailed off, Riveria let her gaze return forward.

Silently, broodingly, she ran the comb once more through Tione's hair before coming to a stop, just as she'd done so many times for Aiz in the past.

"You know anything, Riveria?" Tione asked.

But Riveria didn't reply.

The only thing that changed was the tilt of her head, just enough that she could direct her gaze out the window.

"The fifty-ninth floor..." Riveria finally said. "...There, everything will be made clear."

The sky reflected a brilliant blue in her jade eyes.

"Y'know, yer theory was right on the money, Finn!"

It was out on the main street, with the sun shining down and the sky crystal clear, where an unhurried voice—lazy, almost—announced its opinion.

It was about the same time Riveria and company were having their own conversation up in the parlor room of the manor. Bustling carriages and boisterous demi-humans clattered about the cobblestones, while the prum Finn glanced up at the figure next to him.

"How so, Loki?"

Walking along beside him was none other than the goddess with ginger hair and cinnabar-colored eyes, Loki.

The deity in question glanced down at her follower, hands laced behind her head.

"When we went over everything with Gareth and Riveria! Said it yerself, didn'cha?"

It had been six days now since Aiz had gotten them involved in that incident down on the twenty-fourth floor.

Loki had been discussing it together with the three faction leaders in their home's office, and it was then that Finn had said it. They still knew nothing about that creature Levis, and they were still in the dark regarding that new species of monster and their strange, richly colored magic stones.

"We simply don't have the knowledge to pacify that many monsters. Doing so—"

—is nothing more than a fantasy, was how Finn had finally completed his sentence in an attempt at masking his true feelings.

"But you actually wanted to finish that sentence like this, yeah?" Loki brought it up again, refusing to let sleeping dogs lie. And then, in a perfect imitation of Finn, "Doing so would put us on par with those monstrous underground dwellers."

The prum's shoulders visibly slumped. Loki had seen straight through him.

"It seems even a god like you could take a stab at where that was heading."

"And what a stab!" Loki teased, a playful smile gracing her lips. "What's left of the Evils—they ain't people *or* monsters. They're phantoms. Which is why this whole thing with the crystal orb turned into such a big to-do. Finn, whaddaya think is down on the fifty-ninth floor, huh?"

During their encounter on the twenty-fourth floor, Levis had told Aiz: *"Go to the fifty-ninth floor. Should answer a lot of your questions."*

And that's where they were going on their expedition. To the new depths beyond the farthest they'd ever tread—the fifty-ninth floor.

Just what exactly awaited them there?

"I doubt someone like me could even hazard a guess," Finn countered, his answer purposefully vague as a sort of riposte. He gave his thumb a little lick, intent on keeping his thoughts firmly to himself.

"Though I will say that we might finally have met our match."

And it wasn't just a single entity, either. It was a giant shadow made of countless, erratically overlapping lines.

A presence entangled in the expectations of many…or something like that, Finn believed.

"Ain't that the truth," muttered Loki under her breath.

Finn watched her out of the corner of his eye, his thumb beginning to throb.

"Hey, Finn…care if I speak freely?" Loki asked abruptly.

"What is it?" Finn looked up to see her stop short a few feet in front of him.

She turned around.

In that single moment, the air between them changed, almost as if she'd taken off some kind of mask. The corners of her mouth curled upward.

"This is why I can't leave this world alone."

"…"

"Hybrids aren't humans or monsters. Even for us all-knowin' gods, entirely unexpected things're happenin'—like an 'unknown' that deities themselves can't predict."

Loki's eyes widened just slightly, revealing a twinkle of delight. It was almost as though she was drunk on some sort of high-grade wine.

She could sense the unknown she had thirsted after for so long. The feeling of foreboding was enough to make her stomach curl even as the warm sun shined on the tranquil cobblestones beneath her feet. And yet that wasn't enough to stop the insatiable elation from building in her belly.

Loki let out a laugh of pure, unadulterated joy.

Finn responded with a faint smile of his own, watching his goddess in silence.

"'Course, I'm most worried about you guys, yeah? I'm all choked up about it! Make sure ya come back alive, y'hear!" Reverting back to her usual blasé attitude, Loki circled around behind Finn and gave his shoulders a little squeeze.

They were attracting attention now. Finn forced a somewhat sardonic smile.

"No need to worry, Loki. I'm an adventurer, after all," he responded amid the teasing. "I know all too well the feeling of challenging the unknown."

Loki met Finn's upturned gaze, pausing for just a moment before shooting him a grin.

The goddess and prum shared a long history, indeed.

Before long, they had resumed their walk.

The path they followed was Northeast Main Street. It bordered the Industrial District, the city's number two ward and the heart of the magic-stone manufacturing and production industry, and was constantly clogged with freelance laborers from various guilds and familia craftsmen.

Being an area so focused on manufacturing, the majority of passersby were laborers in work attire. Burly middle-aged humans toted tools and materials to this place or that while animal-people studied production orders and shouted themselves hoarse. All throughout the hubbub echoed the clanging of metal on metal, interposed with the crassly shouted songs of dwarves at work.

It was safe to say women and children were a foreign sight in a man's world such as this. Looking decidedly out of place, the petite Finn and female Loki wound their way from the main street to the heart of the district.

Still chatting idly, the two of them arrived at a little bungalow of a workshop.

"—We're here."

In front of the workshop, the building itself in desperate need of a good soot-cleansing, stood a goddess with hair of blazing vermilion.

She directed her left eye, of the same brilliant hue as her hair, toward Loki and Finn. Her right eye was currently hidden beneath the large eye patch that sheathed half her face.

"Mornin', Phai-Phai. Or should I say 'afternoon'?"

The woman in front of them was none other than Hephaistos, world-renowned goddess of the forge and timeless leader of *Hephaistos Familia*.

"Phai-Phai," as Loki called her, raised a hand in greeting.

Even with the impressive jet-black eye patch, her divine beauty left no doubts as to whether she was a goddess or not. Her ensemble of white tunic paired with black trousers and gloves exuded an air of rustic masculinity, which, when coupled with her stunning visage, no doubt marked her as the sort of person inclined to care for others.

Hephaistos responded to Loki with a greeting of her own, red hair swaying slightly as her lips formed a weak smile.

"Sorry for calling you all the way out here like this, Loki."

"Think nothin' of it! We're the ones draggin' yer mates along on our expedition to keep our weapons all nice 'n' shiny, after all."

Loki Familia had sought *Hephaistos Familia*'s help on their upcoming expedition.

Finn had come to Hephaistos (via Loki) to request provision of a High Smith in hopes of staving off wear and tear for their weapons during their expedition.

Hephaistos had agreed, so long as her followers were guaranteed the drop items from the Dungeon. Thus, an alliance had been forged between the two familias.

"Your acceptance of our proposal means the world to us, Lady Hephaistos."

"Oh? Such gratitude from a prum of valor like yourself is a distinction all its own. It brings me nothing but honor to help you and your familia on your trek through the Dungeon." Hephaistos's eye crinkled in response to Finn's deep bow.

"Your words are too kind, milady." Finn's eyes closed at the goddess's dignified demeanor.

"This is the first time y'all are meetin', right?"

"It is. Though we've greeted each other many times in the past, this is the first time we've spoken face-to-face, I believe," Finn said.

"Let's continue this conversation inside, yes?" Hephaistos suggested before guiding Loki and Finn toward her workshop. The two followed her into the building, surrounded by the clamorous clanking of metal on metal.

"We've been asking her again and again to have a meeting before the expedition...Finally had to just come here ourselves. She really doesn't ever leave her workshop, does she?"

Loki just laughed. "She's just like you, Phai-Phai! A real craftsman at heart. Seems the apple don't fall far from the tree after all, eh?"

"I suppose some things never change."

Hephaistos let out a sigh, which elicited another chuckle from Loki and a quirk of the lips from Finn.

Immediately upon entering the doorway, they were greeted with the strong smell of iron, which permeated the air of the workshop and the considerably sized smithy connected to it. Lacking sufficient magic-stone lamps, the space was shrouded in dim shadow, the main source of light coming from the brilliant red flames of the roaring furnace.

Now that they'd entered the building, the mad *clang, clang* of metal on metal they'd been able to hear outside besieged their eardrums all the more. It was there, farther inside the workshop, that they saw her.

She was facing away from them, surrounded on all sides by some of the biggest tools they'd ever seen and pounding animatedly at an ingot on her anvil with a hammer.

Ember after ember from the nearby furnace singed the copper skin of her cheeks; sweat poured from her face in rivulets, adding still more to her aura of gallantry. While her disciplined features lacked the feminine allure of a woman, there was a different sort of beauty about her—ferocious, like a blazing pyre: the epitome of a craftsman.

She took no notice of Hephaistos and the others, eyes glued to her anvil as the hammer descended with one mighty strike after another.

Finn and Loki came to a stop a few steps away from the forge. Hephaistos gestured silently for them to wait, and they complied with a nod, simply watching over the lone smith at work.

The woman's ebony ponytail shuddered, and with one final clang of the hammer, her hand came to a stop. Without missing a beat, she snatched the completed sword body from off her anvil with a pair of tongs.

There was a hiss, followed by a plume of steam. A honed, polished blade came into view. A novice watching could have no way of knowing how long she'd spent on the weapon as she slapped together the hilt and flange. In a flash, the sword was complete.

She spent a moment scrutinizing the crimson blade in her hand before finally letting out a sigh.

"Tsubaki." Hephaistos beckoned the woman with long black hair flowing down her back.

The one she'd called Tsubaki turned around.

"Oh?" As though noticing them just now, her right eye widened in surprise. Almost instantly, her face broke into a broad smile.

"How many weeks has it been, my goddess? Need something? No, wait! Take a look at this magic sword I just whipped up. I'm pretty confident about this one."

As old as the woman looked, you'd almost think she was a child by the way she gleefully held out her sword, all smiles.

"I was just here two days ago..." said Hephaistos, responding to the woman's endless stream of words with a sigh. "We need to discuss your upcoming expedition with Loki's team. I told you this, right?" The hint of frustration was tangible.

"Ohh!" Tsubaki bellowed in what seemed like acknowledgment. She walked over to them with a laugh. "That's right, that's right!"

"Good to see you again, Tsubaki."

"Well, if it isn't Finn! Tiny as ever! When you're cooped up in a shop all day, ya start missin' the warmth of other people. C'mere and gimme a squeeze, would ya?" Tsubaki exclaimed before approaching the prum with her arms outstretched.

"I'm afraid I'll have to decline," Finn said with a wry smile. "Tione would have my head if she found out."

The woman let out a bellow of laughter.

Tsubaki Collbrande was the captain of *Hephaistos Familia*.

Not only did she command the virtual army of High Smiths that made up the familia of forge work, she herself was the most skilled smith in all of Orario.

© Kiyotaka Haimura

She was a half-dwarf, her parents a human from the Far East and a dwarf from the continent; she boasted a set of graceful features reminiscent of her eastern origins. Standing at a good 170 celch, she was fairly tall with long arms and legs, no doubt thanks to her human blood—a quality that apparently made her the envy of her short-limbed dwarven brethren.

Her work wear boasted the eastern flair of her mother's homeland, the bottom consisting of a brilliant red *hakama* and the top consisting of nothing but a bleached cloth pulled tight around her ample bosom. As for why she kept her copper-colored stomach and shoulders bare in spite of the constant assault of embers, well, Finn had once heard her explain that the forge was "damn hot!"

Topping everything off were a shapely red right eye and, most notably, a jet-black eye patch nearly identical to Hephaistos's—the only difference being that it covered Tsubaki's left eye instead of her right.

"By the looks of it, ya made somethin' ridiculous again, didn't ya, Cyclops?"

"You know I don't like that name, Loki! Makes me feel like some kinda monster! How'd you like it, huh?" Tsubaki's face soured as Loki snickered at the newly finished sword in her hands.

"Cyclops" was the title given to Tsubaki by the other deities.

Being both a smith and a Level 5 adventurer, with the combat skills to prove it, made her a bit of an oddity if not an outright demon.

The peerless combat skills of the almost excessively unique craftsmen (Tsubaki included) was just one of the many reasons other factions rarely attacked *Hephaistos Familia*—that and its establishment as an invaluable familia of smiths.

Loki snickered somewhat lecherously. "I will say yer lookin' as busty as ever. Look! Practically fallin' outta that thing you call a shirt!"

"Want 'em? You can have 'em! These two lumps of fat do nothin' but get in the way at the forge. Don't need 'em!"

"Guh-hah!" Loki nearly choked. She hadn't expected her obscene remark to be met with such scathing retaliation.

Tsubaki just cackled, the twin mounds in question bouncing somewhat stiffly within their cloth restraint.

"Shall we get back to the subject at hand?"

"Let's. Time is of the essence, after all."

Ignoring Loki in her plight, Finn and Hephaistos attempted to steer the conversation back on track.

"Yes, ma'am!" Tsubaki nodded between mouthfuls, snacking on a piece of soot-covered jerky that had been sitting on her desk for who knows how long while she'd busied herself at the forge.

And with that, once Loki had recovered, the deities and captains of both familias, shrouded in the gloom of that dim workshop, dove straight into discussion regarding their upcoming expedition.

"Look, I'm just gonna ask ya straight—how many High Smiths ya givin' us?"

"Hmm…Looking at smiths who are not only experienced crafts-men but able-bodied adventurers, as well…I'd say we have about twenty, Tsubaki included. Every one of them is at least Level Three, so you can have faith in their abilities," Hephaistos replied.

There was no telling what might happen upon entering the Dun-geon. It would be to their advantage to have party members who could not only maintain their weapons but take care of themselves in a pinch.

"That's reassuring. Though I have to ask—will you be joining us, as well, Tsubaki?" Finn inquired.

"For sure! I wanna see those depths for myself. That and, if at all possible, I'd like to be the one nabbin' any new materials," Tsubaki replied, brimming with curiosity as to what awaited them beyond the floors her own faction had traversed. She shot them a smile devoid of worry. "It'll be a great opportunity!"

"And what of our Durandal weapons?"

"A-OK there! Five of 'em, each one prepped personally!"

"Nice, Tsubaki. Thank ya."

"Can I ask you two to give Bete Loga an earful for me? Near impos-sible request he gave me! Comin' to me cryin' that his poor Frosvirt was all in pieces—took me forever to rebuild! Damn werewolf."

Knowing they'd have those caterpillar monsters to deal with from the fiftieth floor onward—nasty critters that secreted corro-sive, weapon-destroying fluids—Finn and the others had left their

Durandal Superiors with Hephaistos and her crew. This included the weapons for each of their top-class adventurers excluding Aiz, who already had Desperate, and Riveria, who was simply a magic user.

Tsubaki had already finished up all the Durandal weapons, so when Bete had come to her with his Superior, Frosvirt, completely destroyed after their bout with Levis on the twenty-fourth floor, she'd been put out, to say the least. Apparently he'd come running immediately after the incident, demanding personally that she "fix it before the expedition!"

Tsubaki had been working day and night without sleep readying the equipment for their main party. Finn and Loki both made sure to offer her additional words of thanks.

"Though, really, I'm not sure that magic sword was necessary..."

"Yeah, we did already order a bunch o' Superiors from y'all, and yer stuff ain't exactly, uh, cheap..."

"Come now. Surely a familia like yours should have no problem getting a loan." Hephaistos's left eye crinkled in mirth.

It was true that a magic sword, what with its instant, long-range capabilities, would be a good candidate for taking on those caterpillars. But magic swords were already expensive enough, let alone a top-tier model from *Hephaistos Familia*.

"G-go easy there..." Loki replied with a forced laugh.

"Though I gotta say, when it comes to craftin' magic swords...you could do better than me," Tsubaki mumbled to herself.

"What, do you mean there's someone better than you in that familia of yours?" Finn posed, to which Tsubaki nodded happily.

"Someone far better at forgin' magic swords! Fact is, I don't think there's anyone what knows more 'bout magic swords than that person in the whole world."

Both Finn's and Loki's eyes widened in surprise.

Tsubaki Collbrande was the finest smith in all of Orario.

Hearing that there was someone even better than her, the master smith, was a shock, to say the least.

"For you to talk about them like that, they must be someone, indeed. Who is it?"

As though waiting for Finn to ask just that question, Tsubaki chuckled gleefully.

"Listen and be amazed! It's none other than that ol' blue blood—"

"That's enough, Tsubaki," Hephaistos interrupted. "You know as well as I that our colleague would prefer their lineage kept a secret."

Left Eye Patch grumbled sullenly in response to Right Eye Patch's stern admonishment.

"Come ooooon! We got nothin' to lose! Lemme tell 'em!"

"Good grief! It's this kind of self-centered carelessness that's already sent people to him asking about magic swords. Remember how angry he was?"

It was clear to Finn and Loki that things were a bit complicated among the members of *Hephaistos Familia.*

Tsubaki, however, showed no signs that she'd actually taken Hephaistos's scolding to heart.

"Such a waste! All that talent and he ain't even usin' it. Makes no sense to me." Tsubaki sighed, her gaze falling to the red blade in her hand—the magic sword fresh from the forge.

Then, in that moment…

The air around her hardened.

"Whether it's blood or somethin' else, if we don't invest everything we got, us little folks'll never get close to the domain of the gods. Things like all-powerful weapons ain't nothin' but dreams," Tsubaki concluded, voice low. The ravenous glint in her right eye was enough to shame even the nearby furnace.

It was the same glint Loki and the others had seen so many times in the eyes of adventurers like Aiz, who constantly aimed higher and higher.

The look of pride, a thirst for more, and the insatiable perseverance of a craftsman.

Tsubaki knew that if she didn't bet everything, she'd never be able to forge a piece worthy of the gods, let alone one that surpassed them. It was something only she could know, having reached the highest pinnacle one could as a craftsman.

Tearing her gaze away from her creation, Tsubaki glanced over at Hephaistos and let out a bold peal of laughter.

Hephaistos slumped her shoulders with a sigh at her follower's bald-faced aggression.

"That's craftsmen for ya. Must be tough, Phai-Phai."

"Mmn...At any rate, shall we return to the issue at hand?"

Steering the conversation back on track, the quartet moved on to sketching out the expedition.

"Is the plan to meet in front of Babel, then? And enter from there together?"

"Yes. Once inside the Dungeon, my team and I will do our best to protect the rest of the group. While this may need to change in emergency situations, for the most part all combat should be left to us."

"We'll help with half of the supplies. We've come this far already—might as well share the load."

"Thanks, Phai-Phai. Appreciate it."

The four of them ran through their respective final checklists before bringing the meeting to a close, and then Finn and Loki bid the others farewell and left the workshop behind them.

Preparations for *Loki Familia*'s expedition were well under way.

"Hey, uh...Miss Aiz? There was something I wanted to talk to you about!"

They were four days into their training, having just completed a rather strenuous practice bout atop the city walls.

It was just a bit before sunrise—their decided-upon time for wrapping things up—when Bell approached Aiz, considerably red-faced and flustered.

"It's, uh, well...tomorrow, see? My supporter won't be able to go to the Dungeon tomorrow because of issues with her lodging, so, uh...I was thinking maybe I wouldn't go, either, so, uh...well...I was just thinking that...that maybe tomorrow we could...Instead of just in the morning..."

"...Train...all day?" Aiz finished for him.

"Y-yes!" Bell stuttered with boisterous nods of his head.

Aiz slid her sword back into her scabbard before letting her gaze travel skyward and quietly contemplating.

She was supposed to be training Lefiya then...but Lefiya and Aiz were part of the same familia. They could get together whenever they felt like it.

Plus, to be honest, Aiz wanted to spend more time with Bell to improve his combat skills.

The short time they had before the sun rose wasn't enough.

Which was why, with a silent apology to Lefiya, Aiz agreed.

"Very well."

That was the story Aiz personally relayed to Lefiya, apology included, and which was also the reason the elf wasn't able to train with her today.

Three days remained until the expedition.

It was supposed to be Lefiya's fourth day of training, as she was one day behind Bell.

But that morning found her walking despondently down the busy main street in a tremendously bad mood.

Her azure eyes sat almost entirely still in their sockets, and her normally graceful elven features exuded a kind of silent animosity. From the demi-humans engaged on the sidewalks to those she passed in the street, everyone averted their eyes.

She gripped her beloved staff tightly to her chest, resentment saturating her very being.

"He's not even part of our faction...he's not even part of our faction...he's not even part of our faction...!"

Disgraceful! Shameless! I can't believe it!

Each tear-choked condemnation muttered under her breath was directed at that boy.

The impudence of haggling for a full day of the Sword Princess all to himself. She could feel the anger building up inside her just thinking about it. Unable to raise an objection to Aiz, Lefiya's blame was, instead, being launched at the boy in continuous tear-laced salvos. *Is he really such an absolute nitwit?!*

The path she currently trudged along was on North Main Street, not far from her familia's home.

She was on her way to the Dungeon to do a bit of training on her own—what other choice did she have? The cerulean sky stretched odiously above her, shining down on the bustling cobblestones.

"—Viridis?"

It hit her ears just as her vision had practically darkened in rage.

The sound of her last name.

"Hmm?" She spun around to find a young elven girl standing a few steps behind her.

She had long jet-black hair reminiscent of a shrine maiden's, and her eyes shone like a pair of scarlet rubies.

Snow-white battle gear enshrouded her slender figure all the way to her neck, topped with a short cape. Beside her, a golden-haired god waited patiently.

The sight of her made Lefiya stop short in surprise.

"Miss Filvis..." she muttered under her breath.

The girl in white, Filvis, wore a startled look of her own.

A Level 3 magic swordsman and the captain of *Dionysus Familia*, she'd fought beside Lefiya and the others on the front lines during the incident on the twenty-fourth floor some days ago.

This chance meeting brought both of them to a stop. As passersby jostled them on all sides, the regal blond god—Dionysus himself—opened his mouth to speak.

"This is the colleague you spoke of, Filvis? The Thousand Elf?"

"Y-yes, she is."

Lefiya stood rooted to the spot. This was her first time meeting the god of *Dionysus Familia* in the flesh, and she found herself at a loss as to how to react.

Dionysus, however, just smiled, examining her with his glass-like eyes.

"I've heard so much about you from Filvis. Could I interest you in a cup of tea, perhaps? I'd been hoping to show you my appreciation."

*   *   *

The three of them made their way to a bustling outdoor café on a small corner of North Main Street. From their round table facing the road, they were surrounded on all sides by the sounds of busy footsteps and lively voices.

"It's my understanding that you looked after Filvis down on the twenty-fourth floor. I'd like to once again offer you my utmost gratitude. If it weren't for you, I might have lost her, and for that, I am in your debt, Lefiya Viridis."

"I-it is nothing, really. I've lost count of the number of times Filvis has saved me…"

Lefiya felt terribly obliged at Dionysus's words of praise.

Dionysus had ordered them tea and fruit tarts. The sweet smell of pastries mixed with fresh red and blue berries was enough to make Lefiya's mouth water.

"Loki would surely wring my neck if she heard this was how I thanked you," the golden-haired god joked somewhat strangely.

Lefiya's impression was that he was a most refined and sociable god.

At the same time, there was something inscrutable about him. In fact, those glass-like eyes of his seemed able to peer straight through to her soul. He was a kind of all-knowing, ever-prudent godly presence, and she could see why he had offered his ill-tempered evaluation of Loki as "a shrewd deity."

Filvis sat in silence as the two of them conversed, having been forced to accompany them. She hadn't touched her tea or the tarts and simply glanced back and forth between Lefiya and Dionysus.

"…I believe I have a solid grasp of what happened down there by this point, but I'm interested in hearing from others who took part. How do you feel about the events on the twenty-fourth floor?"

Their pleasantries finished, Dionysus's face hardened.

Instinctively correcting her posture, Lefiya took a few moments to think through her response. While it was true Loki mostly thought of the other god as nothing more than a parasite of sorts, the two had been comparing notes more and more often since the Monsterphilia—or so she'd heard. There was no way Dionysus hadn't already met with Loki regarding the recent events at that place in the Dungeon.

Thus, there would be no harm in talking to him. After judging that to be the case, Lefiya relayed her opinion as a firsthand witness.

"—Magic stones inside beings even the gods know nothing about? A crystal orb that can make monsters mutate? The whole thing… Just thinking about it makes my head hurt."

Dionysus listened to Lefiya in silence before bringing his forehead to his palm with a heavy sigh.

As Filvis watched, those glass-like eyes of his came to meet Lefiya's.

"Thanks to the information you and the others brought back, we've made progress in identifying the true identity of our enemy. A third power linked to the remnants of the Evils, the being referred to only as 'Her' by Olivas Act…Lefiya Viridis, I must tell you—the sense of imminent danger I feel is all too real." He continued, hardened features suppressing his feelings. "Almost as though the very peace of this city itself is silently being eaten away from the inside out…"

Lefiya had heard from Filvis that a member of *Dionysus Familia* had been killed before the Monsterphilia. Remembering this, she listened quietly to Dionysus's every word.

"Though the bulk of the responsibility may end up falling on *Loki Familia*, we, too, would like to do everything we can. You may come to us whenever you're in need."

"Th-thank you. Thank you so much." Lefiya averted her gaze in response to the god's offer.

The sounds from the bustling street enveloped them during the lapse between their words.

"Come to think of it, how are the preparations for your expedition coming along? I heard the lot of you will be on your way to the depths before long," Dionysus said cheerfully, in perfect contrast to their previous topic as he brought his tea to his lips. He was catching furtive glances from the female customers around them.

There was something strange about his smile—a sickly sweet mask—that put Lefiya on edge. She responded carefully, deliberately leaving out the finer details of her familia's goings-on.

"Things are progressing according to plan. We shall leave in three days."

"Three days..." Dionysus murmured with a faint smile. "Filvis has been worried, you know. About you and the expedition."

Lefiya and Filvis both gave a start.

"She's been talking about you constantly since the incident on the twenty-fourth floor. More than she talks about herself, even."

"M-Master Dionysus!" The elven girl in question rose from her chair, causing Lefiya's eyes to widen in shock. With her voice caught in her throat, Filvis's normally white cheeks flushed with pink, and her eyes looked everywhere except at Lefiya.

"This is the first time I've seen her let anyone affect her like this in quite some time. I would imagine you're the type of person cats take to, yes?"

"Um...What exactly do you mean by...that?"

At Lefiya's perplexed inquisition, Dionysus's lips curled upward in a cheeky grin befitting a god.

"When Filvis first joined the familia, her fussiness was positively off-putting. So much that she wouldn't let anyone get near. Quite like a cat, you see."

"I am...not sure I understand what you're saying. What does that have to do with the current situation?"

Dionysus seemed to be enjoying himself thoroughly, shoulders shaking in mirth. The way he ignored Filvis's appeals as he revealed her past gave the impression of a mischievous child.

Even Lefiya couldn't help chuckling to herself at Filvis's panic.

Try as she might to suppress her emotions, she simply couldn't keep it together under the stares of the other two.

Already her face was beaming a brilliant shade of red.

"Might I ask what your plans are for today?" Dionysus asked gently, his gaze soft as he took in the two elves.

"Today? I, uh...was planning on heading to the Dungeon for a bit of magic training."

"I see..." Dionysus brought a hand to his slender chin. "If it wouldn't be too much trouble, perhaps you could take Filvis with you?"

Lefiya and Filvis were taken by surprise once again.

"What do you think?"

"I-I suppose it would…be okay…" Lefiya murmured.

"W-wait just a minute, Master Dionysus!"

But even as Filvis raised an objection to Lefiya's tentative consent, Dionysus interrupted her with an assurance of his own.

"Don't worry about me. Go help her."

"B-but I…"

"Don't let me stop you from strengthening your bond with one of Loki's people. In fact, I've already made it known that you should do everything in your power to cooperate with them. You wouldn't go against the will of your god, would you?"

Cutting Filvis's flustered protests short with a single smile, he turned his gaze to Lefiya.

"Lefiya Viridis, if it's not too much to ask, I would hope that you and Filvis could get along. There's a bit of a rift between her and the others in our familia." With a hint of fatherly love in his eyes, he added: "I would love to see her smile again."

With that, Dionysus rose from his chair.

"If you'll excuse me," he said before exiting the café and disappearing into the crowd.

The two elven girls were left alone at the table.

Their eyes met. Filvis's lips parted in resignation.

"If…if it really isn't too much trouble, I'll join you," she said, face red and eyes averted.

"…All right. We'll go together." Lefiya could feel her own face begin heating up at Filvis's embarrassment. She cracked a sweet smile.

"…"

After parting with the elves, Dionysus was quiet as he made his way from the busy street to a small alley situated neatly in the crack between two buildings.

The narrow corridor was dim compared to the earlier brightness of the main street.

And for a moment, it was silent. Then…

"—What an adorable relationship those two have."

The teasing, provocative voice of one of his fellow gods came from in front of him.

"Do you need something, Hermes?" Dionysus replied indifferently, almost as though he'd already been alerted to the other's presence.

The owner of the voice emerged from the shadows to approach him.

A set of lightweight traveling attire graced his frame, and his orange eyes complemented his tangerine hair.

The finespun gentleman with eyes as sharp as arrows raised the brim of his winged hat and gave a laugh.

"How goes it, Dionysus?"

Dionysus's eyes narrowed at the simpering god as his masklike smile came into focus.

It had been Hermes's gaze on his back that led him to hand off Filvis. An honest girl like her would only get in the way as he attempted to *wheedle out his fellow god's true intentions.*

You couldn't let your guard down around Hermes.

He'd come to inherit a sort of shrewd handyman-type presence among the other gods, and he had no qualms about dealing with all manner of clients—a fact that was particularly apparent at this moment.

Hermes's smile deepened, the gloom of the back alleyway crowning his head.

"I merely wanted to talk. You're free at the moment, aren't you?"

"So you accost me in an alley? A fine place for an ordinary little chat."

"Now, now, no need to raise your hackles." Hermes raised his hands in harmless insistence.

Dionysus just snorted. Everything about the overly theatrical god was suspicious.

"Don't tell me you're Ouranos's little dog now. You done with Zeus? You can't have expected that I didn't notice you and that old fossil colluding together."

"You're quite mistaken, I assure you. I'm just the middleman."

"Oh, give me a break! I hardly trust either of you," Dionysus retorted, considerably harsher than normal.

Hermes hunched his shoulders.

"Let's start with the Monsterphilia, hmm? What exactly are Oura-nos and the others hiding? If you're so intent on gaining my trust, you had better start talking."

"Hiding? What could they possibly be hiding? And if they are, I'd be first in line to want to know," Hermes replied airily, his grin never faltering.

"Then we've nothing to talk about," Dionysus finished with a cold glare and turned on his heels.

"Whoa, whoa, whooooooa! Stop for a moment and just listen to me, would you, Dionysus?" Hermes dashed forward to stop Dionysus in his tracks, then gently wrap his arm around the other god's shoulder. He brought their faces together.

"I lost children myself down on the twenty-fourth floor. I'm just as much a victim here as you! If there really is something happening in Orario…then you can bet I'll do everything in my power to find out."

"…"

"Come now. As fellow gods from the heavens, you'll tolerate a bit of idle chatter for me, won't you?" Hermes's orange eyes narrowed slightly as they peered into Dionysus's clear ones. His voice lowered to barely a whisper. "In fact, I've prepared us some grape wine just for the occasion. Who knows…? Maybe my own lips will loosen after a bit of savory drink."

"…I'm very particular about my grape wine, you know."

Both their mouths curled up into identical crescent moons.

"…Ha-ha-ha-ha-ha."

"…Heh-heh-heh-heh."

The two gods exchanged laughter darker than the shadows in the alley.

Then they took off down the road, arms around each other's shoulders, before disappearing into the gloom.

"Talk about ominous…"

A dejected mutter could be heard above the two deities.

A female figure squatted atop the buildings above the alleyway—the chienthrope thief and member of *Hermes Familia*, Lulune.

Beside the girl, whose dog tail hung low with apparent exhaustion, was a beauty with aqua-blue hair framing her silver glasses.

The edges of Asfi Al Andromeda's white cloak fluttered in the breeze.

She was not only Lulune's captain but also the worldliest member of the entire *Hermes Familia*.

Witnessing the almost sinister back-and-forth that had taken place below them just a moment before, she could only offer a sigh.

"Their hearts are as black as you can get…C'mon, Asfi. Can't we just go home?"

"…No. We keep on." Asfi responded to her colleague's appeal with a tired slump of her eyelids. She pushed her glasses up the bridge of her nose.

Then the two girls tasked with keeping an eye on their god stealthily followed in Hermes's and Dionysus's footsteps.

"Just who does that human think he is?!" Lefiya said, voice sharp as a thorn, as the two elves bathed in the phosphorescent light of the Dungeon's mazelike walls. They were on the Dungeon's fifth floor. Shortly after parting with Dionysus, they had set out on their way to the upper levels for Lefiya's magic training, as planned.

As the two of them passed by one lower-class party after another, Lefiya relayed every one of her pent-up grievances about the human Bell to her fellow elf.

Filvis, upon grasping the situation, couldn't resist shooting her disgruntled comrade a wry smile. "This reminds me of my own familia. We had someone like Aiz, too, who was always taking care of the other members. You should have seen the fights I used to have with my friend over her…" A hint of nostalgia tinged her voice, her gaze pointed forward.

The wistfulness coloring Filvis's features, marbled with just a bit of sadness, was enough to bring Lefiya's tirade to a halt.

An older member of her familia…A friend she used to constantly argue with…Could she have lost those companions during the

Twenty-Seventh-Floor Nightmare? The tragic event that had stolen so many lives?

Lefiya was silent for a moment; then, in a deliberately boisterous voice, she began her diatribe anew, going on first about Aiz and the others, and then about the boy and his many faults. She wouldn't allow her kin to succumb to her grief.

Filvis responded with a smile, her deep-red eyes crinkling.

"Right, then. It was Concurrent Casting you were practicing, was it?"

"Indeed! I attempted to chant while Aiz attacked me..."

Lefiya and Filvis approached the center of the room—the place in the western part of the Dungeon's fifth floor that Lefiya had grown so used to these past few days—before the two faced each other.

Filvis's slender chin tucked inward in contemplation as she listened to Lefiya recount her training.

"In my role as captain, I often make use of Concurrent Casting. Mastering it would indeed be of great value to you..."

As a magic swordswoman, Filvis occupied the role of High Balancer, an elite position in the center of formations, where something like Concurrent Casting was virtually a requirement. In fact, when it came to frequency of use, Filvis topped even Riveria. That she just so happened to be Aiz's replacement in today's training session was quite a lucky coincidence for Lefiya.

Even as Filvis stood there looking mildly troubled, Lefiya knew she had to have her as her teacher.

"If you have even the briefest word of advice you could give me—a trick, perhaps. Something that could give me an advantage..."

"A trick? But aren't you studying under Riveria? Mixing her instructions with mine could very well lead to confusion..."

There was no one Filvis respected more than Riveria, the greatest magic user in Orario and, moreover, a high elf. She was probably afraid anything she might tell Lefiya would clash with Riveria's teachings.

She was silent a moment. Then, finally, she gave a little nod, as though reaching a decision.

"I've never trained anyone before, so I've no confidence when it comes to giving instruction..." Filvis's eyes rose to meet Lefiya's. "But perhaps you'll let me speak as a fellow magic user. Viridis, throw aside attacking and defending."

"What?!"

"Mages aren't naturally inclined toward hand-to-hand combat. Superficial attack and defense will only lead to failure, like sharpening a dull, damaged sword for reuse. You must, instead, devote yourself fully to pure evasion. Divert your attention for nothing but the casting of your spell."

There were four main elements to keep in mind when attempting to chant concurrently during a battle: attacking (and defending), moving, evading, and chanting. What Filvis was telling her now, however, was to forget about the first element. To give up on trying to attack and defend.

Truth be told, chanting was the only element that mattered for pure magic users fighting as the rear guard. As a magic swordswoman who'd struggled her way through the front lines of battle, Filvis spoke from experience when she explained that sloppy hand-to-hand combat could lead to more than a simple magic misfire—it could lead to a magic self-detonation.

When you were trapped, just evade, evade, and evade some more.

"Concurrent Casting is supposed to be easier for those on the front lines to learn. Magic users in the rear guard, valued for their firepower capable of changing the tides of battle, must begin by mastering their technique above all else. Keep in mind that magic power encompasses more than simply the strength of your spell."

Adventurers on the front line needed to be constantly moving, engaged in a sort of sword dance and prepared to tackle even the most unforeseen of circumstances. After that, all that was left to do was throw one new element into the mix—chanting, for instance. This made it much easier for them to not only learn Concurrent Casting but to master it. And that wasn't even going into their magic output, which was remarkably low—a desirable trait when one's magic output was like a bomb waiting to go off.

And so they would freely alternate between attacking and defending, all the while hurling their spells.

That was the typical image of Concurrent Casting. It was a world that belonged to those on the front line, magic swordsmen like Filvis, and—

"This is something you shouldn't try to imitate," Filvis warned.

That makes sense… Lefiya thought.

It was true that in her practice battles with Aiz, her chants had failed more than once when she was trying to defend herself. Her priorities had been out of order, focused on the wrong element.

There would, of course, be attacks she wouldn't be able to evade, but she needed to drill into her mind that moving and dodging needed to command her full focus.

"Becoming a mobile artillery battery may be every magic user's dream…but for most, it's a luxurious fantasy."

Taking out enemies on the front lines like Filvis, loosing powerful spells one after the other—there were few aside from Riveria, the strongest magic user in all of Orario, who were able to accomplish such a task.

The first thing rearguard magic users like Lefiya needed to prioritize was invoking magic at all—as her fellow elf so eloquently explained.

"Now then, there's no point talking if we aren't going to put it into practice. Shall we begin?" Filvis pulled out her wooden wand.

Lefiya readied her own staff in response. "A-all right! I'm ready!"

Thus, Lefiya's Concurrent Casting training began anew, only this time with Filvis instead of Aiz.

"I know I said to toss aside all defensive maneuvers, but you should keep a minimum level of personal defense—blocking my attacks, for instance."

"R-right!"

Brandishing her nonlethal wand as opposed to her usual sword, Filvis began chanting.

She came at Lefiya with sharp movements, quickly eliminating the space between them, and Lefiya shifted her focus to ward off each incoming attack, using every bit of staff technique that Riveria had hammered into her.

"Radically short chants like mine unleash a surge of magic power, and they must be invoked without pause, but there's more to it than just short and long chants."

"…!"

"Don't rush in without thinking. No premature loading of magic power into your spells. Wait until the chant's second half rolls around before letting it go."

"I understand!"

Filvis's theory was right on the money—Lefiya received more and more signs that she needed to place greater emphasis on when and how she used her magic power, as well as how she wove her spells.

It also helped that Filvis could control her attacks far better than Aiz.

Though the strikes of her wand were relentless, peppering Lefiya as she dashed about wildly, none of them were overly ruthless, and they always led directly into her next move. It was almost like she was the conductor of some symphony, each wave of her baton indicating where her next spell would land.

Their spells were the music, and the footsteps became a dance.

Like a pair of forest fairies, hands entwined in the meadow, they danced gracefully as one led and the other followed. They formed a studied waltz beneath the phosphorescent light of a secluded nook in the Dungeon.

This time for sure…!

Lefiya regained her footing after her last failed attempt at chanting, pure power building up behind her eyes.

The steps of the dance brought her nimbly across the floor, her lips weaving together the words to her next song—and something responded deep inside her. She managed a considerably longer chant than she had the first time around.

Still, if she had to be completely honest, Filvis's attacks couldn't live up to Aiz's.

Compared to the lightning-fast strikes of the Sword Princess, which were practically invisible to the naked eye, Filvis's wand was clear as day.

Which was exactly why Lefiya had more breathing room.

"Loose your arrows, fairy archers. Pierce, arrow of accuracy—Arcs Ray!"

It was during their twentieth spar when Lefiya was finally able to let off a spell, properly using Concurrent Casting.

The completed missile of her Arcs Ray flew from the tip of her staff.

The beam of light shrieked past Filvis with a high-pitched screech, the elf jumping aside to avoid it, and crashed into the Dungeon wall to leave behind a crack.

"I…I did it!" Lefiya muttered in awe, her breath labored.

She'd been able to cast a spell.

Hugging her staff to her chest, her face broke into a grin of pure joy.

Of course, the spell she'd managed to cast didn't even begin to approach the power of what she could do with both feet firmly rooted to the ground. With her magic power suppressed just to pull it off, her Arcs Ray had done barely more damage to the far wall than a sword could achieve with a few slashes.

Filvis's slower attacks had to be taken into consideration, as well. In her current state, Lefiya wasn't able to accomplish something like this against monsters in a real fight—the kind she'd face in the Dungeon depths.

But none of that mattered to Lefiya. The results she had produced today were big.

The fact that she'd been able to concurrently cast even one spell in battle was enough to plant a seed of confidence deep down inside her chest.

All the training she'd received from Riveria, even the lessons she had with Aiz—all of it led her to this point, and the pure exhilaration pumping in her veins was enough to set her cheeks ablaze.

"A flawless chant. Don't forget that feeling," Filvis commended her.

"I won't! Thank you so, so much!"

A song had been infused into her dance. Lefiya was so happy, it felt like she would burst.

Watching the girl from the corner of her eye, Filvis wasted no time moving on.

"Shall we turn things up a notch, then?"

"Wh-what?!"

"Wait here a moment, would you?" she asked before turning on her heels toward the exit.

Lefiya cocked her head in total confusion as Filvis vanished down the passageway, leaving her completely alone. She had no other choice but to wait as Filvis had requested.

It didn't take much longer for the sounds of monsters falling to echo off the Dungeon walls. Ten of them, to be exact.

And then, five minutes later, she heard *it*.

"Wh-what on earth…?"

The ground shuddered beneath her, followed by the repeated croaking of a great many frogs.

Closer and closer, the quakes and monster cries approached. Then—

From the entryway emerged Filvis—dragging behind her what appeared to be an entire horde of monsters.

"?!"

"Time for round two, Viridis. Only this time, it won't be me you're fighting."

Filvis dashed past the still-in-shock Lefiya, leaving the croaking mass of reptilian frog shooters nowhere to leap except straight at the less experienced elf.

"EH, EHHHHHHHHHHHHHHHHHHHH?!"

—*A pass parade?!*

The teeming throng of some twenty monsters leaped at Lefiya en masse. She simply turned around and ran.

The frog shooters cared nothing about her sheer terror and fol- lowed behind her in a swarm.

"You're not to lay a finger on those monsters, Viridis!"

"What?!"

"Use your magic! You can only kill them with a concurrently chanted spell!"

Filvis's instructions brought Lefiya to a halt—she'd been fully prepared to go hog wild on the lot of them, fighting off the Level 1 creepy-crawlies with her staff.

"You and I both know the monsters on this floor can't do you any real damage. Perfect for a bit of Concurrent Casting practice, no? I used to do this sort of thing all the time before I mastered the skill," Filvis called out from her spot a considerable distance away.

What are you, a teacher from hell?! Lefiya wanted to scream, but even she could understand where Filvis was coming from. Quickly, she began chanting a spell.

The frog shooters drew near, forming a menacing circle around Lefiya as she focused solely on evading, rather than countering, their incoming attacks. Just because the frogs were barely stronger than low-level monsters like goblins and kobolds, that didn't mean she could fend off a relentless swarm of them coming at her from all sides.

"*Loose your arrows, fairy archers. Pierce, arrow of*—Nngah!"

One of the giant, single-eyed beasts lashed out a tongue from its mouth and landed a direct hit on Lefiya's face, cutting her chant short.

Wet, sticky saliva coated her cheeks. It was just as Filvis had said—the attack didn't do much damage, but their long-range capabilities certainly didn't make the fight any easier.

"*Take it up a notch*" is right!

Not only did she have more enemies to deal with, she also had to guard herself against ranged attacks from farther away.

There couldn't possibly be a more suitable enemy in the whole Dungeon for mastering Concurrent Casting.

"*Proud warriors, marksmen of the forest…*" Lefiya began, doing her best to ward off both the body slams and the tongue slaps from her surrounding foes.

"*Take up your bows to face the marauders. Answer the call of your kin, nock your arrows…*" she continued, injecting fire into her words even as the blows rained down and sweat dribbled off her.

Casting her field of vision wide, Lefiya dedicated just enough focus to moving and dodging. She was the unshakable tree.

Everything she'd learned from Aiz, Riveria, and Filvis—it was all strung together, everything reflected in the way she moved.

"*Bring forth the flames, torches of the forest. Release them, flaming arrows of the fairies—*"

Again and again, her spell was interrupted, and the chant failed. But still, she didn't give up.

She wouldn't allow herself to give in.

"Fall like rain, burn the savages to ash..."

In her eyes she could see the girl she longed to become, standing atop the ledge of success.

And she could feel the boy—probably giving it his all at that very moment even as he ran himself ragged and the metallic taste of blood invaded his mouth.

I won't lose to him.

Determination coursing through her veins, her body set alight with sheer, fiery willpower, Lefiya loosed a mighty roar.

"—Fusillade Fallarica!"

She completed her spell.

Dodging incoming body slams, parrying the multitude of tongues flying at her, Lefiya jumped back as a brilliant, golden magic circle formed beneath her feet. Then a barrage of flaming arrows rained down on the teeming mass of frog shooters.

The frog shooters' skin and bulbous single eyes glowed a brilliant red before the raging magic storm swallowed them.

Everything within the spell's large blast area erupted in flaming agony, followed by the roar of tens of hundreds of explosive blasts.

"..."

Filvis, who'd been fending off additional incoming enemies to prevent them from interfering, narrowed her eyes at the spectacle. She said nothing.

Lefiya stood authoritatively amid the embers, char, and residual magic, her staff clenched in both hands as she inhaled and exhaled.

"It seems you're getting the hang of it" were Filvis's first words as she started toward Lefiya.

The frog shooters decimated, a breath of calm had settled upon the room.

"Th-thank you so much! It is only thanks to your help that I was—"

"Oh, please. The foundation was there long before I happened by. This is nothing but a result of your own hard work."

Still gripping the staff, Lefiya felt her cheeks grow warm from hearing the friendly words of praise. The things Aiz and the others taught her had finally started to take root. Not only was she being commended, it felt like her mentors were, too, and the thought manifested as a mixture of pride and happiness bubbling up inside her.

Filvis's eyes softened as she noticed Lefiya's bashfully downturned gaze. Remembering her exhausted reserves of magic power—and the fatigue that would come with it—she invited her onetime pupil to take a seat on the ground.

The two faced each other in the center of the room, shoulders relaxed.

"But it is true, Miss Filvis. Your instruction was so easy for me to understand. Even I felt like things would turn out well in the end. Don't you think you have a natural gift as a teacher?" Lefiya continued, refusing to let the topic die.

"...It was a happy accident. I have no talent when it comes to guiding others," Filvis retorted curtly, though her brusqueness was more a side effect of her embarrassment than a cold refusal. She closed her eyes.

Lefiya couldn't resist a small smile, seeing the pink that tinged the other elf's sullen features.

Though she'd already sensed it before their training began, the two of them really were growing closer.

The cold distance between them at their first meeting had all but evaporated.

Exchanging thoughts, feelings, making it through the fight on the twenty-fourth floor together—their hearts and minds had never been more closely bound.

Perhaps it was as Dionysus had described, and Filvis had let Lefiya into her heart.

The thought made Lefiya incredibly happy.

But she couldn't help the little voice inside her craving more.

A desire that only Filvis could fulfill.

"I, uh...Miss Filvis?" Lefiya began as her cheeks reddened, drawing the gaze of her fellow elf.

"What is it, Viridis?"

"I was wondering if...perhaps...you could call me Lefiya from now on?"

Filvis froze. Then she, too, turned a brilliant shade of red.

An awkward silence passed over them as Filvis faltered, the true meaning behind Lefiya's request sinking in.

"I-I can't."

"Oh, please!"

"I said it's not possible!"

"I am begging you!"

"Stop hounding me!"

"I shall hound all I like!"

The pair were practically shouting at each other, their faces flushed.

Filvis found herself overwhelmed by Lefiya's request, her body pressed forward and her voice shrill.

Finally, she turned away, averting her gaze.

Upon seeing this, Lefiya realized she might have gone too far and quickly reined herself in.

Filvis still refused to meet her eyes. Her lips parted once, twice, and then, in the tiniest of frail voices, so soft it was hardly even there—

"—L-Lefiya…"

Her entire profile was dyed a vivid, radiant crimson all the way to the tips of her elven ears.

Hearing her name, Lefiya felt her face grow steadily brighter, until it practically sparkled, and she let out a jubilant "Thank you!" A gratified smile was plastered across her face.

Filvis still refused to lift her head, which elicited a mirthful giggle from the other girl as happiness flooded through her.

The two elves, different though they were, sat there in comfortable companionship, the walls of the Dungeon all but forgotten.

"Can I…ask you something?" Filvis asked.

"Hmm? What is it?"

"You…truly plan on joining the expedition, don't you?"

A lull settled over them as Filvis finally returned to her usual self.

The expedition she referred to was, of course, the upcoming *Loki Familia* expedition.

"…Yes. I'll head for the Dungeon's uncharted depths with Aiz and the others."

The journey would take place in a mere three days' time.

Riveria and Finn had told her directly that she'd be joining the main party aiming to reach the fifty-ninth floor—they'd need the combined forces of the entire faction to take on this venture into the Dungeon. She'd act as both a sort of stalwart fortress and rearguard assistant to Aiz and the other first-tier adventurers.

Hearing this, Filvis averted her gaze, ruby eyes pointed toward the ground.

"Ah..." came the single word from between her thin lips.

She was quiet for a moment, a glimmer of anguish leaving a trace on her features, as though she were desperately trying to keep her feelings sealed inside.

As Lefiya watched, her eyes finally cracked open.

"You are able to re-create...summon the magic of other elves, yes?"

"Huh? I, uh...Yes."

Filvis rose to her feet, looking down at Lefiya.

Lefiya responded instinctively with a nod of her own. Even her alias, Thousand Elf, had its origins in this technique—the Summon Burst.

"If it's not too much trouble, could you tell me the requirements?" Filvis requested.

Lefiya pushed herself to her feet. She was hesitant at first—her magic was supposed to be kept secret, after all—but ultimately, she trusted Filvis, and she began explaining it.

The magic-summoning technique, Elf Ring.

It was limited to elven magic, and it required a two-part chant and an expenditure of Mind to perform. As far as requirements went, it was necessary to have a complete understanding of the desired magic's effects, as well as the proper chant.

Filvis took it all in with a light nod and then began walking.

She stopped an adequate distance away before bringing out a white magic circle and casting a spell.

"Shield me, cleansing chalice—"

Lefiya's eyes widened as Filvis conjured her magic almost instantaneously.

"—Dio Grail!" Her voice was loud, piercing as she invoked the

spell, and with it came a brilliant flash of light that illuminated the space around her.

It was a pure-white barrier, almost like a symbol of the elf's inner spirit and sublimity.

Despite the minimal magic power she'd used, it boasted a radius of over five meders and was accompanied by a flurry of sparks.

It was the same holy radiance that had protected Lefiya and the others down on the twenty-fourth floor, and Lefiya found herself entranced by the beautiful white light for a good number of seconds. The evil-vanquishing shield seared itself into her eyes.

"Miss Filvis, what was…that spell?" she finally asked, dumbfounded, as her fellow elf released the spell.

Filvis lowered her arm before slowly turning around.

"Dio Grail, an ultrashort barrier spell. It protects the caster and their companions from all variety of physical and magical attacks. A magic shield that can drive away evil, cast out demons, and protect what's important."

Filvis explained both the magic's effects and the words of the chant with a soft smile.

"I'm entrusting you with this spell, Lefiya, so…come back alive."

Lefiya felt her eyes well up with tears at seeing the snow-white elf's smile.

"I will!" she responded with a teary smile of her own. Filvis's kindness and protective strength suffused her.

Blue eyes met red ones as the two elves looked at each other with camaraderie and understanding.

On that day, Lefiya not only took a great leap forward on her path to mastering Concurrent Casting, but she also gained a new spell—Filvis's Dio Grail.

"Nngah!"

A scream and a thud.

A head resting on a pair of soft thighs.

"Nngoh!"

A second scream. Another impact.

Again, a lap pillow.

"Nnguh!"

Again and again he was robbed of his consciousness.

Again and again, Aiz's lap.

"Gaargh!"

The blue sky swallowed the boy's screams.

It was a gorgeous day. The midday sunlight poured down across the hustle and bustle of the massive city, its warm, enveloping glow extending all the way to the two atop the city walls.

Aiz ran her fingers through Bell's bangs as he slept peacefully atop her lap, her gaze turned blankly toward the sky. Around her drifted tiny echoes from the busy streets far below.

Her golden eyes narrowed softly amid the wonderfully glorious weather.

It seems I can't control my own strength, after all...

Her eyes wandered before returning to the boy, his eyes still closed. Inside, she could feel her heart sink.

It was the fifth day of their training, leaving only three days before the expedition.

Bell had asked if she could train him for a full day, so Aiz had been doing nothing but engaging him in practice duels since early morning. She was giving it her all, instructing him relentlessly just as Lefiya and Filvis were having their own crash course within the Dungeon.

And yet, try as she might, things hadn't progressed as smoothly as she'd hoped—the number of times Bell had been knocked out was evidence enough of that.

"I can't do it. I'm not like Finn and the others..." Aiz muttered under her breath, shoulders slumping.

Not only was she failing Bell, she was letting Lefiya down as well, having broken their promise to train for the day. She felt hopeless, as though she couldn't face either of them.

The scabbard of her trusted sword, Desperate, lay next to her on the rocks, swathed in a brilliant sheen of sunlight.

And yet...

She felt like she finally understood the meaning behind the smiles Finn and the others had shown her during the training sessions in her past.

Striking her down, lifting her up.

Striking her down, making her shine.

Shaping a person the same way a smith would temper a sword... Slowly changing them into a new form before polishing them.

Perhaps there was joy to be had in that, something only teachers could understand.

Even Aiz could understand that emotion thanks to the boy's swift, palpable growth...or so she felt.

She looked down at the white rabbit running so earnestly up the mountain, determined to reach its peak, never resting or dozing, and before she knew it, she was smiling.

Instinctively, she reached a hand out to run her fingers through his white bangs.

"..."

She waited, and finally, ever so slowly, Bell's eyes fluttered open.

His rubellite eyes stared blankly up at the sky spreading out overhead.

Still a bit dazed, no doubt, from just having woken up, he simply lay atop her thighs...until Aiz abruptly, earnestly—

—dropped her head forward to peer down at his face.

"Are you all right?"

"...Bwah?!"

Seeing Aiz's face suddenly pop into his field of vision, the boy let out a (maybe slightly delayed) yelp of surprise.

He stumbled off Aiz's pliant thighs and shot to his feet before turning around, cheeks burning.

This wasn't the first time he'd woken up like this. Aiz had been doing the same thing every time he lost consciousness since their second-day practice sessions.

While it had its origins in the whole Mind Down incident, now it had become almost natural.

She certainly didn't want to just leave him there on the cold stone while he was out of commission—and besides, it felt pretty good.

It was a relaxing, calming way to release tension and unwind. A gentle, comforting respite between sword fights where Aiz could rediscover that something she'd forgotten so long ago.

Her eyes followed Bell curiously as he stood by fretting—perhaps he was upset—before giving her thighs a soft, inviting pat, seemingly urging him not to get to his feet so quickly.

This only made Bell shake his head fervently.

"You're sure you're all right?"

"...Yes."

Aiz beckoned the frozen boy again, and he took a seat beside her. She glanced over to see him with his head turned, looking in any direction but hers. He pressed his back against the parapet behind him, then pulled away, then pressed against it again, his cheeks still flushed.

Allowing herself a short break, Aiz circled her arms around her knees, close enough that her shoulder was just touching Bell's. She couldn't help the twinge of worry directed at the boy.

"Do, uh...Do you think I'm...getting any better?" he said.

"...Why do you ask?"

"It's, well, I mean...Lately I, uh...keep getting knocked out, so..." he started as though readying himself, his gaze still fixed forward.

While it might have been a bit shallow of her, Aiz couldn't help the little spark of happy surprise that blinked in the back of her head—the number of times Bell had brought up something not directly related to their training was so low she could count it on one hand.

The corners of her mouth trembled slightly, eyes never leaving him as she responded candidly.

"You're growing. Really...To a surprising degree."

"U-um...but..."

"The reason you keep getting knocked out is probably my own fault...I keep mistaking the amount of power I should use."

"That—! It's not—! You shouldn't think that!"

Even as Aiz said it, she could feel her mood sink. Her eyelids drooped with a slow, quiet sadness. Bell turned toward her with a jerk, hurriedly refuting her reasoning.

Even as her shoulders gave the smallest of slumps, Aiz realized she'd come to understand something lately.

Bell Cranell was just a boy.

He grew flustered when something went wrong, became dispirited when he was sad, felt ashamed when something was embarrassing, and was simply joyful, cheeks red and smiling, when good happened.

Sincere, straightforward, occasionally showing off, and always pushing himself past his limits.

A child so surprisingly common he barely fit the mold of other adventurers with their desires for wealth and fame, their dreams and ambitions.

And even if the stuff on the inside—his heart, mind, or spirit—was wrong, his body, his physical abilities weren't those of an adventurer, either. They weren't even those of the heroes he admired.

Even now, as the kind and good-natured Bell attempted to dispel her melancholia, he was still just a boy.

"…"

As charming as she found that fact, she also found it very strange.

Why was it that someone like him, a person so far from what most adventurers were made of, could have achieved such dramatic growth?

Aiz herself was easy enough to understand.

Pressured by the boy's growth, her training grew stricter and harsher with every passing day.

Even considering the rate at which he kept losing consciousness, the extent of his remarkable growth made it difficult for her to hold back.

Bell was racing forward at a speed that more than made up for the inefficiency of her training regimen.

Which brought Aiz back full circle to why she'd considered training him in the first place.

It was all to understand his secret. She hadn't discovered even the faintest clue about the path to a new peak that she yearned for.

The true nature of the growth so contradictory to his character. Aiz questioned it more and more every time she got closer to him.

She paused for a moment, the doubts piling up in her mind, before finally letting her lips part with a tremble.

"…Can I…ask you something?"

"Huh?"

She gazed straight into Bell's face.

And then she asked, with an expression more serious than she herself could ever remember displaying, "Why is it you're able to grow so strong so quickly?"

"Strong…?"

Aiz, who had trouble putting even the simplest of things into words, poured everything into that question

It made Bell stop short in bewilderment, almost as though such a question had absolutely nothing to do with him.

Aiz herself knew it was a long shot, but she fervently wanted to ask it.

As though that need had gotten through to the flustered Bell, his brows furrowed in intense concentration as he seriously thought it over.

At long last, he began to talk.

"…Well, there's someone I'm trying to catch up with, no matter what it takes. And…somehow in all that running…I ended up here…" He threw a glance at Aiz, his cheeks reddening as he incoherently expressed his thoughts.

"…I guess…I have a goal in mind…that I have to accomplish at all costs."

Aiz's golden eyes widened.

Deep down inside, she felt the words of the oath she had made in the past burn in her heart before quickly growing cold.

Her golden gaze met his rubellite eyes momentarily, then she silently looked skyward.

"I see…" Her eyes took in the blue of the overarching sky as she wrapped her arms lightly around her knees.

The breeze combed through her long golden hair.

"…I understand." As the cerulean sky reflected in her eyes, the words fell from her lips.

It might not have been the answer she wanted, but it was an answer she could understand.

He'd told her that not too long ago, hadn't he? That he, too, had an objective.

Just like her.

A goal that she had to accomplish at all costs. A far-off height that she needed to reach.

"Me too…"

—*I have a wish.*

The words that slipped from her mouth disappeared in an instant, swallowed up by the sound of the wind as her eyes remained fixated on that blue expanse of sky.

It was a cold wind, blowing strong from the west.

The same rush of air a swordswoman like Aiz was so used to hearing.

She sat there motionless, the wind playing with her hair as she stared up into that great big sky as though it were liable to swallow her whole.

"I-I, uh…" Bell began.

"?"

"I…Never mind. It's nothing…"

Even as Aiz curiously tilted her head to the side, Bell tucked whatever he had planned to say back deep within his chest.

Aiz was incredulous, but she didn't pry and let her eyelids close instead.

She had a hunch that not even Bell himself was aware of his own improvement.

From what she had gathered—from what she had no choice but to gather—all Bell was doing was racing forward as fast as his legs would take him.

She knew all too well that those rubellite eyes of his couldn't lie or swindle or hide things.

He told the truth in its entirety, a fact that should have left her wallowing in her own misery. Instead, however, a smile rose to her lips.

...Such nice weather.

As her conversation with Bell ground to a halt, her eyes crinkled at the warm sun pouring down on them.

The sky was so blue today, tiny white cirrocumulus clouds swimming freely in the clear expanse.

From the city's eastern district came the echoing sound of the noontime bell, the clear ringing joining the pleasant sunlight wrapping around them.

"Mmn..."

At that moment...

A tiny murmur escaped from Aiz's petite lips.

She instantly flung a hand to her mouth, but it was too late.

The warm, sunny weather had enticed a yawn from her.

"...?" Right next to her, Bell noticed and turned to her with a start. His expression was a mixture of curiosity and surprise.

Aiz returned her hand to her side, recomposing herself as if nothing had happened.

Uh-oh...

But even as she did, her heart silently muttered.

I'm...I'm sleepy...

In the midst of all that warm, wonderful sun, Aiz's eyelids were fighting a losing battle.

Waking up before sunrise to train Bell and then training Lefiya in Concurrent Casting until the evening hours—she felt like she'd done nothing but eat, sleep, and train for the last five days with not even a moment's rest. Even the time she spent asleep was shaved down as much as possible.

And now this sunlight, so warm, so narcotic, had become her worst enemy.

Apparently even first-tier adventurers could still succumb to this type of fiendish weather.

How long would she be able to keep this up? This unmoving gaze of rigidity? Her normal, static features so devoid of emotion?

She'd been working so hard these last couple of days, and the lethargy tugging at her entire being was all too real.

"Perhaps we should…practice our napping skills."

"Huh?"

It was out before she even realized it.

Her mouth was running away from her.

"You need to be able to sleep anywhere, you know. Even way down there in the Dungeon."

"…"

"It's an essential skill. A quick way to restore your stamina."

Still her mouth continued to run.

Aiz refused to look at him, her eyes pointed straight ahead as she talked, but she could feel his gaze on the side of her face, questioning, no doubt confused.

She was making things up and she knew it, but as much as she was sweating on the inside, it was too late to backtrack. So she emphasized the importance of it all the more, this "sleep training," as she called it.

There was a chance he might believe it, naive as he was, and Aiz held onto that tiny sliver of hope.

"Are you…by any chance…sleepy, Miss Aiz?"

Nope.

He'd seen through her so easily. She could feel the heat building in her cheeks.

"—It's training." Aiz turned her head toward Bell with an almost audible snap.

"R-right."

Bell found himself unable to keep from nodding at the kind of sheer force only a first-tier adventurer could possess, a tiny trickle of sweat forming beneath his temple.

And as they sat there, staring at each other, eyebrows raised, their cheeks turned a brilliant shade of red.

"So…uh…we sleep…here?"

"Yes," she replied in a hurry, thanks to her embarrassment.

She gave a terse nod before lying flat on the stone floor with a tiny *thump*.

Just about ready to give herself over to the drowsiness that had so suddenly overcome her being, she caught a glance of Bell next to her, motionless.

"What's wrong? Can't you sleep?"

"N...no, I can't..."

She was on her side, and he lay down next to her on his back.

Throwing a glance over at Aiz only to have their eyes meet, he hurriedly returned his gaze to the sky.

Already on the verge of sleep, she watched as he squeezed his eyes closed in a forced effort to make himself sleep before quietly letting her own eyelids fall.

Slowly, slowly, her consciousness drifted off to sleep.

She could hear someone. A voice was reading a story.

It was a tale she knew by heart. One she'd heard time and again.

It delighted her no matter how many times she listened.

Her mother's voice was soft like the wind, steeped in love, affection overflowing as she recited the words.

Her father's voice was loud, clumsy as he laughed, his kind eyes watching over both of them.

This was her favorite time. When the three of them could share: her mother, her father, and her—Aiz.

When she raised her eyes from the words of the story, she was met by the most wonderful sight.

Everyone she loved, a whole room of people, had joined her mother and father, all of them smiling, all of them laughing.

A beautiful, compassionate high elf, an adult prum the very same size as her, a dwarf with his great big mouth open, laughing heartily.

And so many more. Animal people, Amazons, and humans alike surrounded Aiz and her family.

Aiz felt her cheeks turn pink with warmth, and she stood on her tiptoes, hands waving as she grinned broadly.

Such a tender moment. An irreplaceable bond. A precious place.

But in a single moment, everything changed.

A black cloud formed beneath their feet.

From a giant rift in the floor came the oozing black nightmare, swallowing up the world once so filled with light.

So black, so black, so black, the shadowy blob canceled out every bit of light.

In the midst of all that darkness, Aiz could only watch, speechless, as her father walked away.

Armor shrouded in a thin black scarf. A long silver sword.

Her father held that gleaming silver blade in his hand as he faced the writhing shadow.

Father!

She ran after him, desperately calling out to him, but he didn't turn around.

He grew farther and farther away, and her mouth twisted downward in an ugly frown. Just as she turned around to call for help—everyone had vanished without a trace.

In their place were weapons. A multitude of them.

Swords, spears, axes, staffs, shields.

They protruded from the ground like gravestones, forming a circle around her.

Aiz found herself lacking words, captivated by her surroundings. There was no one in sight, not even her father. Everything was consumed by the endless darkness.

Encircled by the meaningless, broken weapons, she called out their names again and again. Her father, her mother, everyone she knew.

And then came a powerful wind.

As it tousled and whipped her golden hair, she turned around to see *her* on the far side of her field of vision.

With the same long golden hair flowing down her back—her mother.

Her back was to Aiz as she confronted something writhing in the midst of the darkness.

Before Aiz's call could reach her, the shadow flared its gills.

A swarm of new shadows sprang forth, entangling her mother, arms outstretched, swallowing her whole.

Tears flooded Aiz's golden eyes.

She screamed, and suddenly, in front of her appeared a single sword protruding from the ground.

It was identical to her father's, a silver sword covered with cracks.

Aiz pulled that decrepit weapon from the ground and gave chase.

—*Wait for me!*

She was no longer a young girl. She was the Sword Princess. And she raced forward, cutting her way through the darkness.

—*I said WAIT!!*

Again she yelled at the silhouette of her mother as it melted into the darkness.

I'll make it there.

I'll come for you.

And I'll definitely bring you back, I swear.

She vowed to the figure already swallowed by that black vortex.

Then she swore to herself. To the young girl left behind, tightly gripping her sword.

And then.

A brilliant wave of white light slammed down on top of her, obscuring her vision.

"…"

Her golden eyes cracked open silently.

She blinked a few times to fight off the residual unease of the dream.

There weren't any tears.

But her vision was slightly blurred.

Still on her side, she gave her eyes a stealthy wipe of her arm.

"…?"

She was getting her bearings and returning to consciousness when she heard something.

A series of soft, sleeping breaths that belonged to someone else.

She glanced to her side and found the boy splayed out on his back, eyes shut tight.

Bathed in warm sunlight, he was fast asleep without a care in the world, tiny snores whistling past his lips.

Blinking several more times, Aiz felt a smile coming on.

They were unusually far away from each other, weren't they? Finding it rather curious, Aiz slowly slid herself closer to Bell's side.

And then they lay there, the two of them, side by side on the stone floor.

The boy's sleeping face was even more cherubic than when he was awake.

Aiz reached her hand out gently, as though tenderly handling some precious treasure.

Her fingers touched his cheeks. They were so warm.

The heat passed from his skin to the tips of her fingers.

His lips parted at the pressure. "Forgive me, Grandfather..." he murmured, as though he were having a dream of his own.

Aiz smiled.

The way she'd done so long ago, when she was carefree and young.

His white hair contrasted so distinctly with the terrifying black shadow of her dream, and she let her fingers run through his bright locks again and again, her eyes crinkling.

As unnerving as her dream had been, her heart was already calm.

She had a white rabbit to lead her tiny self out of wonderland.

That time of tenderness she was supposed to have lost so long ago wrapped around her now like a comforting blanket beneath the gaze of the blue sky.

It was nearing sunset.

The streets of Orario were stained a pinkish red as the sun began its descent toward the distant horizon.

Set against that vibrant sun, a fierce duel was taking place atop the city walls.

The boy and girl came close, then separated, over and over again. Night had almost fallen.

A pair of eyes watched their match from far above, perched at the city's highest pinnacle that stood nearest to the stars.

"While I can't say I'm displeased that she's drawing out that child's radiance..." The image of the golden-haired, golden-eyed swords-woman was reflected in silver eyes with every scabbard strike. "...This intimacy they've formed worries me."

There was a twinge of jealousy in her voice as she clenched a fist by her side.

"Especially if it should end up interfering in his trial." Her silver eyes narrowed. "Allen," a high, soprano voice ordered the petite man from up ahead.

"Yes?"

"A bit of roughhousing never hurt anyone. Give her a warning."

"Understood." The man replied courteously, his cat ears and tail twitching.

Something feels off, Aiz thought between strikes, bathed in the light of the setting sun.

"Bell. You've really taken a beating this last hour. Are you sure you're all right?"

"I'm...I'm fine! Really!"

Their arduous training atop the city walls had acquired an audience in the form of a young goddess.

A few hours ago, after their so-called "nap training" had ended, the two of them had decided to head down into the city for a bit to shore themselves up with a meal.

It was when they stopped to purchase Jyaga Maru Kun, Aiz's favorite food, that they ran into none other than the goddess of Bell's familia, Hestia.

The young goddess was working at the stand when the two had waltzed up, unassumingly, to buy themselves a few of the meaty potato snacks. Needless to say, they'd nearly gotten their heads bitten off once Hestia's rage had been ignited. While the reaction was to be expected—seeing her own child hanging out with a member of another faction they weren't even close to was enough to make anyone fly off the handle—something about the adverse reaction hinted at a residual grudge on the part of the goddess.

At any rate, after a bit of explaining from Aiz and a bit of desperate persuading from Bell, Hestia had finally, reluctantly, agreed to let them continue their training.

There was one caveat: "You have to let me sit in on today's training session!"

Which was why the young goddess (and Bell's new guardian, so to speak) had accompanied them to the top of the city walls. She needed to make sure nothing happened to her adorable little follower, after all!

The goddess Hestia...What was it Loki always called her?

Aiz threw a quick glance at Hestia in the far corner between her bouts with Bell.

The young goddess boasted delicate features that toed the line between adolescent and young lady. Possessing twin pigtails done up with blue blows that matched the color of her eyes, she sported a surprisingly ample chest despite her petite stature.

"Hey! Watch what you're looking at!" The girl raised her hands in objection to Aiz's wandering gaze, her breasts swaying with the movement.

The sight of all that bouncing finally reminded her what Loki's epithet was: *"That busty Jyaga Maru midget tramp."* Now she had a pretty good idea why Loki and Hestia had never really gotten along.

All the more reason why Aiz couldn't tell Loki and the rest of her familia about her training sessions with Bell.

"Nnguh!"

"You're sure you're all right?"

"P-perfectly fine!" Bell responded, recovering immediately from a particularly damaging blow from Aiz.

He was being even more stubborn than usual, as though he were especially motivated.

As proof, he'd yet to lose consciousness even once since Hestia had joined them atop the wall.

Like he was determined not to lose face in front of her.

"You can do it!" came Hestia's cheers of support as he received hit after hit from Aiz.

As much as the corners of Aiz's lips wanted to creep upward, she held them still—nothing but a humorless solemnity graced her features as she swung her scabbard in relentless onslaughts.

The sheer determination behind his every strike and block, his every desperate flail of his dagger only spurred them on faster and faster.

The high-pitched clangs of their colliding weapons echoed out into the sky above.

Time drifted like the clouds in the evening sky, forgotten, and before long, the dark blue of twilight had overtaken them.

"...Shall we end on that note, then?"

"Ah, sure. Thank you for...for everything."

Aiz lowered her scabbard, looking up at the moon overhead, and Bell felt his strength leave him.

His body was peppered with bruises, but she had to hand it to him—he'd remained conscious the entire time. Even now, he continued to fight off what must have been an overwhelming urge to collapse. Aiz narrowed her eyes as she gauged his current state and then began packing up her things to head in for the night.

"Good work today, Bell! Feels good getting the stuffing kicked out of you now and then, doesn't it?"

"L-Lady Hestia, I-I was really trying my best out there!"

"So many hits and not a single drop of blood or tears! Miss Wallen-whatever-her-name-is doesn't think much of you, nope! She doesn't, she doesn't!" Hestia rushed to Bell's side, a giant grin on her face as she violently pounded him on the back.

At the same time, Aiz calmly slid Desperate back into its scabbard.

She could still remember the violent reactions whenever Hestia had seen her strike her follower in the past.

—*"Just what do you think you're doing?!"*

—*"Keep your hands off my Bell!"*

Strangely, though, she'd been remarkably calm and composed during this most recent training session.

In fact, she seemed almost elated at Bell's battered, bedraggled state—or perhaps at Aiz for doing the battering and bedraggling.

Giving the young goddess a curious cock of her head, Aiz turned her gaze away from the parapets to take in the city below.

It had grown considerably late by this point. The streets were filled with the dazzling glow of magic-stone lamps and the bustle of adventurers returning from the Dungeon.

Time had gotten away from Aiz. She'd been training since the morning, after all, and though she'd already told Tiona and the others she probably wouldn't be back for dinner, she had a feeling there'd be a few scolding remarks from Riveria's general direction.

Quickly gathering up her things, she vacated the premises with Bell, still wounded by Hestia's comments, in tow.

They took the stone stairs down to the city proper.

After countless steps, they ducked under a door at the base of the wall and emerged into a back alley at the edge of the city's north-western district.

"U-um, Lady Hestia? We're outside now, so could you...maybe... let go of my hand?"

"Are you crazy, Bell? Look how dark it is here! You need to hold my hand tight to make sure I don't trip or anything!"

The three of them made their way through the streets beneath the darkness of the twilit sky, Bell and Hestia's lively exchange in sharp contrast to Aiz's still calm.

—Then her ears perked up as her intuition as an adventurer alerted her to something.

"..."

She became still, eyes shifting back and forth to examine her surroundings as Bell and Hestia carried on their horseplay beside her.

It was a fairly wide road, deserted aside from herself and the others.

Put another way, it was too quiet.

The complete lack of even a single other person was almost abnormal. Everything was submerged in the murk of nightfall, the stars and moon above providing the only light. Not even the surrounding buildings offered any illumination from magic stones.

A stealthy glance to a side of the road revealed a fancy magic-stone lamp pole that appeared as though it'd been smashed with some sort of blunt weapon.

—*We're being watched.*

A back alleyway devoid of life, purposefully blanketed in darkness.

Aiz's delicate brows slanted sharply. She could feel someone watching them.

Next to her, Bell sucked in his breath, his embarrassment from Hestia's grip on his hand cut short the moment he noticed Aiz's face. Not wasting a moment, he looked around to investigate their surroundings.

Meanwhile, Aiz came to a stop, staring long and hard at a corner at the side of the road.

"—"

"—ngh!"

"Whoa!"

Bell immediately froze as well, prompting a surprised gasp from Hestia, still unaware of the situation.

Aiz watched the path before them.

She peered into the shadows permeating each and every narrow crack between the countless dwellings lining the wide road.

She pierced the darkness with her glare: *Come out, now.*

And it did. At length, the one who had been observing them emerged from the shadows.

A catman...

Clad in black armor, black linens, and a black visor, he seemed to melt into the darkness itself.

He was male—that much she could tell—and slightly shorter than Bell, but the metallic visor covering his upper face made it impossible to discern his identity.

The light of the moon illuminated the black and gray fur of his feline ears and tail.

From his right hand protruded a silver spear that was at least two meders long.

He radiated bloodlust, like a cat unable to stop itself from killing a mouse despite its owner's scolding, and Aiz felt herself instinctively revert to Sword Princess mode.

"_____"

There was a *thud* as he kicked off from the stone. He was by Bell in an instant.

Time seemed to stop. The appearance of the shadow in front of him was so sudden, Bell didn't have a chance to respond.

The catman's spear came at him in a flash—but so did Aiz's already unsheathed sword, Desperate, blocking the strike with lightning speed.

"—Gnngh!"

"?!"

The spear was knocked away.

The Sword Princess would not be ignored. The silver flash that was her sword struck again at his spear, now raised in self-defense. Sparks went flying as she drove him away from Bell.

The young catman flew backward, and Aiz took a silent step in front of Bell, who was still in shock.

Her golden eyes were steely as she stared at him, an enemy who'd cleared out this stretch of alley to lie in wait for them.

He showed no signs of answering for his actions now.

Their eyes locked.

Then they simultaneously leaped forward.

"H-hey, hey, *hey*!!"

But the fierce duel had already begun.

By the time Hestia had recovered enough from her gaping astonishment to let out a yelp, Aiz and the catman were entangled in a furious whirlwind of blows.

Racing forward, pulling back, leading then countering, give and take, back and forth, again, again, again. The two upper-class adventurers collided in a ceaseless rhythm, oblivious to the lower-class boy and powerless goddess rooted to their spots on the sidelines.

Their speed increased even further, as did the rhythm of their alternating strikes.

—Who is this guy?!

Aiz's eyes narrowed. Physical skills on par with her Level 6 abilities? Mastery of the spear that could easily rival her swordplay?

It was at that moment that she felt it. A presence from far above.

Four small shadows emerged atop the three-story building overlooking their duel.

He had friends after all, huh? Even in the midst of her fight she could sense them, and she expanded her field of awareness.

Then the four of them dropped in without a moment's delay.

Sword, hammer, shield, and ax all fell upon the battlefield.

"—Miss Aiz!" Bell cried out from the sidelines once he noticed the surprise attack, but Aiz would not be daunted. She would show them she was every bit the War Princess that so many adventurers feared.

With an attack that broke the sound barrier, she fended off her feline opponent before using the momentum to propel her sword upward for a sudden second strike.

She then turned toward the four incoming weapons, her entire body a bow and her sword the arrow, taut and trembling with the full force of her might. She released.

"!!"

A flash. Her sword drew a brilliant crescent in the sky overhead.

It carved through space with such speed it left a silver afterimage in the air, repelling four attacks at once.

There was a metallic clash as their arms flew back. The four attackers landed on the ground, fear and dismay coloring their features.

Aiz's golden hair still billowed from the movement. Behind her, the catman hissed.

"Tch...Monster."

The golden-haired, golden-eyed swordswoman's technique and strategy were even more impressive than her nominal Status.

Even Bell trembled at her display of sword prowess. The incredible number of battlefields she'd crossed in her lifetime was readily apparent.

The additional attackers, who had approached from opposite the catman, finally came into view beneath the moonlight—four prums, all clad in the same black armor and visors as their feline companion.

Aiz squinted at the residual tingle in her fingers, left over from the earlier impact. She swung her sword in front of her, and it answered with a crisp *swish* as it sliced through the air. On her one side was the young catman; on her other, four short prums, overshadowed by their disproportionately large weapons.

And then they were off, all six of them moving at once, as though they'd been given some sort of signal.

"!!"

They came at her from both sides in a pincer attack, but Aiz stood her ground, undaunted.

Just like the catman, the four prums boasted abilities and skills that could only be described as first-tier. The five of them surrounded her, delivering wave after wave of attacks in a ferocious barrage that left Aiz with nowhere to move. Giving up entirely on attempting to evade their attacks, she instead focused on fending them off, using Desperate to intercept and repel every enemy strike.

It was a moonlight raid in the blackest night.

As the ceaseless noise of metal on metal echoed throughout the isolated back alleyway, Aiz fought tooth and nail against her attackers, her sword forming a barrier around her.

What were they trying to accomplish? Was it her they were aiming for? A surprise attack against one of *Loki Familia*'s elites?

Just as her mind began running wild at what these mute attackers could want, one of the prums—the one holding an oversize sword—called out from beneath his visor.

"Consider this a warning, Sword Princess."

"You'd do well not to do anything rash from now on."

The hammer-wielding prum spoke this time but provided no further context. Aiz's eyebrows rose in uncertainly.

"What are you...talking about?!" she shot out between the report of blades.

"Lock yourself away in the Dungeon, little doll. Hide yourself away on this expedition of yours..." the young catman hissed cruelly, "...and *die*."

Aiz found herself at a loss when she heard the feline's words. But she didn't have time to dwell. There was a sharp scream from behind her.

"B-Bell!!"

?!

She whirled around instinctively, still fending off her attackers, to find Bell and Hestia surrounded by yet another group of black-clad soldiers.

There's even more?! She moved to help them only to have her path blocked by a spear.

"...?!"

"If you refuse to listen, we'll be forced to take drastic measures," the catman spat coldly.

Standing there, she could hear sounds of fighting from Bell and Hestia's direction. The quartet of black-clad soldiers leaped at them, as if to deliver a warning to her.

She could feel her patience growing thin. Try as she might to escape the circle her attackers had made around her, she simply couldn't break through.

The attacks came at her faster.

So fast, her golden eyes widened in surprise. The five shadows were coming at her even more relentlessly now.

—I knew it. It's them.

It came to her like a flame, scorching the inside of her chest. Talent like this could only point to one familia.

The other great faction long thought of as the counterpart to *Loki Familia*.

Led by that beautiful goddess, their members boasting war records that could rival Aiz's own.

The first-tier adventurers—

—Vana Freya and Bringar!

The former was a Level 6 bearing the alias of a chariot and thought to be the best in all of Orario; the latter, a group of Level 5 prums with combat abilities far exceeding Level 6 and near-perfect coordination.

Aiz found herself immobilized by the relentless, multihit counterattacks of the four-man prum troop. At the same time, the catman sped up, his agility surpassing hers even after her recent level-up, and his perpetual barrage forced her to block more with her sword. She was holding back, inner turmoil forbidding her from revealing her true strength, her spell Airiel. She wasn't about to allow even a single part of its chant to grace the ears of her enemy.

But she was outnumbered. Even Aiz didn't stand a chance against five first-tier adventurers at once.

And if they were to realize that, the battle would be over very quickly.

"We'll say it again. This is a warning."

"Dig too deep and we can't guarantee your life."

It came from the hammer- and ax-wielding prums this time, further drawing out the battle.

Aiz felt her expression falter as they continued to gain the advantage, and the young catman shot her a look of pure ice from beneath his visor.

"If you get in her way—we'll kill you." With a terrifying slash, his spear grazed the front of Aiz's silver breastplate, leaving a scratch on its surface.

Silver sparks danced before her eyes.

"—Miss Aiz!"

Then she heard it.

The boy's frightened shout.

Aiz whirled around to find Bell with his right arm thrust out in front of him.

He'd already finished off the four black-clad soldiers, with Hestia on his left arm and Aiz's current attackers in his sights.

The five first-tier adventurers turned toward Bell. Aiz seized that moment to escape from the circle.

Bell wasted no time. His voice roared through the air like the sound of a cannon.

"FIREBOLT!!" he screamed, forgoing the chant, and six flaming bolts of lightning immediately followed.

The sparking conflagrations overlapped, piling on top of one another as they hurtled toward the attackers before swallowing them whole.

The explosion was instantaneous.

A wave of voracious heat mushroomed out from the impact zone, practically throwing them backward. The flaming sparks exploded into cinders that rained down from the sky, staining the faces of Bell, Hestia, and Aiz—now a safe distance away—a brilliant crimson.

The crackling embers bloomed around them.

For a moment, at least, the obsidian attackers had been shaken off, lost in the sea of flame brought to life in that small street corner.

"I…I cast a spell without chanting…"

"You'll wanna report that. Someone's going to be pleased as punch."

Meanwhile, the five attackers leisurely walked out of the flames, not bothered in the least by the magic attack of a low-level adventurer. The four prums even had strangely pleasant smiles on their faces.

Aiz readied herself, but just when it seemed it would return to blows, the five assailants lowered their weapons.

"That's enough. We're leaving."

At the young catman's command, the four prums scattered.

Fearing the flames would draw unwanted attention, they moved quickly to retrieve the black-clad soldiers Bell had trounced earlier.

Aiz saw no reason to recklessly pursue their attackers. She did, however, keep Desperate at the ready even after they disappeared from view, waiting until their presences were far, far away before finally letting out a sigh.

Sliding her sword back into its scabbard, she made her way over to where Bell and Hestia were staring blankly, completely overwhelmed.

"Are you injured?"

"I-I'm fine! I'm more worried about you, Aiz…"

"I'm also unhurt."

Aiz glanced at Bell, Hestia still fretting over him.

Though Bell's magic hadn't done any real damage to the attackers, that didn't mean it had been pointless. In fact, his move had helped her out of a pretty tight situation.

Aiz still found herself a bit in awe at the boy's unique fast-casting magic she'd first witnessed down on the tenth floor. She parted her lips in thanks…only to see the white-haired boy avert his eyes, softly biting his lip as though something still weighed on him.

It was a curious look, and Aiz found herself wondering what it could mean until he opened his mouth.

"Those people…who were they? And why would they attack us like that out of the blue…?"

Bell asked with a sort of forced composure, as though hiding his feelings.

The way he was acting bothered Aiz, but she responded to his uneasy question all the same.

"Surprise attacks like this aren't uncommon."

"They aren't?!"

"No. Though it is rare outside the Dungeon…"

While Bell yelped with surprised, still ignorant when it came to power struggles between factions, Aiz's mind raced with questions once more.

Had they been targeting her while she was cut off from the rest of her familia?

She thought back to their warning. Had she pissed off some faction without realizing it? And had Bell and Hestia simply gotten caught up in the whole thing?

She certainly couldn't think of anything she'd done that would warrant a vicious attack like this, but the fact that she'd put the other two in danger filled her with self-reproof.

"Can you think of anyone who'd wanna attack you, Wallen-whatever?"

"…Too many, in fact."

Aiz was hesitant to answer so directly but also realized it wasn't exactly a secret with her familia.

"Geez! Must be tough in *Loki Familia*," Hestia muttered in awe as Aiz thought back to her attackers' warning.

"If you get in her way—we'll kill you."

Still unsure what the young feline could have been referring to, she tucked the words away for later all the same.

Retaliating at the faction level would only exacerbate the situation, something she was sure her opponent was trying to avoid, as well.

Which meant she'd need to leave it be for now, as much as it left a foul taste in her mouth.

The flames from Bell's spell had calmed down to something on the level of a bonfire. People were starting to gather, though, so Hestia suggested they skedaddle.

Aiz nodded, hoping to avoid any unnecessary trouble herself. Still exchanging words with the young goddess, she started toward a small alley.

—Only to realize Bell wasn't following them.

"…?"

Still rooted to the spot, he was simply staring off into space.

"What's wrong…?" Aiz called out behind her.

Bell turned around with a start. "Huh? Ah, no, it's…it's nothing. Nothing at all." He quickly dashed over to them.

Aiz glanced in the same direction Bell had been so intently staring.

Toward the center of the city.

Where the tall white tower gazed down at the trio from its spot in the night sky.

"Ottar's somewhere in the middle levels?"

Raul Nord, member of *Loki Familia*, spun around.

It was evening, only two days remaining until the expedition.

They were in Guild Headquarters, currently teeming with adventurers on their way back from the Dungeon. Armor-clad demi-humans bustled around the wide marble lobby as they went about their business,

whether it be cashing in their monster loot, reporting to their advisers, or collecting rewards for completed quests.

Standing in front of the giant bulletin board that was decorated with official Guild proclamations and quest notices, Raul turned his gaze toward the incoming bearer of information.

"Is that true, Aki?"

"Yes. Well, at least that's what a couple of adventurers were saying earlier. Not sure how much stock you put in it, but quite a few folks have seen him now."

The cat girl in black—Aki—flicked her slender obsidian tail that was the same color as her waist-length hair.

A number of *Loki Familia* adventurers were at the Guild collecting intel that could prove useful during their upcoming expedition.

Irregulars along their planned route, overlapping schedules with other factions, potential presence or absence of floor bosses— investigating these things was important work and couldn't be neglected if they wanted to ensure their expedition's smooth progress.

And it was this exact job that'd been entrusted to *Loki Familia*'s lower-ranking members.

"Mister Rauuuuuul! Looks like ol' Goliath's reared his ugly head on the eighteenth floor again. Everyone's just lettin' him be, assuming we'll take care of him as we go through."

"The Guild's saying Babel can't get all the salamander wool and undine robes we ordered! What should we do?"

"Just…just hold on a second, will ya? Give me a moment!" Raul thrust his hands out to stop the barrage of incoming information, his brow furrowing in overwhelmed aggravation as he pleaded silently for a chance to collect himself.

Raul Nord. Human. Twenty-one years old.

His big forehead was crowned with a crop of spiky black hair. A man of medium build and average stature, his features only further emphasized his humanness and utter ordinariness. Even now, standing flustered in front of his companions, he made for a fairly boring, uninteresting addition to the familia.

That being said, he was still a Level 4, second-tier adventurer.

Born the third son of a poor farming family, before he was even eight years old Raul made what he called "the biggest decision of his life" by leaving his country home. Like so many others, he arrived at Orario filled with big dreams and just a little manly ambition. Before long, he found himself inducted into *Loki Familia*.

He turned out to be a natural, and by forcing his way onto the battlefield behind Finn and the others, Raul got to where he was today. For a reason even Raul himself couldn't fathom, first Finn, then the other elites in the familia began putting a great deal of trust in him, which was why he often found himself tasked with supervising other lower-ranking members, whether in administrative tasks like this or dealing with issues in the Dungeon.

That same human, so scatterbrained when compared to the pioneers of such a great familia, was currently attempting to prioritize the incoming information from his fellow familia members one at a time.

"Uhhh…Right! Aki! We were talking about Ottar…"

"He's been spotted hunting monsters around the seventeenth floor these last couple of days. Right, Leene?" Aki turned to glance at her colleague next to her.

The bespectacled girl with her hair pulled back in a braid responded with a nod and a hesitant "Y-yes."

Ottar the Warlord…captain of *Freya Familia* and the strongest warrior in all of Orario.

At the same time, he was one of *Loki Familia*'s longest-standing foes.

Ottar had commanded the top spot on the familia's blacklist for as long as Raul could remember.

It seemed a bit strange that *Freya Familia*'s captain, of all people, would be camping out in the middle levels where he'd overpower every monster he came across…

"…What's that guy up to, I wonder." Though even as he muttered it under his breath, Raul knew there was no one in the vicinity who could supply him with an answer.

The other familia members around him glanced back and forth at one another, starting with Aki, who simply shrugged her shoulders.

"What's goin' on here, huh?"

"Ah! Sir Gareth!"

The dwarf made his way through the hustle and bustle to where they were standing next to the giant bulletin board.

Gareth was one of the heads of *Loki Familia*, and the great dwarf warrior exuded the aura of a seasoned soldier. He naturally drew the gazes of the nearby adventurers, their eyes filled with a kind of awe.

Raul filled the dwarf in about Ottar.

"So the old bloke's muckin' about the middle levels? Hmm...Bah! I wouldn't give it a thought!"

"Really?"

"That's right! Don't let it bother ya, yeah? Even if the fella's there on official orders, he's not one to favor plannin' 'n' all that. I don't think we've got to worry about him interferin' in our expedition," Gareth mused. "'Sides, what with the Guild encouragin' exploration in the depths, he'd be takin' a risk himself attackin' a familia doin' just that," he continued, running a hand through his beard.

Raul and the others found themselves agreeing with the old dwarf—he was one of their familia's leading authorities. Of course, thanks to Aiz's silence, none of them knew about the vicious attack against her that had occurred just the night before, which meant they weren't particularly on guard when it came to *Freya Familia*.

"What brought you here, then, Sir Gareth?"

"Right! Got done carryin' everything back to the manor. Expedition's gonna start right on time the day after tomorrah. Gotta inform the Guild, y'know?"

Raul and company followed Gareth to the counter in the lobby as the dwarf filled them in on the familia's preparations. It seemed everything was in order, including the weapons—and the magic sword—from *Hephaistos Familia*.

When a high-ranking faction such as *Loki Familia* went on an expedition, it was essential that they report the details to the Guild—everything from their start date to how long they planned to stay down in the Dungeon. They were a valuable military power to Orario, after all.

If something happened to them and they didn't return from the

Dungeon, the Guild would oftentimes send in search-and-rescue parties.

"By the way, how're you kids doin', huh? Restin' up properly 'n' all that?" Gareth turned toward Raul and the entourage of other familia members trailing behind them.

"Ha…Ha-ha-ha…Ha-ha-ha-ha-haaa…" Raul laughed weakly.

Even with the expedition right around the corner, he and the other low-ranking members were finding every chance they could get to train, none of them wanting to look bad in the face of Aiz's recent level-up. As they walked, Aki looked purposefully in the other direction, and Leene refused to meet Gareth's eyes.

Gareth, in turn, could do nothing but sigh, the same as a certain high elf had earlier.

"I've already gotten an earful from Mister Bete, actually…" Raul admitted. The memory of the werewolf standing over him with a sardonic laugh as tears pricked the corners of his eyes was still fresh in his head.

"Ain't gonna do ya any good now, moron!"

"He and Miss Aiz…they went up against some pretty powerful enemies down on the twenty-fourth floor, didn't they?" Raul whispered quietly in Gareth's ear.

It took Gareth a moment, but finally, he nodded. "…Aye, they did."

As one of the familia's elites, he'd already heard all about the incident a few days prior.

"Bete hasn't changed a bit since they got back," Raul muttered, thinking back to his show of arrogance—par for the course for him—back in the manor.

Gareth, however, remained quiet. He knew that the werewolf had actually been training harder than anyone else the last few days.

Blaming himself entirely for what happened, and stubbornly hating to lose, he'd been exercising on his own in secret, careful to make sure Raul and the others had no idea what he was doing.

And Gareth had been helping him train in a little shed just outside the city in the wee hours of the morning.

"Haah…Kids these days…"

"?"

Gareth let out a deep sigh, to which Raul eyed him curiously.

Before long, they made it to the counter where a young receptionist sat waiting.

"Report from *Loki Familia*. Just wanted to let ya know we'll be settin' off on our expedition in two days like we tentatively reported. Here's our application."

"Wonderful! Understood."

Misha Frot cheerfully replied as she accepted the application parchment from Gareth.

She was a short little thing, reaching only 150 celch, topped with a mop of pink hair. Answering Gareth with a youthful voice that matched her cherubic face, she rose from her chair and straightened her posture.

Placing one hand over the other with a smile, she gave the dwarf a deep bow.

"We will be awaiting your safe return. May the fortunes of war shine upon you." It was a prayer for the brave adventurers' triumphant return, spoken not only as an employee of the Guild but as a fellow citizen of Orario.

Then she stamped the expedition application form with the crimson Guild seal.

"*Loki Familia*'s expedition will be carried out as planned."

The nearby torchlight responded with a spark.

The voice of the elven Guild master, Royman Mardeel, echoed throughout the dim underground space. The floor was covered in large slate blocks and four torches illuminating its large altar, giving off the feeling of an ancient temple.

His corpulent, fleshy body, completely unbefitting of an elf, knelt in front of the colossal two-meder figure of Ouranos. The old god nodded slowly from his seat at the center of the altar.

"You may leave."

"Y-yes, my liege."

As the austere voice of Orario's founding god boomed around him, Royman's bulbous body quivered. Silently, he stepped back from the altar, making his way out of the chamber and back up the stairs to the surface.

Ouranos remained motionless in his spot atop the great stone pedestal, his blue eyes staring after Royman's retreating form long after the other man had left.

"...They'll be going through with it after all?" came a voice from the darkness once Royman was out of earshot.

It was Fels who stepped forward, dark robe slicing through the veil of concentrated darkness in the corner of the chamber.

Blackness shrouded the cloak all the way down to his ornately patterned gloves, leaving absolutely no skin visible. Fels was like a ghost in the flickering torchlight—appearance, race, sex, every possible aspect was left as an enigma.

"Indeed. It would seem Loki, too, desires information on the recent string of violence," Ouranos replied without even turning his head.

Thus began the colloquy between the venerable god and his closest adviser, deep in the prayer room below Guild Headquarters.

"What do you think, Ouranos? Could the key to everything truly lie within the Dungeon's depths? On its fifty-ninth floor?"

"That is what I believe, though I cannot be certain."

"A god's hunch, sir?"

"Yes."

Their words were short, punctuated with flickers from the nearby torches.

At Ouranos's terse response, Fels nodded.

"Understood. Shall I arrange for a set of eyes to watch them? I'm sure whatever is down there will be of great interest to us."

"See that you do," Ouranos replied to the black-robed Magus's suggestion.

"Allow me to go over all our information. Let me know if I'm missing anything."

At the old god's nod, Fels continued from within the folds of the shadow-filled hood.

"First, we have what was revealed to us on the twenty-fourth floor by that creature-woman with the red hair, Levis."

"The one manipulating the viola and protecting the crystal orb..."

"Indeed. In addition, if we believe what we learned from the ringleader of the Twenty-Seventh-Floor Nightmare, the reanimated Olivas Act...both the fetus and the vibrant magic stones within that new species of monster all originate from the being referred to simply as 'her.'"

"She" was the one who had revived Olivas Act from the abyss of death by implanting within him a vivid magic stone, giving birth to a new human-monster hybrid. The red-haired woman, Levis, was also such a creature. By assimilating magic stones, she and her kind could morph into all-powerful enhanced species—beings that surpassed the limits of both mortal and divine knowledge.

It seemed these creatures, "her" especially, had used their ability to control monsters and set off this string of incidents dating all the way back to the Monsterphilia.

"'She's sleeping deep within the earth,' 'She wants to see the sky'... That is what Olivas Act said according to *Hermes Familia*. From that we can infer 'she' inhabits the Dungeon's lower depths..."

"Then is she like the monsters of the Ancient Times, craving the light of the upper world?" Fels responded to Ouranos's words with a well-placed conclusion.

There was a high chance that whatever awaited *Loki Familia* on the fifty-ninth floor, where the creature Levis had directed Aiz, had something to do with "her."

"The relationship between Aiz Wallenstein and the crystal orb is but one piece of the puzzle."

"..."

Aiz had reacted so strongly upon first coming into contact with the fetus back in Rivira on the eighteenth floor, she'd collapsed. The fetus, too, had responded to Aiz's magic.

At Fels's words, Ouranos ever so slightly averted his eyes.

Enshrouded in deep shadows broken only by the flickering torches, he stilled his tongue as though searching his thoughts for an answer.

Fels continued in spite of the old god's brooding silence.

"Next, we have the remaining Evils. While we do know they're ghosts from ages past, we don't know who is leading them. All we can confirm is that they were seen capturing violas on the twenty-fourth floor and carting them off to who-knows-where."

The many factions that sided with both them and the Guild had conspired against and destroyed this radical group.

Under the direction of gods who referred to themselves as "evil," they'd stood for the downfall of order, inciting rebellions all across Orario with schadenfreude as their one clear objective. They simply wanted to watch the world burn.

The Evils familias had been eradicated, and every single one of the "evil gods" sent back to the heavens. It wasn't clear whether these newly discovered "remnants" were actual survivors of the group or simply recent followers eager to carry on their work.

Everything about the group remained a haze—how many familias were connected to it, the organization's scale, and even the gods leading it were a mystery.

"Forces on the surface cooperating with 'her' and her followers below to obliterate Orario…Could this be what's tying all these events together?"

"It would come as no surprise to me if the remnants of the Evils had an alliance with the underground powers…or perhaps were being used by the underground."

Fels's voice reverberated across the altar, then Ouranos's.

It could very well be that the two groups, Levis's followers and the Evils remnants, were both using each other, but before Fels and Ouranos could reach a conclusion, there was an interruption.

"…May I ask you something, Ouranos?" Black robes swishing, Fels turned toward the venerable god in his spot atop the altar.

Ouranos replied affirmatively with a simple turn of his head.

"During the incident on the twenty-fourth floor, the red-haired woman uttered the name of a person…Well, the name sounded very much like that of a god—Enyo.”

It had been among the information they'd received from the chienthrope.

"—*While not complete, it's grown enough! Take it to Enyo!*"

That was what Levis had said to that figure in the mask and hood—possibly one of the Evils—upon acquisition of the crystal orb.

"This 'Enyo' is probably an important character. Does the name ring a bell?" Fels asked in an attempt to confirm Lulune's report.

"…I don't recall ever having heard of a god by that name," Ouranos replied before continuing. "However…the word *enyo* does exist in the language of the gods."

His blue eyes narrowed.

"It means 'destroyer of cities.'"

It was the day before the expedition.

Which meant it was the last day of training.

Two shadows overlapped atop the stones of the great wall on the city's outer rim, bathed in dawn's first light from the east. The woman, long golden hair spilling out behind her, struck forward again and again, and the boy, white hair fluttering this way and that, followed her every movement in fierce pursuit.

They performed violent back-and-forth offense and defense between scabbard and dagger as they had each day before.

As the magnificent dawn cresting the far mountains painted Aiz's face, she studied the boy in front of her.

Each time she went for an opening, he blocked.

As she raised the speed of her attacks, the number of his blocks increased.

It was the defensive technique she'd taught him.

Repelling enemies' attacks from the side or an angle, rather than from the front.

In terms of defense, he'd certainly met his goal for their training.

The boy put everything he had behind his strikes, behind the technique he'd seen, felt, and learned over the course of their duels.

"—*Nngh!*"

There was a kind of brazen vigor imbued in his skill with the dagger.

Even as the relentless string of attacks carved away at him, he kept up his blocks, deflecting blow after blow.

And then.

The boy did more than defend. He attacked Aiz for the very first time.

"…!" Aiz's eyes opened in surprise.

Bell's dagger streaked at her, its blade flashing beneath the morning sky.

It was easy to block, but that didn't change the fact that the boy had been able to get a strike in at all.

Aiz stared at him wordlessly. The boy's breathing was haggard, and his dagger arm hung limply at his side.

His body was littered with bruises, but his face held the same look of determination he'd had since their first day, rubellite eyes shining with an unfading brilliance.

All of a sudden, the morning sun beamed toward them, the resulting radiance flooding Aiz's field of vision with white.

The boy stood there, haloed in pure-white resplendence. A sort of euphoria escaped Aiz's lips at the sight, and she smiled from the bottom of her heart.

"That's it, then, I guess…" Aiz whispered with a sigh.

The sun was already peeking over the majestic mountains of the eastern sky, almost like a signal that their week of training had come to an end.

Aiz turned toward that sight, squinting at daybreak's glorious fire. The boy did the same before turning back to her and bowing his head.

"Thank you. Thank you for everything," he said, bending at the waist and facing the stone beneath his feet.

Their one week together had been short. Too short, it seemed, and as Aiz looked back over their seven-day tryst, she felt her heart and mind flood with emotion.

She hadn't uncovered a single thing about Bell's uncanny growth.

However, without even noticing it, she'd learned how enjoyable it was watching him improve from one day to the next, what it felt like to have her heart flutter, and the pure bliss that came from knowing she could teach another.

And for Aiz, who'd known nothing but combat for as long as she could remember, this made her happy.

It had been a path of joy and sorrow, frantic worrying, despondent wallowing, profound thinking, and utter happiness that had brought the two of them to this point.

She embraced this time, this irreplaceable moment they had shared, deep within her heart.

After a while, Bell rose, his white hair fluttering in the breeze and making him look even more like a rabbit than usual.

Their eyes met.

"I would also like to thank you. It was…fun," she said quietly, voice reverberating with a warmth that surprised even herself as her eyes softened.

She smiled once more, the two of them bathed in morning's first light.

Bell's face instantly reddened, his mouth opening and closing wordlessly as he stared at his feet. Seeing this only made her smile widen. If there was one thing that hadn't changed during their week of training, it was his constant embarrassment.

Who knew the white rabbit could be so shy?

"…Good luck…with everything."

"…Thank you."

Aiz slowly tore her gaze away before turning around.

It was time for the two of them to begin running again. With those last few words, she began to pull away, knowing she'd regret it if she allowed herself to pause here.

This wasn't good-bye.

From here on out, the two of them would be facing their own objectives, aiming for their own separate peaks.

"…"

Aiz walked a few steps along the top of the wall glowing in sunlight, then slowly turned back around.

The boy had already turned his back to her, far off now as he ran along his own path.

Inhaling a deep breath of all that vast morning blue, she curled her lips into a smile.

"…See you again."

And then, turning her back to the boy, she ran.

Her sunny-blond ponytail spilled out behind her as she dodged.

Deep below the surface, closed off from the sky, her voice sang out, reverberating off the Dungeon walls. Again and again the sword flew at her, but her voice never faltered.

Staff clenched in her hands, Lefiya wove her spells, her lips constantly moving.

Stepping, evading, dodging the relentless attacks of the golden-haired, golden-eyed swordswoman, she took advantage of every opening she found, taking only the minimum hits necessary to keep the incoming strikes from influencing her chants.

Just like the first day of their training, she refused to back down or close her eyes in fear.

She focused on every attack, vision wide, picturing her next movement in her mind to ensure the words of her chant remained unbroken.

Deep inside her she could hear the words of her many teachers.

The soul of an unshakable tree and the chanting techniques she'd learned from Riveria.

The Concurrent Casting Filvis had helped her master.

She threw everything out in front of her in a single attack on the swordswoman she so revered.

"Loose your arrows, fairy archers. Pierce, arrow of accuracy…"

In a dance, she wove her song between the steps of her opponent's sword waltz.

As the magic circle formed beneath her feet, Lefiya completed her chant, unleashing the spell.

"—*Arcs Ray!*"

A brilliant arrow of light shot forth from the circle.

Aiz stepped deftly out of the way as it shrieked by to explode against the Dungeon wall.

Chunks and pieces of the wall went flying as smoke rose up from the resulting rift. The damage was great, greater than before—evidence of her increase in magic strength from her training with Filvis two days prior.

"Whoa..." Aiz let out an awed mutter of surprise as the two of them stared at the wall.

The elven magic user herself just smiled faintly at the improvement in her Concurrent Casting, her breath still ragged.

"Impressive, Lefiya. You're really getting the hang of this."

Lefiya laughed bashfully. "Only...thanks to everyone's help, truly. The credit isn't mine to claim..."

She wouldn't have been able to master the skill if even one of her teachers had been missing.

Everything was a result of her practice duels with Aiz and Filvis as well as Riveria's tutelage. They were the women who had guided her as she'd fought so desperately to keep up.

"Of course it is," Aiz countered with a smile in response to Lefiya's red-faced modesty.

Aiz's heartfelt praise, however, made Lefiya only more embarrassed.

"Miss Aiz...I have been working very hard so that I can support you and the others in the expedition," she explained, hugging her staff to her chest as she met her tutor's gaze directly.

She didn't want to waste what Aiz and everyone had done for her or slow them down. She wanted to be helpful and make a difference.

"I know." Aiz nodded at the elf's bold-faced oath of determination.

Lefiya could see her own conviction reflected in those golden eyes.

Then finally, her lips parted. "Could I ask...What's become of that human?"

The area around Aiz's eyes softened. "He's also been trying very hard."

It was the day before the expedition, so this would be both Lefiya's and the boy's last day of training.

Aiz's face had appeared refreshed, almost invigorated after ending her early morning training session with that boy. Her usually stark, emotionless features were tinted with joy.

"I see…" Lefiya answered quietly at Aiz's response, both verbal and visual. Lowering her gaze, she focused instead on the bluish-white pallor of the magic stone affixed to her staff.

She'd never quite been able to erase that boy from her mind.

Even now, at the end of her training, she couldn't keep herself from thinking about him.

"What with the expedition tomorrow, why don't we head back early?"

At Aiz's suggestion that they vacate their Dungeon training room, however, Lefiya's head rose, and she interjected with another suggestion.

"Actually, I…I would still like to do a bit of fine-tuning on my own."

"Sure…It's fine. Just don't push yourself too hard, okay?" Aiz responded, not pressing her further.

She excused herself from the room, almost as though sensing something in the elf's demeanor, and left Lefiya alone among the phosphorescent walls and ceiling.

She closed her eyes, taking a deep breath.

At length, she began to perform once more, staff gripped between her hands and the songs of her people on her lips.

Periodically double-checking her movements, periodically releasing a beam of light at an oncoming monster, she trained.

As long as time permitted, she reviewed and practiced again and again and again.

"…I should head back," Lefiya muttered some hours later as she drew a pocket watch from her clothing and checked the time.

Her silver elven pocket watch, crafted to resemble a tree and leaves, indicated it was already well into the evening hours.

Shutting the lid with a *snap*, Lefiya took off for the exit, stopping just in front of the door for a last look at the room where she'd spent so many hours training during the past few days.

I learned so much here, she thought with a faint smile. This would be the last time she'd leave.

"Perhaps I stayed a bit too long..." Lefiya mused before leaving that western room on the Dungeon's fifth floor and dashing toward the surface.

Thinking back to how enthusiastically she'd taken Aiz's words to heart, she returned to the floor's main route, currently flooded with other people. She progressed to the upper levels, taking out the odd monster or two and passing a good number of her fellow adventurers along the way.

Maneuvering through Onset Road, as the large passageway on the first floor was called, she proceeded up the spiral staircase to the large hole that led to the surface and emerged on the ground floor of Babel Tower.

She was just about to make her way through the gate and into the sprawling Central Park when she ran into a familiar face.

"Ah!"

"Ah!"

Their short cries of surprise overlaid each other as their gazes met.

She saw those unforgettable rubellite eyes and hair as white as virgin snow.

He hefted a giant backpack on his shoulders and stood beside a young werewolf girl with long grayish-brown hair. *One of his adventurer companions?*

On his way back from the Dungeon, no doubt, he appeared completely spent, but after crossing paths with Lefiya, the two of them stopped short.

The werewolf girl eyed the two of them curiously as other adventurers bustled around them.

Lefiya was the first to move.

Eyebrows rising, she raised a slender finger and pointed it with an almost audible *SNAP* at the bemused boy.

"I won't lose!"

The boy simply stood there, bewildered, with his eyes as round as saucers. Lefiya ran.

Out through the gate, into the park as the eyes of the baffled werewolf girl and her fellow adventurers seared into her back.

The conviction she was saving for tomorrow's expedition and the resolution she'd made to that boy.

Holding those two feelings close, she bolted through the square that was all awash in reds. In and out, in and out, she weaved through the crowd.

She ran toward the fiery crimson of the setting sun and didn't look back.

"If you would, please, Lokiiiiiii!"

"Fer cryin' out loud! Just how many of you guys are out there?!"

Night had fallen.

A mighty roar bellowed from Twilight Manor, home of *Loki Familia*.

The cry originated in Loki's bedroom atop the centermost spire in the outcropping of towers. A line of the goddess's precious little followers had formed outside her door at the peak of its winding staircase.

"This is ridiculous! How could this many of ya need yer Statuses checked?! The night before the expedition, even—good grief!"

It was true—every single one of them was waiting for a turn to update their Statuses. Men and women alike had flocked to Loki's tower in hopes of applying their excelia before tomorrow's expedition.

Loki had specifically warned them not to wait until the last moment to update their Statuses in order to avoid this, but her advice had fallen on deaf ears. Consumed by the need to train, they'd beaten themselves up, polished their skills, and collected every last bit of excelia they could until the last second possible. Though the feeling was understandable, so was Loki's lament.

"Damn training craze, damn Aizuu…" Loki cursed the golden-haired airhead under her breath as she diligently went to work updating Statuses for that girl's brethren. She wasn't about to turn them away, given even the tiniest boost could mean the difference between life and death on the rigorous expedition ahead.

"Gods-dammit! Not even enough time to cop a few feels!"

"Thank yoooooou!"

Loki could practically feel tears of blood running down her face as she remorsefully watched a beastwoman exit the room with her tunic removed, taking that smooth curve of her back and those beautiful breasts with her.

It was a veritable frenzy, and she barely had room to breathe. No matter how many of her followers' Statuses she updated, the line outside her door refused to shorten. That was the problem with having a big familia—it was a lot of work, too.

The short hand of the clock made first one circle, then two as it neared midnight.

"I'm...I'm done!"

As the last gentleman took his leave with a word of thanks, Loki gazed out at the complete lack of people in front of her door.

Pushing it closed, she heaved a sigh that was equal parts delight and relief.

Not more than a second later, the door burst back open, almost as though it'd been planned.

"Yo, Loki! Update my Status, will ya?"

"Guh...Beeeeeeeete..." Loki collapsed onto her bed upon the young werewolf's entrance. "Can't ya see I'm dyin' here?"

"How the hell was I supposed to know, huh?" Bete responded, indifferent to the silent tears Loki cried into her bedsheets. He pulled a chair over next to her and sat himself down.

"If only I coulda ended with someone like Aiz...Least then I coulda gotten a little thrill as a reward. But no...It had to be Bete..." Loki grumbled to herself.

"Screw you." Bete pulled off his battle jacket. "It takes you, like, one second, so just do it already!"

"Yeah, yeah."

Bete turned his bare back to Loki, surrendering himself to the goddess's touch.

Unlocking and quickly raising the crimson hieroglyphs on Bete's back, Loki proceeded to update his Status.

"Comin' here after everyone else has already left…You wouldn't happen to be trainin' by yerself all secret-like, are ya?"

"How the hell did you know?!"

Loki just snickered. "My little secret."

The goddess out of sight behind him, Bete didn't even try to keep the exasperation from his face.

She grinned to herself before running her finger, wet with ichor, over his back.

"I bet some of those kids who're scared of ya now would come right up to you if they knew 'bout your secret training sessions. So out of character, y'know? Some people go fer that. That's a comfortin' thought, ain't it?"

Bete let out a sharp laugh. "What do I care about making friends with weaklings?" The werewolf so feared by everyone beside the familia elites simply scoffed, briefly muttering, "Stupid," as Loki's finger continued to flow across his back without pause.

His amber eyes stared angrily at the far wall.

"It's us strong folks' duty to look down on the small fries from on high. Our right."

"…"

"If we don't laugh and spit on 'em, who will? We'll just end up with a buncha idiots who don't know their place," Bete continued, voice dripping with irritation. "They should be lookin' up to us so much they break their necks. Those namby-pambies…They're so weak, it's disgusting."

Though he didn't say it explicitly, it was clear his words were aimed at the throng of familia members desperately struggling to catch up after Aiz leveled up.

Loki was silent as she listened, staring at Bete's finely chiseled back and the faint scars that covered his skin. She closed her eyes before letting out an abrupt puff of laughter.

Finishing his Status update, she translated the results into Koine.

"Yer abilities have really shot up, Bete."

"How much?"

"'Bout three levels."

"Shot up, my ass!" Bete snatched the translated update results from her hands with a howl.

"Nah, come on! Fer a Level Five to get these kinda results on their own, it's really somethin'!" Loki assured him with a laugh.

The werewolf just huffed and puffed, his eyes burning holes through the form. "This ain't shit…"

Glancing around at the wine bottles and other knickknacks proliferating Loki's room, he lit the candle on her desk before burning the update form.

"…Yeah, yeah, we get it. You're a tough guy."

As Bete pulled his jacket over his shoulders and headed for the door, Loki called out from her place on the bed.

"Tough enough to protect everyone down there. You'll do that fer me, yeah?"

Who knew how many dangers awaited them on their upcoming expedition? As the goddess's words reached his ears, the werewolf stopped in the doorway and glanced back over his shoulder.

"…Ha. You didn't choose a buncha asses, ya old hag."

Now it was Loki's turn to look surprised, rarely as it happened. Bete just grinned.

"They may be chumps, but they ain't cowards. They can take care of themselves."

Loki looked long and hard at her ever-disobedient child.

Then she smiled.

She woke up on her own.

It was morning. The day of the expedition.

Aiz slowly cracked her eyes open at the sun filtering in from the crack between the curtains.

Pushing herself up from her bed in her room at the manor, she threw a glance first at Desperate leaning against the wall, then out the window, her eyes narrowing.

There was nothing but clear blue sky as far as the eye could see.

*   *   *

"Leeeeet's do this!"

"Do you have to be so loud? Just shut up and get ready…"

Tiona and Tione emerged boisterously from their beds in their two-person room.

It was time to get their things ready. The expedition they'd been waiting for had finally arrived. As the older of the two wrapped her battle clothes around her ample chest and slender legs, her younger sister—already changed—opened up their chest's shelves and began tossing items out left and right, stuffing anything they might need into her pack.

As Tione grumbled and complained, the floor quickly became buried in Tiona's possessions.

Her pareu swishing back and forth, Tiona turned finally to collect her large double-edged sword from its spot against the shelf.

"This expedition is our chance to catch up with Aiz!"

She gripped the oversize weapon by the handle, its blades glinting with a brilliant luster.

"Lefiya, I'm heading out!"

"Ah! All right! I will be there shortly!"

Lefiya hurriedly returned to her preparations as her roommate stepped out the door.

Turning to the mirror, she set to work on her long golden hair, holding the silver barrette accessory between her teeth to free her hands until she could tie it back in her usual ponytail.

Once everything was secured, she took a last look in the mirror and nodded with a little "Okay!"

"…"

She rose from her chair with her staff, Forest's Teardrop, already at her side and glanced down at the palms of her hands.

As though checking the magic strength her brethren—no, her *friends*—had bestowed upon her, she squeezed her hands into tight little fists.

Then, head popping back up, she slung the cylindrical supporter's backpack over her shoulder and took off out the door.

*   *   *

"Ah! Bete!"

They were out in the garden of the manor, carting some of the large-scale cargo and other materials.

The lower-ranking members of the familia were at work gathering everything from tents and spare armor to the thirty-plus weapons (magic sword included) they'd be taking on the expedition, inspecting and organizing everything accordingly.

Everyone, willing or not, was nervous and excited about the big day, and in the midst of all the chatter, Raul, in charge of instructing his fellow familia members, spotted Bete emerge from the tower's entryway.

His gauntlets and silvery metal boots shone brightly in the sun.

"G-good morning!" Raul took the initiative and greeted the werewolf, easily the most restless of all the other first-tiers.

"Well, aren't you all takin' yer sweet time?!" Bete spit his response at both Raul and their surrounding colleagues.

They visibly shrank back, since Bete himself was already greatly feared among the lower-ranked members, and Raul could feel the sweat forming on his temple as he forced a laugh.

"Ah-ha-ha-ha…"

In spite of everything, the fact that Bete was no different from normal even before the big expedition was almost strangely calming.

"Aiz and the others aren't here yet?"

"Th-they aren't, sir! I've received word that Miss Tiona and her sister are currently eating breakfast in the mess hall, but it seems Miss Aiz is still in her room," Raul continued, pushing forward despite the surrounding atrophy.

Bete came to a stop. "Really? She's not gonna eat anything? That goddamn woman…" he muttered, cursing under his breath as he turned around and headed back the way he'd come.

Raul didn't know if the werewolf was on his way to eat or headed up to Aiz's room, but either way, as he watched Bete walk away, he found himself thinking the strangest thought.

What a nice guy…

*   *   *

"…"

Finn was down on one knee, hand to his chest in his room, located in the manor's northernmost tower.

He was silent, eyes closed, a grand tapestry covering the wall in front of him and a statue of a goddess occupying a spot atop the nearby shelf.

Both the tapestry, woven in gold and silver, and the plaster statue, a spear in its hand, portrayed the same woman—the fictitious though greatly worshipped goddess of the prums, Phiana.

"You up, Finn?…Oops, sorry. Didn't mean to intrude."

"No, it's fine. I'm finished."

Gareth and Riveria made to leave as soon as they saw Finn kneeling in front of Phiana, but Finn stopped them before they could retreat, opening his eyes and pushing himself to his feet.

Concluding his prayer, he turned away from his beloved goddess to face his two closest friends.

"Prep work's finished. Everything's packed 'n' good to go."

"Understood. Thank you, Gareth."

"We were hoping to have a final meeting before heading out. We need to organize everyone into the two parties we'll maintain until the eighteenth floor," said Riveria.

Finn walked over, and they formed a circle. The three heads of *Loki Familia* quickly busied themselves making their final check before the expedition.

"How is everyone doing, Riveria?" Finn inquired, wrapping up their meeting.

"I worry about their constitution, considering how much they've been training lately…but I don't see it becoming a problem. They're all in top physical condition."

"We got ourselves a bunch of young hot shots, that's why. Morale is high."

As voices began drifting in from the direction of the garden, Gareth crossed his arms in front of his chest, eyes narrowing.

"Aiz and the rest of the young'uns have finally grown up…Just us three fogies still around to remember what it was like back then," he mused, thinking back to when their familia had first formed.

"We're not retired yet, Gareth," Riveria replied, closing her eyes with a smile.

As Finn looked up at the two of them, he felt his expression slowly change.

"The day has finally come. Today, we'll take on the unexplored depths left to us by Zeus and Hera...If we prove successful, our names will be known across the world once more."

There was a glimmer of steadfast resolve in the prum's green eyes, the strong ambition to restore his race's renown in the back of his mind.

"You haven't had enough yet? There isn't a prum around that doesn't know your name, Finn," Riveria commented.

Finn, however, just closed his eyes and shook his head.

"As far as famous prums in Orario, I know only Bringar of *Freya Familia*...But as for my brothers who live outside the city, I have very little renown."

The number of prums with any sort of reputation in not only Orario but the whole world was few enough to be counted on one hand. As Finn relayed this, his eyes dropped to his fist.

"Prums need a chance to shine, an opportunity to wave their banner of courage."

They had to have the kind of hope personified in Phiana, who had supported them since the Ancient Times.

And we'll spare nothing, no matter the sacrifice, as long as it's for the sake of that hope—his heart added.

"It doesn't end here. No matter what awaits, I shall press forward." Finn raised his head, resolve coursing through his petite figure.

Gareth looked down at the tiny adventurer and stroked his beard with a laugh.

"Good gracious...You really haven't changed a bit, Finn. More ambition in those pint-size bones of yours than some men got in their whole bodies. And never givin' a damn what others think about it, either!"

"And here I've been trying to mellow out," Finn responded with his shoulders slouched.

"You, Finn? Don't make me laugh!" Gareth's lips turned upward together with his beard.

As Riveria gazed down at the two of them, a nostalgic look came over her. "...To think that the three of us who used to do nothing but quarrel among ourselves would spearhead a Dungeon crawl together. A funny world it is sometimes."

The proud, versatile high elf; the crude, disparaging dwarf who hated her; and the prum stuck between them, a never-ending stream of sighs passing his lips.

As the three of them thought back to the days that led them to this moment, they shared a sudden smile.

"Let's do this, yeah? It'll be a breath of fresh air," Gareth said, extending an arm.

Finn and Riveria, despite their wry smiles, imitated the dwarf and dropped their hands atop his in the center of their circle as though they had planned to.

The same ritual they'd performed so many moons ago on the day of their oath.

It was Loki who'd forcibly encouraged the three of them to put their bickering on hold long enough to join hands like this and share their aspirations.

"To heated battles."

"To an unknown world."

"To the revival of my race."

The dwarf, elf, and prum spoke in turn before bumping their fists together.

Their intentions spoken, it was time to end their walk down memory lane and become the familia leaders they were.

"Aiz and the others will be waiting. Shall we go?" said Finn.

Riveria and Gareth nodded, and the three left the room.

"Speakin' of...Finn, how goes, uh, that other objective of yours?"

"Yes, your successor...A bride who can produce an heir."

"Unfortunately, I'm not exactly blessed when it comes to romance. If you two happen to find anyone nice, do introduce me?"

"Tione would murder me. I must politely decline," replied Riveria.

"Same here, friend," added Gareth.

The three demi-humans chatted idly with spear, ax, and staff in hand as they made their way over to their waiting comrades.

Sunlight poured down on Central Park from the clear blue sky above.

It was the intersection of Orario's eight main streets, making it a hub for adventurers even in the early morning hours.

Armored boys, girls, and heroes alike passed through the square on their way to the Dungeon, their supporters trailing behind them. In the midst of the swarm of races on their way to the great white tower, Aiz, too, found herself heading toward that great skyscraper.

After gathering everything in front of the manor, Finn led the *Loki Familia* troupe to Central Park via North Main Street. Accompanied by load after giant load of equipment and materials, they stopped a short distance from Babel's northern entrance and awaited further orders.

Even crying children were silenced by the sight of their flag, emblazoned with the emblem of the Trickster. As the largest familia in the city, they drew attention and buzz from all sides as they stood there waiting for the command to depart.

"Oh-ho-ho! If it isn't the Sword Princess! Been a while since we crossed paths. How ya been?"

"Miss Tsubaki…"

Aiz was staring up at Babel and its backdrop of blue sky when Tsubaki's voice sounded out next to her.

She glanced over to find Tsubaki Collbrande, ever-present eye patch over her left eye, closing in on her with an amiable smile on her face.

Just as Aiz was wearing armor and bearing her sword, Tsubaki was bedecked in her own Dungeon gear. Her armor was a mix of island and continent styles—bright-red pleated trousers from the East called *hakama* concealed her legs from the shins up, while battle clothes covered her upper torso and ample chest. On top of that, she wore gauntlets and shoulder protectors.

Her upper and lower halves were every bit a fusion of East and West.

At her side in its obsidian scabbard was her long *tachi*. Accompanying her were the many High Smiths who would be joining the expedition.

The confederation of *Hephaistos Familia* and *Loki Familia* was complete.

"It will be a pleasure working with you," Aiz began, having been told by Riveria some time ago that the smiths would be joining them.

"You bet! Just leave things to me! No need for the fancy words, though! We're itchin' to get down there, too, so we're scratching each other's backs for sure," Tsubaki responded good-naturedly, not even trying to hide her own familia's intentions.

Aiz could only smile wryly at the other woman's boisterous laughter.

All of a sudden, Tsubaki looked away with an "Oh!" of surprise.

"There you are, Bete Loga! You break that Frosvirt of yers again, and I'll never forgive you, ya hear? I had a hell of a time fixin' it!"

"Whoa, whoa, whooooa there! I hear ya loud and clear, okay? I won't break it! Damn! Get away from me!"

Eyes locked on Bete, Tsubaki made a beeline toward him. He cried out, beads of sweat dotting his temples as the smirking woman closed the gap between them far too much for his comfort.

Aiz looked on curiously as the fearless spectacle drew the awed gazes of everyone around them, only to be approached by a new shadow.

"How fares the Sword Princess, hmm?"

"...Miss Lulune?" Aiz turned around to find herself face-to-face with the young chienthrope girl. She stared at her in puzzlement, with no clue as to what a member of *Hermes Familia* would be doing there. "Why are you here...?"

"Thought I'd wish you well and all on your expedition, I guess. You have saved me more than a couple of times in the past." Apparently she'd determined just when the two familias would have some free time before departing for the Dungeon and timed her entrance accordingly. Though she quickly added that she had no intention of overstaying her visit lest she trouble the actual expedition participants.

"Take these. A little something to eat I like to bring with me when

I'm exploring ruins. One of these'll keep you full for a whole day. And, uh, don't worry—there's nothing weird in 'em or anything."

"...Thank you." Aiz smiled softly at the offered pouch of block-shaped rations.

While members of both familias were currently absorbed in the exchange happening between Bete and Tsubaki, Lulune plopped the bag into Aiz's hand—with an unexpected *clink*.

Concealed beneath the bag was a single crystal.

"From our friend in the black robes," she whispered so softly only Aiz could hear.

"!" Aiz's eyes widened with a start.

"Black robes" could mean only one person—the hooded character Aiz and Lulune had both been seeing more and more of recently.

Aiz had trouble containing her surprise as she looked down at the blue crystal—a request from the mysterious shaman.

"I checked it out already with Asfi, and it seems pretty normal... Seems our friend just wants you to have it on the fifty-ninth floor, is all," the thief explained, recounting what she'd been told as she discreetly handed Aiz the crystal. "Toss it if you want. Your call." After she finished speaking, Lulune took a step back.

Aiz found herself at a loss, which only made Lulune laugh, her brow wrinkling.

"I really did just wanna come see you off, though, you know...even if it may not seem like it with the request and all. Once you come back, we'll go for that drink, got it?" Her tanned skin flushing slightly, she brought a finger up to sheepishly scratch at her cheek. "Catch ya later!" she finished before turning around and walking off with a swish of her tail.

Aiz watched her disappear into the crowd, then she returned her gaze to the pouch—and crystal.

The orb itself was tiny and blue, connected to a chain. After a moment's glance, Aiz fastened it to the loin guard of her armor.

Did she completely trust that hooded figure? No. But this was a good-luck charm given to her by a friend who came all the way down here to see her off.

The little blue crystal glittered atop the silver gleam of her loin guard.

"Was that Miss Lulune just now? What could she have wanted with Miss Aiz?"

Lefiya ruminated on this as she caught a glimpse of the exchange between Lulune and Aiz.

Surrounded by Tiona and Tione—who were endlessly chattering—and the other familia members, Lefiya cocked her head to the side in curiosity.

"Miss Lefiya!"

"Hmm? Miss Amid?" She turned around to find a beautiful silver-haired human with features so delicate they resembled a doll's.

The *Dian Cecht Familia* healer bowed her head, having joined the group via Northwest Main Street.

"I couldn't be here waiting for you on account of *Miach*—I mean, a certain familia taking up my time with their new merchandise contract, but it seems I've still made it on time. This is for you."

"Are these…potions?"

"They are, indeed. Our very own high-magic potions."

Amid handed her a small pouch filled with a variety of test tubes.

At the surprised expression on Lefiya's face, she continued. "A farewell gift for your expedition, yes?"

"Amid! You came to see us off! But what gives? How come only Lefiya gets a gift?" Tiona butted in, overhearing Lefiya and Amid's conversation.

"Surely someone like you doesn't need potions, Miss Tiona," Amid responded with a little snicker.

"What's that supposed to mean?!"

"I was merely joking," the healer replied before she pulled out an even larger pouch than the one she'd given Lefiya. "You'll find a few high potions and elixirs inside. Share them with everyone, would you?"

"Thank you, Amid. This is wonderful. And so many, too," Tione replied appreciatively, to which Amid only shook her head.

The kindhearted healer looked at each of them in turn before offering them a deep bow.

"May the fortunes of war shine upon you," she said before taking her leave.

Lefiya, Tiona, and Tione glanced down at the healing items they'd received before raising their voices in thanks.

All around them, too, similar exchanges were taking place.

Personal acquaintances and friends alike showed up to send off their *Loki Familia* comrades with a smile and a few words of encouragement.

Humans and demi-humans from all around were there to support and salute the adventurers on their journey to the unknown.

"Brothers! Sisters! The expedition begins now!" Finn called out from in front of the assemblage.

Everyone turned to face the familia leader, Babel to his back and Gareth and Riveria to either side.

"We'll be splitting into two parties as we enter the Dungeon! Riveria and I will lead the first, and Gareth will be leading the second! We'll rendezvous on the eighteenth floor and continue together to the fiftieth floor! Our goal? To venture into the unexplored depths—the fifty-ninth floor!"

Everyone's ears—Bete's, Tiona's, Tione's, Lefiya's, Tsubaki's—buzzed with Finn's proclamation.

As Aiz joined the others watching the three familia leaders, her mind was already racing at the thought of what awaited them in the den of monsters beneath that great white tower.

Within the Dungeon's dark depths below the earth.

"You are adventurers! Warriors no less brave than the heroes of old! Conquer the vast unknown and return with fame and fortune!"

From the main streets, the square, in every corner and window, citizens, adventurers, and everyone else in Orario watched over them, eager to see *Loki Familia*'s departure.

"Sacrifices will lead to nothing but false honor! Everyone, pray with me now! Make an oath to the light of the surface—you will come back alive!"

As the members of both familias raised their fists, Finn sucked in his breath. Then, as though communing their short departure with the blue sky stretched out above their heads, he gave the order.

"Expedition team—move out!"

Their battle cry shook the very heavens.

Aiz stared at the sky overhead, surrounded by the shouting cries of her peers.

Loki Familia's expedition had begun.

"This is gonna be interestin'!"

The manor's central tower...

Having sent Finn and the others off from their home earlier, Loki now stood on the roof, looking toward the city's center as the cries of war echoed around her.

"Could it be calamity that awaits them? Or perhaps..."

The underground shrine beneath Guild Headquarters...

Ouranos turned his brine-colored eyes skyward as the torchlights flickered around him.

"Yes...Show me."

And atop the highest floor of the great white tower.

Unbeknownst to all, the beautiful goddess smiled down on them.

Thus, the threads of a new Dungeon epic were spun beneath the gaze of the gods.

The majority of the two factions' heavy hitters were in the vanguard party—the first team to dive into the Dungeon.

Given how unpredictable the Dungeon was, it would be their job to take care of any Irregulars that popped up along their route. They would act as advance troops, ensuring the safety of the heart of the expedition by clearing the way for the party following them with the materials and spare equipment.

Those on the vanguard team led by Finn and Riveria included

Aiz, Bete, Tiona, Tione, and seven more of the familia's most distinguished first-tier adventurers. They were joined by a slew of second-tier adventurers, such as Raul, who'd be acting as supporters.

Gareth, the remaining first-tier adventurer, as well as Lefiya and the other magic users, would follow behind in the second larger party.

"Hey, hey, Tione! What are all those people from other familias doin' here? They're not, like, supporters we've hired or something, are they?" Tiona asked, glancing behind her. The two parties had split to avoid the chaos of the narrow upper-floor passageways as they made their way into the Dungeon. She'd only just now noticed *Hephaistos Familia* smiths traveling along behind them.

"Don't be an idiot, Tiona. Have you already forgotten what happened during our last expedition?" her sister replied in exasperation.

"?"

"They're smiths, Tiona," Riveria explained with a great deal more politeness.

"Ah!" Tiona burst out, suddenly understanding. Considering she'd played no part in the expedition preparations—and consequently knew nothing of the trouble that had gone into them—she'd had no idea members of *Hephaistos Familia* would be joining them.

Ten *Hephaistos Familia* smiths had joined the fifteen *Loki Familia* adventurers. The smiths had been split up between the two parties with their captain, Tsubaki, accompanying their current group as a member of the vanguard.

"That's pretty crazy, though, you know? *Hephaistos Familia* High Smiths? Together with us?"

"Yes, and Lady Hephaistos is doing us a big favor, so let's try and avoid any blunders, hmm, Tiona?" Finn responded with an amused laugh, watching the girl spin about excitedly at the news of their new companions. He'd been the one who'd gone to Hephaistos directly, after all.

"I know, I know!" Tiona replied with a laugh of her own as she sprinted ahead to wrap her arms around Aiz's shoulders from behind. "Did you hear that, Aiz? Huh? Huh? High Smiths from *Hephaistos Familia* are joining us!"

"Yes, I heard...Pretty neat," she responded playfully to the naive

Amazon hanging off her back. Like the others, Aiz already knew that the smiths would be joining them, but she couldn't keep a smile from gracing her lips at Tiona's enthusiasm.

They soon arrived at the Dungeon's seventh floor.

Surrounded by the greenish walls and ceilings of the Dungeon's passageways, they continued along unhindered, their cheer almost strange considering the fact they were on an expedition.

"Hell yeah! If they're from *Hephaistos Familia*, we at least don't hafta worry about them slowin' us down! What a relief!" Bete bellowed next to them, his ears twitching, which garnered a laugh from the High Smiths behind them.

"There it is! Bete's famous ego!"

Tiona narrowed her eyes at the werewolf's pompous grin.

"Is it even possible for you to be nice, Bete? Do you get some kinda thrill looking down on everyone else? I hate people like that!"

"You got it all wrong! You actually think I like looking down on bottom-feeders? Don't make me laugh! All I do is call it like I see it," Bete responded with a snort, explaining himself the same way he'd done for Loki only the night before.

Still attached to Aiz's back, Tiona let out a squawk of anger that sounded very much like a monkey.

The werewolf's goading only elicited angered grumbles from those around them.

This was a sight they were more than used to.

"What can I say? I can't stand weaklings! Lookin' at 'em floundering away makes me laugh so hard I can't stop!"

"That sounds like nothing but the arrogance of a strong man looking down his nose at others," Riveria responded.

Tiona added, "True! You were one of those 'weaklings' once, too, you know!"

"I'm just sayin' they need to know their place, is all!"

As Aiz listened to the three of them squabble, a thought came to her mind.

Know your place—the thought morphed into words that she muttered beneath her breath.

One's place. It was neither pitying, nor insulting, nor shocking. It was simply something you knew.

It was the same thing that had been hammered into that boy so many times he'd verbally renounced his place. What had been running through his head? How had he felt? What was it that had pushed him to that point?

She thought of those rubellite eyes she'd seen back at the bar, liable to burst into tears at a moment's notice.

How had he overcome things after being looked down on, scorned, spit on by Bete? Or perhaps it was that very contempt that spurred him forward?

Had he hated himself so much that his anger became a spring, propelling him steadfastly, obstinately higher and higher?

Wait, could it be—?!

What if that boy's goal he "needed to accomplish at all costs" included Bete somehow?

For some reason, the shock hit her with a *slam!* She found herself suddenly unable to support Tiona's weight, staggering forward. Ignoring the other girl's curious expression, Aiz attempted to keep her knees from collapsing.

I'll have to ask him sometime... she thought even as her hair stood on end at the possibility she had stumbled upon. She lowered her gaze, memories of her past week with the boy trickling through her mind.

I wonder what he's doing right now...

Perhaps he was still running the same as he always was.

Maybe fighting with the things she'd taught him in his thoughts.

His face flashed through her mind, just a little bit tougher than it had been before, when suddenly, her head shot up with a *snap*.

"...Seems like there's four of them."

"Huh? Is this what they mean when they say 'speak of the devil'?"

Tiona, who was still glued to Aiz, and Bete both reacted.

Everyone's eyes turned toward the right-hand side of the oncoming intersection, where four adventurers quickly drew near, looking decidedly worse for wear.

They were throwing furtive glances behind them, almost as if they were running away from something.

"Hmmmm? They look in a hurry. Think we should see what's wrong?"

"No. Parties aren't supposed to interfere with one another within the Dungeon."

"Hey, guuuuys! What's up?!" Tiona called out to the quartet, ignoring her sister's restraint.

"…Idiot."

Finally noticing Aiz and the others, the surprised adventurers came to a halt in front of them.

"Wh-who're you? W-wait a minute! The Amazon?!"

"Is that Tiona Hyrute?!"

"Which can only mean…*Loki Familia*! I-it's their expedition!"

Upon realizing their identity, the quartet immediately began shrinking back.

"Come ooon! Why is it always me…?" Tiona grumbled to herself at the use of her alias and the fear behind it. The speaker's eyes were still fixated on her.

Bete, on the other hand, turned to the four to ask what they were doing.

They were briefly indignant at the werewolf's scornful inquiry…but then they seemed to remember their situation, bodies giving a tremble.

"…There was a minotaur!"

"…Huh?"

"A minotaur, you fool! That great bull of a monster was prowling around the upper levels!"

Bete came to an immediate stop at the adventurer's strangled, cracking voice.

The others, too, were overcome with a kind of shocked pallor. For a mid-level boss to be appearing on the upper levels was an irregularity, indeed.

Aiz felt her right arm begin to tremble at the mere mention of the word *minotaur*.

For some reason, the image of Bell's face welled up inside her once more.

"...I apologize, but could you perhaps give us some more details? Please tell us exactly what you saw," Finn said, speaking for the rest of the group.

"S-sure..." replied what seemed to be the leader of the quartet before beginning his story. "We were exploring the Dungeon, same as always, when we saw him—a minotaur! In one of the passageways between the rooms," he continued, face pale. "He was...*attacking some kid with white hair*! We'd have done something, but one howl from that beast and we got the hell outta there!"

—BA-DUMP.

Aiz's heart gave a jump inside her chest.

It felt like her entire body was suddenly soaked in sweat.

Forgetting to breathe, she desperately tried to comprehend the words she'd just heard.

A kid with white hair...a human?

The more they spoke, the fiercer, more painfully her heart pounded.

No longer able to keep herself out of the conversation, she pushed toward the adventurers.

"The minotaur! Where is it?"

At the sound of her voice, everyone stopped.

Tiona, Tione, the adventurers, and the entire expedition.

Time itself seemed to come to a halt before the swordswoman's bloodcurdling gaze.

"Where did you see that adventurer being attacked? Tell me!"

"Th-the ninth floor...but you'll have to hurry..."

She ran.

No sooner had the words reached her ears than she was off, racing at lightning speed down the passageway the adventurers had come from.

"Aiz?!"

"What the hell are you doing?!"

But Tiona and Bete were already far behind her.

Ignoring her comrades, forgetting the expedition entirely, she listened to only the accelerated pounding of her heart.

She was spurred on by emotion, by confusion, by a sense of impending danger.

That thing—it's attacking him!

She didn't have time to check if the information was true or not. All she could do was run, her feet slamming against the earth.

Bisecting any monsters unlucky enough to get in her way, she didn't falter, didn't lose steam. Straying from the standard route, she found herself on the aforementioned ninth floor in the blink of an eye.

The moment the Dungeon's walls changed, an unnatural silence struck her ears.

Total quiet.

As though every monster had hidden itself away and stilled its breath in fear of some maverick beast.

No sooner had the thought crossed her mind than the roar of a crazed bull echoed through the far-off passageway, confirming her fears.

No!!

In the midst of the fading cry came the faint sound of a person's scream. Aiz felt her blood begin to boil.

There was no doubt about it. That was Bell being attacked.

A Level 1 adventurer like him would be helpless against the minotaur. No matter how much he'd trained with Aiz, the levels of their abilities were worlds apart.

She was fighting against the clock now. Every second counted.

Still uncertain as to the boy's exact location, she relied solely on sound as she sprinted through the maze—only to come face-to-face with a prum covered in blood.

"?!"

"P-please...H-help...!"

Blood poured from the gaping wound on her forehead. As she let out her desperate plea, she slumped to the ground at Aiz's feet.

Tears clouding her unfocused chestnut eyes, she placed her hands on the ground and continued with a haggard bellow.

"P-please save him! Save Master Bell!"

"!!"

Grief flooding through her, Aiz knelt down to take the girl into her arms.

"Where is he?"

"On the…standard route…Room E-16…" She lifted a trembling hand to point in the direction behind her, relaying the area number designated by the Guild's map data. And, indeed, droplets of blood speckled the ground, highlighting the path the prum had taken in her search for help.

Aiz took off with a grunt, carrying the girl in her arms.

She raced past room after room, the passageway's phosphorescent glow lighting her path.

"Help…Please…" Continual, incoherent mumbles came from the prum in her arms. Aiz tightened her grip, fingers digging into the girl's side and heart weeping as she followed the trail of blood.

Just when she'd plunged into the final room before her destination—

"—Stop."

There came a single command.

"—"

At that one word, Aiz screeched to a halt.

She was in a large rectangular chamber devoid of monsters or her fellow adventurers. There was only him, standing in the middle of the room.

His mighty, armored frame like a megalith. His height spanning well over two meders.

His four brawny limbs rippling with muscles like steel.

A pair of boar-like ears, evidence of his boaz heritage, underneath his cropped rust-colored hair.

And his eyes, the same color as his hair, directed straight at Aiz.

"…The Warlord."

Aiz's eyes flashed as she took in the sight before her.

As though in response to Aiz's hoarse whisper, the man's eyes narrowed.

The captain of *Freya Familia*—Ottar.

A first-tier adventurer and the mortal enemy of *Loki Familia*.

Why is he here—?

Aiz found herself at a loss, unable to comprehend the situation.

It didn't make any sense. What was he doing here, and why would he be trying to impede her way?

As the weak breaths of the girl in her arms reached her ears, an uncharacteristic level of emotion permeated Aiz's features.

The boaz warrior was simply standing authoritatively in the center of the room.

He was in front of the only road leading to her destination, his giant back blocking the entrance to the passageway. His armor was unbelievably thick, and an enormous knapsack was slung from his left shoulder.

As their gazes intertwined, he took a hold of the bag with his boulder-like fingers and tore it from his back.

Clang, clang, clang! From the torn cloth rained a multitude of weapons, falling to the ground with a ferocious series of clatters.

"I challenge you…Sword Princess."

"?!"

Aiz's bewilderment became all the more apparent.

Ottar, on the other hand, simply reached down to grab a giant sword from the pile and silently pulled it from its sheath.

"Why are you doing this?!"

"Does one need a reason to kill a longstanding enemy when coming face-to-face with her in the Dungeon?"

There wasn't a hint of trepidation in his steely voice.

At a time like this?! Just as Aiz's mind raced to figure out what the boaz could be thinking, a sudden thought flashed through her head—the attack from three days ago and its accompanying warning.

"You'd do well not to do anything rash from now on."

"If you refuse to listen, we'll be forced to take drastic measures."

"Dig too deep and we can't guarantee your life."

"If you get in her way—we'll kill you."

Vana Freya, Bringar, and now the Warlord.

They all belonged to one familia and had given the same warning.

It can't be, it can't be, it can't be.

Their objective was none other than—

"Drop the girl." Ottar's eyes pierced through the prum in Aiz's arms as he readied his greatsword. "Or she'll die."

An intense intimidating aura swelled up around him. There would be no escaping a fight now.

From his stance alone, it was clear he wasn't letting anyone through. Aiz curled her lips in resentment but did as she was told.

Placing the girl on the ground, she pulled Desperate from its scabbard.

She could no longer let her attention be divided. Carrying baggage into a battle would do nothing but ensure her defeat.

The soldier in front of her was stronger than Finn, Gareth, or Riveria—he was truly the strongest adventurer in all of Orario.

The reigning crown. The sole Level 7.

The Warlord—Ottar.

"Come, Sword Princess," he beckoned, his voice backed by the roar of the ferocious bull in the passageway behind him.

Aiz's golden eyes flashed as she sliced the air in front of her with her sword.

"Stand aside!"

The roars of the bull and the screams of the boy ringing in her ears, driving her forward, she charged.

It was the Sword Princess versus the Warlord.

The battle between the two strongest first-tier adventurers in Orario had begun.

She launched herself into it full force, unembellished.

A diagonal cut from the shoulder, so fast it was barely perceptible.

"—Tepid."

"!!"

The boaz deflected her full-powered attack with his large sword as if Desperate were nothing more than a twig.

Her body off-balance from the ricochet, she suppressed her awe, allowing the momentum of her deflected sword to spin her around for another attack.

But once more, it was blocked.

Sparks flew. She gave up on finesse and simply went for speed.

"Aaaaaaaaaaaaaarrrrrggggghhh—!!"

Her sword struck again and again in a merciless string of attacks.

The boy was in danger. Her mask had been discarded—she was the Sword Princess now, and the rousing flurry of sword slashes elicited a mighty yell from the depths of her throat.

Each and every one of her countless strikes was a killing blow as she bared her fangs at Ottar.

She was a Level 6 now, and she had the Status to prove it.

Pouring every ounce of her top-class strength and speed into her strikes, she showered the man in front of her with silver sparks.

"Those moves—ah, yes. You did recently reach a new level, didn't you?"

"—"

But still, she was blocked.

Every single one of her attacks was turned aside.

His defense was impenetrable.

Against the onslaught of inescapable strikes, Ottar still shot her down.

Without even taking a step, he summoned pinpoint accuracy and mountain-like fortitude to render each of her attacks useless with naught but the sword in his right hand.

Desperate let out high-pitched screams as it got knocked about. She had to wonder how the soldier even knew about her level-up considering it had never been officially announced, but she quickly suppressed such thoughts.

With a slash that sliced through the very air itself, Ottar's sword drove her away.

"~~~~~~~~~~~!"

She barely managed to slip Desperate between the other sword and her chest, but it still hurled her backward with the force of a rushing river.

Her feet dug into the ground. When she was finally able to bring herself to a stop, she found herself directly in front of the young prum girl she'd left on the ground. As she let her eyes follow the path she'd taken, her thoughts became a mix of astonishment and terror.

In that single defensive blow, he'd sent her back more than ten meders.

"—Ngh!"

But she didn't allow herself to remain dazed for long. Taking up her sword once more, she began her attack anew.

There was no time to gawk. No time to delay.

Her enemy was blocking that passage of shadows, and she would give everything it took to reach it.

She attacked from the side, from below, trying every angle she could to get through that impenetrable defense.

"Just how strong will you become, Sword Princess?"

"...?!"

His sword met hers, bigger yet somehow faster than her Desperate. She tried moving, feinting, and attacking from every possible direction, but the impregnable fortress remained unscathed.

Aiz couldn't contain a shudder at the contrast between his words and attacks.

His sword skills were terrifying enough as it was, but adding to them the pure power of his physical abilities made them all the more so. It was as though she'd changed places with Bell, no longer the teacher but the student.

He really was a megalith.

He didn't so much as twitch at Aiz's amped-up speed or the hurricane of sword strikes that came with it.

Like a mighty boulder amid the raging wind, he was calm and composed.

He was a wall, and the wall wouldn't budge. Guarding the path behind him, he refused to take even a single step, repelling Aiz's attacks time and time again but never instigating any of his own.

This...This is...!

A Level 7.

No—this is the Warlord.

It had nothing to do with levels, but the brute strength of one well-trained warrior. Aiz bit down on her lip.

"Nngh!"

With a loud noise, she was pushed backward, landing a ways away. Once again, the gap between them had widened.

This happened four times in the span of a single minute.

Her hand was already starting to tingle around the hilt of her sword. Gaze fixated on the expressionless boaz, her eyes flashed.

—*I have to get through.*

—*I need to save him!*

—*I refuse to let him die!*

Without revealing her connection with the boy, she used it as an impetus to kick off from the ground, becoming the wind.

She unleashed the magic she'd sworn to herself never to use against another person.

"*Awaken, Tempest!!*"

She was on fire.

She would do anything to reach the boy.

Wreathed in the blessing of the wind, halfway into her charge she disappeared into the gale.

The time for hesitation was gone. She lunged toward the soldier in front of her, holding nothing back.

"Nngh!!"

The gale strike screamed from her sword.

Ottar's rust-colored eyes narrowed sharply, his hand turning into a blur.

The first strike was blocked.

Her eyes widened at the sight of his sword meeting Desperate, but she didn't stop there.

The current still flowed through her, and her next strike came at him like a literal storm.

They clashed head-on.

"—"

Aiz could barely believe what happened next.

Her enemy followed her every move, her every raging wave, and deflected each and every gale-like strike.

His sword absorbed the shock of her violent tempest. Though his enormous frame trembled slightly at the fury of her raging winds, he refused to retreat or stand down. Even when it seemed he would give in or that she had the upper hand, his incredible maneuvers, gargantuan strength, and even the gauntlet on his left hand all worked in sync to create continuous blocks and attacks.

The extraordinary feat of technique and strategy shut out Aiz's storm in its entirety.

Their levels of experience were simply too different.

Not even her Airiel, the magic that could put their abilities on the same playing field, the blessed winds that had helped her overcome countless battlefields before, could daunt him.

It was a cultivated mind and body that separated them.

Endless training substantiated with physical ability and combat skill.

—*There's no end to this.*

As her flurry of strikes continued, each one punctuated with a tempestuous screech, Aiz found herself in awe of the soldier's features.

There had never before been an opponent she couldn't best once she unleashed the power of her wind—save that monster hybrid Levis, whose mere existence surpassed human knowledge.

But even she was paling in comparison to the boaz before Aiz now.

This wasn't just endless, it was preposterous.

He was practically a god.

This talent, this steadfast exertion, this unwavering determination— he was every bit the modern-day hero.

Ottar the Warlord was, beyond a doubt, the epitome of greatness.

"Hnngh!"

"Guhh—!"

Not missing a beat, the flash of Ottar's sword caught her armor of wind.

With one direct attack, he overcame her current and Desperate, cleaving all the way to Aiz herself.

The staggering force carved Aiz's thin frame into the Dungeon floor. Once more, she was propelled backward, fists clawing at the ground, hurtling over the top of the downed prum girl until finally—she hit the wall.

Stepping away from the edge of the room, she set aside her sword.

The current was with her. Her golden eyes pierced the soldier on the other side of the room, the man himself bewildered by her response.

She would use it. She would finally use it. Her secret weapon.

The voices—?

From deep, deep within that passageway of darkness…

The voices had stopped.

The constant roar of the mad bull, the desperate cries of the boy fighting for his life—all of it.

Aiz's face contorted like a child on the verge of tears. She found the hilt of her sword once more, gripping it tightly.

—Out of my WAY!

Heart screaming, she cast her trump card.

"*—Li'l Rafaga!!*"

The wind flashed.

A divine wind shot forward, making a beeline toward Ottar, so massive that it could never be used outside the Dungeon walls.

The speed at which that leviathan wind sliced through the room made Ottar's eyes widen.

Muscles protruding from his massive shoulders, he gripped his sword in both hands.

The boaz soldier swung his great silver weapon down diagonally at the incoming strike.

"Huuurrrrrraaaaaaaaaaaahh—!"

He roared.

Voice exploding from his throat like the crazed call of a monster, he met the cyclone head-on.

It was the first time the soldier was forced to use both hands, to rely on his full strength.

Aiz's vision became a blur of wind, and she saw Ottar's armor get torn from his frame.

The impact was incredible. As the air current raged and the ground sank beneath his feet, a tremendous explosion rocked the room.

The recoil from the resulting shock wave sent both of them flying.

The two attacks had neutralized each other.

© Kiyotaka Haimura

"…"

Aiz looked up in a daze from where she'd landed on her rear end in the middle of the room.

The control she'd been able to keep over her strength for so long, the promise she'd made to herself never to use it against another person—

—She'd broken it.

She'd used her finishing move.

Her pure, unfiltered strength.

"…"

Ottar silently peeled himself off the passageway wall before returning to his place in front of the entrance.

He'd lost his armor, a section of his battle clothes was ripped, and scrapes littered his cheeks and shoulders, but that was it.

Tossing aside his sword, now heavily damaged, he grabbed a new one from its place poking out of the ground.

The wall towered over them, calm and composed.

The single path behind him was still so far, far away.

"…Ngh!"

She didn't let the shock afflict her for more than a moment.

Grabbing Desperate from where it had stabbed into the floor, she renewed her charge.

Ottar responded in kind, his sword at the ready.

"Let me through!"

Sweat flying, she cut at him ruthlessly with unrelenting strikes of her blade.

Ottar didn't respond. It was only through his continued ripostes that he made his resolve known.

The armor-less, injured soldier versus the unscathed yet single-mindedly slashing girl.

Step after step, their violent dance continued in an attempt to see who would yield first—when suddenly…

"—?!"

Thunk! There was the sound of someone leaping, and Aiz saw a shadow fly over her head, straight toward Ottar.

Down came the double-edge blade with a ferocious, air-splitting slice. The boaz responded in surprise, raising his sword to meet it.

"What in the world is goin' on here?!" Tiona cried out in surprise after landing back on the ground, her attack deflected. She wasted no time setting her sights on her companion's opponent.

Aiz could do nothing but stare in shock at the Amazonian girl who'd caught up with her, flourishing her oversize weapon.

"The Amazon...!"

Aiz took off at once, as the berserker immediately prepared her next attack, and for the first time a crease formed between Ottar's brows. His defense was already shaken by the sheer destructive power of the Amazon's Urga, and he was late in responding to the incoming rain of sword strikes.

His endurance waned. He grabbed for his third sword—a long one, this time—and wielded it in his left hand as he used it to push back the leaping Tiona.

Only...

As soon as she was gone, he was met with another shadow, this one speeding toward him along the ground. Ottar gritted his teeth.

"Boar bastard—!"

It was Bete this time, delivering a full-bodied kick to the man he'd always considered his rival.

Ottar raced to defend himself. No sooner had he blocked the kick than he was met by a pair of whirling Kukri knives.

"Gnngh...!"

"What in the world is going on here?!" demanded Tione in a voice identical to her sister's as she joined the fray.

It was four against one now. A trio of first-tier reinforcements.

It reminded Aiz of her moonlit battle against the black-clad attackers, only now it was time for the city's strongest adventurer to experience the relentless waves of attacks from *Loki Familia*.

From Urga's wild swinging to Frosvirt's incessant thrusts to the quick, intersecting slashes of the Kukri knives.

Even the impenetrable defense of the unshakable Level 7 was liable to start coming apart at the seams.

"Nngh!"

Aiz took advantage of that split-second opening and dashed forward. She dived toward that single gap behind the boaz's mighty frame.

"—Oooaaaarrrggh!!" With lightning-fast reflexes, Ottar steered his longsword toward the side of Aiz's head—

Only to find a pair of fang-like silver boots digging into his steely arm.

"Just try and look away from me, porky!"

"Vanargand...?!"

Bete's kick effectively put a stop to Ottar's attack.

Riding on the assistance of her companions, Aiz charged, disappearing down the passage the boaz had been so adamantly guarding.

—*I'm through!*

Scraping together every last ounce of strength she could muster, she raced down the path.

"...!"

Ottar's features distorted upon witnessing the golden-haired, golden-eyed girl rush past him.

As he staved off the incoming attacks of Tiona and her friends, the natural-born soldier could tell already that even if he were to follow in immediate pursuit, there was no way he could overcome the god-like speed of the Sword Princess before she reached her destination.

"And here I was just thinking that my thumb was awfully itchy. I suppose this is all part of the bargain, as well?" The voice of a boy came from the direction of the standard route leading to the eighth floor, directly opposite the opening Ottar and the others were occupying.

The boaz narrowed his eyes at the blond prum and his long spear.

"Hey, Ottar." Finn posed, almost as though greeting an old friend.

"...Finn?" Ottar silently lowered his weapon.

Around him, the trio of first-tier adventurers remained at the ready. From behind Finn emerged another—a high elf of unparalleled beauty.

Realizing he was more than outnumbered, the boaz conceded, his fighting spirit gone.

Their opponent having lost his malice, Tiona, followed by Bete, took off after Aiz down the passageway.

"Riveria! Help that prum girl!" she called.

"We still have no idea what the hell is even going on!" Bete shouted.

"Y-you two…!"

As Tione's face twitched at her sister's (and comrade's) temerity, Finn and Ottar faced each other. The two familia captains began to speak. Tione couldn't leave the one she cared so much about, and Riveria was already at work tending to the blood-covered prum.

"As Bete so eloquently put it, I'm still a bit foggy as to what's going on here. Would you mind filling me in on why exactly you chose this time and this place to take up arms against us, Ottar?"

"There's no incorrect time and place to challenge an enemy."

"Indeed. Then would it be safe to take this as the will of not only your familia but your god, as well? Is Lady Freya hoping for all-out war between us?" Finn asked with a smile, to which Ottar remained silent.

The sharpened tip of the prum's spear gleamed in the Dungeon's light.

"…I was acting independently," he finally uttered, voice low.

Abandoning his weapons, he began walking forward. Even as Tione's eyes narrowed into tiny points, he proceeded toward Finn and the others undeterred.

He walked right past Finn, Tione, and Riveria, who had finished casting her healing magic on the downed prum and was waiting beside Finn with one eye closed.

"So long as you're going to form your little clique, I've no chance of winning," the boaz said coolly the moment he passed them by.

"Good to know. We're not keen on taking up arms against you, either," Finn replied.

Saying nothing else, Ottar made his exit, taking the same path Finn and the others had.

He proceeded down the narrow, dim passageway, leaving his long-standing foes behind.

"This failure will come back to haunt you," he muttered to himself, still losing blood from the abrasions littering his body and his fist curled as tight as a boulder. The self-condemning words dripped with profound significance.

Eyes pointed straight ahead, he didn't look back.

"We'll just say you were oblivious to your own incompetence."

From behind him came the far-off roar of a crazed bull echoing throughout the Dungeon, accompanied by the shouts of a certain set of adventurers.

"Remove your shell, renounce all others, and confront the adventure. Focus on nothing but the path ahead."

His eyes flashed at these final words.

"Only then can you win her favor."

Light up ahead was leaking its way into the single dim passageway.

"…!"

Aiz hastened at the sight, and she practically flew down the path.

Plunging into the room, her field of vision expanded instantly, eyes first locking on to the minotaur in the middle of the room, and then the boy lying faceup on the ground a good distance away.

Aiz's breath caught in her throat.

The minotaur making its way toward the boy quickly became aware of Aiz's presence. At the same time, Aiz checked the boy for signs of life; relief flooded through her when she confirmed the faint rise and fall of his chest.

A flurry of emotions welled up in her own chest, but she pushed everything away and became the Sword Princess again in an instant, steering her gaze toward the minotaur.

…?!

The aberrant beast, equipped with an adventurer's sword, came to a stop at Aiz's overwhelming intensity, its fur bristling.

She didn't even pause to ascertain the situation. She rushed forward, placing herself in the bull's path with her back to the downed boy.

The remnants of her Airiel created a soft breeze, fluttering the leaves of the flowers growing from the room's floor.

"—"

She felt a presence behind her. A gasp.

The boy had woken up, no doubt. Tossing aside her grief and sorrow, she reinforced her grip on the hilt of her sword and stared daggers at the bull in front of her.

"G-guwoh!" came the clearly terrified noise from the monster, to which Aiz did not respond.

Her silence revealed the anger in her armor-clad chest.

And as that anger built, her current began to dance as well, stirring the grasses of the room with tiny, subtle shudders.

The spirit of her honed blade swirled together with the wind.

"There she is! Aiiiiiiiz!"

"Tch, all that for this boring thing?"

Tiona and Bete, quickly followed by her sister and the others, made their way into the room, footsteps echoing and eyes veering toward the minotaur.

Aiz still had no idea what was going on. What were Ottar and the rest of *Freya Familia* trying to pull? Had they somehow tamed the minotaur? She did know one thing, though—she would take care of this monster and she would do it now. She wasn't about to let the boy be injured further.

Rustle, rustle.

There was a sudden fluttering from the grasses directly behind her.

Throwing a quick glance behind her, she saw the dazed boy, the worn-out Bell, pushing himself up to a sitting position.

"...Are you all right?"

—*Are you all right?*

Just like the first time they'd met.

She'd said the same thing to him when she saved him from the minotaur.

A sigh of relief passed between her lips.

"...You fought well."

—*You fought very well.*

Slightly different this time.

Back then, she'd added a few words of praise and sympathy, the boy having survived his fight against the minotaur.

Kindness filled her heart.

"I'll take care of things now."

—And take that thing out.

Canceling her magic, she instead directed all her power into the sword in her hand.

But the moment her foot touched the ground to rush forward…

Suddenly…

Huh?

A resounding *thump* rang from the ground.

And it wasn't from Aiz.

It wasn't from the minotaur, either. Or from Tiona and the others.

Thud, came the noise from someone.

And they were right behind her.

As they kicked themselves up from the grass.

"?!"

Aiz spun around. At the same time, a hand grasped hers.

Her golden eyes widened in surprise.

He was standing.

The boy had recovered and risen to his feet.

Despite the cuts littering his body, his rubellite eyes were glinting, staring past Aiz and focusing on the minotaur.

She could feel the heat radiating off his hand, currently clasped tightly in her own.

"…No."

Aiz gazed in astonishment as he pulled her back.

Propelled by sheer will, he advanced in front of her.

"I don't need Aiz Wallenstein to save me anymore!" he bellowed from the depths of his lungs.

As though showing off. As though declaring his will. As though hoisting the flag of his unyielding ambition.

At the sight of the boy, obsidian knife readied in his hand, the minotaur's eyes widened—before crinkling in savage mirth.

Coming to some kind of accord with the boy, it turned its large sword in Bell's direction.

Why? How...?!

This was unbelievable.

Aiz had told herself so many things.

That he was just a boy.

That he was kind, innocent, a child.

That he didn't have the makings of an adventurer.

—So how?!

And regardless.

He had risen to his feet.

That same boy.

That same child who would never have what it took to be an adventurer had risen to his feet via pure determination.

"Gngh!!"

Blood pouring from his unarmored limbs and frame quivering, the boy awoke from within.

This was his enemy and his alone, and he unleashed his attack, brutal and pitiless.

No—!

—Wait!

Aiz launched herself forward, the words forming between her lips, when—

She saw another back overlap the boy's. A back she hadn't seen in a long, long time.

"—Stay there, Aiz."

It was her father's, from the last time she'd seen him.

"—"

The back of the man who'd left her with those words, wind sword in his hand, before leaving for battle was overlaid atop the boy's.

The boy and the hero were one.

Eyes opened wide, she found herself unable to move.

It felt like her heart and body weren't connected. Little Aiz was frozen in place.

—*Ah.*

Then she understood.

As she was confronted with that image, as her memories came to life before her, she understood all too well.

He'd broken free of his mismatched mold and become an adventurer.

He'd taken his first step along the path to becoming a hero.

"I challenge you…!"

Thus, the boy…

…Faced the adventure.

The same way her father had thrust himself into that jet-black vortex.

The boy faced that mighty bull of red.

His fight with the minotaur rekindled the image from her past that had been seared into her eyes forever.

Aiz couldn't stop him. She simply stood there, rooted to the spot.

She was unable to move, incapable of even uttering a sound.

Everything seemed so far away, the noises around her all but gone, and nothing but that fight reflected in her vision.

The mighty sword of the raging bull versus the flying dagger of the boy, roars versus screams, melted into every one of their back-and-forth attacks.

Sparks flew, blood spattered, and the high-pitched, metallic clanks of weapon on weapon echoed again and again.

They were evenly matched.

A one-on-one fight to the death.

As the one who had taught him how to fight, Aiz could barely believe her eyes at the deadly battle taking place in front of her.

Wagering everything he had, the boy was determined to take the bull down.

"—Outta the way, Aiz! I've got this!" Bete's voice came like a slap from behind her as its owner rushed forward.

The werewolf unable to condone weaklings was already fully prepared to save Bell.

"Yo! Airhead! What the hell are you just standin' there for...?" he started, before screeching to a halt right beside her.

He was looking at her golden eyes opened wide in consternation.

"...Huh?"

Bete realized it, too.

"Huh? Wait, isn't that...?"

"...Who said he's a Level One?"

Tiona noticed it. Then Tione.

"If my memory serves me correctly..." Even Finn put two and two together. "Isn't that the same kid Bete called a complete beginner only a month ago?"

His incredible growth—the amazing transformation he'd achieved, becoming an adventurer, determination and ambition screaming from his throat.

"*Gwwwwwwooooooooaaaaaaarrrrghh!*"

"Ahhhhhhhhhhhhhhhhh—!"

The mighty roar broke through.

Man and monster clashed, continuing their battle of speed and strength.

Before Aiz even realized it, everyone had gathered around her.

Bete, Tiona, Tione, Finn, and Riveria with the prum girl in her arms.

No one said a word, simply watching the battle take place from as close as possible.

Just like Aiz, her eyes trembling as she found herself transfixed by the scene in front of her.

They were captivated, watching with bated breath.

"Argonaut..." Tiona murmured gently.

It fell from between her lips, almost like a sigh.

It was a story.

A nursery tale about a young man dreaming of becoming a hero, misguided by the malicious intentions of others and his own hapless fate.

A legend about how he was loved by a ghost, brought down a mighty bull, and saved a princess.

It was one of her favorites among the stories her mother had told her.

"I always loved that fairy tale..." Tiona murmured, the words buzzing in Aiz's ears.

She had her arms around her chest, almost as though imagining the story playing out atop the scene in front of her.

That's right.

This was one page of that epic.

Though the level of the fight might have been nothing for the first-tier-adventurer audience, somehow, none of them could pull their eyes away from the spectacle.

They'd forgotten it.

The beloved familia myth, ever watched over by the gods.

"—nngggghh!!"

The battle raged.

Neither side would give in. It was a ferocious back-and-forth. Faster and faster.

Man and beast carved away at each other's lives in a duel to the death.

The boy flung himself at the mad bull with every ounce of strength and spirit he could possibly muster, putting to use everything Aiz had taught him.

It was a desperate, all-out effort lacking prudence or pride. An insatiable hunger for victory.

His technique.

Tactics.

Quick thinking.

Weaponry.

Magic.

It was all for this. Everything pumping into this single fight.

"*Firebolt!*"

And again.

"*FIREBOLT!*"

His body surged, his weapon sailed, and his magic flared.

He let out a ferocious roar—wielding his god-blade as he summoned forth fire and lightning.

"*FIIIIIIIIIIIIIIIIIIIREBOOOOOOOOOOOOOOOOOOOOOOOOOOLT!!*"

There was a mighty blast.

——————————*?!*

As the boy's obsidian knife plunged into the bull's frame, the point-blank explosion assailed it from the inside out.

Flames erupted from within the minotaur's body, and the beast gave off a violent cry of agony before disintegrating into a thousand tiny pieces of flaming debris.

A charred piece of the bull tumbled across the grass, and its magic stone somersaulted through the air before embedding itself in the ground.

The bull warrior was gone, not a trace remaining, leaving only the boy.

"He...He freaking won..." Bete muttered in wonder at the victorious boy's back.

"...There's nothing left...Mind Down."

"He fainted while standing..."

Tione and Tiona mused, just as astonished, at the sight of the motionless boy, still gripping his dagger.

"..."

And Aiz—

Seeing that back, having surpassed its limit.

That figure, having given everything he had.

That face, having overcome the adventure.

—found herself flooded with emotion and scenes from her past.

Bell Cranell.

It was a name Aiz would never forget.

The back that overlapped her father's.

The page in the legend.

The greatness that had been achieved.

Today, an adventurer who'd taken his first breath—had obtained his first qualification for hero-hood.

LAST
CHAPTER

TO
ADVENTURE

Гэта казка іншага сям'і
для прыгод

© Kiyotaka Haimura

It was noisy as they set up camp.

Voices called out orders here and there, and boots hastily clomped about to fulfill those orders. Iron stakes were thrust into the ground and laced with rope as tents popped up one after another.

They'd made it to the Dungeon's fiftieth floor.

Loki Familia was busy setting up their camp at a monster-free safe point—a large-scale respite between the legs of their expedition.

As planned, the two parties had reconvened on the eighteenth floor before making their way to the depths—this fiftieth floor included—together.

The vast forest around them was dyed gray as though covered in the volcanic ash of a recent eruption. Clear, branching streams of green like veins on a leaf flowed among its mighty trees, and high above them, dozens of meders or so, an abundance of great stone pillars like stalactites shone down on them with a soft phosphorescence.

The spot *Loki Familia* had chosen for their base camp was atop a giant boulder looking down on the ashen forest.

From within that dim twilight, as magic-stone lanterns swayed atop tents and stacks of cargo, a commotion far different from the usual hustle and bustle of work was brewing.

"What is up with Bete and the others?"

"That's what I wanna know…"

"They're even more intense than normal…"

Raul, Aki, Leene, and the other second-tier members could be seen with their heads low, furtive whispers passing among them. In their sights were the Amazonian twins, the werewolf, and the others in the collection of first-tiers.

Tiona was pacing back and forth, Urga in her hand as she let out one frustrated moan after another. Tione, too, was silently spinning her Kukri knives around and around and around. And Bete was busy terrifying *Hephaistos Familia*'s High Smiths with his menacing expression.

All of them were on edge, no one saying a word as they simply paced about the perimeter, which, in turn, was making the lower-ranking members restless. Finn and the others, currently issuing orders just outside the headquarters, heaved weary sighs at the young first-tiers.

Even Lefiya, busy hauling cloth for the tents, threw a worried glance at them—and Aiz.

"…"

Aiz paid her no heed, gazing down at the scenery below from her spot atop the boulder a short way from camp.

As her eyes took in the vast forest, her mind was somewhere far different—lost in memories of the event she'd witnessed up on the ninth floor.

—The minotaur was defeated.

The boy Bell had fought the great bull on the ninth floor.

That accomplishment, performed by a lower-level adventurer, left everyone in silence. Nobody moved. Nobody could look away. And Aiz's eyes were glued to his back.

The boy had spent his entire self and had fainted right then and there, yet remained standing.

As he stood, frozen like a statue, his bare back revealed his Status.

Through his tattered linens, through the blood and dirt, the Falna revealed something extraordinary. Aiz's eyes sharpened like swords.

Every single one of his abilities had reached S.

It was a Status that defied every rule in the book.

The lingering vibrations of the shocking truth of hieroglyphs refused to dissipate. He had broken past all limits. As the reality struck home, the pounding of her heart and rush of her blood buzzed in her ears.

Not even realizing it, she took a step toward the boy.

She took one step, then another. The grass folded beneath her feet.

Her breathing stopped. The Dungeon's phosphorescent light washed over her face. The boy's back grew larger and larger in her field of vision.

Finally, she came to a stop.

Next to the boy, the young prum girl had collapsed onto the ground, her strength depleted from loss of blood. But Aiz paid her no mind, her golden eyes focused on the spectacle in front of her.

At the ability and skill slots of his Status, hidden by blood, dirt, and bits of torn undergarments.

She wanted to know.

Her one true wish drove her to learn about the secret to his growth, and she raised her arm.

Ever so slowly, Aiz extended her hand toward the frozen boy's back.

"—Don't. To go any further would be improper."

"!"

Riveria appeared next to her, grabbing her wrist.

Aiz's shoulders gave a start. She'd been so absorbed in those hieroglyphics, she hadn't even noticed the elf draw near.

She turned her head to meet Riveria's jade-colored gaze.

Eyes moving back and forth like a lost child's, she finally hung her head.

"...I'm sorry."

"..."

Relaxing her arm, she let it drop, and Riveria released her wrist.

Tiona, Tione, Bete, and Finn simply watched in silence as the two women hid the boy's secret from view.

Riveria immediately began tending to the boy, and Aiz did whatever she could to help. She covered his bare shoulders with a light tunic, averting her gaze from his cut and bruised features behind his bangs, as if in apology.

Soon, Aiz had him on her back, while Riveria carried the prum girl in her arms.

They went to Finn, asking if they couldn't transport the two wounded to Babel's infirmary.

Upon receiving his permission, they started for the surface, and Finn and the others headed back to the main route to meet up with the others.

Aiz said nothing as they made their way to the infirmary, concentrating on nothing but the weight of the boy on her back.

Once there, they laid the two of them on a pair of infirmary beds before leaving them in the charge of the clerk. Then they instructed the messenger sent from the manor to relay the information about the minotaur's appearance in the upper levels and accompanying details to the Guild.

Just as the messenger was leaving with Riveria's report, a certain young goddess came barreling into the infirmary.

"Where's Bell?!"

Struggling to breathe and completely exhausted, Hestia looked back and forth between the two beds containing Bell and the prum girl.

She must have heard he'd been carried out of the Dungeon, because she was still dressed in her shop uniform. With giant, sloppy tears she clutched the boy's peacefully sleeping face to her chest.

Aiz and Riveria were already at the door, ready to leave, but they turned to the newly arrived goddess and explained the situation.

"…Thank you. Both of you," she said after listening quietly.

Then the two of them left her in peace.

It hadn't taken them long to reconvene with Finn and the others down in the Dungeon, now accompanied by Gareth and the rest of the rearguard troops.

After reorganizing their expedition party on the eighteenth floor, they had departed for the depths.

Witnessing Bell's adventure had lit a fire in the bellies of the first-tiers—Tiona, Tione, Bete—and they'd practically launched themselves on every monster they'd come across. As a result, they'd progressed much faster than anticipated, reaching the fiftieth floor in only around six days. This intensity and complete disregard for the lower-ranking members baffled Raul and the others—they knew nothing about what had happened on the ninth floor.

I...

The ceaseless soliloquy had dominated Aiz's mind since that day.

The boy's gallant figure. His driven heart, burning bright.

That back the same as her father's from her memories.

His Status that defied limitations—and the possibilities it entailed.

Aiz's heart swirled with emotion as the scenes raced through her head.

Once they were finished setting up camp, everyone in *Loki Familia* settled down for dinner.

Making a large circle around the campfire in the middle of the tents, they helped themselves to their meal as they'd done many times already throughout the expedition. The food was lavish—a show of appreciation and a morale boost to the members who'd made it all the way to the fiftieth floor that included such luxuries as mruit and other Dungeon-grown fruits and dried meats, as well as soup from a giant pot.

Even *Hephaistos Familia*'s High Smiths had joined the circle of boisterous eating and drinking.

"Why's everyone been so weird for the past fifty floors?"

As a few guards patrolled the environs, Tsubaki sat herself down with a *thud* in front of Aiz and the others, jerky hanging from her mouth and bowl of soup in her hand.

It turned out that the High Smiths under her command were plenty strong enough and had no need for protection. As they deftly dodged the occasional surprise attack with a variety of martial arts, they always calmly followed *Loki Familia*'s commands, and not even Irregulars could throw them off guard. Tsubaki would sometimes even stray from the group upon catching sight of rare monsters in hopes of snagging their drop items and had no trouble bashing the poor creatures to smithereens with her *tachi*. Eventually she did stop, but only after ignoring so many warnings that Riveria finally gave her a wallop with her staff. At any rate, despite everything, the whole group managed to make it to the fiftieth floor without losing a single person, High Smiths included.

In response to the unabashed question from the half-dwarf in black, Tiona paused between greedy gulps of food to open her mouth.

"We saw this amazing adventurer on our way to the eighteenth floor. Haven't been able to sit still since!"

"That so? Who was it?"

"Uhh…Crell Banell?"

"Ho-ho…I'll make a note of that one."

The weapons master jotted down the "amazing adventurer's" name at Tiona's half-baked response. All the while, Aiz simply sat next to them, silently replenishing her nutrients.

Still deep in thought, she ate nothing but one of the ration blocks Lulune had given her.

"Let's begin our final meeting, then, shall we?" Finn said, and the group, now finished with their meal, started making their final checks.

Everyone in the circle cleaned up their utensils, ears keen.

"As was communicated previously, only a select few will be continuing on past the fifty-first floor. Everyone else, *Hephaistos Familia* included, will remain here to guard the camp."

They wouldn't be able to take anyone below a certain level of ability, not even supporters. The larger the group, the more time and energy it would take to dole out orders. They needed a party that would be light and agile, which was why only the familia elites would be making the trek to the untraversed depths.

The rest of the crew would stay back to protect the base camp, which would serve as a sort of depot for the departing party.

"The party will include Riveria, Gareth…"

They wouldn't set out until tomorrow, once they had gotten plenty of rest.

After Finn finished listing the seven names of those who'd take part—the familia heads and elites, all of them first-tiers—the supporting members were called forth.

"As for support members, those joining include Raul, Narfi, Alicia, Cruz, and Lefiya..."

Lefiya had already known she'd be joining, but somehow, hearing her name made her throat buzz with an inaudible scream.

In a lineup of Level 4 supporters, the Level 3 elven magic user couldn't help the butterflies fluttering in her stomach.

"For those remaining in the camp, should any of those new species of monster spawn nearby, fend them off from afar via magic swords and spells. Do not let them close to the camp. I'm leaving you in charge, Aki."

"Yes, sir!"

They would need to be on the watch for the caterpillar monsters and their acidic venom, Finn continued.

The catgirl, who had been assigned to a position of leadership as opposed to support like Raul, rose to her feet in acknowledgment.

"Tsubaki will also be joining the party to tend to our weapons."

"Leave it to me, boss!" Tsubaki replied with a smile and a nod. Rather than fearing the unknown, the Level 5 smith's heart appeared to ache with excitement at the opportunity to explore the Dungeon's unexplored depths.

Once all the directives had been issued, Tsubaki rose from her cross-legged position on the ground with a burst of energy.

"Well, then! Shall we go ahead and hand things out?" she proclaimed abruptly to Finn and the others, her eyes directed at the baggage of her fellow High Smiths. The group began pulling out cloth-wrapped weapons and handing them to their respective owners.

There were five of them. One for each of the first-tier adventurers, excluding Aiz and Riveria.

"As requested...your Durandals."

Finn, Gareth, Bete, Tiona, and Tione each took hold of a bundle, pulling away the cloth to reveal the weapons underneath.

They were met with the glimmer of finely honed silver.

"I call it the Roland series. Each one of them comes exactly as ordered."

None of the first-tier adventurers could tear their eyes away from their weapons.

Finn with his long spear, Gareth with his mighty ax, Bete with his twin blades, Tiona with her giant sword, and Tione with her halberd.

It was a set of gleaming, indestructible armaments that only a master smith like Tsubaki could ever hope to create. Five beautiful works of art, their blades imbued with hidden power and durability.

As the weapons' owners tried out the feel of the Roland series in their hands, those around them let out sighs of wonder at the beautifully crafted Superiors.

"Thank you, Tsubaki. These are exactly according to specification." Finn shouldered his long spear with a smile.

"Durandal, huh? A lot lighter than I expected!" Gareth exclaimed as he held his giant ax aloft with one hand.

"What, you didn't request something like that other stupid thing you call a weapon?" Bete mused, sheathing his twin blades as his thoughts went to Tiona's oversize (and nonstandard) weapon, Urga.

"Didn't have much of a choice! Got told she wouldn't be able to finish everyone's stuff on time for the expedition if she had to make something like my Urga," Tiona responded with a frown as she swung her large Durandal sword through the air.

"A-a halberd, Miss Tione? Really?" Raul eyed Tione's two-meder-plus weapon as beads of sweat formed along his hairline.

"Well. You know. Figured something like this'd be better against the critters we'll be up against past the fiftieth floor," Tione replied, nonchalantly giving the mighty weapon a test slash. It cut through the air with a crisp *slice*. "It really is light," she murmured, eyes narrowed.

"I used only the best materials! And took care to make each one as powerful as could be. There's a few differences here and there depending on the shape, but I can guarantee at least second-tier attack power outta each one of 'em," Tsubaki said with a satisfied nod, watching them hold her weapons.

While Durandal weapons could maintain their sharpness after countless violent battles, their attack power wasn't as high, which was the reason she'd waited until right before their main mission—their advance to the fifty-first floor and beyond—to pass them out.

While their new weapons were still attracting lingering excitement from the other familia members, Finn finally opened his mouth.

"Very well. We should adjourn to make final preparations for tomorrow. We'll set out during the guard change at four AM."

At the prum's orders, the group began to disperse.

Some of them left for their assigned tents, some went to check on the status of the guards, and still others made their way to the High Smiths for a bit of discourse.

Aiz, too, got to her feet, fully prepared to vacate the premises. Until.

"Sword Princess," Tsubaki called out before walking over to her. Her finger was pointed at Aiz's waist, the uncovered red eye honing in on what dangled there.

"Lemme take a look at that weapon of yers. It could use a bit of ser-vicin'," she said, referring to Desperate, Aiz's weapon of choice for the past fifty floors. While the Dungeon's monsters had done their fair share of work on it, it was the fight with Ottar that had really worn the blade down. A craftsman like Tsubaki could tell with a single glance that it needed repairs.

"...Thank you," Aiz responded with an obedient nod.

With the meeting adjourned, the middle of the camp was empty.

Surrounded by tents, Tsubaki procured her portable furnace and whetstone before taking Desperate from Aiz. She first stripped from her armor—down to nothing but her usual *hakama* and chest wrap—then got to work, ample cleavage and tanned skin bare.

Aiz found a small pedestal and sat herself down in front of the weapons master.

"So that little girl's all grown up and representin' the city, huh?"

Around them, others were starting to do the same. Groups of adventurers came to the High Smith in hopes of sharpening their weapons, watching over her as she did her work.

Among this assemblage of weapon-fussy adventurers, Tsubaki started up a conversation.

"I shoulda called dibs on ya, yeah? What a waste," she said with a laugh, busying herself with the blade. She explained that she'd never been able to get herself a skilled customer like Aiz, even outside her normal contracts. Despite the words of remorse, she didn't seem particularly regretful.

The craftsman who'd made a name for herself long before Aiz had even joined *Loki Familia* seemed to be in a rather nostalgic mood.

"Ten years ago—wait, was it nine? Anyway, back then you were like a naked sword."

"..."

"Fighting, fighting, fighting no matter how much damage your blade took. I remember thinking to myself, *That girl's gonna get herself killed!* Such a little tyke, you were..."

Aiz listened in silence as Tsubaki talked.

"I'm gonna be frank with ya, Sword Princess. Back then, I would never have imagined wantin' to craft a weapon for you," Tsubaki confessed, looking down at the dulled sword in her hand. "Most adventurers of character'd be champin' at the bit for a smith the moment they found somethin' glittery to make it from, but not you, Aiz," she continued as she honed Desperate's blade. "Which is only natural! Haven't you ever wondered why those folks who've never handled more than one sword don't make themselves new ones?"

"I..."

"I'll tell ya why! 'Cause those folks don't think of themselves as weapon users. They themselves are the weapons under construction!" Tsubaki continued before Aiz could finish her hesitant thought. "You know, all the gods found it *very* ironic when they gave you that alias, 'Sword Princess.'"

"..."

"They just wanted to see when you'd finally break," Tsubaki said with a rather malicious grin, glancing up from the sword to the girl.

The girl who, until only a few years ago, had kept fighting and fighting with that worn-down, chipped sword.

All of a sudden, the words Loki had instilled in her rose from the back of Aiz's mind.

"Those who push while runnin' full-out will always trip."

The memory of her goddess's advice playing in her head, she glanced up at the woman in front of her now, her gaze meeting Tsubaki's right eye.

"But you've changed now." Tsubaki laughed softly.

"Huh...?"

"You've mellowed out. People who don't know you might still say you look like a doll, but your face really is softer." Tsubaki's eye narrowed as though she were some sort of all-seeing oracle.

Aiz's expression, on the other hand, clouded at the smith's words.

Even Aiz had come to realize it—the fact that she, herself, was no longer a sword.

Hearing from someone else that she'd "changed" was more evidence than any that the girl she'd once been, who'd fought and fought and fought without looking back in order to achieve her heart's desire, was somewhere in the past.

She couldn't help the anxiety bubbling in her belly. Her attachment to her dream was waning, though she'd once have done anything to achieve it.

Her thoughts drifted back to her fight with Ottar, to the boy's limit break, and, finally, she couldn't take it anymore.

"Do you think I've grown...weak?" she asked Tsubaki.

If she wasn't a naked sword any longer, did that make her nothing but a beast with broken fangs?

"You've gotten stronger, haven't ya? Just look at yer level! Up and up and up." The half-dwarf guffawed.

"That's not what I mean," Aiz responded, her voice unusually hard.

That expressionless exterior referred to as a "doll" by so many was cracking.

I...

—I wonder if I'm paying for my past.

She thought back to her father, how she'd seen him along with the boy's back, and how happy that made her. *Is this enough? Is this truly all you can do?* asked the impatient voice in her head.

As Aiz's gaze turned downward, Tsubaki just smiled, eyes closed as she continued sharpening the girl's sword.

"Well, you're plenty sharp enough now, I'd say. I think it's just that you found your scabbard." Tsubaki continued with a smile as Aiz raised her head. "When you're safe in your sheath, you don't need to stay as sharp as a tack. Then, whenever you cross an enemy to kill, you can flash right out at 'em."

A scabbard. A place to store a blade. A place of rest for a sword like Aiz.

Tsubaki's eyes bored into her as she spoke.

"What it all comes down to is yer friends."

Loud noises clashed against the Dungeon ambience.

Grunts accompanied the *whp, whp* of a large silver blade sweeping through the air. The copper-skinned girl's long pareu fluttering, she practiced her dance of swords beneath the starlike phosphorescence of the Dungeon's domed ceiling.

"Grrr...It's just not right! This isn't Urga!" Tiona grumbled, the large Durandal sword, Roland Blade, in her hand and her head tilted in displeasure.

She was training by herself atop the flat rock overlooking the underground woods along the camp's eastern border, forcing her muscles to adjust to the new weapon she'd be using against the caterpillar monsters.

Each of her lightning-fast test slashes left afterimages hanging in the air.

Blood rushed to her tanned limbs with the effort, tinting them a faint pink, and the muscles of her abdomen tensed as sweat tickled her belly button. Finally, with a breathy sigh, she brought an arm up to wipe at her face.

"Didn't I tell ya to get some rest, Missy?" a dwarf asked, exasperation evident on his face.

"Huh? Oh, Gareth." Tiona glanced over, resting her sword on her shoulder. "But I can't help it! I'm all wound up. Can't sit still."

"...'Cause of that lad you saw, hmm?"

"Yeah!" she responded with a happy nod.

Gareth hadn't been with the vanguard group at the time, but he'd heard about what happened from Finn. He could only sigh at the girl in front of him overflowing with even more energy than usual.

Though Gareth had no idea who this mysterious adventurer could be who Finn and the others kept talking about, he had a couple of choice words he'd like to share with him. Mostly in regard to what he'd done to his companions.

"I mean, it was just *so* amazing! Like a hero straight out of legend!" Tiona continued boisterously, unaware of the dwarf's inner grumblings. "He went up against that big thing even knowing he was no match! And, and guess what? He beat 'im!" Her cheeks red and her face alight, almost as if she'd been the one to perform the feat herself, she laughed skyward.

Beyond the mass of phosphorescent columns lining the domed ceiling.

Toward that floor high, high above them where the boy had proved victorious.

"No matter what happens tomorrow, no matter what enemies we come across, I'm gonna fight—just like that boy!...And I'm gonna protect them. Aiz. Lefiya. Everyone."

Her eyes narrowed as she gazed up at the stardust radiance.

Defeat wasn't an option in her mind. They would return to the surface. Every single one of them.

As Gareth looked at her, he couldn't help but chuckle. "Seems I'm just worryin' for nothin', huh?" he muttered with a wry smile, hand going to the ax on his back.

As he readied the mighty Durandal weapon in his grip, Tiona looked at him curiously.

"Shall we have a go, then, eh? Come!"

"Really?!"

"Only if you promise to cool off afterward and get some sleep."

Gareth chortled lightheartedly, to which Tiona responded with a wide grin.

"Okay!"

With a mighty swing of her sword, she was off, and the practice bout between Amazon and dwarf began in an instant.

It wouldn't be a lullaby that rocked her to sleep that night but the violent clashing of weapon on weapon.

"I will not slow down Aiz and the others...I cannot slow them down..."

Mumble, mumble.

Lefiya was alone in her tent, talking to herself.

She'd been chosen. She would accompany them on their trek to the unknown. The unexplored depths where nothing but danger awaited, and where she'd have to provide protection for Aiz and the others.

Again and again she mumbled the words to herself, like a mantra, her eyes closed in meditation. She would need to be able to put everything she had on the line tomorrow. She needed to be perfect.

"...I cannot fail...I simply cannot fail...Not tomorrow..." Her concentration had already derailed, the curse-like words spilling from her mouth only building the pressure inside her.

Her every muscle had locked itself in place. Her heart felt liable to burst from her chest. Anxiety flooded her entire being.

"A little tense, are we?"

Lefiya let out an "*Eep!*" as two hands came down on her shoulders. She sprang to her feet, whirling around in a flurry of surprise.

"Miss Tione! When...When did you get here?!"

"I've been here a little while now..." Tione responded, somewhat bewildered at Lefiya's reaction.

"W-well, uh...Why are you...here?"

"Mmn, was feeling antsy. Thought I might go swing the iron a bit like that idiot sister of mine, but, well...the captain needs me," she replied, fingers threading through her long black hair.

When Lefiya shot her a puzzled look, Tione peered back at the elf in an equally inquisitive manner.

"So…what were you doing, hmm?"

"Me? I, well…I was…meditating…to ensure I do not fail tomorrow…" she responded somewhat vaguely, head pointed toward the ground. Realizing her abilities might not be equal to those deep floors, her voice grew smaller and smaller, trailing off into nothingness in front of her first-tier companion.

Tione could only sigh at her worked-up subordinate. Drawing close, she took Lefiya's cheeks in her hands.

"Huh…?"

"Lefiya."

"Wh-what is it?"

Lefiya's face reddened at the sudden touch. Tione's fingers curled softly against her skin.

"Remember what Aiz said back on the fifty-first floor? That we'll protect you, so you can just lie back and take things easy."

Lefiya found herself gazing up in wonder at the other girl, the warmth from her hands filling up her cheeks.

Tione's words were like a gentle whisper, an older sister's admonition.

"And what is it that'll save us?"

"…My magic," Lefiya replied, bringing a smile to Tione's lips.

Soon, Lefiya was reaching for her in an embrace considerably more restrained than Tione's, to which Tione responded by running her hands through the girl's hair with a gentle coo. Despite her embarrassment, the tension left Lefiya's shoulders at the Amazon's words, at the warmth radiating from her skin.

The contact between them was like that of close sisters. "Th-that tickles!" Lefiya giggled, leaning backward, before both of them went tumbling to the ground with flustered *eeps*.

Golden hair mixed with black atop the cloth of the tent floor, their gazes turned skyward, and mirth lit up their eyes.

"If you're feeling nervous, I could sleep here with you?"

"I…That is…are you sure?"

"Of course! I can never get any sleep in that tent with Tiona talking the way she does and moving around in her sleep."

Tione brought her forehead to Lefiya's with a little clunk, returning the flush to Lefiya's face and eliciting a smile.

Perhaps, for just a moment, she could forget about tomorrow and the journey into those uncharted depths.

And then she'd fulfill her role in hopes that she'd be able to play and laugh and joke just like this once more.

"If you want, we can sneak into the captain's tent. I'd definitely be able to fight my best tomorrow after a night with him in my arms."

"I am not so sure that's a good idea..."

"Not good...This is not good!"

Frantic muttering came from within one of the camp's large shelters.

It was a group tent for the familia's male members, and one of them, Raul, was currently fretting even more than a certain elven magic user.

He was off in a corner by himself, legs trembling as he sat in a chair. The mix of men and women in the tent, currently taking a break with a card game, threw him occasional looks of concern. Raul was currently the only person in the tent who wasn't part of the defense party that would stay behind to guard the campsite.

Indeed, he was the only one of them who'd accompany Finn and the others into the uncharted depths.

"Take it easy, Raul! Pull yourself together!"

"A-Aki..."

The catgirl had been inspecting her one-handed sword and round buckler when she'd taken notice of Raul's pathetic visage, and the sight prompted her to approach her male companion. Her slender hand gripped his shoulder, drawing his glance upward.

Raul's face was pale, almost ghostly. Aki's brow furrowed.

"This isn't the first time you've gone past the fifty-first floor, yeah? And you came back alive, didn't you? Have a little faith in yourself!"

Raul could only hang his head at the black catgirl's forceful words of encouragement.

"I'm a mess..." came his choked reply.

Anakity Autumn.

She was a Level 4, second-tier adventurer of *Loki Familia*, the same as Raul, and known by her friends as Aki on account of her name being hard to pronounce.

Her shoulder-length black hair matched the alluring black fur of her ears and tail. Her slender elegance was enough that the womanizing goddess Loki had scouted her personally. Highly capable, with the Status to prove it, she'd been tasked by Finn to lead the party that would remain in the camp.

Raul had always thought her a far superior adventurer to himself. Calm, cool, and collected, with guts like iron, and always available for a little advice and encouragement, even now—it was easy to see why she'd been put in charge while the first-tiers were away.

"But...but last time one of those new species almost killed me! What if...What if this time they finish the job? Aki...If I don't come back, would you...send the money I've been saving in my room to my family back home...?"

"Not this again!"

Having been inducted into the familia at around the same ages, Raul and Aki made up what was known as the "second team," which supported and sustained Aiz and the others in the main party. They'd been called upon their fair share of times to accompany the first-tiers on whatever venture they were planning.

Overhearing their conversation, another girl in the tent timidly raised her hand.

"Is...Is it really so dangerous down there? Past the fifty-first floor?"

Leene raised the question, her braided pigtails dangling behind her.

Her inquiry sparked another series of tremors all across Raul's body.

"It doesn't matter how many lives you have, it's never enough," he replied, voice trembling. "Descending into the fifty-second floor is like descending into *hell itself*. Everything you thought you knew about the Dungeon is rendered completely moot."

There was gravitas in his voice that plunged the entire tent into silence.

Every one of the lower-ranking members had shut their mouths. Even Aki had zipped her lips, saying nothing.

It was so quiet, you could hear someone gulping toward the back.

"—Raul, you shouldn't scare them like that. It's your duty as their superior to encourage, not start a panic."

"M-Miss Riveria! I'm…I'm sorry…"

The high elf pushed open the flap of the tent before entering.

Every elf in the tent snapped to attention as the vice-captain's eyes scanned the room. Raul just hung his head apologetically.

"You have nothing to fear, I assure you. Even if one of those new species were to appear, you'll be able to pick them off from afar before they can draw near. Or are you saying you won't be able to handle that?" she asked provokingly, staff in her hand and jade-colored hair swaying. "All you need do is wait patiently for us to return. In fact, you should be excited, I would think. We'll be bringing back souvenirs from the fifty-ninth floor, after all," she added as a playful aside quite removed from her usual demeanor.

The tent was silent for another moment. Then its occupants burst into laughter.

"We'll be looking forward to it, Miss Riveria!"

"Yeah! Bring me back a giant bone, please!"

"You nitwit! How are they gonna carry that back?"

The bustle returned to the tent in an instant. Riveria just smiled at the boisterous group.

It appeared the vice-captain had come specifically to ease the tensions of her fellow colleagues. She'd known the unease would be even greater than normal among the lower-ranking members, what with the Irregulars looming over their heads—the caterpillar monsters they'd encountered on the last expedition especially.

No doubt Finn and Gareth were also making their rounds, offering advice and calming words to the other members and younger first-tiers.

At least that was what Raul presumed, and considering how long he'd known the trio, he was probably correct.

Next to him, Aki nodded, probably thinking the same exact thing.

*And then there's me…*Raul thought. He'd never be able to do something like that.

He had no backbone. No ambition. But even as that unshakable sense of inferiority permeated his very being, as he looked up at Riveria, something changed. He could be like that. He *would* be like that. Like the great leaders of their familia.

Curling his hand into a little fist, he mouthed a silent "I can do it."

Then he rose to his feet with a sudden burst of energy. "We're starting a card tournament to celebrate the eve of the raid! Everyone, place your bets—you might go home with the jackpot!"

Taking advantage of Riveria's encouragement, he took control with a surefire strategy—no one could resist a bit of morale-boosting gambling.

And it worked. All around him came cries of affirmation as his fellow colleagues latched on to the idea.

"Don't get carried away!"

"Nngah!"

The high elf's staff came down sharply on the crown of the misguided youth's head.

"I-I'm sorry!" The pathetic apology was followed by peals of laughter.

"…"

Bete was glaring at the scenery in silence.

He was standing along the western edge of the large, flat boulder that formed the foundation of their campsite. Standing alone, perpendicular to the cliff face, he gazed at the landscape below.

Reflected in those amber eyes was the mighty opening in the Dungeon's western wall.

"If you're here to gimme a pep talk, don't even bother," he suddenly spoke upon sensing the nearing presence behind him; he didn't even turn around.

Finn's small shoulders hunched slightly in the ceiling's dim light.

The young werewolf could already sense the prum's intentions, cutting him off before he could think of offering him a word of advice or encouragement.

"What are you looking at?"

"You can't tell? Where we're headin' tomorrow—the nest of those filthy, disgusting monsters."

Bete continued to stare at the passageway leading to the fifty-first floor, not even glancing his way, so Finn changed his line of questioning.

"Where have you been looking these past six days?"

—Bete's fist clenched with an almost audible choke.

Six days ago. The day of the incident on the ninth floor.

It was the back of that boy, the boy who'd overcome adventure, that was seared into Bete's amber eyes.

Both his fists were clenched. A fierce light bloomed in his gaze, directed at that opening.

"I wanna be on the front line tomorrow, Finn."

What with his quick speed, Bete was usually placed on the midline as a sort of shortstop.

The front line was reserved for Aiz and Tiona. Bete's request meant one of them would have to switch.

"I wanna be able to let loose. I wanna plow through them with everything I've got and not have to hold back and lead the way. And if any of those new species or that creature-lady shows up? Hah! I'll kill 'em. I'll kill 'em all!" He followed up with an almost bestial laugh.

Finn just nodded. "All right."

They stood there, the two of them, gazing off into the eternal blackness of that looming passage.

That great tunnel to the unknown was quiet, like the calm before the storm.

"…"

Aiz glanced about at her companions and fellow familia members, before returning her gaze to Tsubaki in front of her.

"It's not that you've gotten any weaker, per se. You've just got more to protect now. And you don't like bein' protected yerself," Tsubaki continued with a smile, finally putting down her portable furnace and whetstone as she finished up her maintenance work.

Aiz took the proffered sword from the smith.

"..."

She looked down at her hands, then at the newly sharpened blade and its restored luster.

Then, silently, she slid the gleaming silver sword back into its scabbard.

There was a mighty roar.

The death cry of a monster in the darkness reverberated loud enough to split eardrums. Then came the sound of fresh meat being torn and ravaged, followed by cries of pain that were just as quickly cut off.

Cries, then silence. Cries, then silence.

Amid the unsettlingly frequent monsters' screams, all that was left was the countless bluish-purple crystals shedding their soft light in the darkness.

A slender set of fingers reached out to pluck one such crystal from the clumps of ash, and a pair of jaws closed around it with a *crunch*.

"**What are you doing?**" demanded a sudden voice in the darkness.

It had an eerie, disquieting tone, as though multiple voices had been layered on top of one another—at times male, at other times female. The woman it was directed at turned with a flick of her bloodred hair.

"Exactly what it looks like I'm doing: eating," Levis responded coldly, her green eyes turning toward the visitor.

They were occupying an unknown room in the Dungeon, with naught but a single passage offering them entrance. The phosphorescent light emanating from the walls was anemic at best, and everything was masked in boundless shadow.

A sea of ash coated the ground beneath their feet.

Monsters' carcasses. A multitude of them. The remains of unlucky beasts, magic stones stolen from their bodies and their bones turned to mountains of ash, piled on top of one another. They'd been captured, then slaughtered, and their executioner was currently grasping one of the bluish-purple crystals before nonchalantly popping it into her mouth.

Crunch, crunch, crunch. The sound was dreadfully unappetizing as she ground the stone between her teeth.

The monsters' cores had become her meal.

Her visitor—a mysterious hooded figure in a bluish-purple robe and strangely patterned mask—lashed out in irritation at the spectacle.

"The Sword Princess and her friends have already begun their descent. Why have you not done anything?"

"You know as well as anyone that this body consumes *dreadful* amounts of energy," Levis replied languidly to her companion's criticism.

"..."

She turned her back on the visitor, slender limbs and ample chest on display beneath tattered battle clothes that appeared to have been stolen off the corpse of a dead adventurer.

The masked figure gazed in silence at the collection of dragons impaled atop greatswords from their backs to their stomachs, littering the environs like test specimens. They writhed in agony, unable to escape the deeply buried blades.

Levis thrust a hand into the bodies of the monsters still in captivity, ignoring their screams and freeing them of their magic stones as blood gushed from their wounds.

"I was gravely injured thanks to Aria and her friends. I need to rest," she finally added, implying that fighting against Aiz now would only lead to defeat. "I consumed a great deal of energy up on the twenty-fourth floor. These monsters will help me recover my strength." As a human-monster hybrid and an enhanced species, she had the ability to consume other monsters' magic stones.

The callous creature-woman returned to her meal of bluish-purple crystals.

"**Do what you will. But if problems should arise…**"

"They're strong, those brats. They'll make it to the fifty-ninth floor where that awaits, mark my words…even if we have to bring Aria's corpse there ourselves."

The masked figure's tongue hissed in response. "**You intend to defy Enyo?**"

Levis spun around, her eyes narrowed. "Use me all you want, I don't care. But in return, I shall do as I please."

"**You…!**"

"Do let Enyo know, as well, would you? That I may need to act on my own from time to time." She turned her back on the hooded figure and made her way toward the center of the room. "We're done here. Leave me."

Drip, drip. Droplets of blood landed at the hooded figure's feet as though punctuating Levis's words.

The heads of viola flowers writhed atop the ceiling, monsters ensnared in their countless tentacles.

Vines squeezed around one of the pitiful offerings, oozing blood, before dropping it at Levis's feet with a dull *thud*. Then she began to feast, both on the monsters caught in her violas and the dragons impaled atop her weapons.

The masked figure turned away from the ghastly meal, bluish-purple robe trembling in disgust as the screams began anew.

From the midst of the camp and its many tents enshrouded in the dim phosphorescence of the Dungeon's walls, the lid of an elven pocket watch, emblazoned with a leaf and tree, closed with a *snap*.

The eyes of a great many adventurers went to their weapons.

Swords, wands, double-bladed edges, scimitars, silver boots, staves, axes, spears.

As the Trickster flag smiled comically over the headquarters of the camp once more, a certain prum captain opened his mouth.

"We leave...*now!*" The quiet order issued from between his lips, and soon *Loki Familia*'s elite party, led by Finn, was off, leaving the camp.

Accompanied by the shouts of their comrades and High Smiths who would stay to guard the base, they made their way down the flat rock face and toward the great forest of ash.

Their party totaled thirteen—seven fighters, five supporters, and one smith.

Bete and Tiona would form the front line while Aiz, Tione, and Finn would cover the middle.

Behind them in the rear guard were Riveria and Gareth. Despite a few alterations to the lineup, it was still *Loki Familia*'s first-tiers' golden formation. Two supporters had been added to every line, carrying extra weapons and items. Tsubaki, who'd be looking after everyone's weapons, was positioned along the midline with Finn.

The whole lot of them, including supporters loaded down with giant backpacks that contained oversize weapons and shields, made their way to the giant opening in the Dungeon's western wall.

"How come I have to be with Bete, huh?" Tiona grumbled, giant Durandal sword atop her shoulder and supporters nervously silent next to her.

"Ah, shut it, ya stupid Amazon," Bete snapped with his own disgruntled frown, not even looking at her. With Frosvirt on his feet, new twin Durandal blades—Dual Roland—strapped to his waist, and over ten magic daggers filling both leg holsters, he was equipped from head to toe.

"Geez, you guys are sure a lively bunch at all hours, aren't ya!" Tsubaki laughed at the two bickering attackers as she placed her hand on the hilt of her *tachi*.

"I'm afraid it's not our best side..." Finn wryly responded from next to her.

"Lefiya, your breathing is awfully shallow. Loosen up a bit, all right?"

"R-right, Lady Riveria!" Lefiya responded, doing as the high elf next to her in the rear guard instructed.

On the outside, Riveria appeared every bit the calm, composed high elf she normally was, but the glint in her single opened, jade-colored eye seemed to remind Lefiya not to forget her "unshakable tree."

"Sure, you don't need to be actin' like those clowns at the front, but you do still need to be ready as a primed cannon, so to speak. As a magic user, ye've gotta have nerves o' steel. To be ready for action when the time comes. You, too, Raul!" Gareth added with a stroke of his beard from behind the two elves, his loud voice directed toward Raul's slinking back on the midline.

"M-me?!"

They truly never changed, all of them. Among the usual banter of their fellow first-tiers, the long-haired Amazon and the golden-haired, golden-eyed swordswoman occupying the party's midline turned back toward Lefiya. Tione shot her a wink without breaking step, and even Aiz flashed her a small smile.

Lefiya responded instinctively with her own smile and a happy nod, readjusting the cylindrical pack on her back and devoting herself to the party's progress. The magic stone atop her staff emitted a soft pale-blue light.

"That's enough idle chatter. Focus on preparing for the battle ahead," Finn instructed as the group emerged from the ashen forest in front of the large opening.

The passageway connecting the fiftieth and fifty-first floors slanted sharply just inside the gaping hole in the western wall. Staring down what could almost be described as a cliff face, they could already make out the shapes of monsters in the darkness below.

Everyone quietly readied their weapons. Then Finn gave the order, long spear in his hand.

"—Bete. Tiona. You're up."

And they were off.

The ferocious duo of werewolf and Amazon went speeding down the slope.

The rest soon followed, and with that, their attack on the unexplored depths had begun.

In the blink of an eye, Bete's silver boots and Tiona's greatsword took care of the monsters that had spawned just outside the safety point.

"We'll continue down the main route as planned! Don't let any of those new species get close!"

The Dungeon's layout took a turn for the unusual between the fifty-first and fifty-seventh floors—in the so-called deep levels. The flat planes that made up the ceilings and walls were drawn in a deep graphite color, stretching out between rooms in an intricate series of halls and passages.

It wasn't the architecture itself that differed so greatly from the upper levels at the start of their journey, it was the sheer scale of it all. The floors down here were in a league all their own, spreading out in front of the racing party as they heeded Finn's every command.

They couldn't afford to fight unnecessary battles or waste items.

They sped through the Dungeon with nothing but the unknown, the fifty-ninth floor, in their sights.

"They're coming from the passage up ahead."

"Front line, keep moving! Aiz, Tione, they're yours!"

"Roger that!"

Aiz's honed swordswoman's intuition had already anticipated the monsters spawning up ahead as Finn called out.

Just as Aiz had predicted, a fissure formed on both sides of the passage as the front line passed by, bursting open to reveal a swarm of black rhinos. Not wasting a moment, Tione's twin Kukri knives and Aiz's Desperate made quick work of the spawned rhinoceros monsters.

"There's a few strays back here, gents!" Gareth shouted from the back of the group as he dismantled the incoming monsters with his ax.

The Dungeon roared around them. Monsters came at them from all sides in an effort to hinder their progress.

From the side, from intersections, from the ceiling, from the walls.

Encounter after encounter. The menace of the Dungeon's depths.

The rate at which the black rhinos and deformis spiders attacked them from every angle was incomparable to anything they'd had to face on the upper levels.

Again and again they came, but the party of adventurers refused to back down.

"Grrrraaaaaaaaaaaaarrrrgghhhh!!"

Bete flung himself at the monsters blocking his path, his flying kick melding seamlessly into a whirling mass of flashing boots that sent the surrounding monsters sailing. The feral wolf Vanargand mowed them down one after another, paying no heed to the carcasses piling around him.

With relentless speed, he went from one monster to the next, hitting and running, hitting and running. His kicks flailed wildly and carved the way forward for the rest of the party, leaving decimated monsters in his wake.

"M-Mister Bete is even worse than usual..." mumbled his fellow frontline supporter with a shudder as blood sprayed and corpses practically rained down from the sky.

Just as the gulp left his lips, a raging Amazon flew by, her own sword swinging wildly. "Stop acting like you own the place, Bete!!"

"Heh. He's even more impressive in real life!—Oh! Lucky!" Tsubaki watched the scene unfolding along the front line as she deftly took care of an incoming black rhino with her *tachi*, then grabbed the black rhino horn it dropped. The smith tossed it into her backpack with a smile of delight.

There was a flash as she whipped her *tachi* from its scabbard with a speed and artistry that made the draw a technique all on its own.

It was so fast not even Raul, running alongside her, could see the movement of the blade.

"Miss Tsubaki, how are you so strong when you're just a smith...?!" He groaned.

"Come now! A craftsman has to test her work, don't she? Gotta see how many monsters that weapon of yours'll cut through and make sure it'll cut and cut and cut all the way to the innermost depths! Getting stronger just happened along the way."

"That's only mildly terrifying," Raul replied in horror to the natural-born smith's explanation.

Tsubaki, however, had nothing but drop items on her mind and darted in and out among her surrounding supporters at will, only aware enough to the point that she wouldn't impede the group's progress.

"Lefiya, don't cast your spells at random—you'll only draw the attention of those new species. Leave the fighting to Aiz and the others for now. Wait until the new species finally arrive, then unleash your magic!" Riveria advised Lefiya as the two of them ran side by side along the rear guard, surrounded by their fellow party members.

"U-understood!"

Keeping the aspiring magic user under her close supervision, Riveria turned her ever-watchful jade-colored eyes toward their surroundings. The two magic users would act as the party's firepower, but for now they could only have faith in their companions and wait until the time was right.

"Narfi! My Urga!"

"Coming up!"

Tiona tossed her large Durandal sword behind her without even turning around. The Level 4 supporter girl accompanying her on the front line responded by passing her the double-bladed Urga.

Wielding the massive adamantine sword in her hand, she stared down the impenetrable wall of monsters in front of her and then charged.

She screamed past Bete, taking out a good twenty monsters in a single thrust.

"Leeeeeeeeeet's do this!!"

Using her entire body, she used every drop of strength in her bones to perform a massive circular swipe.

She became a spinning top, bisecting every monster in the passage with her mighty double-edge blade.

Cries of agony filled the room as a whirlpool of blood rose up around the Amazon. From the newly cleared path, she could already make out the raucous noise of more monsters on the move.

"—Here they come! The new species!"

The wide hall quickly filled with yellow-green blobs.

Their skin was a ravishing swath of colors, their bodies like wide, flat arms, resembling stingrays. And their fleshy legs, multitudes of them lining their either side, sent them careening forward like battle tanks on the move. On top of all that, within those bodies was corrosive acid capable of melting anything and everything.

They'd finally encountered them. The caterpillar monsters *Loki Familia* had prepared for the most.

"Change formation! Tiona, pull back!" Finn shouted through the din. His orders were immediately carried out.

No sooner had the words left Finn's mouth than Aiz was leaping forward, switching places seamlessly with the retreating Tiona.

"*Awaken, Tempest!*" she called out with a lunge, activating her Airiel and running shoulder to shoulder with Bete.

"Aiz, send some my way!"

"—Winds!"

At Bete's request, she focused the power of her wind into his metal boots.

The werewolf, his Frosvirt now wrapped in Aiz's current, grabbed the twin swords from his waist.

Armed with Durandal blades and protected by the wind, the two of them launched themselves at the massive swarm of caterpillars.

"*Gwwwwwwwwwuuuuuuuoooooooooooooooohhhhh!*"

A thunderous scream shook the walls.

Corrosive acid shot from the caterpillars' mouths, only to be deflected by the armor of wind as Aiz and Bete dashed forward. Durandal weapons sliced the monsters' bodies into countless pieces.

They didn't allow the acid to reach their companions in the back, either. Nothing the caterpillars tried worked—whether shooting everything they had straight at the incoming adventurers or exploding in bursts of sprinkling acid. Bete's lightning-fast legs took out caterpillar after caterpillar as Aiz's equally quick sword strikes split their large bodies in half. Their Durandal weapons held strong, showing no signs of breakage.

Loki Familia would not be brought down by this new species.

Not after all the measures they'd taken. Not with their coordination and teamwork. They mowed through the caterpillar monsters with their tremendously effective armor of wind, delivering wave after wave of killing blows.

They brought the enemy's attack to a screeching halt.

"Fading light, freezing land. Blow with the power of the third harsh winter—my name is Alf."

"Everyone, evacuate!"

From behind the combatants, Riveria finished her Concurrent Casting in the blink of an eye.

At Finn's cry, the front and midlines scattered, forming what could only be described as a living gun muzzle.

And forming the body of the gun was a jade-colored magic circle.

From the silvery white staff there—from the first-tier magic user's weapon Magna Alf—surged a brilliant flash of snow.

"Wynn Fimbulvetr!!"

Three snowy tendrils shrieked through the passageway.

Every monster caught in the bluish-white blast froze instantly. Aiz and Bete watched the long, straight passageway in front of them transform into a glacial world of blue from their places of refuge within one of the side tunnels.

The frozen caterpillars and other monsters caught in the blast became a gallery of ice sculptures.

"Damn, that was intense! If only we could produce that kind of magic from a magic sword, yeah?" Tsubaki remarked as she gazed out over the ice-hardened Dungeon floor. She rubbed her arms with a shiver. "Wow, it's cold."

"The day that happens is the day I lose my job," replied Riveria with a little smirk.

Once Aiz and Bete had rejoined the others, the whole party took off down the pass, shattering the petrified monster statues just in case as they ran.

No new monsters could spawn from the ice- and frost-covered walls, either, so the group made their way along the main route quickly, continuing down the stairs to the lower levels.

"There'll be no replenishing from here on out," Finn said as he turned back toward the rest of the party making their way down the wide, long staircase leading to the fifty-second floor, implying that if any of them had any items to use, they needed to do so now. As none of the adventurers had taken any damage, however, none of them moved.

They stood there quietly, offering him nothing but shared looks of tension.

Tsubaki, on the other hand, the only one not of *Loki Familia*, glanced dubiously at her anxious companions.

"Let's go."

With the short command from Finn, they continued down the stairs.

The Dungeon walls of the fifty-second floor boasted the same graphite color as the walls of the floor above, and the party sped past them at an even faster pace.

"Avoid combat wherever possible! Simply repelling the monsters is fine!" Finn never stopped giving instructions.

The relentless encounter rate from the floor above had yet to change, but they continued their dash all the same.

"Ooh, lookit that drop item!"

Tsubaki brought down a monster with her *tachi* in mid-run, her eyes sparkling at the tantalizing prize that fell from its carcass. Raul, however, would have none of it.

"No stopping!" he called out and grabbed her wrist as she attempted to break from formation.

"Nnguh!" the smith grunted as the item on the floor stayed right where it dropped. "But whyyyyy?! S'not like I've ever been down this deep before. What's the worst that could happen?"

"We're going to be *sniped*," Raul replied, cold sweat working its way down the sides of his face.

"Sniped?" Tsubaki threw a wandering eye at the changing Dungeon landscape around them as they continued their dash.

Glowing phosphorescence. Countless tunnels. Plenty of monsters attempting to get close to them. But at least with her quick glance she couldn't make out any suspicious characters waiting to pick them off.

Just as she was about to question what Raul could possibly mean, she noticed it.

It wasn't just Raul. All the supporters looked scared to death as they struggled to keep up with the first-tiers.

Their faces were pale, and almost tangible panic was building just beneath their skin.

"Keep up the pace!" Gareth shouted from the very back, urging them on.

No one said a word. They didn't even breathe. The only sounds were their thundering footsteps constantly plowing forward and the roars of monsters they warded off one after another. A very strange, very disconcerting unease had settled over the party.

It was then, just as Tsubaki was finally picking up on the sense of malaise, that she heard it.

An ominous scream reverberating up through the ground.

"...A dragon's howl?"

The ear-splitting roar of the king of monsters.

Though Tsubaki could sense the mighty beast's presence, it was true that there were no signs of it in their immediate vicinity.

"Finn," Riveria called from the back of the group, to which Finn responded with a nod.

"Right—we've been *spotted*." The prum's eyes narrowed to an infinitesimal degree. "Run! RUN!!"

The shout propelled them forward, further accelerating their pace.

As the front line heedlessly warded off monster after monster, Tsubaki's eyes scanned the vicinity. "Where's it comin' from...?" The ceaseless cries of the mighty beast were throwing everything into chaos. Riveria's heavy breathing behind her sounded practically in her ear.

But the source of the roars wasn't around them. No, it was coming—

"—*From below?*" Aiz's mutter from the front of the midline completed her thought. "It's coming." The Sword Princess's eyes turned as sharp as swords.

"Bete! Change course!" Finn urgently commanded, and the were-wolf at the front led Tiona and the rest of the following party away from the main route and into one of the tunnels.

It was then that it happened.

"_____"

The ground exploded.

"~~~~~~~~~~~~~~~~~!"

Flames erupted from the earth, followed by a crimson shock wave.

The backs of the front line, the faces of the midline, and the weapons of the rear guard—everything was bathed in a fiery red hue.

Tsubaki's right eye widened as far as it would go, her face and eye patch wreathed in a fierce conflagration.

It was as though an enormous land mine had just detonated beneath their feet. Flames enveloped the Dungeon floor, swallowing the monsters in front of them and extinguishing them without a trace.

The pyre wound all the way to the ceiling and then burst through the rock of the fifty-first floor above their heads.

With the massive explosion right in front of them and the waves of heat pushing them back, the supporters had to stifle the screams of terror building in their throats.

"Make a detour! To the western route!!" Finn's commands pierced through the din, directing the party farther away from the main route and down another wide passageway—only to be met with another sudden explosion that shook the Dungeon's walls.

"Riveria, hurry! We need a protection spell! If we draw more of those caterpillars, so be it!"

Forgoing a verbal affirmation, Riveria began casting her spell. *"Tree spirits, hear my prayer. Gown of the forest!"*

"How many of them are there?"

"Six? No, seven at least!" Tione shouted back as her eyes focused on the ground below.

The vibrations practically knocked them off their feet as the relentless waves of heat came at them from all sides.

© Kiyotaka Haimura

Again and again the explosions continued, blazing-hot winds and flaming fragments driving them back as Finn gave command after command in rapid succession.

Finally, the dragon's roars became all too distinct. The next series of explosions shook not only their current floor but no doubt every surrounding floor, as well.

The floor opened up; large sheets of rock crashed down to the floors below. A *massive crimson fireball* lit up the adventurers' vision, bursting through the ground to perforate the ceiling overhead.

"So that's what y'all were talkin' about…!!" Tsubaki exclaimed, a smile overtaking her face as though she finally understood.

Lefiya, on the other hand, currently running for her life a short distance away, was so pale it seemed as though the color had been drained from her face.

This… This is…

She'd heard about it. She'd even prepared herself for it.

But seeing it right in front of her, right here, right now, she couldn't stop shaking.

Her heart felt like it was going to beat out of her chest as the rest of the rearguard party scrambled about her in mass confusion. Even first-tier adventurers could do nothing but run for their lives from the roar of this abominable beast. As the raging tide of blazing heat continued and continued, she felt a scream of panic build up inside her throat—until her blue eyes saw it.

"Raul, get outta the way!" Gareth called out from the back, already having noticed it as well.

"Huh?!" Raul cried out, but it was too late. As the bundle of thick thread shot out from one of the tunnels in the side wall, he didn't have time to react.

Lefiya quickly extended a hand as the spectacle unfolded in front of her.

"Mister Raul!"

Right behind him, she shoved him out of the way, backpack and all.

He stumbled forward and the incoming thread wrapped around Lefiya's arm instead.

It had her. With an almost audible yank, she was snatched away from the group.

"Lefiya!" Tione screamed as the massive thread of the deformis spider dragged her toward its hole.

Lefiya's face distorted in panic as the giant spider monster reeled her in, its jaws open wide—only to burst into flames.

One of the many explosions causing the floor to swell had erupted beneath it, disintegrating the spider in the blast.

"_____"

Lefiya was left suspended in the air.

Then she plunged toward the gaping hole in the floor below as waves of smoldering heat assaulted her body. After a moment of weightlessness, she fell headfirst, as if the thread from the blazing spider was pulling her into the mouth of that endless abyss.

It was then that she saw it.

Deep. It was so deep. Too deep.

The hole created by that giant fireball had *punched through floor after floor after floor*, creating one long vertical descent into oblivion.

And as she fell, she saw the bottom—from which red dragons gazed up at her, smoke hissing from between their countless fangs.

Her azure eyes trembled. Her body began to shake. A very real, guttural terror overtook her entire sense of being.

It was true. All of it.

The volley of explosions assaulting the party again and again and again—were coming from far below them.

They were being targeted by enemies some hundreds of meders beneath their feet.

They...really...

The ominous roars had been a harbinger of the dragon artillery to come.

The enormous flares, capable of blasting through countless layers of thick rock, had been picking off the expedition.

Monsters even more powerful than those inhabiting their current depth were attacking them.

Monsters that ignored the ability levels required to reach each floor.

That ignored the very floors themselves.

Urrghh...

As the dragons eyed her from far, far below, the voice of her companion floated through her mind.

—*"Everything you thought you knew about the Dungeon is rendered completely moot."*

—*"Descending into the fifty-second floor is like descending into hell itself."*

Lefiya finally understood what Riveria and Raul had been talking about.

Compared to the Irregulars of the upper levels, this one was in a class all its own. An unbelievable phenomenon.

It was of a different scope.

A different scale.

An entirely different level of peril.

Was this even the Dungeon anymore?

It wasn't possible!

This was beyond ridiculous—it was insane!

They'd truly descended into hell!!

"*Guuuuwwwwwwwwwwaaaaaaaaaaaaaaaaaarrrrrrrrrrrrrrggg ggghhhhhh!!*"

Lefiya's face morphed into an expression of pure despair as the mighty dragon roars shook the air around her.

In the midst of the nightmarish scene, her body hurtled down toward those monstrous dragons.

The impossibly long, impossibly wide tunnel created by the countless flares trembled.

—In the past, it had been *Zeus Familia* that had ruled over Orario from on high.

It was they who held the record for farthest floor reached. It was they who'd nicknamed this area of the Dungeon "The Dragon's Urn."

It was so named because of the valgang dragons inhabiting the fifty-eighth floor, the bottom of the "urn."

They were monstrous red dragons boasting heights of some ten meders when standing on their hind legs.

She fell toward those dragons now. They awaited her as she sliced through the air, her bangs whipping back and forth as she plunged in a free fall down that massive hole.

Other monsters caught in the blast fell, too, tumbling around her as she froze in fear.

I've seen this before. In a dream…

A terrifying dream where she'd fallen from a great height.

Only now, in reality, there was something even more horrifying awaiting her than the hard surface of the ground.

She couldn't move. Not even a single finger. She was overcome with a primeval fear as one of the valgang dragons below opened its massive jaws.

Its maw was like a gun barrel, only it wasn't bullets loaded in its magazine but a blazing red ball of flame that dyed the dragon's mouth a brilliant crimson as it aimed directly overhead.

It was going to destroy them all in one giant flare—every one of the falling monsters, and Lefiya with them.

""LEFIYA!!""

"?!"

In that instant.

She heard her name breaking into the impossibly long stretch of frozen seconds.

Looking up, she saw them practically throw themselves over the side of the hole.

"You're not slowin' us down, you big, ignorant blockhead!"

Tiona, Tione, Bete.

They launched themselves off the side of the tunnel walls, speeding down toward her.

The sight of the first-tiers racing to save her made her eyes fill up with tears, warping her vision.

"Veil Breath!!" The translucent, ringing name of Riveria's spell came from the fifty-second floor less than a second later.

The four of them, Lefiya and her three rescuers, were quickly surrounded in warm green gowns of light—Riveria's protection spell that would safeguard them against all incoming attacks.

Armed with the blessings of Orario's strongest magic user, Tiona, Tione, and Bete raced down the wall to make it to Lefiya's side.

"_____—Aaaaahhh!!"

In that same instant, however, the mighty red dragon released its flame.

The massive fireball, boasting a diameter of over five meders, launched from the dragon's mouth and bathed Lefiya and the others in a fierce vermilion hue. Tiona leaped from the wall, giant silver sword at the ready.

"Ya bastaaaaaaard!!"

In a swipe that utilized her entire body, she gripped her Durandal sword in both hands and aimed it at the incoming fireball.

The explosion that followed was astronomical.

The two forces had offset each other.

In a crushing blast, the inferno came to a screeching halt in front of Lefiya's eyes.

"Miss Tiona—?!" Lefiya began to scream, but before she could even finish, the Amazon appeared from within the brilliant flash.

"Yeeoouch!" was her only reaction; otherwise she was completely unharmed and wreathed in embers. Lefiya's eyes widened in surprise. The logic-shattering berserker was as lively as ever even as steam rose from her skin.

With Riveria's Veil Breath canceling the majority of the fireball's damage, she'd pulled through without a single scratch. Her Durandal weapon, too, was unharmed. The silver glint of its surface was no less brilliant than before.

"Tione! Bete! There's a wyvern coming!" Tiona cried out, sensing movement from not only the valgang dragons down on the fifty-eighth floor but on the fifty-sixth floor, too.

Dragons began flying out of the tunnels lining the hole like ants crawling out of their nest, mighty wings flapping.

These ill wyverns, bluish-purple dragons boasting heights of some three meders with their tails included, only further emphasized the

Dragon Urn's name. As the great red dragons on the fifty-eighth floor bombarded the adventurers with fireballs, these flying creatures took advantage of the resulting tunnels to launch their own direct attack.

Dragons poured out from the fifty-sixth and fifty-seventh floors one after another, and Tiona and Bete took off running.

"Tione, protect that numbskull!"

With a speed that seemed to ignore the fact that he was falling, Bete kicked off from one of the large stone sheets and shot upward like an arrow to bring his twin blades down on one of the wyverns.

He drove both swords into the monster's eye sockets and then kicked off its body as it let out a scream of agony. He sprang from one dragon to the next with jarring blows that sent them spinning into their nearby brethren.

He used the momentum from his jump to land on the wall, dodging the wyverns' rapid salvo of fireballs before leaping back for another attack.

Tiona, equally undaunted, launched her own attack and sliced an incoming wyvern's wings from its body.

The falling wyvern bodies acted as a shield that protected them from the second wave of explosive fireballs from the valgang dragons down below.

"W-wuaah…?!"

Tremendous explosions. Plummeting monsters. The painfully loud cries of howling dragons.

The out-of-this-world spectacle taking place before her made Lefiya shake so hard she couldn't stop.

"Breathe, girl!" screamed Tione, currently falling alongside her.

"!"

"Don't be afraid! We'll protect you!"

The halberd-wielding Amazon and her intense look caused a flutter in Lefiya's chest.

She thought back to the night before and the time they'd shared in her tent. Now surrounded by Riveria's green armor of protection and touched by the indomitable mettle of the first-tiers refusing to allow this predicament to play out, she let out a grunt to banish the fear from her body.

Nodding in Tione's direction, she tightened her grip on her staff.

She stared down into that infernal abyss at the monstrous red dragons lying in wait, her hair whipping wildly in the wind.

"Aiz, don't!!"

—Meanwhile, back on the fifty-second floor…

Finn commanded Aiz to hold back as she prepared to follow Tione and the others into the great hole.

"If Raul and the others fall in there, we'll never be able to protect them all! You'll stay with us as we continue along the main route to the fifty-eighth floor!"

"…!"

Her lips curved into a tormented frown, her feet still poised on the edge of the hole, but she did as she was told.

Even if Lefiya and the others did land somewhere midway down the tunnel, there was no guarantee they'd be able to find them in the complex labyrinth of the Dungeon. If they could all just make it to the fifty-eighth floor, which comprised nothing but a single grand hall, they'd be able to reconvene without troubling themselves. Tiona and the others knew this, too. Or, at least, they should.

In addition, the tremendous strength Aiz could employ against the caterpillar monsters would greatly hasten the party's descent. It was essential that she remain with the main party if they had hopes of making it to the fifty-eighth floor quickly.

"Gareth! I'm leaving Bete and the others to you!"

"Roger that!"

Already armed with his standard battle-ax and grabbing his Durandal ax from one of the supporters, Gareth took off after Lefiya and the others in Aiz's stead.

Finn quickly set forth reorganizing the rest of the party, not even waiting for Gareth to leap into the hole before ushering them onward.

"It…It's all my fault…" Raul fretted, unable to shake off his own failure and the horrifying turn of events it had caused.

"No need to fret. Save that for when you receive your punishment later. For now, though, focus, yes?"

The thought of Riveria's punishment sucked the color right out of Raul's face, leaving him no room for self-reproach. Even the remaining three supporters could do nothing but send him looks of pity.

With Aiz now in the front line, the party sped its way through the passageways of the fifty-second floor.

"Ha-ha-ha! Looks like I'm stuck in a crazy place again!" Tsubaki hacked away at an incoming monster with her *tachi*, ever-present smile plastered on her face.

One party had become two.

The two parties followed two separate routes, racing their ways to the fifty-eighth floor.

Tiona continued her assault on the wyverns amid the barrage of valgang dragon fire from down below.

The walls, the floors, the very neck of the Dragon's Urn itself grew increasingly more damaged with each of the mighty fireballs, and the actors in the airborne skirmish—both the adventurers and their twenty monster enemies—were dyed a deep red as the flurry of attacks continued.

"Gah! One of those beasties is fast! Nngh!"

"Shit, it's not one of those enhanced species, is it?"

Jumping from wall to wall, Tiona and the others waged a splendid fight worthy of their Statuses, but even they had their limits. They couldn't fly, after all.

The wyverns, boasting a pair of wings as forelimbs, were incredibly fast, but there was one that was especially swift, even among its own kind, and it was currently waging war on Tiona and Bete. As they attempted to block the claws and teeth that accompanied each of its lunges, the wyvern would simply switch to its tail, knocking their weapons out of the way and barraging them with bullets of fire. As the protective Veil Breath surrounding them visibly withered, they found themselves hacking away at the air more often than not as cuts started to litter their bodies.

An enhanced species was a creature that had attacked a great many other monsters and stolen their magic stones, and this king of the skies—fiercer, more powerful than its fellow wyvern brethren—had its flightless adventurer prey in its bloodshot eyes, intent on ripping them to pieces.

The rest of the bluish-purple-scaled dragons doubled back for another counterattack.

"Tione! Toss me!" Lefiya called out, noticing the dragons congregating around Bete and Tiona below her.

"!"

Tione responded by grabbing her hand and flinging the newly fearless girl in the direction of the wall.

Generously bending her knees, Lefiya mimicked what she'd seen from the first-tiers and somehow managed a successful landing before running down along the wall's surface.

"Unleashed pillar of light, limbs of the holy tree. You are the master archer," she began, weaving her spell as she fought against the pummeling pressure of the wind. Her eyebrows bristled.

She couldn't only be protected. She didn't want that.

She had to save them. Her magic had to save them!

Calling upon the unshakable tree inside her, she chanted concurrently as her feet pounded against the wall.

"Loose your arrows, fairy archers. Pierce, arrow of accuracy."

The wyverns noticed her chant and aimed their stones of flame in her direction. She kicked off from the wall, narrowly avoiding the rain of fire while doing everything possible to keep from releasing her net of magic.

She raced, voice ringing loud and sonorous as she thought back to her training with Aiz and Filvis.

Tiona and Tione were flabbergasted at the sight of the magic user moving and dodging, never breaking her chant. Even Bete was in shock, his lips curling upward in a laugh.

She could do it!

She could do it!

She wasn't afraid!!

Her heart trembling, she pointed her staff, and a magic circle lit up with a glimmer.

"Arcs Ray!!"

The maximum-power arrow of light blasted out in a brilliant flash.

The enormous, needlelike flash of magic careened straight down toward the flock of dragons.

But she had only one target in sight.

The bloodshot eyes of the enhanced wyvern widened as the light arrow veered toward it.

Beating its massive wings, it attempted to escape the incoming bolt.

"—TUUUUUUUUURN!!" the magic user roared, causing the arrow's trajectory to warp.

What was once a straight path became curved, the auto-follow properties of the projectile spell sending it chasing after the dumbfounded dragon.

It evolved into a sort of dogfight, a high-speed midair skirmish. The arrow of light nibbled and gnawed at the great wyvern king, taking out the wings of any other dragons that got caught in its path.

Finally, it connected.

"Guuuuuwwwwwwooooooooaaaaaagh!"

With a dazzling glare and an agonizing scream, the wyvern king turned to ash, its magic stone destroyed.

Ash rained down the neck of the Dragon's Urn to the base below. Tiona gave Lefiya a fist pump of victory, and Bete threw her a momentary smile before the two of them returned to their attack on the remaining wyverns.

Her body instilled with a fiery passion, Lefiya moved immediately to her next chant herself.

"Don't think we're gonna let you outshine us!" Tione licked her lips with a smile at the young magic user. She ran along the wall as she once more let loose with her throwing knives. One of her blades impaled the eye of a wyvern, sending it careening to the ground with a scream of anguish as she flourished the halberd in her other hand.

She'd already been having a hard time smothering the fire in her belly at witnessing that boy's adventure up on the ninth floor. This new predicament was only throwing kindling on the fire, and she liked it.

"_____—*Guuwoohh!!*"

One of the wyverns blew flames in her direction as she propelled herself from the wall and tumbled through the air before zipping toward the beast like a speeding bullet. Halberd whirling wildly, she deflected every flaming hailstone in the incoming storm.

"This is pretty convenient!" she said with a smile. The Durandal weapon dispersed the approaching fireballs before she continued with a downward strike.

The stupefied wyvern's skull exploded upon impact, spraying spinal fluid everywhere. Tione used its carcass as a stepping-stone to propel herself farther, using the long reach of her halberd to take out all the nearby enemies with a single strike.

"Though lacking a little on the power side of things," she added as the blade of the halberd got stuck in the body of a wyvern halfway through its swing, eliciting a distressed moan from the unfortunate beast.

Using the pole arm to pull the wyvern toward her, she snatched a Kukri knife from her side with her other hand before driving it into the beast's long neck, relieving it of its head.

"*WUUUUAAAAAAAAARRRRRRRRGGGHHHHH!!*"

"I thought you were dealing with those fireballs, Tiona!" she yelled in exasperation as a valgang dragon on the fifty-eighth floor roared, sending up another flare.

"There's only one of me, y'know?" Tiona shot back, her body singed as she went from one fireball to the next, offsetting each one.

Tione simply stuck out her tongue as she gave another swipe of her halberd.

Tione Hyrute—the Jormungand.

A first-tier adventurer who was feared by even the gods themselves and who got stronger the angrier she became.

Ignoring the look of disbelief from Lefiya, she charged the incoming fireball head-on.

"You're really starting to get on my nerrrrrrrrrrves!!" she screamed. The incensed Amazon smashed the red-hot ball of flame to pieces with her Durandal weapon.

"—I'm gonna kick yer heads in, ya big red bastards!" Bete continued his own attack against the wyverns as the explosion lit up the sky over his head. His eyes were focused on the very bottom of the long vertical tunnel.

He could make out four valgang dragons some two hundred meders below him on the fifty-eighth floor.

Returning his twin swords to his sides, he prepared for his arrival at the base of the Dragon's Urn.

"Hey! Do somethin' about those fireballs, would ya? Even just one of 'em!" he shouted at Tiona, who was currently falling alongside him.

"You ask as if it doesn't hurt like hell when those things hit you!" she screamed back in annoyance, sword flying. Already having taken out a good number of the massive flares, her body and armor both were looking considerably charred. Her tanned skin was practically cooked in some places, smoke rising in tiny wisps from her countless burns.

"Aw, shut up an' just do it!" Bete barked indifferently. "Here we go!"

"You'll pay for thiiiiiiiiis!"

Two pairs of eyes met four as they set the dragons in their sights. Bete pulled one of his magic daggers from his leg holster.

The amber blade atop a golden hilt crackled with an electrical spark as he attached it to his right Frosvirt. The topaz embedded in his long boot absorbed the electrical shock, and the magic dagger crumbled in his hand.

Almost instantaneously, a sheath of lightning crackled to life around the silvery white boot.

"WUUUUAAAAAAAARRRRRRRRGGGHHHHH!!"

Four fireballs came at him at once.

The four valgang dragons, their necks craned straight upward, shot off simultaneous blasts of pure flame.

The gaps between them were infinitesimal. Kicking off one of the stone sheets, Bete dodged the first one, and as the second one threatened to swallow him whole, Tiona smashed it away with an upward swing of her sword.

"Aaaalley-oop!!"

The explosion was massive. Using the Amazon's assistance, Bete landed back on the wall.

Then he bolted forward in a burst of speed.

He aimed for those tiny, tiny gaps, gauntlets singeing as he broke through the incoming wall of fire. The surge of electricity crackling from his Superiors seared the startled eyes of the valgang dragons.

But he didn't stop.

Drawing a path of light behind him, he sped along the wall and came at the dragons like a supercharged bolt of lightning.

He covered the distance in an instant—the whole of that great, gaping hole that spanned the entire way to the fifty-eighth floor, the Dragon's Urn.

With an enormous spurt of energy, he launched himself.

Setting his sights on one of the mighty red dragons directly below him, he practically morphed into a flash of lightning and drove his Frosvirt into the beast's body.

"Die."

It exploded.

The heel of his Frosvirt dug into the valgang dragon's face as the resulting flash lit the tunnel on fire.

It was massive. The attack power of the magic dagger together with his Frosvirt combined to form an electric kick that instantly disintegrated the dragon's head. Its body fell with a slow slump.

Like a crumbling tower, the dragon's monstrous ten-meder frame sank toward the ground and caused the walls, the floor, and the ceiling to shake with a thunderous roar.

Bete landed just off to the side, his gaze turning upward as the other dragons howled in confusion.

"I'm back, you bastards…"

The fifty-eighth floor. The deep levels.

Similar to the forty-ninth floor—the Moitra wastelands—it was one big, wide-open space. No labyrinthine tunnel. No maze. Nothing to block their view. The graphite-colored walls and ceilings came together to form one massive rectangular room.

This fifty-eighth floor was the deepest floor *Loki Familia* had ever reached.

The last time they'd been down here, they'd been completely depleted of stamina and items (equipment included), and had had to abort their raid.

Faced now with the overwhelming sight of the valgang dragons looming high overhead, coupled with the other innumerable monsters littering the fifty-eighth floor, the lone werewolf simply let out a sadistic laugh.

"Aaaaaaand…second!" Tiona landed next to him on the ground of the fifty-eighth floor.

The eyes of every monster on the floor turned simultaneously toward the two adventurers—valgang dragons included.

In less than an instant, a new shadow appeared overhead.

"Fall like rain, burn the savages to ash."

"Run!!"

From above their heads came the majestic call of a chant, followed by a sudden shout of warning.

Bete and Tiona looked up just in time to see Tione and Lefiya appear through the hole in the ceiling, the former fending off an attack from a wyvern while the latter pointed her staff toward the floor.

Bete and Tiona cleared the area immediately, ignoring incoming attacks from the surrounding monsters as the midair spell reached its culmination.

And then.

"Fusillade Fallarica!!"

A torrential deluge of fire arrows rained down on the fifty-eighth floor.

Agonized screams swelled amid the storm of magic. While the red scales of the valgang dragons seemed to simply absorb the legion of fire arrows, the other monsters weren't so lucky. Pint-size, midsize, and even the giant monsters of the depths found themselves wreathed in flame under the powerful, Mind-heavy area attack that raised the bar when it came to skills.

Tens if not hundreds of monsters turned to ash around them, their carcasses joined by the wyverns falling from the sky with rustling wings. The whole of the fifty-eighth floor transformed into a bed of corpses.

"Lefiya! Tione!" Tiona ran over to the two girls, somehow having managed to escape the blast radius of Lefiya's spell.

"W-we're alive..." Lefiya muttered in blank amazement. Tione's arms swept around her as she landed.

"That's what you have to say after that magic you just used?" Tione responded with a smile.

Their happiness, however, was short-lived.

"Those damn dragons blocked it, though. We can't let 'em attack Aiz and the others," Bete informed them, his twin swords at the ready. He was prepared to take on anything, his sharp amber eyes scanning the perimeter.

Embers continued to dance in the black smoke rising from the charred wasteland of the fifty-eighth floor.

Lefiya's spell had taken out a good portion of the monsters, and there was no chance of them reviving, but there were still plenty more enemies scattered about the great room. Wyverns began popping out of the many holes littering the ceiling, and even more important, the remaining valgang dragons were still standing strong—seven of them.

The awesome, floor-disregarding firepower of those dragons was still a threat. They needed to keep the beasts from hunting down the rest of their party, who were no doubt making their way through the Dungeon passageways above their heads at that very moment.

"Agreed. Like I would ever let someone attack the captain."

"Lefiya, heal up if you need to," said Tiona with a growl. The two Amazonian sisters stared long and hard at the valgang dragons, Durandal weapons—halberd and sword—resting on their shoulders.

"S-sure!" Lefiya responded. She grabbed the cylindrical backpack from off her shoulders and hastily rummaged through it. Her breaths growing shorter and shorter, she finally found it—the high-magic potion with the *Dian Cecht Familia* seal—and gulped it down.

"B-but…will we really be able to take out seven of them?" Lefiya asked hesitantly, eyeing the scene in front of them.

"If we can't, we're pretty much done for, so why talk about it?"

"Pretty much, yeah."

Bete and Tiona replied similarly.

The ominous red dragons practically radiated enmity; the wyverns circled overhead, their great wings flapping; and the myriad other monsters still lurked about the floor—even a large group of Moitra formoires were coming at them.

As Lefiya looked out over them, she found herself more than a little overwhelmed. Bete and Tiona, too, despite their casual responses, knew there was no room for error.

The group of first-tiers stared out across that landscape of certain death, their faces taut.

"…How long do you think we'll still have Riveria's Veil Breath?" Tiona mused, her voice low.

"That old bag's spells usually last about an hour…so maybe two or three more fights?" Bete replied.

The repeated, fierce attacks from the valgang dragons and wyverns had considerably chipped away at the gowns of light currently protecting the group and left them visibly dimmed. One more direct hit from one of those fireballs would obliterate it completely, no doubt, and fry Tiona and the others in the process.

"…Once we've taken care of those dragons, we should probably hide out in one of the tunnels on the fifty-seventh floor until the captain and the others get here, yes?" Tione proposed, eyes veering first to the northern staircase leading up to the fifty-seventh floor and then to the southern staircase leading down to the fifty-ninth floor.

Sticking around only to face the murderous wrath of the monsters on their every side wouldn't be a wise decision.

Lefiya and the others nodded in agreement.

"*WUUUUAAAAAAAAARRRRRRRRGGGHHHHH!!*"

One of the valgang dragons finally let out a roar, signaling the start of their second battle.

The monsters moved almost simultaneously, and Tiona, Tione, Bete, and Lefiya readied their weapons before taking off at a running dash.

Only then—

"———*Gwuuoooh?!*"

A shadow appeared from overhead, flying down and instantly shattering the head of one of the valgang dragons.

"————"

There was a thunderous boom as the beast's giant frame came crashing to the ground.

The red dragon's head went flying. All movement came to a halt. Not only the adventurers but also every monster in the room stopped in confusion.

Silence filled the room. Then the falling shadow, the dragon's killer, rose from the carcass of the dead beast, slowly pulling his ax from the remains.

"You buckwheaters still alive, are ye?"

The old dwarf soldier peered out at them from beneath his helmet. Lefiya and the others simply stared at him in surprise, eyes wide.

"Ga…"

"…reth?" Tiona finished Lefiya's hoarse murmur of wonderment for her.

Tione and Bete, too, were rooted to the spot in amazement as the two axes of the first-tier adventurer, Gareth Landrock, glinted in the dim light.

"W...*wuuuuuuuaaAAAAARRRRRRRRGGGHHHHH!*"

One of the other valgang dragons let out a roar of fury at the death of its kin.

Almost as if on cue, every monster in the hall began rushing toward the lone dwarf who'd appeared at the center of the dragon cluster.

"Gareth!"

"Gramps!!"

As Tione and Bete let out simultaneous screams, Gareth flourished his mantle—then vanished.

Kicking off the ground with enough force to crack its surface and uncanny speed for a dwarf, he was suddenly at the feet of a valgang dragon.

The first-tier adventurer was a Level 6, and it showed. Eyes flashing, he plunged his twin axes into the dragon's foot.

"——————*Gwwuh!*"

In a burst of flesh and blood, the dragon sank to the ground, unable to so much as retaliate.

It was so quick and so sudden that Tiona and the others could only let out audible gulps.

The valgang dragons, boasting enormous wings for forelimbs just like the wyverns, had no way to fight back. They possessed no means of attacking at close range. They specialized in long-range magic salvos with nothing but their long fat tails to swing around when it came to close-quarter combat, which made the area in front of them the one place a hopeful attacker could be safe. In addition, jumping atop one of the dragon's chests supplied protection from fireballs, as its fellow monsters wouldn't want to risk friendly fire.

The dragons found themselves at a loss, and Gareth took advantage of those few moments to launch forward once again.

In one hand was his Grand Ax, its weight rivaling even that of Urga, and in his other, the Durandal-made Roland Ax—both of which he suddenly tossed aside.

His hands now free, he took hold of the tip of the fallen valgang dragon's tail.

"Hnngh…Gnnngh…Huuuuwoooooaaaahh!!" he grunted, using every muscle in his body to haul the tail, dragon and all.

Fingers digging into the hard red scales, he lugged the giant frame of the valgang dragon step by step by step.

His face flushed a brilliant red, veins bulging out across his forehead. The incoming hailstones of fire from the wyverns overhead didn't so much as faze him.

Then he let out a mighty cry of bravado:

"…HnnnnnnnnnnnnnggrrrraaaaaaAAAAAAAAGGGGHHHH!!!"

As his upper half twisted beneath the weight, the dragon's body rose from the ground.

—He couldn't possibly be…?!

But he was. The awed premonitions of Lefiya and the others were right on the money.

Gareth began to spin. And with him, of course, spun the valgang dragon, the dwarf's hands still clenched around its tail.

The monstrous ten-meder frame of the beast was whirling through the air at the hands of a lone dwarf.

"*Gw-gwwwuuooooohhhhh!*" the creature screamed in response.

The dwarf spun that great dragon like a giant hammer, his already awe-inspiring might further amplified by the unique strengthening skill characteristic of the dwarves.

"Oh, crap!" Tione cried out.

Which was quickly followed by a scream of "Everybody down!!" from Bete, and the four adventurers dropped to the ground.

?!

Three times. Four times. Five times. Six times, Gareth spun that dragon around.

And with each spin, his speed increased, along with his destructive potential, knocking back any monsters that tried to approach. The cyclone even repelled other valgang dragons that got too close.

Gareth Landrock. First-tier adventurer.

A veteran soldier of herculean strength who truly embodied the dwarven race. His power and endurance rivaled not only the strongest in *Loki Familia* but all of Orario itself, and despite being a natural-born attacker, he'd come to rule the very back of the rear guard as an impenetrable wall. His fists were like hammers, smashing every enemy in his path, and his burly frame was like the world's sturdiest shield.

His ability to plow through enemies and absorb any attack was what had inspired the gods to give him his alias—Elgarm.

It was said that he could carry a damaged galleon to shore single-handedly—a great dwarf soldier worthy of standing alongside Braver and Nine Hell.

"GwwwwuuuuuuooooooOOOOOOOOGGGGGHHH!"

The sounds of pulverized monsters, echoing death cries, and the ferocious vortex filled the room.

Gareth and the dragon had transformed into a veritable tornado, driving back every monster in their vicinity.

"Off yooooooooou...GOOOOOOOOOOOOOOOOO!!" he shouted, releasing his grip on the dragon's tail.

The enormous centrifugal force sent the enormous missile flying at an upward angle to collide with the flock of wyverns overhead.

The hammer that was that great flying dragon drew an arc in the sky, smashing through the wyverns and into the wall with a giant explosion.

There was a thunderous crash, almost indiscernible from a meteorite strike, and the stone crumbled at the place of impact.

"...N-no way!"

Tiona raised her head from the ground and wiped at the dust covering her cheeks.

She saw the five remaining valgang dragons splayed out with their tongues dangling from their mouths. She saw the scattered monsters, already barely resembling their original forms. And she saw the final crimson dragon, its head stuck in the rock along the far wall.

The others—Bete, Tione, and Lefiya, the three of them still flat on the ground—could only stare at the storm-strewn landscape, their faces twitching.

"I could use...a really strong drink right about now...Some proper dwarven stuff..." said the storm bringer himself, breathing heavily, before taking out a high potion and gulping it down in place of liquor.

Roughly wiping off his mouth, he turned his gaze to Tiona and the others, who were still hugging the ground with befuddled expressions.

"What do ye think yer doin' down there, kids? They'll be comin' again soon enough. On yer feet!"

As though in response, a crack appeared in the far-off wall.

The holes in the ceiling were steadily growing in number, and another wave of wyverns was already on its way.

Gareth grabbed his two axes from the ground and prepared himself for battle.

"...Are you...sure you cannot handle things yourself, Sir Gareth?"

Lefiya got to her feet unsteadily before joining the rest of the group.

"Don't be an ass! Ye think I can pull somethin' like that off again?" Gareth brushed her off. "'Twas nothin' but a fluke." He crossed his twin axes in front of his chest. "We've gotta hold out till Finn and the others get down here, ye hear?" His armor was visibly charred from wyvern fire, his mantle tattered and torn. Cuts and bruises adorned his skin.

As Bete and the others saw the damage he'd taken from that outrageous feat he'd just accomplished, they came to a realization.

The reason he normally didn't display this magnitude of strength was because he was always in the rear guard, making room on the front line for them.

And the reason he did this was to protect Bete and the other first-tiers, as well as Raul and the other younger members of the familia.

Gareth turned around to glance at Bete, at Tione, Tiona, and Lefiya, his teeth bared in a broad grin.

"Come now, lads 'n' lasses! Where're those terrors I'm so used to, huh? Up and at 'em! Raise some hell! Or are ye gonna let some old man show ye up?"

At the dwarf's challenge, Bete and the others each raised an eyebrow before responding in kind.

"You gone senile or somethin', Gramps?"

"As if I'd lose to you!"

"After seeing that, I realize more than ever that I am in no shape to be a leader."

Their respective words of youthful vigor prompted a laugh from Gareth.

"Kids these days."

Seeing the others flourishing their weapons, Lefiya, too, readied her staff.

"Hmph. Those our new species?" Gareth muttered, watching the northern staircase leading to the fifty-seventh floor. Repulsive shadow after repulsive shadow gushed from the entryway, and he narrowed his eyes at the sight of their unsettlingly vibrant yellow-green skin.

"The...the path to the fifty-seventh floor..." Lefiya moaned, her voice hoarse.

"Completely plugged up, yeah? Ye gods, if it's not one thing, it's another...Stay close, you lot!" Gareth replied before bounding off with a burst of energy.

While the terrors of the uttermost depths nearly robbed them of their breath itself, the first-tier adventurers had no choice but to follow along after the dwarf.

"We're changing formation! Aiz, you're on the front line!" Finn ordered almost immediately after Gareth dropped down the hole to save Lefiya.

The two groups now separated, Finn and the others in the main party began making their way through the fifty-second floor, taking out swarms of monsters along the way.

"Raul, you and the others stay on the midline and provide assistance to Aiz! Riveria, you're now in the rear guard!"

"R-roger!"

"Understood."

Finn flourished his Durandal spear as he sprinted alongside them, backing up Aiz on point and attacking everything beyond the reach of her sword. Quickly ordering the emergency change in formation from his spot on the midline, he used his cultivated leadership to propel the party continuously forward. Despite the situation developing around them, the powerful voice of their leader helped assuage the unrest and low morale enveloping the party, guiding the adventurers along the path.

Knowing all too well that following his instructions was the surest way of staying alive, Raul and the others made the change without fuss.

"I apologize, Tsubaki, but could I borrow your strength?" Finn asked, his eyes fixed straight ahead.

"No problem, boss!" Tsubaki nodded in response. She slid her *tachi* from its scabbard in a flash, bisecting a nearby monster and joining Finn in supporting Aiz from the midline.

Aiz led the way with Raul and the other three supporters directly behind her. Finn and Tsubaki guarded the group on its sides while Riveria protected them from the rear.

The supporters now forming the center of the party, they upped their pace to race down the tunnels of the fifty-second floor even faster than before.

"Whatever you do, don't stop!"

Still dodging the incoming fireballs from below, they took out only the monsters directly impeding their way forward.

They couldn't leave anything to chance when it came to beasts that could attack without regard to floors. The flares of those valgang dragons would take care of any monsters they failed to kill.

Getting to the fifty-eighth floor was their top priority, and every move was to that end.

The depths of the Dungeon were vaster than the entire city of Orario. As map data unfolded within his head, Finn tossed out order after order, leading them through the complex maze via the shortest route possible as they continued to dodge salvos from the dragons beneath their feet. Meanwhile, Raul and the other supporters had free hands, so they gathered around the one supporter toting the large-scale weapons and used daggers and spears to provide continuous support to the front line.

Riveria's Veil Breath enveloped the entire party. Just as it had with Lefiya and the others, the full-body protection magic glowed along the surfaces of their bodies, warding off critical attacks from their surrounding enemies time and time again.

"*WUUUUAAAAAAAAARRRRRRRRGGGHHHHH!!*"

An array of atrocious monsters blocked their path.

Venom scorpions, thunder snakes, silver worms—the threat of these monsters was so clearly different from that of the previous floors, it was as though they'd passed some kind of invisible line of demarcation. Together with the fireballs of the dragons some multiple floors below, the sheer number of these powerful beasts was what had kept Aiz and *Loki Familia* from progressing farther into the Dungeon's depths…until today.

"Finn! Nine of them!"

"We'll break through here! Aiz, they're yours!"

Following Finn's carefully calculated shortest route, Aiz shot forward.

The roars of the incoming monsters blasting her from all sides, she responded with a scream of her own.

"*Awaken, Tempest!!*" she shouted, activating her Airiel before swinging her sword into the mass.

It slipped past the oncoming needles of poison, past the electrifying sparks of lightning attacks. In the blink of an eye, she'd mowed down all nine enemies.

The flash of her sword morphed into an undulating wave of air, and their bodies exploded upon impact, scattering into the wind. Her armor of wind, now coupled with the green light of Riveria's Veil Breath, screamed as she shot forward.

"Aiz's level-up is really saving our skins," Finn muttered, watching as the Sword Princess plowed her way through the wall of monsters, then proceeded to annihilate every other obstacle in one relentless wave after another.

"I've seen her do some foolish things, so the matter is rather complicated," Riveria replied as she thought back to Aiz's defeat of the floor boss Udaeus.

Aiz's Level 6 abilities, coupled with the output of her strengthened Airiel, gave her an uncanny strength when it came to breaking through enemies. She plowed through the cumbersome venom scorpions and thunder snakes in a manner resembling Gareth's. Wrapped in winds and bearing the bulk of the front line all by herself, Aiz carved her way through the passageway, leaving piles of monster carcasses behind her.

"Are...are we even necessary at this point...?" Raul mused as he and the other supporters gazed at the sight with a shudder.

"Raul, ready a magic potion!" Finn barked, prohibiting them from turning into mere spectators.

"R-right!"

The rate they were exhausting themselves wasn't even comparable to the previous floors. If Aiz continued mowing down monsters at her current speed, her power would be gone in a flash. Sensing the condition of their sole vanguard fighter, Finn ordered for replenishment. Raul responded by quickly fishing through his bag for the item in question.

"Narfi, Alicia, Cruz! Your magic swords!"

"Roger!" the three responded in unison.

"The moment Aiz pulls back to recover, attack!" Finn commanded while taking out more monsters with his spear.

The three other supporters—human, elf, and beastman—readied their equipped magic swords. Following Finn's command, they flourished said swords the moment Aiz, covered in sweat, retreated to the midline.

The instant, chant-less bursts of magic exploded across the path in front of them, wiping out any monsters there.

Aiz grabbed the magic potion from Raul mid-run, finishing it off quickly before returning to the front line. The blazing fires from the magic swords had swallowed up the monsters during her brief respite.

"Those attacks from below have stopped. Y'think Gareth and the others…?" Tsubaki murmured as they continued along tirelessly, with Aiz at the helm. And it was true: the quakes, shudders, and shocks had stopped.

"Most likely. We should take advantage of the opportunity and make haste." Finn nodded in response.

It would seem Gareth's group had fallen all the way to the fifty-eighth floor and already mopped up—or at least drawn the attention of—the valgang dragons deep beneath their feet.

In their place, however, wyverns were starting to emerge from the deep vertical tunnel made by the dragons' blasts and closing in on the party. The winged dragons came and went as they pleased via the neck of the Dragon's Urn.

Despite the continuous attacks from above as they moved between tunnels and rooms, Aiz's wind and Finn's commands helped the party fend off the dragons until, finally, they found the staircase leading to the floor below.

In a flash, they descended to the next floor.

"The fifty-third floor…!" Raul let out a breath of air that could have been excitement or could have been fear, still haggard from their inordinate speed.

Next to him, Finn narrowed his green eyes, studying the perimeter.

"I don't see any of those new species…?"

Apparently, the magic from Aiz's Airiel wasn't enough to draw the magic-sensing caterpillar monsters out of hiding.

Finn gave his thumb a little lick as the party dashed their way through the temporarily encounter-free—and unsettlingly quiet— Dungeon floor.

"Who's going to join us, then, I wonder." A small smile rose to his lips as the throbbing of his thumb foreshadowed the coming Irregular.

Almost as if on cue, a swarm of caterpillar monsters appeared to block their path.

"Th-there they are!" Raul cried out.

"No, wait. There's something…" Riveria's face turned grim as she eyed the scene in front of them.

From among the deluge of caterpillars filling up the wide passageway, an especially large one appeared, bearing a figure in a bluish-purple hooded robe.

"The guy from the twenty-fourth floor…!" Aiz's memory flashed at the sight of the figure shrouded completely in cloth and its mask decorated in strange, ominous designs.

A conspirator of that creature Levis, no doubt, who'd appeared during their earlier fight and absconded with the crystal orb.

"Is that a…person?" asked Tsubaki, her right eye narrowing in suspicion at the eerie figure standing, unshakable, atop one of the monsters.

With boots on its feet and silver gloves on its hands, it seemed every bit a human.

It raised its right hand at the incoming party.

In sync with the movement, the herd of caterpillars arranged themselves into line after line, adjusting the heights of their heads into low, medium, and high, almost like a flight of stairs.

"Kill them."

The entire herd opened their mouths, releasing a simultaneous flood of corrosive acid.

"Nghh!"

"Alter course! Find a cave and run!!" Finn called out the second the tsunamic wave of acid came toward them. The rest of the party responded equally as fast, diving into the nearest hollow they could find.

Behind Riveria, the last to evacuate, the passageway filling up with corrosive acid looked like veins flooded with thick, dirty mud. In a mere moment, the walls, the ceiling, everything began melting upon contact with the monsters' fluid. An acerbic *hissssss* joined the resulting plumes of smoke and strange, nostril-stinging aroma.

"A…A mass acid attack…?!" Raul groaned, his face tight.

To think those monsters could be manipulated to pull off a

massive concentrated attack. Not even Aiz's wind would be able to absorb all that.

The faces of the supporters paled as they watched the indefensible attack wash through the passageway, melting away the very Dungeon itself.

"Everyone, on your feet. They're coming!"

Raul and the others leaped up at the sound of the multitude of legs scrambling toward them through the corroded tunnel. At Finn's command, they dashed toward the front of their small cave, Aiz at the lead.

"Controlling those new species as if they were soldiers…Could our hooded friend be the same as that woman?" Finn muttered under his breath as he shot forward, spear in hand.

"…!" The words made Aiz's brow tremble.

That woman could only mean Levis. If this being was the same as Levis, that would make it another creature.

Her heart cried at the thought that Levis might have a partner also able to control the vibrantly colored monsters.

"Strange place for whoever he or she is to turn up, though," Finn continued.

"Then what the hell is this person?"

"Simply put, a tamer," Riveria responded, not bothering to mince her words.

"You gotta be shittin' me! They can control monsters like *these*?!" Tsubaki replied in shock.

Raul and the other supporters couldn't contain their own gulps of surprise at the thought of someone able to control such a giant army of monsters from the depths. No sooner had the short hitches of air left their throats, however, than said army of caterpillars reappeared from the direction of their route.

"Hit the dirt!"

The sound of the massive acid attack swallowed up the supporters' screams. Aiz and the others were forced to change course once again as the spectacle from before repeated itself all over again.

"A-again?!"

"They're coming from that direction, too?!"

—Raul and the other supporters screamed as the caterpillar monsters closed in on them from all sides. The hissing noise of the acid shooting from their mouths, the smell of decay, and the anguished screams of other monsters caught in the attack echoed around them as Finn gave order after order, leading the party through the fifty-third floor at an incredible speed.

"Don't let them escape, my virgas."

The hooded figure continued doggedly behind them together with its army of caterpillars, now joined by a swarm of violas.

"We're being herded...!" Riveria grimaced, taking note of the way their every path kept getting blocked by monsters.

"To think we'd end up having to deal with strategizing monsters," Finn added with a nod.

The army of caterpillars and their hooded ringleader were most certainly shepherding the party, and the net encircling them seemed to be getting smaller and smaller and smaller as they stopped the party's advance again and again. It was almost as if they were being driven into a corner, and the thought that this could all be a part of that creature's plan brought cold drops of sweat to the foreheads of the entire party.

...The question now is, what is that thing looking for? Aiz, perhaps? Finn thought, throwing a glance behind him as anxiety settled over the group.

He saw the hooded figure giving orders from atop one of the large rushing caterpillars. He could feel the focus of the being's gaze, despite the mask that seemed to block its vision.

Could it be it was targeting the golden-haired, golden-eyed swordswoman hidden in shadow at the front of their desperately racing group?

Was it attempting to take her alive, the same as Levis and her friends?

Or did it simply regard *Loki Familia* as an enemy and wish to annihilate them?

For a brief moment, their gazes met—Finn's and the hooded figure's—and the prum's eyes narrowed.

"Finn, we're being cornered!" Riveria cried out upon realizing their enemy's intentions herself.

"..." Finn laid out the map of the fifty-third floor in his mind. The moment he determined their current position and its nearby locations, he raised his head. "Aiz! Turn left!"

Aiz darted into one of the countless byroads and tunnels splitting off from their current path, leading the party down a long, straight tunnel.

Halfway through their reroute, however, Finn called out again.

"We'll ambush them! About-face!"

Raul and the others were taken aback at the sudden order but did as they were told all the same—they had faith in their leader.

Bearing with him, they forced themselves to a screeching halt and then turned on their heels. The moment Aiz and Riveria found themselves in their new, reversed positions, the hooded figure appeared with its army of monster soldiers along the way they'd come.

Aiz strengthened her Airiel at the sight of the overwhelming swarm of monsters.

"I need three shields lined up now!" their captain cried, to which his party members quickly complied.

The supporters other than Raul peeled off the large shields attached to their backpacks, bringing them together in front of the incoming monster army to form a gapless three-man barrier.

"Aiz!!" Finn shouted again, not wasting a single instant.

Aiz threw a glance back at him in confusion. Then, suddenly, she understood.

Grabbing her knees tightly, she somersaulted backward.

Leaving behind a crack in the Dungeon floor, she flew through the air to land not on the wall but on the supporters' shields.

The moment her feet slammed onto that wall of shields, she readied Desperate, and the massive air current around her undulated as she flourished her sword of silver.

It took a moment for the shock of it to reach the supporters, who cringed as they stooped with a sort of fixed determination. Raul even lent his own support, using his shoulders to help prop them up.

An instant later, Aiz let it out, the name of that skill passing her lips.

"Li'l Rafaga!" She kicked off from the shield to unleash a missile of wind.

"?!"

The oncoming hooded figure gave a surprised shudder.

Leaping forth from the shield, Aiz released that great, spiraling arrow of wind. The creature, realizing it had nowhere to run, could only let out a cry at the approaching attack:

"Virgas!"

The response was immediate: the caterpillars released another of their simultaneous acid attacks.

Acid met wind in a violent blast, but the wind won.

"_____"

The hooded figure beat a hasty retreat as Aiz's attack forced back the caterpillars' acidic onslaught.

Leaping into a corner of the ceiling, it watched as the vortex swallowed the massive swarm of caterpillars.

It made a clean sweep of the entire column, tearing through it in one giant blast, then continued on toward the hooded figure as a powerful, raging gale.

"No way…" the figure muttered beneath its mask as the shock waves hit it and whipped its cloak about.

"We've bought ourselves some time!"

"—ngh!"

It was a long spear that came at the figure this time. Finn, not allowing the enemy to find its footing, followed right on the heels of Aiz's Li'l Rafaga as the swordswoman raced deep into the passage with a mighty explosion.

The hooded figure somehow managed to ward off the incoming Durandal spear with a flourish of its metal gloves.

"Seems that even among you creatures, some are stronger than others."

"—Ngh!"

Finn continued his close-range assault as his opponent kicked off the wall and landed on the ground.

The hooded figure defended itself desperately, its metal gloves coming up to block the onslaught of thrusts again and again, unable to land an attack of its own against the prum's overwhelming spearmanship.

Finn could tell instantly that the creature in front of him couldn't hold a candle to Levis. He'd fought against the red-haired woman on the eighteenth floor, after all.

The hooded figure, unable to keep up with the increasing speed of the attacks besieging the lower half of its vision, let out a shout.

"Violas!!"

Countless yellow-green tentacles rose from the ground to thwart the relentless spear strikes.

Finn took a step back as the flowers surged toward him. From the ceiling, from the walls, from the ground, their innumerable tentacles punched through the earth and rose from holes, coming at him like a sickening green rain. And as he blocked those incoming attacks, his spear a raging whirlwind, the hooded figure lunged forward to counterattack.

It was a rapid-fire back-and-forth as the two opponents set aside everything else in their immediate vicinity. Amid the sounds of Aiz finishing off the caterpillar monsters farther down the long path, they relocated the battle to a side passage, silver spear meeting silver gloves in a violent riposte.

The hooded figure summoned forth a massive tentacle strike from its viola allies, about to add his own attack to the mix—when…

"Gggnh!"

It came like covering fire. A single arrow plunged into the figure's shoulder.

"I…I hit him…" Raul murmured in wonder. He stood a considerable distance behind the two duelists with his bow readied to fire.

The hooded figure yanked the arrow from its shoulder, fingers curling around the wood and breaking it with a fierce *snap*.

"It...It didn't even faze that thing!" Raul cried out despondently.

Finn, however, just smiled as he wiped out the remaining tentacles. "You did well, Raul!"

An instant later, a figure in a red *hakama* shrieked down the cleared passageway.

"Mind if I take a stab at this fella?"

"———!"

Her black ponytail fluttering behind her, Tsubaki sprang forward, landing directly in front of the masked creature.

The hooded figure, still off-balance from the earlier attack, didn't have time to react before the half-dwarf, her right eye narrowed, unsheathed her *tachi* at godlike speed.

It was a direct hit.

"**Guuwwwwwwaaaaaaaaaaaaaaaarrrrghhh!!**"

The creature's right arm went flying, metal glove and all.

It let out a scream of anguish as the limb danced through the air. Tsubaki readied herself for a second strike. The killing blow had failed only due to her opponent's split-second dodge.

But then.

"**—Devour!**" it shouted, drawing one of the violas toward it.

And before Tsubaki's blade could reach its target, the repulsive flower had swallowed the hooded figure whole.

"What the—?!"

The flower let out a scream as the sword sliced at its long body, before scuttling away with the creature in its mouth.

One of its tentacles snatched the arm still flying through the air before the whole thing disappeared into a nearby cave. Tsubaki, befuddled as ever, made to follow, but not before a certain high elf finished casting her spell.

"*—Wynn Fimbulvetr!!*"

Out shot the three tendrils of icy snow.

The magic froze the entirety of the cave, all the way to her main target deep within its confines.

The escaping viola, its back turned to the cave's opening, was instantly encased in a world of solid blue ice.

Tsubaki dashed forward in high spirits, her prey now frozen in its tracks.

"...Huh?"

"What is it, Tsubaki?"

Tsubaki had cracked open the flower ice sculpture, *tachi* at the ready and looking for the hooded figure, but she now stood rooted to the spot in wide-eyed surprise.

Riveria raced over, leaving Finn, Raul, and the others to fend off the remaining monsters, only to be met with the same astonishing scene.

"Nothing but a...robe?"

"How could it possibly have escaped?!"

Indeed, as the two of them stared into the shattered mouth of the viola, all they found was an empty robe and a frozen, cracked mask. Even the severed arm was gone; nothing remained but the metal glove and strip of cloth that had once covered it.

"Could it have escaped during that one instant our vision was obscured by my blizzard?" Riveria mused in pure amazement.

"There's no way! That'd be the fastest escape I've ever seen..." Tsubaki muttered somewhat bitterly next to her.

The two women raised their heads to find another ever-so-narrow path shooting off from the side of the tunnel, connecting itself to the intricate remainder of the Dungeon.

"Riveria. Tsubaki," Finn said from behind them. The prum was followed by Raul and the other supporters, along with Aiz, having returned from her caterpillar extermination. Riveria and Tsubaki turned to face him.

"I apologize, Finn...we've allowed it to escape."

"Whadda we do? Follow it?"

Finn glanced down at the frozen body of the viola, studying the bluish-purple robe and metallic glove for a moment before shaking his head.

"Our priority now is to reconvene with Gareth and the others. We should hurry to the fifty-eighth floor."

"Understood."

None of them were about to argue, not when their companions' safety was at stake.

And so, with the presence of the creature they'd let escape still on their minds, the group began making their way down to the lower floors once more.

"Aiz, if you could take the front line again?" Finn asked.

"Of course," Aiz responded with a nod.

The adventurers raced off, leaving the hooded robe hidden beneath snow and frost behind them.

A fierce battle was raging on the fifty-eighth floor.

The group of adventurers clashed against monster after monster in an attempt to survive, but the path to the fifty-seventh floor—their only path of retreat—was blocked by the incoming swarms of giant caterpillars.

The caterpillar monsters had formed a multitudinous herd, attacking not only Gareth's party but other monsters in the vicinity, as well. Their innate ability to sense magic and magic stones was leading them to the battlefield in droves.

From the caterpillars spitting out their corrosive acid and devouring their unlucky prey whole—magic stones and all—to the ferocious monsters attacking with teeth and claws, indifferent to their own dissolution, to the flock of wyverns overhead, pelting them with salvos of fireballs, it was an outright free-for-all.

Thunderous roars, bestial cries, and dragons' breaths mixed throughout the fifty-eighth floor.

"Is this normal for the floors down here?!"

"How the hell am I supposed to know?!"

As friendly fire pervaded the area, Tiona and Bete mowed down the monsters around them to advance on the newly spawned valgang dragon that had just burst through the Dungeon wall. In an attempt to prevent its massive fireball from obliterating friend and foe alike, they charged the great red beast and took it down with an icy kick from Bete's magic-charged boots and a series of killing blows from Tiona's massive Durandal sword. If they had to thank those caterpillar monsters for one thing, it was that they'd made it a lot easier to move about the battlefield.

The two of them deftly dodged the incoming blasts of corrosive acid as the brutal three-way battle continued.

Lefiya, currently under Tione's protection, avoided casting anything too recklessly lest she draw the attention of those caterpillars.

At the same time, Gareth was fighting with a sheer intensity, his mantle fluttering wildly. "Do these brutes ever stop fighting?" he mused, taking out one enemy after another with his two axes. Each mighty swing of his weapons made an impact like a bomb.

A nearby swarm of caterpillars responded by unleashing a burst of corrosive acid.

"Show me somethin' I haven't seen before!" he shouted before quickly dodging, slamming his Grand Ax into the ground with a brilliant flash.

The sheet of rock crumbled, bits and pieces of stone flying off to hit the caterpillars like explosive missiles. Their bodies crumpled, riddled with holes and leaking acid on the ground below.

The dwarf soldier's Durandal ax took care of the remaining caterpillar with a massive upward swing.

"Grrraaaagh!!"

"*Gunngh!*"

The beast didn't even have a chance to respond. The longitudinal swing cut it in half.

They'd been fighting for nearly eight hours now, and the dwarf's ferocity had yet to wane. *And yet, these uncanny beasts…* Gareth eyed the monsters suspiciously from beneath his helmet. He was studying their movement. *Comin' from the northern tunnel they might be; we've somehow reached the hall's center. We're movin' south.*

He threw a glance behind him to where the droves of caterpillars continued to pour out of the tunnel leading to the fifty-seventh floor.

Ahead of him and to the south was another tunnel—the path that would lead them to the next floor down.

These brutes aren't fixin' to reach the fifty-ninth floor themselves, are they? Tryin' to move even farther downward?

Could the caterpillar monsters rampaging about these depths be attempting to return home?

Gareth narrowed his eyes at the entrance to the unknown, shrouded in darkness, then wrenched his gaze away, his thoughts returning to the battle at hand.

"Th-they're still coming!" Tione cried out with a curse, sweat forming along her neck and temple as another of the great red dragons spawned on the Dungeon floor.

The young adventurers couldn't hide their fatigue as the long battle continued. Bete's tongue practically lolled from his mouth, Tiona's wrists trembled, and Lefiya's breath sounded ragged and strained.

Gareth, however, as tough as ever and showing no signs of weariness, dashed forward toward the newly spawned valgang dragon breaking through the floor—until.

"Wynn Fimbulvetr!"

The massive blizzard descended on them from the northern tip of the hall.

It froze everything: the valgang dragon and the massive swarms of monsters still littering the area. And as Tione and the others watched in awe, a golden flash reflected in their saucerlike eyes.

"Ngh!!"

A golden-haired, golden-eyed swordswoman shot forward like an arrow, shattering the valgang dragon ice sculpture.

Desperate sliced through the frozen dragon's neck, separating its head from its body and sending chunks of ice to the ground below in great, thunderous crashes.

"Miss Aiz!!"

"Riveria!"

Lefiya and Tione cried out in simultaneous jubilation at the sight of their companions.

Aiz came to a stop in the middle of the hall with Riveria, Finn, and Tsubaki hot on her heels. Even Raul, completely unharmed along with the other three supporters, dashed forward to join them.

"Captaaaaaaaaaaain!!" Tione called out, her energy restored in a flash.

"Save the celebration for later!" Finn replied, only half acknowledging her before barking out commands to the others. "We still need to finish off the remaining monsters!!"

The powerful sound of their leader's voice stoking their spirits, Bete and the others joined forces with Aiz and set their sights on the monsters still roaming the open space.

The supporters' protection glowing bright, it didn't take long for the carcasses of the caterpillars and wyverns to pile up, mountain upon mountain of ash littering the ground.

"Miss Aiz! You aren't hurt?" inquired Lefiya.

"I'm fine, yeah...You guys made it through?"

"By the skin of our teeth! All thanks to Gareth." Tiona, this time.

There wasn't a presence to be felt; the party had seemingly reached a long break from the encounters. Even the many holes perforating the ceiling thanks to the valgang dragons had sealed themselves up, leaving the fifty-eighth floor in silence.

The reunited Aiz, Lefiya, and Tiona brought their hands together joyfully.

Finn and Riveria checked on Gareth while Tsubaki, laughing about one thing or another, gave Tione and Bete a resounding series of pounds upon their backs. Tione just smirked, though Bete shot her a look of hate. Meanwhile, Raul and the other supporters passed out healing items from their backpacks, tears trembling in their eyes.

"Oh-ho-ho! This a fang from one of those crazy dragons that kept blastin' away at us? And what's this? A scale?! You've just gotta let me take these back!" Tsubaki pulled out first a valgang dragon fang and then a red scale from amid the plethora of drop items littering the strewn monster carcasses, her face alight with excitement.

Finn, however, didn't share her exuberance. "I apologize, Tsubaki, but you'll have to wait. Something that big will only prove a hindrance as we explore further. Perhaps on our way back?" He kindly reminded her of what should have been obvious.

The party made their way toward the southern end of the room where Finn instructed them to take a short break.

"Though we were forced to take separate routes, the entire party made it to the fifty-eighth floor. I'm not sure whether this is a good sign...or quite the opposite," Riveria mused.

Bete just snorted. "So what? It's not like it's our first time down here."

"You say that as if you weren't gasping for breath about five minutes ago," Tiona sarcastically replied.

"Pretty sure that was you!"

Lefiya, Raul, and the other supporters let out a chuckle as the duo went off on each other as usual. A relaxed atmosphere had settled over the party.

They drank leisurely from potions and magic potions. Aiz finished off the last of her block-shaped rations from Lulune. And Tsubaki whipped out her smithing tools to perform emergency maintenance on the adventurers' weapons.

It was a momentary respite for the group as they sat in a circle, the uncharted depths right in front of their eyes.

"..."

"Captain? Is something wrong?" Tiona piped up as Aiz and the others enjoyed their moment of downtime.

The prum was standing with his back to the group, spear at the ready as he stared down the gaping darkness of that large hole to the south.

He seemed fixated on it, gazing deep into the void that would lead them to the fifty-ninth floor.

"According to the records left behind by *Zeus Familia*, the Glacial Territories await us beyond that passage...".

"I-indeed. It's said that glacial streams run across the land, making it hard to advance, and bitterly cold winds make it hard to even move your body..." Tione continued his thoughts.

"W-we brought plenty of salamander wool! We had to request some from other factions, but we should have just enough for all of us, supporters included." Raul stood up in a hurry, snatching the crimson fabric from his backpack. Salamander wool was a type of fire-element armor with cold-resistant properties.

Finn didn't move, his green eyes, like the surface of a lake, still fixated on the passage in front of him. Finally, he spoke.

"If the cold is so intense it can freeze even first-tier adventurers... why can we not feel it now? Sitting here with the entrance in front of our eyes?"

Tione and Raul shuddered in simultaneous bewilderment at Finn's inquiry.

It was true. They were waiting right in front of the passage that would lead them to the fifty-ninth floor, yet none of them felt even the slightest breeze of chilled air from the large hole before them.

Listening in on their conversation, first Aiz, then the others, rose one by one with their weapons readied.

"You sayin' somethin's up?" Bete mused, staring at the dark hole.

"No idea...but I wouldn't think *Zeus Familia* to be one for exaggeratin' things," Gareth replied as he adjusted his helmet.

It was evident from everyone's faces that this wasn't something they could just ignore.

"..."

Just as a strange feeling of tension began to brew within the party, Aiz remembered something.

What someone had said to her some twenty days ago up on the twenty-fourth floor.

—*"Aria, go to the fifty-ninth floor.*

—*"Things are getting interesting right now. Should answer a lot of your questions."*

That was what that redheaded non-human woman had told her.

That there was something down there on the fifty-ninth floor.

Something she sought.

As she stood before the hole that led to the very depths of the earth, she unconsciously adjusted her grip on the handle of her sword.

The crystal hanging from its chain around her loin guard gave off a faint glow, almost as though humming to life.

"Wh-what do you think we should do, Captain?"

"…The salamander wool should prove fine. We leave in three minutes." Finn gave his thumb a little lick. His gaze was still sharp as he took in the tunnel before them.

The rest of the party quickly finished up their preparations, bringing their moment of rest to a close. Then, equipped with their weapons and reestablishing their formation, they approached the giant hole.

"Strange. It's not cold at all…" Tiona observed as Raul and the other supporters lit their portable magic-stone lanterns to ward off the enveloping darkness.

"…In fact, I would almost say it is…muggy," Lefiya finished her sentence, the inklings of sweat dotting their skin.

None of them knew what to say about this unexpected humidity, and a vague apprehension shushed the group. They continued down the long, long staircase to the floor below, senses keen to even the slightest noise.

Clink, clink.

Their footsteps echoed throughout the stairwell.

Farther and farther they descended into the darkness.

Toward a light at the end of the tunnel.

"Finn, this is…" Riveria began.

Finn nodded at the voice of the high elf from behind him. "Indeed. From here on out, we enter a land that no one, not even the gods themselves, have witnessed—the unknown."

And with that, they reached the light.

Descending the last stair, the group stepped out onto the fifty-ninth floor and into the unknown depths.

"_____"

They found themselves at a loss for words as they took in the scene before them.

There were no glacial streams.

No soaring mountains of ice. No frozen rivers of blue.

No. Reflected in their eyes were masses upon masses of the strangest plants and vegetation they'd ever seen, a landscape altogether divergent from the floors above.

"A...jungle?" Tione gazed around at her surroundings in wonderment, still gripping her Kukri knives.

This room, even bigger than the fifty-eighth floor above their heads, overflowed with green trees and vines. Immediately in front of them was a forest of soaring trees. At their feet were a lush green bed of grass and trembling rings of richly colored, poisonous-looking flowers. It was an enclosed room with four far-off greenish walls towering high, and all shapes and sizes of flower buds dangled from the greenery.

"Is this like the...twenty-fourth floor...?" Lefiya murmured, her voice trembling as she hugged her staff to her chest.

Even Bete narrowed his eyes as he looked out across the spectacle. The sight closely resembled the pantry on the twenty-fourth floor after it had been taken over by violas and become a plant.

Aiz was quiet as she gazed across the landscape. Meanwhile, Raul raised his gaze from among the flustered supporters.

"Do you...hear that?"

A strange noise was coming from the floor's center.

It sounded like something chewing. A crumbling noise followed by an occasional high-pitched, trembling voice.

As the mysterious noise continued, obscured deep within that dense jungle, all eyes of the frozen party went to their prum leader.

Spear in hand, Finn gave the order:

"Forward."

That was all it took for the group to move.

Bete and Tiona took the lead as they made their way along the jungle's one road, almost like a pathway carved through the trees.

Everyone's eyes shifted back and forth from one tree to the next, keeping watch lest something spring forth. Lest they lose their wits.

A phosphorescent glow shone down on them from the ceiling some ten meders above their heads. This tiny glimpse of the Dungeon walls peeking out from so much green thickness was all they had to remind them that this strange floor was even in the same labyrinth they'd come to know.

Minutes passed as they continued through the trees, the ever-loudening sound in front of them drawing them forward.

Then, all of a sudden, the jungle disappeared around them, opening up to reveal—

"…What…is that?" Tiona asked as she readied her Urga.

It was a large, open hall of ashen earth, devoid of trees.

And at the center of that barren wasteland was a multitude of caterpillars and violas.

It was a nauseating, gut-wrenching amount, and they were all gathered around something—a woman with a giant plantlike lower half.

"Is that one of those crystal-orb monsters?" Gareth asked, wrinkles forming in his cheeks.

"Has it…absorbed a titan alm?" Riveria added, identifying the large, vegetative monster that called the deep levels its home. Known as the Corpse Flower King, it preyed at will upon adventurer and brethren alike.

The caterpillars were extending tonguelike organs from their mouths, offering up the vivid magic stones at their tips to the female body of the titan alm. The violas, too, had opened their giant, gaping jaws to reveal the magic stones in their mouths.

The woman fed upon the stones with fervor.

Her body very much resembled the female caterpillar they'd encountered up on the fiftieth floor. As its countless tentacles devoured the vibrantly colored offerings, the caterpillars and flowers, now devoid of their magic stones, rotted and turned to ash, one by one.

"You're kidding! It's already gobbled up that many monsters?" Tsubaki's right eye widened as she took in the monstrous pile of ash, almost like salt, around the creature.

It was then that Lefiya and the others noticed it.

The ashen ground they were standing upon at that very moment was actually the *countless carcasses of monsters* turned to ash and piled up beneath them.

"Shit…!" Finn's face skewed as the rest of the party trembled in fear.

"An enhanced species…?!" The tattoo on Bete's face twisted with his grimace.

"＿＿＿＿＿＿"

And Aiz.

She could hear her own heartbeat.

It was screaming, so loud her ears felt liable to burst.

Her blood was churning at the sight in front of her.

Only then.

Something changed. Just as Finn and the others were about to respond.

"————*Ah.*"

The faintest noise rose from the creature's grotesque head as it raised its upper body.

Only halfway through its feast on the surrounding monsters, it began to writhe like a worm.

"————*Ahhhh.*"

The repulsive-looking upper half still trembling and squirming, its flesh suddenly bulged.

She released a sigh of ecstasy. Finn and the others watched in amazement as the most beautiful woman they'd ever seen was born, emerging from all that ugliness like a butterfly from its cocoon.

"————*AhhhhHHHHHHHHHHHHHHHHHHHHHHHHHHHHH HHHHHHHHHH!*" came the scream of pleasure.

The adventurers had to slam their palms over their ears at the overwhelming, high-frequency sound waves that threatened to rupture their eardrums.

The woman, having risen from that husk of flesh, bent backward and directed her eyes to the heavens.

Long glossy hair descended along the curve of her back.

Covering her supple arms, her curvaceous chest, and waist was a gown of brilliant colors.

The gorgeous face of the woman gazing up at the ceiling, still shuddering with pleasure, could rival even a goddess's.

She was green. Every inch of her, from her hair to her skin.

Everything apart from her eyes, which were pools of gold that lacked pupils and irises.

It wasn't only her upper, human half that changed, either. Her abnormal lower half also underwent a transformation, now sporting enormous petals and a multitude of tentacles.

From the middle of that fifty-ninth floor, the gargantuan half-monster, half-goddess let out its first cry.

"Wh-what *is* that thing?!" Tione groaned, still holding her ears against the creature's raucous cries.

But no one knew what it was, even as it continued its song of rapture. All anyone could do was look on in horror.

"...No way," Aiz said from among the din.

Forgetting to cover her ears, she simply stood there in blank astonishment.

Her lips were trembling, her ears buzzing, the rapid churning of her blood having reached its peak.

There was no way. Could that...? Could it possibly...? Could it really be—?!

The questions ran through her head one after another, her body swaying in resonance with the blood pounding through her veins.

Could she be feeling the same thing? Could she?

"She" turned away from the ceiling, head swiveling on her neck as she directed her eyes toward Aiz.

"*Aria—! Aria!!*" she shouted, her voice filled with joy.

Again and again, that strange, abnormal creature screamed the name.

And when Aiz's eyes met those golden ones, she knew.

Her body froze in terror as her trembling lips parted.

"A...spirit?!"

"—Ouranos!" Fels whirled around at the image reflected in the crystal—the "eye" currently fastened to Aiz's loin guard.

They were in the Chamber of Prayers beneath Guild Headquarters.

Ouranos simply narrowed his eyes from atop his pedestal, both at the black-cloaked figure's cry and at the scene taking place within the crystal.

"It is true, then," he muttered. "I hadn't wanted to believe it. Could this really be one of the spirits of old that descended alongside us to Orario's surface? That carried out our will and assisted the heroes?" His brow furrowed as he took in the sight of the laughing woman in the crystal.

—The spirits had acted as an antenna for the gods, carrying out their will between the time of their descent and the Ancient Times.

They were weapons released by a number of the gods to act as the civilized people's guides, to expel the monsters from the surface world.

Something like the Falna of the present day.

The spirits bestowed humanity and many of its heroes with their divine protection. The voices of those women accompanied those heroes as they exterminated monster after monster.

Many of the spirits were sent into the Dungeon, into old Orario, the main source of the monsters, which was how the labyrinthine epic—the *Dungeon Oratoria*—came into being.

Its tales, still passed on today, recounted the history of those heroes who were guided by the gods via the spirits.

Fels took everything in with a strained gulp and returned his attention to the crystal.

Powerful spirits of the Ancient Times. Then this creature here, in the crystal, could only be—

"—A being that descended into the Dungeon, was presumably consumed by a monster, and yet has maintained its own sense of self for all these years."

"That would mean it's been alive for over one thousand years!"

"Indeed. And its current state depends on that of the monster that consumed it..."

It was survival of the fittest. Monsters had always followed such reason.

This spirit absorbed by a creature, too, had become a monster governed by primordial desires—feeding, stealing, indulging.

"An amalgamation of a child of the gods...and a monster. Is this, too, what this world holds in store?" Ouranos muttered, eyes closed as though holding something back.

Finally, his eyelids rose to form a narrow gaze as he took in the visage in the crystal.

"That which you see there…is already corrupted."

"A spirit?! That freaky-looking thing?!" Tiona exclaimed in response to Aiz's muttered words.

The group of adventurers couldn't help but tremble as they took in the sight of the hauntingly, venomously beautiful woman.

It was almost as if she'd forgotten who she really was, wrapped up in her gown of many colors and residing atop the colossal chassis of a monster.

It was a strange combination of repugnant beauty and odious sanctity.

The party found themselves at a loss against the sheer dignity of the corrupted spirit and the overwhelming sense of aversion it engendered.

"Those new species…were they merely more of that thing's tentacles?" Finn narrowed his eyes at the some ten-meder aberrant standing before them.

It was a good guess, considering how the caterpillars and violas had focused their attacks on other monsters. Perhaps magic itself was the necessary energy for this creature to survive.

Preying on monsters, collecting magic stones, and finally returning her to her true form. They really were nothing but "tentacles," extra appendages doing the spirit's dirty work.

Across from Finn, *she* continued to laugh. Again and again she called out to that certain swordswoman.

"*Aria! Aria!!*"

Her voice, almost like a child's, faltered as she awkwardly formed the words.

"*I missed you! I missed you!*"

"…?!"

"*Don't you want to be together forever?*"

Tiona's and the others' heads turned instantly at the words. Lines of tension appeared across their faces as though they already had an idea of where this was heading.

"—*Won't you let me eat you?*"

And then the spirit smiled.

Instantly, the remaining caterpillars and violas turned toward them with ferocious jerks, setting their sights on the adventurers—on Aiz—as though manifesting her dark will.

At the same time, there was a thunderous boom from the direction of the exit as the opening closed up with green flesh.

"Everyone, prepare for battle!!" Finn instantly commanded.

It was enough to stir them despite the confusion, and the party was unwavering despite their lost escape route. Tiona and the others readied their weapons.

She let out a sharp peal of laughter, and the battle began.

"*Ruuuuuaaaaaaaaaaaaaaaarrrrrrrrrrrrrgggghhhhh!!*"

The mass conglomeration of well over fifty caterpillars and violas rushed the group with a mighty roar.

The adventurers responded by unsheathing their Durandal weapons at the vibrant yellow-green masses.

"You want me to move up, Finn?" Gareth shouted as he jumped forward.

"Like this is any different from before! Time to squish some bugs!!" Bete followed suit, the two of them dodging the incoming acid and slicing the caterpillars into bite-size pieces.

Among the cacophonous cries of agony, Aiz remained rooted to the spot, heart pounding painfully against the walls of her chest. Quickly, she shook off the feeling of dread and forced herself back into the proper headspace before diving into the battle.

Flourishing her Desperate, she flew into the swarm of enemies, her body and sword a vortex.

"Lefiya, aim for that woman! Raul and the others will assist the rest of the group with their magic swords!!" Finn rattled off command after command with the same precision he enforced against floor bosses.

"U-understood!"

"R-roger!" Raul replied before he and the other supporters took off.

Staff at the ready, Lefiya began her first chant. Simultaneously, the group of supporters brandished their long magic swords and unleashed a volley of instant magic attacks.

Using the salvo as cover fire, Aiz dashed forward, pushing back the swarm of caterpillars.

"Like hell I'm just gonna stand around like some spectator!" Tsubaki announced as she plunged her blade into the throng of violas, her *hakama* fluttering.

"*Heh.*"

There was movement from the direction of the reborn spirit as her army of monsters was slaughtered around her.

Myriad tentacles rose from her titan-alm lower half, whipping forward with a wild celerity.

Tiona and Tione responded to the tentacle onslaught with a swift counterattack of their own.

"" "This thing's tough!" "" The faces of the twin sisters twisted in identical grimaces at the speed and power of the incoming attack.

The shock was enough to rival Udaeus's pile-driver attack, and both sisters' hands tingled around the grips of their weapons. Even as they went to work pruning the raging appendages, the massive feelers remained unscratched.

The true deluge of tendrils was focusing its attack on Aiz some one hundred meders away. Combining their attacks with their companion's, the two sisters fought back unforgivingly against the relentless cat-o'-nine-tails-like thrashing.

"Riveria, hold off on your spells!" Finn called out, stopping Riveria as she moved to join the battle.

"What?!"

The prum hadn't even turned around. His back was to her, and his right thumb ached. There was a hint of distress permeating his voice.

"My thumb! It won't stop throbbing...Something's coming!" Finn's usual mask of leadership was beginning to crack. "We have to be prepared for anything!"

His instincts weren't to be taken lightly. He was the one person there most attuned to the battle.

And the creature—that goddess-like beauty—just smiled coyly in affirmation.

"Arise, flames."

In an instant, the spell was cast.

"A chant?!"

A kind of stupefied terror shot through the group like a bolt of lightning as a magic circle formed around the spirit's massive chassis.

In a flash, the brilliant red light of her spell rose up from the ominous pattern on the ground, enveloping her entire body.

"A monster? Casting a spell?! You've gotta be kidding me!" Tione cried out in exasperation.

It was impossible. It was unthinkable that a being that survived on instinct and brutal destruction possessed the ability to cast any sort of magic.

The reason and intelligence required of magic was a domain limited to people and people alone—it was not a realm where monsters could tread.

It might have been a spirit, but this thing still had the body of a monster!

The magic circle of crimson widened.

Then it burst, an outpouring of magic power surging forth from its light.

Finn's eyes widened in surprise, but he formulated an order all the same. "Riveria! A barrier!" His voice had an edge to it the others had never before heard.

Instantly, Riveria began casting a spell, the desperation evident on her face.

"The rest of you! We need magic! Throw out everything you've got!" Finn's commands continued one after another. Raul and the other supporters let out a roar with their magic swords as Lefiya voiced a spell.

"L-let her have it!!"

"*FUSILLADE FALLARICA!!*"

The supporters unleashed a simultaneous barrage from their magic swords as Lefiya released her fire arrows by the hundreds, all of them careening toward the spirit.

The entire floor was bathed in light. In response, the creature gathered its ten gargantuan petals frontward to protect her lower half. Smile never faltering, she continued her chant, and in front of her erupted a thunderous explosion, its shock waves leaving behind flash after brilliant flash.

Lefiya and the others peered through the din of stray blasts tearing the ground and hurling fragments of hard earth, only to find the flower petals—and subsequently the spirit herself—unharmed and untroubled.

Tsubaki laughed. "Didn't work, huh?"

They'd failed.

Not even Lefiya's tremendous firepower could penetrate that thing's exterior, and that thought alone was enough to convince them their every attack was useless. Lefiya, Raul, and the other supporters could only look on in terror as Tsubaki stared daggers at the creature's impenetrable armor of flower petals.

"What's that thing made of, anyway…?" she murmured under her breath.

"*Rage, rage, RAGE! Vortex of fire! The crimson wall! Hellfire's roar! May the ardor of the gale plunge the world into grief and misery! The sky shall burn! The earth shall ignite! The seas shall boil! The fonts shall churn! The mountains shall erupt! All life shall turn to ash! May the lives of the great ones serve as atonement for the coming choler and grief—!*"

"*Dance, spirits of the air, keepers of the light! Forge thy pledge with the forest's protectors and envelop us in the psalm of the earth! Surround us!*"

The two spells were chanted at the same time.

The ominous song met the sweetly ringing translucence of Riveria's protection spell—both elves' eyes trembling in horrified wonderment at the length of the spirit's chant.

It was a protracted spell song.

Unbelievably long yet so fast, it overcame even Riveria's rapid-fire words. A colossal mass of magic power surpassing human knowledge, unattainable by humans, cocked and loaded with the utmost of swiftness.

As the spirit's alluring features crinkled in delight, the high elf's visage twisted in alarm.

"We can't even get close to it…!!"

Aiz, Tiona, and the others were still attempting to attack the creature directly, struggling to ward off the throng of tentacles as the magic shook the entire floor. The great, sweeping assaults mowed down everything in their path, monsters included, not allowing the adventurers to advance even one step forward. They already had their hands full keeping the tentacles and monsters away from Riveria.

The monster still chanted. *"Your envoy beseeches you, Salamander! Incarnate of fire! Queen of flame—!"*

Tiona and Tione slashed again and again at the oncoming tentacles.

Gareth, Bete, and Tsubaki faced off against the swarm.

Raul, Lefiya, and the other supporters unleashed arrows and magic in fruitless onslaughts.

And Aiz. The rain of whipping tentacles still approached her, relentless in its pursuit.

The spells and endless throng of tendrils made for an impenetrable wall of armor protecting the spirit.

Everything came at them at once—an opponent that could attack, defend, and chant all at the same time—and as Finn took in the battle before him, he could feel his teeth grind with increasing ferocity.

"—Retreat! Pull back to Riveria's barrier!!" He gave the order, knowing all too well where things were heading.

Still backed by Lefiya's and the other supporters' cover fire, those on the front line made their way back to Finn. Riveria completed her chant the moment they arrived, almost as if she had planned it.

"Materialize, mighty barrier of forest's light, and lend us your protection—my name is Alf!" With a wave of her hand, Riveria completed her chant—the ultimate protection spell. *"Via Shilheim!!"*

A jade-colored magic circle formed beneath Riveria's feet, the light gleaming before transforming into a dome-like green structure. It surrounded all thirteen of the adventurers, Riveria included.

It happened at the same time. The exact moment that the high elf's physical- and magic-attack-canceling barrier erected itself around them…

The spirit finished her own chant.

"Fire Storm!"

The world turned red.

"_____"

It was a massive inferno, akin to a fire elemental.

A raging, broiling wave of wind. A tsunami of flame. A river of incendiary crimson that closed in on Riveria inside her barrier.

It swallowed everything. The monsters. The magic dome with the adventurers inside. The entire floor itself.

"~~~~~~~~~~~~~~~~~~~~~~~!"

The impact was sensational. A thundering boom as hellfire met barrier, joined by Riveria's anguished cry as she struggled to support her staff with both hands.

Screams of agony surrounded them as everything outside the barrier fried instantly, and Riveria's jade eyes dilated to their limit.

The party found themselves petrified as they watched the world turn to a living hell past the safety of their barrier.

And then.

Crack.

A splinter formed in the barrier of the strongest magic user in all of Orario.

"The shield…?!"

In front of them, above them, to their left, to their right, spiderweb-like cracks ran the entire length of the wall of light. Raul's and Lefiya's faces lost all color.

The explosive wave of hellfire closed in on them from all sides.

"—Gareth! Protect them!!" Riveria screamed, the scorching heat all but consuming her.

Gareth responded in an instant and snatched two large shields from the supporters before leaping behind Riveria.

There was a high-pitched shriek. Riveria's Via Shilheim shattered.

"RIVERIA—?!"

Riveria went first.

As she was swallowed up by the massive stream of raging crimson fire, Aiz's scream disappeared into the roiling swell.

Then it hit Gareth with a colossal impact as it slammed into the two giant shields.

"Grrrruuuuoooooooooooooaaaa*AAAAAAAAAGGGGGHHHHH HHHHH*!!" the dwarf soldier groaned as Riveria disappeared into the swirling inferno.

Behind him, Tiona threw Aiz to the ground. Finn and the others were already hugging the earth in Gareth's shadow.

But it wasn't enough. The two shields melted at a laughably rapid speed. Gareth's helmet and armor liquefied around him.

"GRAMPS!!" Bete cried out as the shields disappeared entirely.

Gareth had no choice but to fling his arms out, using his body itself to block the relentless conflagration.

"GGGRRAAAAAAAAAAAAAAAAAAAA*AAAAGGGGGGGGHHH HHHHHHHHHH*!!"

The dwarf's titanic roar met the incoming inferno—

The explosion was immeasurable.

Everything went red. The blast sent Aiz and the others flying back with an incredible force.

Their skin and armor sizzled and charred as the crimson cyclone tossed the first-tier adventurers about, yet somehow they still managed to hold on to their weapons. They couldn't even scream. The charred hiss of flaming destruction enveloped the world around them. Again and again they tumbled along the ground, Lefiya, Raul, and the other supporters escaping the brunt of it thanks to Finn's protection.

The flame purged everything.

"Grrn…hnn?!"

The storm finally cleared to reveal Aiz and the others scattered about like corpses atop the scorched earth.

Nothing remained but charred ash as far as the eye could see. No monsters. No magic stones. Not even the jungle behind them was left. Everything had turned to cinders and dust. The floor of the Dungeon around them had become a different world with nothing but the spirit at its center unchanged.

They'd escaped the full force of the wave, but even the aftershocks had left them in disrepair—their armor and bodies were marred with cuts and burns. Moaning in pain, they shakily peeled themselves off the ground, no one saying a word.

Riveria lay facedown, the magic gem of her silvery white staff cracked. Her robes, made from holy fabrics of considerable magic resistance, were burned to a crisp and lying in tatters around her.

Gareth had tumbled a short distance away, his body charred and lying faceup. He'd held out to the very end in order to protect Aiz and the others, and his armor was painted black.

The elven magic user and dwarf soldier lay motionless. Silent.

Lefiya, Raul, Tiona, Tione, Bete, everyone could do nothing but look on, a kind of crippling despair twisting and contorting their features.

They were gone. All the familia's leaders save Finn.

Two of *Loki Familia*'s strongest warriors had passed.

They'd reached an unprecedented state of emergency.

"Riveria…Gareth…" Aiz's voice was hoarse as the two names passed her lips.

They'd lost their familia's two pillars of support. Morale had hit a new low.

The sight in front of them was enough to break the hearts of the young adventurers.

Even Finn, holding himself up by his charred arms, found his green eyes tightening.

"Moan, mighty earth—"

But it wasn't over yet.

"＿＿＿＿＿＿＿"

The spirit began her next spell, a coy smile playing on her face.

—it was too fast.

Already, the black magic circle was forming beneath her, a deep obsidian color different from the one before.

She hadn't paused even a moment to allow the post-magic rigor to abate before her next chant was well on its way, and the unbelievable spectacle rooted Aiz and the others to their spots.

"Rise, rise, RISE! Husk of the earth! Sheen of iron! Hammer of the cosmos! May genesis's pact upheave rock and stone! The sky shall burn! The earth shall split! The bridge shall rise! Heaven and earth shall become one! May the axes of the ether rain down and bring about calamity's ruin—!"

Another long, protracted chant. But they knew that destruction was imminent.

"Your envoy beseeches you, Gnome! Incarnate of the land! Queen of the earth—!"

There was no hesitation. No pause. She sang the melody bestowed unto her with an incredible facility, bringing it to completion.

It was partly shock that triggered the first-tiers' instincts. The moment they hit the ground running, the spirit let out her final note as a dark cloud of blackest light enshrouded her body.

"Meteor Swarm!!"

The circle flashed, and light shot straight up to coat the ceiling in shadow.

The magic converged, and thousands upon thousands of meteorites formed in the mass of darkness.

"Protect Raul and the others!!" Finn shouted, dashing forward to grab one of the supporters' arms.

And in that moment, the storm began.

"Whuuuaaaaaaaaaaaa*aaa*AAAAAAAAAAAHHHHH!" Raul's scream echoed throughout the fifty-ninth floor as they were caught in a vortex of destruction and exploding bedrock.

Bete grabbed hold of him as the two were knocked off their feet. Aiz grabbed Lefiya, holding her tight as they disappeared into the inky blackness. Tiona and Tione flung themselves toward the remaining two supporters, and Tsubaki used her body as a shield to protect them. The entire Dungeon shook around them as the glimmering black meteors pummeled the earth over a tremendous radius.

Aiz felt her gauntlets go flying, but she paid them no heed, never releasing her grip on the magic user in her arms. As they rode the shock wave, she saw Riveria's and Gareth's bodies being pelted mercilessly by the swarm of black comets.

She screamed, but no sound came out.

Everything was under the control of those savage chains of light.

"...ghn...ah."

"D-dammit...!!"

Bete dug his fingers into the already scorched earth, Raul moaning listlessly in his arms.

A giant crater had formed. The adventurers lay sprawled out a short distance from the massive hole, smoke and inky black particles marbling the air above their bodies. The spirit smiled sweetly at them from atop her massive chassis as first one, then two, then the rest of them began to stir, somehow managing to push themselves shakily to their feet.

Their quick instincts and expeditious defensive maneuvers had allowed them to weave their way through the massive storm of meteorites and narrowly escape with their lives.

"Everyone alive back there?" Tsubaki smiled weakly, her right arm completely carbonized and hanging uselessly at her side.

"Just barely..." Tione responded as she pushed herself free of the supporter she'd been protecting.

Tiona, too, hazily cracked open her eyes. Narfi, in tears, administered a restorative potion for the pain.

"M-Miss Aiz...?"

"Hnngh...hah...hngh..." Aiz could reply to Lefiya's plea only with stilted gasps. The instinctive cast of her Airiel had lasted mere seconds against the direct blast of meteors, and the mix of golden hair atop the two girls' heads was smattered and disheveled.

The golden pools of the spirit's eyes narrowed as she took in the scene before her. Spreading her supple arms, the two great flower buds along her lower half began to bloom.

"Is she…"

"…absorbing magic power?"

First the inky black particles floating around the room, and then the red particles, almost like embers, began drifting back toward that colossal, vibrantly colored ring.

Tiona and Tione could do nothing but stare in wonderment as the spirit recharged her consumed magic power. It was unthinkable—she should have used up almost all her magic reserves by this point, but by reabsorbing the scattered particles, she'd have a full tank. The hearts of every adventurer there dropped into their guts. The spirit devoured everything. Every single particle. Even the jade-colored magical residue left over from Riveria's shattered Via Shilheim.

Once she was fully recharged, she'd be able to ravage them with her dreadnought-like, wide-range annihilation spells once more.

As beautiful as the spirit looked with those particles of light around her, all Aiz and the others saw was the grim reaper's scythe about to bestow the finishing blow.

"*Laa*—…"

The spirit lifted her slender chin, a new melody lilting from her lips.

The high-pitched voice weaving its cherubic song seemed so childlike and innocent, and as she sang, a multitude of shadows formed behind her.

"Are those…monsters?" Lefiya's eyes trembled with anguish as she took in the sight of that vivid yellow-green skin.

They were coming from a massive hole behind her—a hole reaching all the way to the sixtieth floor—a legion of caterpillars and violas all summoned by the singing spirit.

The sight of that great army, of that spirit wrapped in her gown of many colors, dispelled what little strength the adventurers had left.

"Is this the…end?" Tsubaki murmured, supporting her useless arm as her right eye blurred with an unspoken truth.

The others knew it, too. Bete, Tiona, Tione, all of them still kneeling on the ground. The last thing they'd wanted to do was abandon hope, but the current situation appeared beyond dire. Lefiya felt her eyes well up with tears as she bit down on her lip. Raul's and the other supporters' eyes refused to leave the ground.

Still on the floor herself, Aiz kept her hand around Desperate's hilt, her eyes trained on the writhing mass of approaching monsters.

All around her, the weapons of her fellow adventurers lay strewn across the ashen earth.

Swords. Spears. Axes. Staves. Shields.

A desolate scene that brought back memories of her dream.

Though the unbreakable weapons still retained their shapes, their luster had faded to a dull sheen, as though resonating with their owners. With disgusting sounds, the swarm of monsters gathered around their queen, simply staring up at the sea of stars that was the drifting particles of light.

Aiz was silent, unable to so much as lift her blade.

"..."

It was then that it happened.

Finn rose to his feet, wiping his soiled face vigorously.

Step by step, the golden-haired prum advanced.

Farther and farther he continued, past Raul with his head raised, past Lefiya in her bewilderment, past Bete as he turned around questioningly, past Tsubaki with her right eye trained on him, and past Aiz, staring at him wordlessly.

He picked his spear up from off the ground and stood defiantly before the spirit and her army, his back to his companions.

Then he thrust the head of the spear into the ground.

"We're going to destroy that thing."

He made his declaration, green eyes flashing as they stared down the sweetly smiling spirit in front of him.

Tiona and the others let out audible gulps.

He shot a glance back at the stunned adventurers.

"I ask you for courage. Tell me, what is it you see before you?"

A repulsive amalgamation of spirit and monster.

A being that surpassed human knowledge with the ability to command an army of monsters.

"Do you see fear? Despair? Ruin? I see nothing but an enemy we must bring to its knees. We can surely prevail."

A tremble passed through the shoulders of the entire party.

He continued. His tiny frame was all that stood between them and the horror that awaited them.

"We've never needed an escape route. And we don't need one now. I'll clear a path myself with this very spear!" he exclaimed, eyes filled with determination as he looked back at his companions. "I vow in the name of Phiana herself that we shall prove victorious! So follow me!"

Their whole bodies were shaking now. Tiona's, Tione's, Bete's—all of their chests and eyes, their arms and legs quaked violently.

As they gazed at the figure standing before them, Raul curled his hand into a fist, and Lefiya felt her heart well up with courage.

If the ability to incite armies, to uplift, to promote, to demand inspiration no matter the time, no matter the place was a requirement for herohood, then truly, the "Braver" Finn Deimne was more hero than anyone else.

"Or is following in the steps of that boy Bell Cranell too much for you to handle?"

More than anything else, Finn was a prodigy when it came to *lighting fires in people's bellies*.

"_____"

In an instant, Bete and the others were transported to the scene of that decisive battle.

The crazed bull and the lone boy carving away at each other's life force. That true adventurer, wagering everything, his body, his soul, for that one fight.

The lingering memory of that brutal match set their very souls alight.

There was nothing more passionate. Nothing more pure. Nothing nobler.

It was a page in the great epic.

Aiz's eyes widened as the sight of that boy's back played across her mind once more.

The back of that boy overlaid on her father's.

"—Hell if I'm gonna let some pipsqueak like this take me down!!" Bete howled in fury as he rose to his feet.

"...A little full of ourselves there, are we?" Tione responded as she swept her bangs out of her eyes before joining him.

"This is our adventure, too!" Tiona jumped up, a giant smile plastered across her face.

Aiz rose, too, a glint in her eye as she adjusted her grip on her silver sword.

They snatched their weapons from off the ground. Twin blades, halberd, greatsword—they all shone with a renewed brilliance as though filled once more with their owners' fighting spirit.

Raul and the other supporters could only gaze in wonder as, one by one, the first-tiers swelled up with an invigorated dynamism. Gone was the grief and hopelessness. There was only their brilliantly burning spirits.

Bell Cranell...!

Lefiya's heart ignited with a fiery passion as that name graced her ears.

In her mind, she could see him running out ahead of her, and the thought of it stoked the coals already ablaze within her chest. Following in line with Aiz and the others, she tightened her hands around the grip of her staff and rose to her feet.

Raul and the other supporters looked on in mute amazement and then pulled themselves together and leaped off the ground, jaws set.

A kind of immeasurable energy that went beyond limits had seized the party.

"Raul! You and the others will stay behind and back us up! The rest of us will charge that thing! You, too, Lefiya! You're with us!" Finn shouted at the reawakened adventurers, returning his eyes to the spirit still at work absorbing magic power from the air, while the supporters scrambled about to retrieve their scattered weapons.

"Understood!"

Once their armaments had been speedily returned to them, Lefiya and the first-tiers readied themselves for their first—and last—charge.

Finn stood with his back to them as they rushed about. Once he'd received his second Durandal spear, he approached the bodies of the elf and dwarf still lying on the ground.

"Riveria…Gareth…Is this the end?" He averted his eyes, having no desire to see his two friends splayed out like lifeless corpses.

No, the only direction he looked now was forward, at the enemy in front of them.

"If so, then rest. My story hasn't finished."

Voice filled with ambition, with determination, he stepped forward.

He would continue, even if it meant leaving them behind.

"Forward!!" He turned around to issue the command to his companions, now that their preparations were complete.

And then they were off, their hearts raging as they rushed that teeming mass of howling monsters.

Twitch.

The left hand of a certain dwarf trembled at the sound of those rushing feet.

Five fat fingers dug into the ground before grasping it tight.

"Damn cheeky little…prum!" Gareth pushed himself to his feet, a genuinely chagrined smile playing on his face.

He turned to the elf next to him, her own hand stirring as she raised her gaze.

"And what do you think you're doing, elven wench? You think this is the time to be sleeping?!"

"…Silence, you abominable dwarf." Riveria drew her staff to her, chuckling with a bold audacity.

They were back. They were leaking blood and at each other's throats the same as when they'd first met, but they had returned.

"Sir Gareth…Miss Riveria…!!" Raul cried out, tears threatening the corners of his eyes at the tenacity, the fortitude, the unbreakable bond the leaders of their familia shared.

"My ax, boy!!" the dwarf bellowed, and the supporters were quick to toss the legendary warrior his Grand Ax. Then he dashed off after Finn and the others with a raging howl, completely undeterred by the wounds all over his body.

"You all—protect me!" Riveria instructed as she readied her staff, her own body covered in lacerations. She was already summoning a jade-colored magic circle beneath her feet.

"Roger!!" Raul and the other supporters responded in sync, quickly doing as they'd been told.

There was a vivid flash. Her strongest spell began to take shape.

Abandoning all unnecessary movement, the most powerful magic user in Orario focused solely on her chant.

"...Well, I'll be damned!" Tsubaki's eye narrowed as she took in the sight of the reinvigorated *Loki Familia*. "Better be gettin' your act together, too, old girl!" Right arm still dangling at her side, she readied her *tachi* in her left hand and dove headfirst into the throng.

· The final battle had begun.

Light swirled around them in a raging vortex toward the ghastly vessel at its center.

Two hundred meders. That was all that remained between them and the corrupted spirit still greedily devouring magic power, and they made a beeline toward her, weapons flashing.

They moved like the wind. A thunderous howl rose up to meet them the moment they clashed with the massive army of monsters.

"Aiz, save your strength! We'll need you to land the finishing blow! The rest of you, protect her!"

One strike.

They were betting everything on a single strike.

Finn knew that against an enemy like this, one that had countless methods of attack and defenses like a fortress, any chance they could finagle would be momentary at best.

Aiz needed to save up her power, and he and the other first-tiers needed to get her next to that thing at all costs, even if it meant a few sacrifices along the way.

They'd use every ounce of their power to cut a way through the teeming mass and guide Aiz toward the corrupted spirit.

She nodded and activated her Airiel.

"Awaken, Tempest!!"

The flowing armor of wind quickly encircled her body.

The rest of the party changed formation, moving Aiz and her winds of enchantment to the center and placing Finn at the head to form an arrowhead shape.

A silver bolt to pierce the heart of that creature.

"Lefiya, begin chanting something! Anything!" Finn shouted as Aiz began amassing her wind power.

"Understood!"

And then Finn himself began to chant.

"Spear of magic, I offer my blood! Bore within this brow—" The ultrashort chant on his lips as he ran, his left hand was quickly dyed a deep bloodred as it amassed magic power.

He closed his eyes and pressed his thumb, now a brilliant red, against his forehead like the sharpened point of his spear. The moment it touched, the glowing magic power rushed inside him.

"Hell Finegas!"

Finn's emerald eyes burst open, now stained a murderous shade of crimson.

"*—GggwwwwwwwwwuuuuuuuuuooooooooooGGGGGGGHHHH HHH!!*" The usually taciturn prum leader screamed with all the strength and savagery of a feral warrior.

Hell Finegas was Finn's spell for bolstering fighting spirit.

It gave him a lust for battle, drawing out a bloodthirsty passion from deep within him while greatly boosting his abilities.

At the same time, however, it greatly *reduced* his rational thought processes.

—Finn was done giving orders.

Aiz and the others realized that all too well the moment they saw their leader transform into that barbaric soldier.

Everything now was to get Aiz to that spirit, which meant prioritizing abilities over orders.

From here on out, each one of them would be giving their own commands.

Tiona, Bete, and Lefiya silently adjusted their grips on their weapons. At the same time, Finn took back the Durandal spear he'd entrusted to Tione.

He flung himself headlong into the oncoming monster swarm, his tiny frame looking even smaller next to the two long spears in his hands.

All alone he rushed forward, away from the rest of the party, war cry straining his lungs.

"————————————————————HNNGHH!!"

The slaughter began.

Before the caterpillar at the front of the horde could even think of releasing its corrosive acid, the upper half of its body was forcefully wrested from its frame by the prum's Durandal spear. Legs went flying, followed by a hail of fleshy chunks. The spear continued, hitting the monsters to its left, its right, behind it—all of them exploding and scattering in pulpy pops with that single swing of his spear.

The prum hardly took notice of the carnage he'd created, moving fluidly into frenzied slashes of his two spears.

"*Wuuuuuuuuuuuuuoooooooooooooaaaaaaaaaaaarrrrrrrgggghhhh!!*"

The long silver pikes plowed through caterpillar after caterpillar. Finn's scream shook the walls as acid sprayed and splattered. The relentless slashes dug deep into the caterpillars' flesh, all the way to their cores, shattering their magic stones and sending clouds of ash dancing through the air.

He destroyed every one of them in his path. Nothing could touch him. Not the caterpillar's acid. Not the violas' tentacles. He crawled the ground like a crazed beast, bypassing every incoming attack as he robbed the fiends of life with each flash of his spear.

"It's been a long time since I've seen Finn like this...!" Tione murmured as she and the others witnessed the bloodbath occurring before them. Though this certainly wasn't the first time they'd witnessed Finn's berserker form, the inhuman butcher in front of them was so far removed from the leader they knew that they could only look on in awe, eyes trembling. Even the Sword Princess, still surrounded by her armor of wind, found the color draining from her face at the sheer power of their prum leader. In only a matter of seconds, a mountain of carcasses had formed in front of them.

The lancer's howl continued unbroken, his reddened eyes desperately craving, desperately lusting for blood.

He single-handedly plowed his way through the teeming throng, the true point of their arrowhead formation, while Tiona and the others took out any other monsters that drew near.

"*Ah-ha.*"

Still in the process of recharging, the spirit turned her gaze toward Finn and the group in their rapid approach and unleashed a flurry of thick tentacles.

Bete and the other first-tiers fought them back in an effort to protect Aiz. Finn, on the other hand, neatly chopped three of them in half. The sound of it reverberated off the walls as the three fat whips recoiled and twitched. A look of disbelief crossed the spirit's face.

Braver had both a golden spear and a silver spear.

In his right hand was his tried-and-true weapon of choice—the Fortia Spear. Often called the "Brave Fortia Spear," it was a Superior weapon with a golden tip.

In his left was the silver Durandal spear—Roland Spear. Armed with these two spears, Finn was a veritable whirlwind.

"*—But it all ends now,*" the spirit said with pure scorn after her moment of surprise.

The multicolored ring she'd been using to absorb the magic power closed, and she returned her two great flower buds to her lower half. Then she raised her arms, her gown shuddering with the movement.

"*Arise, flame—*"

Once more, the repulsively ethereal voice began to sing. Once more, she began casting her spell.

"More magic?!" Tione cried out in alarm.

"Shit!!" Bete immediately responded as the two of them watched the magic circle begin to form beneath the spirit's feet, accompanied by a brilliant red light.

There was still a good hundred meders left between them and the creature, and a wall of monsters yet blocked their path. There was no way they'd make it in time.

In front of them, the spirit raised her armor of flower petals—ten colossal shields she kept stored behind her lower chassis. Aiz, Bete, and the others could only watch in despair as she began uttering the same protracted chant as before, her iron-wall-like defenses already in place.

"Your envoy beseeches you, Salamander! Incarnate of fire! Queen of flame—!"

The spell was finished before they knew it, magic light swelling up around her. The hearts of not only Aiz and the other first-tiers but Raul's and the supporters' in the back, as well, dropped into their guts.

Then Finn jumped.

Gripping his gold-tipped spear and grinding his teeth together, he hurled himself at the spirit, a prum cannonball.

"AAAAAAAAAAAAAAAAAARRRRRRRRRRRRRRRRGGGG GGGGGGGGGGGHHHHHHHH!!"

There was a brilliant flash of golden light as Braver shot forward.

Then, with a flash of his red eyes, he launched his weapon. The Fortia Spear hurtled forward, puncturing the very air itself and transforming into a beam of light that rocketed straight toward the spirit.

The distance between them might as well not have even existed considering the speed at which that spear traveled. It was to her in an instant.

"Gngh!"

The spear plunged into the spirit's face just as she was about to release her spell.

It sailed past the armor of flower petals so fast it was nothing but a single point as it dove straight into her open, chanting mouth.

It was a direct hit. Passing all the way through her head, the golden tip of the spear protruded out the back near the lower half of her brain stem.

© Kiyotaka Haimura

The spirit bent backward from equal parts shock and awe—Finn had triggered an Ignis Fatuus.

"?!"

The unexpected impact left her faltering, unable to control the magic so close to release.

And then she lost it. The massive net of magic power broke, spilling out unchecked, and she erupted in flames. The explosion was colossal. A giant blast, large enough to mask her entire body, detonated from inside her, and the crimson magic circle she'd summoned fizzled into nothingness.

Aiz and the other first-tiers found themselves in stupefied awe as Raul and the other supporters behind them let out cries of joy.

"NOW!!" Tione screamed, stepping in for Finn, and everyone took off.

Bete and Tiona eliminated the remaining caterpillars and violas surrounding them, allowing the group to finally break through the teeming army.

Fleshy chunks of meat flew around them as a path opened up straight to the spirit.

"Please—give me strength! Elf Ring!!" Lefiya shouted, finishing up her Concurrent Casting the moment they ploughed through the monster obstacles.

Her summon burst was ready. A small, golden magic circle formed around her running feet, waiting for her next command. In a constantly changing battle such as this, she needed to be ready for anything, so she simply held her breath, siphoning more and more power into the spell as she waited for the perfect time to release.

She and the rest of the party upped their speed with the flaming spirit in their sights.

"…"

From within the rising smoke, the spirit swayed, her skin charred and blackened.

A single tentacle rose, curling around the spear currently skewering her throat and tugged it out with a jerk. There was a *snap* as the spear was broken in two.

The pieces of the gold-tipped spear dropped to the ground with a clatter, and then the spirit healed herself with an ignition of magic power. In only a matter of seconds, the gaping hole in her throat was filled with flesh. She smiled.

Still scattering residual magic power from her auto-regeneration, she turned the golden pools of her eyes toward Finn and the others.

"*Pierce, spear of lightning! Your envoy beseeches thee, Tonitrus! Incarnate of thunder! Queen of lightning—!*"

A golden magic circle appeared in front of her eyes.

"A short chant?!" Tiona cried out at the almost instantaneous spell.

Short chants excelled when it came to pure speed, and considering this was a spirit they were dealing with, the power behind it would be nothing to balk at, either—not even comparable to the spells of a normal magic user.

No, this was a spell that could stand up to even the best of the best, and the sight of that loaded magic gun made the eyes of every adventurer there—Finn and his Hell Finegas included—widen in terror.

Brilliantly sparkling beams of lightning burst forth from the midair magic circle.

Time itself seemed to stop as an electric glimmer seared the adventurers' faces.

"*Thunder Ray!*" the spirit screamed.

The all-powerful spell, reserved for the spirits of the Ancient Times, enveloped Aiz and the others with a deafening roar.

"*—Shield me, cleansing chalice!*"

She had to stop it!

The moment the words burst from her throat, Lefiya leaped in front of the others.

The golden magic circle at her feet transformed into a circle of pure white, filled to the brim with the power to save the people she loved the most.

Lefiya unleashed the ultrashort chant of her friend with a speed that surpassed that of her enemy's.

"*Dio Grail!!*"

A snow-white, circular barrier surrounded them.

Less than a second later, the two magic spells collided.

"~~~~~~gnh?!"

Lefiya's body began to sink, both hands tightly gripping her staff.

The massive thunder attack pummeled the round barrier. Then, just like with Riveria's spell earlier, there was a high-pitched screech, and a crack formed across its surface.

It couldn't take much more. Though the spirit's current spell didn't come close to the power behind the earlier protracted chant that had shattered Riveria's Via Shilheim, it still contained incredible force. Lefiya let out a scream of anguish as the white fissure grew with every passing second.

Aiz and the others could only watch as their fields of vision went white. The spirit's magic—magic that could easily swallow them whole—was fully prepared to crush the spell of the tiny elf in front of them.

Lefiya's knees began to give; sparks flew as her barrier screamed.

Then.

"LEFIYA!!"

"You can do iiiiiiiit—!"

Two shadows ran past her, colliding with the barrier.

It was Tione and Tiona. Durandal halberd and greatsword crossing, they slammed themselves against the white shield.

They were supporting her Dio Grail in its attempt to hold back the lightning.

"Tiona! Tione!" Aiz cried out as Lefiya's eyes slammed shut.

The two brave first-tier adventurers used their own bodies as shields, not even caring as their skin instantly scorched under the full brunt of the sparking electricity.

Lefiya's knees screamed at her, so close to giving out beneath her.

Was this it, then? Was this the best she could do?

"—I can do it, too," she whispered as Aiz, Bete, and Finn stood behind her.

In front of her were Tiona and Tione, blocking that omnipotent spear of thunder with their bodies.

Her body ignited. Blood and magic churning, boiling, frothing within her, her azure eyes opened with an almost audible *snap*.

"ICANDOIT,TOOOOOOOOOOOOOOOOOOOOOOOOO——!!"

The two spells neutralized each other.

"!"

Lefiya roared as light burst from the pure-white barrier, pushing back the incoming lightning and erupting in a giant explosion.

They destroyed each other, spirit and elven magic rupturing in a brilliant light storm that sent shock waves rippling from the impact. Tiona and Tione went flying, and even Lefiya herself was sent straight back at an incredible speed.

The other adventurers didn't even look back as the three girls whizzed past them but pushed forward immediately.

"NOW!!" Bete howled as the three dashed ahead, Finn with his spear and Aiz with her accumulated wind power.

Tears pricked at Aiz's eyes, her pupils trembling at the courage, at the sacrifice of her companions, but she stayed on target, nothing but that towering corrupted spirit in her sights as she shifted her grip on Desperate's hilt. She was the Sword Princess..

And only three of them remained.

Only some fifty meders stood between them and the spirit.

"—*Harbinger of the end, white snow.*"

A clear, ringing tune rang out behind them.

From the giant magic circle over two hundred meders away. Standing at the center of that flowerlike magic circle of jade was Riveria, her silvery-white staff, Magna Alf, primed and ready.

The high elf's eyes were tightly shut, her focus on nothing but the spell at hand.

This was it. The most powerful spell of the most powerful magic user in Orario. The true ultimate spell that would take every ounce of Mind she had.

"Get your magic swords ready!" Raul shouted at the other three supporters even as they warily eyed the building waves of magic power forming behind the elf. They needed to prepare for the multitude of monsters drawn to the massive magic power building around Riveria and approaching her without so much as a glance at Aiz, Bete, and Finn. The army of caterpillars and violas kicked up a storm of dust and smoke behind them.

"Aim for the caterpillars! Don't let a single one through! Then we'll take on the violas behind them!" Raul called, sounding more and more like Finn.

The three Level 4 adventurers nodded. They only needed to take out the acid-spewing caterpillars from afar with their ranged weapons. The remaining violas could then be taken out using any means possible.

Gripping their long magic swords with their superior power and endurance, they took aim, then let their power fly.

"Gust before the twilight."

Flame, lightning, ice, then flame again—the rounds of magic ammunition hit the oncoming caterpillars with godlike precision.

Again and again they launched their elemental salvos, the sound of Riveria's chant in their ears. One by one, the caterpillars exploded until finally Raul's magic sword reached its limit and shattered in his hands. He quickly kicked open the backpack next to him and grabbed a bow and arrow.

A true jack-of-all-trades, he deftly aimed his arrow into the throng, shooting first one, then two, then three of the oncoming caterpillars right through their hearts, piercing their magic stones and turning them to ash.

"—Raul! Behind you!!" one of the other supporters screamed. Try as they might to take them out, the army of caterpillars was almost upon them.

"!"

Indeed, when Raul turned around he saw a new swarm of caterpillars and violas a ways behind Riveria but pressing closer every second.

The green wall that should have been blocking their path back to the fifty-eighth floor had gone up in flames together with the rest of the jungle thanks to the spirit's earlier inferno, leaving the passage-way open for monsters from the upper levels.

They were caught in the middle of a pincer attack, and they only had one magic sword left. Raul's voice stuck in his throat—he had no idea how to proceed. It was at that moment that Tsubaki rose to her feet with a swish of her red *hakama*, her right arm fully restored.

"Leave those critters to me."

"Huh?!"

"Toss me one of those, will ya?" she said as she motioned to the weapons left behind by Gareth and the others. Having stripped her-self of her battle clothes to heal her arm, she stood now in nothing but a single cloth. She took first Gareth's Durandal ax, then Tiona's Urga into her hands.

Tan skin bared, she dropped her *tachi* to the ground and took off running.

"M-Miss Tsubaki, you can't!!" Raul wailed as the smith headed straight for the swarm of monsters behind Riveria, ax in her right hand and Urga in her left.

It didn't matter *how* strong the half-dwarf was, there was no way she'd be able to wield Tiona's Urga and Gareth's Roland Ax, two of the heaviest custom-made weapons around, at the same time.

Tsubaki, however, was not one to care about such matters. Ignor-ing Raul's cry, she made a beeline for the oncoming monster mass, dodging a salvo of corrosive acid and promptly dismantling three caterpillars at once with a wave of her ax.

"Like hell I can't," she stated matter-of-factly before blocking another barrage of acid with her Durandal weapon. Or perhaps *block* wasn't the appropriate word, as the mighty swing of the heavy blade never stopped moving and sliced through the skin of one yellow-green caterpillar after another.

Utilizing the subsequent inertia, she sent Urga spinning with nothing but her left hand, slicing and bisecting the incoming violas, tentacles and all.

"Just how many weapons y'think I've made, huh?" She laughed haughtily, continuing her double-fisted slaughter as Raul and the other supporters looked on in awe. "Each and every one of 'em got a thorough test run."

The supporters' faces gave simultaneous twitches. She was absolutely relentless—no doubt having experienced anything and everything there was to experience when it came to armaments in her effort to one day create the ultimate weapon.

They didn't let their wonderment last long, however, and quickly returned to their defensive maneuvers as Tsubaki showed them just what a Level 5 could do, a grand smile playing on her lips.

"Fading light, freezing land," Riveria continued, her eyes closed, as Raul and the other supporters—and Tsubaki the one-woman army—continued fending off the oncoming monster army.

Her words came out faster and faster as the spell of ice and frost formed on her tongue.

"Blow with the power of the third harsh winter—advent of the end."

Only she didn't stop. She continued, transitioning directly into another spell.

"A blaze shall soon descend."

The jade-colored magic circle already formed beneath her grew in splendor as her chant shifted toward magic of complete and total annihilation—her inferno spell.

"Approaching flames of war from which this is no escape. Battle horns blaring on high, all atrocities and strife shall be engulfed."

Concatenated Chanting.

It was a special magic characteristic possessed solely by the high elf queen, Riveria Ljos Alf. A type of chant that could encompass any of the three spells expressed in her Status.

Just as different levels could exist within a single Status, so, too, did three levels of spell exist within her Magic.

From ultrashort chants to short chants, from short chants up to long chants, and from long chants all the way up to protracted chants.

By connecting the respective levels of chants, one could bolster the total magic output, change the magic's effects, and amplify their destructive power.

Offensive, defensive, healing—three different types of magic each with three different levels. This made for nine different spells the high elf could concatenate at will depending on the situation, which was where her alias, Nine Hell, had come from—a name of praise bestowed upon her by the gods.

And a name that struck fear and awe into her many elven brethren. It was the name of the strongest magic user in all of Orario.

"Come crimson pyre, merciless inferno. Become hellfire."

This was no longer simply her ice spell, Wynn Fimbulvetr. With each additional word of the concatenated chant, she focused even more Mind, a colossal amount.

The chant she wove now was a second-tier spell, the longest in her arsenal and boasting the greatest range. It was a spell that would set every enemy within its blast radius ablaze in holocaustic hellfire. The sublimation of ice into flame, short into long destructive power doubling in a spell of catastrophic proportions.

"Purge the battlefield, end the war."

Behind Raul and the other supporters, behind Tsubaki, her silvery-white staff stood ready. A brilliant light flashed from the cracked magic jewel at its tip as the mammoth magic power was released.

Her hair danced in the rippling waves of magic light flowing from her magic circle, and slowly, ever so slowly, she opened her jade eyes.

"Incinerate, sword of Surtr—My name is Alf!!"

It was complete.

As far, far ahead of her, a small white barrier offset the spirit's lightning attack, the magic circle at Riveria's feet grew to encompass the entire battlefield.

The adventurers, the army of monsters, and even the spirit itself—all of them found themselves standing upon glimmering jade radiance.

She had found it. The creature, in the middle of that massive army, threatening her companions even now. Then, she pronounced her spell.

"REA LAEVATEINN!!"

The eruption was immediate.

Inferno-like pyres of flaming destruction rose from the earth and burst forth from the magic circle.

They incinerated everything. The monsters attacking Raul, Tsubaki, and the other supporters, the army of monsters proliferating the perimeter, the violas approaching Lefiya, Tione, and Tiona on the ground—everything was swallowed by those swelling waves of pure hellfire.

And it didn't stop there. The raging flames traveled all the way to the ceiling, to the walls, scorching everything and setting the very air on fire with enough power to rival even the corrupted spirit's earlier firestorm and turning the Dungeon, once more, into a world of blazing red destruction.

"_____"

The spirit somehow managed to react as the radiating pillar of fire and brimstone erupted from the center of the magic circle, encasing her entire body in armor formed of ten giant flower petals.

Separating herself from her lower, titan-alm half, she prepared for the incoming attack.

Then *exploded.*

"~~~~~~~~~~~~~~~~~~~~~~~~~~~~~!"

It hit her ten times. A ten-pillar colonnade of devouring incandescence rocked the spirit's giant frame.

It was incalculably hot. Immensely powerful. Riveria's genocidal spell burned, gouged, charred, then ignited the surface of the armor-like flower petals.

They crackled and popped. The very same petals that had stood up to the magic of Lefiya and the magic swords without taking so much as a scratch now burned whole before falling to the ground.

"Riveria…"

Aiz felt every crevice of her body radiate sensational heat as she watched, surrounded by the high elf's flames of pure magic power.

Then she, Bete, and Finn took advantage of the magic user's assistance and propelled themselves still faster, their eyes flashing.

"…!"

For the first time, the spirit's smile vanished. Her defenses were gone.

Thirty meders remained. Nothing but a few short moments between them and the spirit. They hurtled through that world of fire, and as the spirit looked down on them, her lips tightened in rage.

Long green hair flowing, she opened her mouth.

"——Aaaaaaaaahhhhh!!"

And the earth responded.

From beneath their feet, from deep within the lower floors themselves, a multitude of green pikes burst through the floor as though summoned by that high-pitched call.

"!!"

The tentacles rose up, forming a mighty dome-like barrier some twenty meders wide around the spirit.

Bete's and Finn's eyes widened in surprise, and then the two of them zoomed forward, twin blades and silver spear whirling in an attempt to bring down the wall.

""Gngh!""

But it was no use.

Their blades sank into the green flesh but neither pierced nor cut the mighty shield. The sight of them rushing at it full tilt with absolutely zero effect made even Aiz shudder.

—All the speed, power, and force they'd built up during their charge was effectively nullified.

And now they'd given her a chance to cast another spell. The tables had been turned.

They'd lost their one chance, and time felt like it was screeching to a halt around them. Only then...

A giant whirling blade came rushing past them to collide with the massive green wall.

——*An ax?!*

The mighty ax plunged into the fleshy bulwark, cleaving a massive fissure. Before they could so much as register the surprise, however, a certain dwarf soldier sailed past them and dove at the wall.

"What? Was all that just talk, Finn?" Gareth goaded, the corners of his mouth turned up in a ferocious smile as he yanked his Great Ax from the green tentacles and promptly plunged it back in with another zealous swing.

The rift in the bulwark widened, though Bete and Finn hadn't even been able to make a dent.

And then Finn smiled. Eyes still red and all rational thought supposedly wiped from his mind, he shot his comrade-in-arms a wry grin.

"Don't make me say I knew you'd come."

"Hah! You wish!" Gareth guffawed before taking another whack with his ax.

The resulting clout was enough to shake the very ground beneath their feet. The rift grew larger still. There was so much force behind each swing of the ax that the blade was beginning to crack.

Aiz and Bete watched in wonder as Gareth abandoned the ax and clenched a boulder-like fist.

"Get outta my way!!"

He punched the great green wall of tentacles.

"I said BEAT IT!!"

Another punch. This time, a hole opened up in the fleshy barricade.

"*!*"

The spirit inside moved almost instantaneously.

And a multitude of tentacles suddenly burst through the ground at Gareth's feet.

"_____"

They impaled him.

One, two, three, a whole throng of them pierced through his body and held him aloft as blood gushed out from the many holes.

But even as the red liquid poured from his mouth, the dwarf only laughed ferociously.

"You'll have to do…better than THAAAAAAAAAAAAT!!"

His bellow reverberated off the walls.

Plunging both his hands into the breach as if he weren't leaking a waterfall of blood, he tore at the tentacles.

"Bete! Aiz!!" Finn screamed, and the two responded immediately by diving into the opening the dwarf had created.

Finn followed after, his comrade helping him through with a yank of his hand as he made it through the last of the barrier.

"*Ngh?!*"

They were a mere ten meders away now, and the spirit invested every tentacle she had into intercepting their attack.

The endless giant whips came at them in a frenzy, straight toward Aiz and the incredible wind power surrounding her, but Bete and Finn blocked them.

"Outta my way!" Bete shouted as he whipped out two magic swords from their leg holsters and slammed them down on his Frosvirt. The two boots ignited in the blink of an eye. Re-equipping his twin Durandal blades, he then threw himself at the flailing tendrils, pruning them whole.

"Burn in hell!!" His feet drew flaming arcs in the air as his two swords carved away with great silver gleams.

The four separate killing tools worked in sync, one on each of his limbs, whirling in a veritable blade dance that first lit the tentacles on fire, then severed them with the force of a raging wave.

It was do or die at this point. The two men fought back against the tentacle onslaught with everything they had.

""Guuurrrrrrrrraaaaaaaaaaaaaa*aaa*AAAAAAARRRGGGHH!!""

Their war cries overlapped.

Their armor was gone. Their bodies were riddled with wounds. But somehow they managed it. Twin blades and spear cut a single pathway.

""Aiz, go!!""

She ran.

Down the single path of survival she sprinted to take on the spirit herself.

It was just her and that thing now.

The cyclone of her Airiel versus that massive, towering creature.

As Aiz turned her gaze upward, her eyes met those deep golden pools.

—I am not Aria.

She told herself as she thought back to those first trembling words of joy the spirit had directed at her.

—And I do not know you.

She knew absolutely nothing about this thing besides the fact that the sight of it made her blood boil.

—All I know is that you shouldn't exist.

That much she knew.

Her golden eyes flashed as they took in the maleficent, venomous spirit of chaos before her.

Indeed, the blood running through her veins was already whispering to her.

Telling her to consign this monstrosity to oblivion.

With one swing of her sword, she was off, charging straight toward the spirit.

"...Ah."

The world above her was bathed in red, embers floating in the rising heat.

Lefiya stared up into that oversaturated world as her arms trembled to life.

A searing pain ransacked her body; devoid of strength, her eyes grew hazy and clouded.

Weakly, she raised a bedraggled arm toward the sky.

"Unleashed…beam of light…limbs of the…holy tree…"

She would sing.

It was the only song she had left in her.

A song that *she* could hear, even as she waged war against that terrifying enemy so far, far away.

"Loose your arrows…fairy archers…"

Even if she didn't turn around.

She would hear it, and it would soothe her, protect her, save her as it pushed back the enemy threatening her.

"You are the…master archer…"

Just like a fairy, dancing in the forest. Like a spirit, racing to save the one she loved.

Singing the song only she could sing.

"Pierce…arrow of…accuracy…"

She would deliver her song.

"…Arcs…Ray…"

"—Raaaaaaaaaaaaaaaaaaaaaaaaaaaaaaaaaaaaaaaaaaaaahhhhhhhhhhhh!!"

Aiz leaped.

Finally, the distance between them was gone. Kicking off from the ground, she sailed toward the colossal frame of her opponent.

Then she directed her sword, Desperate, at the main body of the spirit sitting atop the titan alm.

The spirit herself could only look on in blank amazement as Aiz drew near, cyclone-like power coursing through her—and then…

—She laughed.

"_____"

She opened those smiling lips to reveal the inside of her mouth, which housed a tiny magic circle.

The dancing tendrils had been nothing but a distraction to keep them from noticing the magic light forming inside her, the tiniest chant summoning the tiniest cerulean magic circle.

Her silence and expression of shock had only served to camouflage her next attack.

Aiz's features froze in terror upon realizing she'd been led right into a trap.

It was too late now. The spirit released her spell.

"Icicle Edge!"

The resulting pillar of ice was monstrous.

It struck instantaneously, leaving her no room to evade.

A massive blade of blue ice launched directly in front of her eyes.

An arrow of light shot forth from Lefiya's outstretched arm.

The single beam of light rose straight above her head before curving to run along the ground.

"Go..." Lefiya's voice trembled.

Find her. Fly to her.

"GO!!" She screamed it this time, her eyes closed.

The arrow's speed increased, almost as though responding to Lefiya's cry.

"REACH HER!!"

And it did. Lefiya's song reached all the way to Aiz.

And exploded against the incoming blade of ice.

"!!"

Neither Aiz nor the spirit saw it coming.

The arrow of light appeared from nowhere, slamming into the icy pillar in front of their eyes and diverting its path.

The spirit's attack zoomed straight past Aiz, tousling her golden hair, deflected by the final cover fire of a girl who'd refused to stop singing.

The moment Aiz realized what had happened, her eyes flashed. Facing the bewildered spirit, she swung her sword of wind with everything she had.

"Gnnnghhh!!"

"Nnngh!"

With an astonishing reflex, the spirit managed to bring her arms up to block the oncoming sword and its vortex-like gale.

The wind screamed.

As the spirit gripped the body of the sword in both hands, the squall tore her vibrant gown to shreds in an instant.

The sword trembled, imbued with all that massive current, then gave a flash as it plunged straight through the spirit's body.

Crimson blood welled from the creature's green skin.

"—*NO!!*"

Her face contorted in pain and agony as the sword, propelled by the tempestuous winds, bisected her whole. She flung up a single tentacle in immediate response.

The powerful whip was quick to break through Aiz's armor of wind, sending the swordswoman flying.

"AIZ!!"

Tiona and Tione, holding each other up, watched as the golden-haired, golden-eyed girl rocketed through the air in a shower of blood.

As did Riveria, standing there weakly.

As did Raul and the other supporters, exhausted and spent.

As did Tsubaki, supporting herself with her weapon.

As did Lefiya, still splayed across the ground.

As did Gareth, down on his knees.

As did Bete and Finn, sent flying by the flurry of flying whips.

The girl's body whirled as it crossed above the Dungeon floor.

"_____"

But even as blood poured from her head, her perception had not diminished. No, not even a single bit.

Eyes still as sharp as swords, she used the momentum of her flight to travel all the way to the Dungeon's ceiling—then *landed*.

She stood there, upside down, and drew Desperate behind her like a bowstring pulled taut.

"*Rage, Tempest———!!*"

She'd unleash everything.

All the Mind she'd collected within her, everything loaded into the cannon that was her Airiel.

A windstorm more powerful than a typhoon.

"*!*"

© Kiyotaka Haimura

The bloodied spirit directly below her immediately began weaving together a new chant.

"Light, gleam! Tear through the darkness! Your envoy beseeches thee, Lux! Incarnate of light! Queen of refulgence—!"

The ultrashort chant summoned a giant massive circle above her head to oppose the lone swordswoman.

Aiz's gaze met that of the spirit below her, then she pointed the tip of her sword toward the ground.

She was ready.

All eyes were on her.

"Aiz…" Riveria murmured.

"Do it, lass." Gareth's eyes narrowed.

"Go, Aiiiiiiiz!!" Tiona and Tione cried out in simultaneous encouragement.

"Crush that bitch!" Bete asserted.

"It's up to you now," Finn said with a smile.

"—Miss Aiiiiiiiiiiiiiiiiiiiiiiiiiiiiiiiiiiiiiiiiiiiiz!!" Lefiya screamed from her spot on the ground.

And then.

"Li'l Rafaga!!"

She released the storm.

"LIGHT BURST!!" the spirit said as she finished her own spell at the same time.

Spiraling arrow of wind met massive blast of light.

There was a momentary pause.

Then the whirling kamikaze blasted through the gleaming white light, eliminating it completely.

"_____"

The unbreakable sword impaled the spirit from her head to her chest.

A single flash of wind traveled from her seemingly feminine upper half to her monstrous lower half.

As the silver sword sliced her in half, the spiraling gale gouged out chunks of her flesh. The spirit's high-pitched shriek echoed throughout the hall.

Desperate passed all the way through, collided with the hard earth—and then exploded.

The wind thundered as the spirit turning instantly to ash, her magic stone shattered.

The resulting shock waves made the entire floor quake.

Still, the tempestuous gale continued, all the ash rising and whirling like a massive dust storm.

"~~~~~~~~~~~~~~~~~~~!"

The adventurers covered their faces with their arms in an attempt to protect themselves from the violent winds.

As the gale pushed them back, the brilliant flash painted their visions white.

The weapons thrust into the ground began to shake, resonating with the scream of Aiz's sword.

And still the storm continued to rage and howl.

Then…

Once the trembling and the rumbling began to subside…

Tiona and the others looked up from their crouched positions… and saw a shadow moving in the center of that giant crater.

The young swordswoman slowly rose to her feet, pulling her silver sword from the ground.

She turned her golden eyes toward them, her long blond hair practically glimmering in the overhead phosphorescence—and they couldn't hold in their cheers of pure joy.

"AIIIIIIIIIIIIIIIIIIIIIZ————————!!" Tiona shouted as she rushed forward, her body covered in cuts and bruises. How she still had any strength remaining was anybody's guess.

Tione was soon to follow, and Aiz could only smile softly at the broad smiles of her two Amazonian companions. Tiona practically leaped on her as the sisters wrapped her in their arms.

"…Are you all right, Gareth?" Finn inquired as he made his way over to the dwarf.

Gareth glanced up from his spot on the ground, skin and armor stained a bloody crimson. "I seem to remember some prum tellin' me the only thing I had goin' for me was this great lug of a body," he replied, the corners of his mouth turning up in a knowing grin. Next to them, Bete closed his eyes with a laugh.

Far, far behind them, the supporters were hugging one another with tears of relief—even Raul brought an arm to his eyes as he let out a waterfall of manly tears.

"Lefiya, are you all right...?" Riveria knelt down to take the magic user in her arms.

"Lady Riviera...is...is Miss Aiz...?" Lefiya replied from against the high elf's chest as she directed her watery eyes upward.

Riveria turned her gaze toward the swordswoman in question.

"She's fine...thanks to your magic."

Lefiya looked over to see Aiz stumbling beneath Tiona's and Tione's overwhelming embraces.

Aiz, in turn, looked back at Lefiya, golden eyes meeting azure.

Thank you, she mouthed silently.

"Oh..." Lefiya's vision blurred as it took in the sight of that smile.

It was a true, genuine smile from the depths of her heart.

A single tear worked its way down her cheek.

"Goodness gracious! I'd say I've seen about everything now!" Tsubaki rubbed at her eye patch from afar as she watched over *Loki Familia* in their celebration.

Then a childlike smile spread across her face.

The cries of victory echoed throughout the entirety of the fifty-ninth floor.

They'd done it. They'd overcome another expedition. And as the adventurers raised their voices, their weapons gleamed with a brilliant luster.

Aiz pulled her sword from where it stood protruding from the earth in the middle of the hall.

It glinted a dazzling silver in her hand.

Гэта казка іншага свету.

развянчалі сцэнары

The battle on the fifty-ninth floor concluded, *Loki Familia* quickly began readying themselves for departure under Finn's command.

Scraping together what items they could, they somehow managed to get everyone healed—at least enough that they could walk—before the lot of them began making their way back to the fiftieth floor where their base camp awaited.

Knowing they needed to move quickly if they hoped to avoid the next wave of monsters on the fifty-eighth floor, they dashed their way up and through the Dragon's Urn.

"So…does this mean we can think of that creature as part of the advance guard, too?" Riveria asked Finn next to her. They were around the vicinity of the fifty-first floor as the party continued their full-steam sprint toward the camp.

"I would say so, yes." Finn nodded in response as Tiona and the others took out any spawned monsters they encountered along the way with a vocal passion that fully demonstrated the wondrous power of healing items. "There's no doubt about it. Both Aiz and Lefiya already witnessed that crystal orb leeching a monster and transforming into that feminine creature, did they not?"

"Aye, I've heard that, too. Still…" Gareth piped up with a wheezy voice from Riveria's other side, saying nothing about the heavy wounds inflicting his body as he ran.

Neither he nor Riveria could hide their disquietude at the prum leader's inquiry as they continued their exhausting advance.

"Then that would mean…"

"Indeed—"

"—The *main body* of that creature lies elsewhere," uttered the voice in the Chamber of Prayers beneath Guild Headquarters, the torchlights flickering.

Ouranos and Fels had witnessed the entire battle unfold thanks to the magic crystal attached to Aiz's loin guard.

"Then that means whatever it was that birthed that crystal orb fetus...the true form of that corrupted spirit...lies somewhere much farther down. Past the sixtieth floor and beyond..." Ouranos hypothesized, his voice low.

It almost seemed as though the spirit's scream after her defense was shattered by Riveria's spell had actually been a cry for help.

And the wall of tentacles that had risen up to protect her was, in fact, from a floor much farther below.

"Taking into account the way the terrain, environment, and ecosystem of the fifty-ninth floor was also completely transformed, I believe it's safe to say the true form of this enemy dwells much deeper within the Dungeon," Ouranos continued.

Fels listened in silence to the venerable god before responding with a sigh, his black robes shuddering. "This situation is even more unthinkable than we could have imagined."

"Then those hybrid creatures. They're a result of this corrupted spirit, too...To think that one of the spirits of old, sent to save humanity, would end up being the cause of everything threatening Orario now..."

"A bit ironic, isn't it?" Fels murmured languidly. "There have been signs of this *abnormality* for many years now, but we've not been able to perceive its existence until now...Is it just as we thought, then? Could its recent increase in activity be due to Aiz Wallenstein?"

"We can only assume," Ouranos replied with a nod, his brine-colored eyes narrowing. "There are, of course, a number of things we'll need to determine regarding this corrupted spirit's true form; however, that is—"

"—A problem for a later time," Finn asserted as the party hurried its way through the Dungeon's labyrinthine passageways. "What Aiz and the others witnessed up on the twenty-fourth floor...the crystal-orb fetus? Starved for meat and feeding off other monsters? It began consuming magic stones from monsters like those violas and evolved into a woman-like creature just like we saw below—or, should I say, a demi-spirit."

"You don't mean…" Gareth responded somewhat fearfully.

"I do." Finn nodded. "Our enemy is using those portable crystal orbs, growing them using magic, and sending them to the surface… almost as though they're hoping to summon a fully mature spirit aboveground."

Even *Loki Familia*, the strongest familia in Orario, had barely been able to eke out a victory against the demi-spirit on the fifty-ninth floor.

If one of those things were to make its way to the surface—or even worse, if there were multiple crystal orbs already making their way to the surface…

The city would be destroyed. It would never last against one of those feminine creatures, let alone an army.

Riveria's and Gareth's faces hardened at the news.

"It wouldn't be hyperbole to say Orario would be doomed." Finn smiled bitterly as he licked his thumb. It wasn't too difficult at this point to read into just what Levis and the remnants of the Evils were plotting. Riveria and Gareth, too, began to realize the gravity of their situation.

"We need to get this info to Loki. As soon as we're ready, we'll head back to the surface."

"Right."

"Understood."

There were no objections as the adventurers headed for the exit.

"Soooo…what exactly's goin' on here, huh?" Loki eyed the other gods sitting with her at the circular table. She appeared decidedly miffed.

They were at their usual high-end establishment, three of them in total gathered in one of its soundproof rooms.

Across from her sat Dionysus, with his eyes closed, and Hermes, a delicate smile coloring his face.

"We're all victims of the same crime, are we not? So we're all in the same boat. Wouldn't it make sense to share whatever information we can?"

"Enough of the Mister Nice Guy act." Loki didn't even hide her dubious expression as she studied the sweetly smiling Hermes.

Bodyguards for the three gods waited a short distance away from the table against the wall, standing with their eyes closed as they monitored the proceedings in silence. Dionysus had brought Filvis, Hermes had brought Asfi, and Loki had brought one of the lower members of her familia.

"You'll tell me what this is all about, won't you, Dionysuuuuuuuuuus?" Loki pouted.

"I apologize, Loki, but you'll simply have to trust us. I'm afraid I'm as unwilling a participant as you are," Dionysus replied equally as despondently, his eyes closed. Finally, he let out a sigh. "For the time being, shall we return to the conversation at hand?"

Reluctant as she was, Loki began relaying to them what information she knew.

She explained the series of events that had taken place in the mere three days Aiz and the others had been gone on their expedition.

"Even if remnants of those Evils have infiltrated Orario, those creatures and their friends probably reside deep, deep within that Dungeon…Alas, people like me have no way of searching for them! But no! The more I learn, the more serious this situation becomes! So I thought to myself—maybe I shouldn't poke my nose in after all?"

"Oh, please, Hermes. We're beyond your 'explanations' at this point." Dionysus continued, "And yet…this being who'd dare take the name of 'Enyo'…? It's almost like a declaration of war aimed directly at the gods of Orario."

"Could also be a warning to the Guild. At any rate, right now we pretty much just hafta wait fer Finn and the others to return with more info." Loki added her own musings to the pile as the three gods spoke one by one. Their guards continued to stand in silence, simply listening to the discussion unfold.

When it seemed they'd covered most everything, the gods took the conversation up a notch, approaching the main issue at hand—

—What exactly they needed to focus on right now.

"Those black cages the Evils were trying to cart around on the twenty-fourth floor…with the violas inside them…" Hermes pondered.

"I think it's safe to say they were attempting to bring them to the surface via the Babel tunnel," Dionysus replied.

"Yeah, but even *if* the Guild turned a blind eye to 'em, there's no way they'd be able to haul those giant things out without gettin' seen…yeah?" Loki said.

The three of them exchanged glances.

"Which means…"

"I'd say so." Loki nodded toward Dionysus before continuing. "Babel's not the only one. There's another one—at least one more." Her red eyes opened from a pair of thin slits as she got to the core of the matter. "One more entrance."

That one and only giant tunnel leading into the Dungeon might not actually be as "one and only" as they thought.

Almost as though confirming her suspicions, a tiny throb began pulsing, on-off, in the back of her mind. Her godly intuition was never wrong.

Tione • Hyrute

BELONGS TO:	*Loki Familia*		
RACE:	Amazon	JOB:	adventurer
DUNGEON RANGE:	fifty-ninth floor	WEAPONS:	Kukri knives, halberd
CURRENT WORTH:	14,050,000 valis		

Status   Lv.5

STRENGTH:	A 824	ENDURANCE:	B 769
DEXTERITY:	B 781	AGILITY:	B 785
MAGIC:	G 207	PUMMEL:	G
DIVE:	G	IMMUNITY:	H
HEALING POWER:	I		

MAGIC:	Restrict lorum	• Restraining magic. • Restricts the target, movement based on a certain chance. Success probability increases with user's magic stat.
SKILLS:	Berserk	• Attack power increases upon taking damage. • Effects increase based on anger level.
SKILLS:	Backdraft	• Dramatically increases user's strength when on the verge of death.

EQUIPMENT: Zolas

- A set of Kukri knives.
- Crafted by *Goibniu Familia* for 58,000,000 valis.
- First-tier weapon. Can also be used as a throwing weapon. Great utility in many situations.
- Made using the Wyvern Fang drop item. Relatively easy to make so long as the resources are available, which is why she carries a number of spares.

EQUIPMENT: Filka

- A throwing knife. Effective against monsters on the lower floors.
- Used by a certain Amazonian tribe. Commissioned by Tione from *Goibniu Familia*.

TIONE HYRUTE

Afterword

The first act of this spin-off is now complete.

There've been a few more ups and downs than the original series, but I was given the opportunity to write not only what I wanted to write but what I wanted to read, which is what brings us now to this fourth volume.

I'm often hit with ideas when I'm taking a walk or listening to music. They suddenly appear in my head like scenes from a manga or movie.

Scenes like…the main character going up against an unbelievably powerful bull; a leader, his back to the viewer, encouraging his stricken subordinates in the face of an all-powerful enemy; a heroine unleashing the final blow from the sky after her companions have cleared the way for her.

I have a habit of coming up with plots based on these kinds of powerful scenes that spring into my head and that I, myself, want to read. The characters, the world, the details of the setting—all of that takes a back seat as I write whatever it takes to reach those scenes I already have planned in my head. Calculating backward, in a way. Rather than starting from the story's foundation, I start from the points I want to reach.

This terrible practice—or should I say author's weakness—can make it very difficult to get the opening of a story up and running when writing for publication. I've been thinking about this method of writing a lot lately; however, every time my characters arrive triumphantly at the goal I've set for them, every time they exceed my expectations, I think to myself how glad I am that I made it all this way.

The fact that I've been able to continue this series like this via my own selfish methods is only thanks to the support and encouragement of my readers. I can't thank you all enough for sticking around with me as long as you have. I'll continue doing my best to write stories you guys will think are exciting and fun.

On that note, there are a great many people I'd like to thank who have made this book possible.

My editors at GA, Otaki and Takahashi, my illustrator, Haimura Kiyotaka, who once again colored my book with his fantastic illustrations, and my stakeholders—it was only thanks to all of you that this book reached publication, and for that, you have my undying gratitude. I hope you'll continue to be there for me along the rest of this journey together with my readers.

I know I wrote this same thing in my afterword for book seven of the main series, but I really feel like these last couple of books have gone by in a flash—books five, six, seven, and now this fourth book of the spin-off series—which is why I'm considering taking a short breather before diving back in. At any rate, I'm just glad that I'll be able to continue this little side story as it moves into the second act.

All the best.

Fujino Omori